A TEXAS
Promise

Printed in the United States of America

First Printing, 2019

978-1-7327562-2-9

Sycamore House Publishing

P.O. Box 344

De Leon, Texas 76444

www.lauraconnerkestner.com

For my husband John Alan Kestner,
quite simply the nicest guy I know.

For Coby, Jay, Charlie, Josie, Jordie, Burt, Mall
Cole, Emily, Audrey, Ryan and John Ryan—collec
the biggest blessing in a truly blessed life.

For Mama and Daddy. Thank you for the love, a
for the Texas pride and the Okie determination.

ACKNOWLEDGEMENTS

Thank you to Kathy and David Prickett, Debra Owen, Charlotte Jacks, Sue Keith, Karen Keith, Donna Irby, Tricia Hopkins, Sylvia King, Jordan Atkins, Coby Sauce, Audrey Gibson, Emily Atkins, Bob and Kathy Tarpley, Rachel Spencer and Madalene Spencer for reading this book and offering feedback.

A special thanks to Karen Wright and Mary Yantis, two ladies who wield red pens with an expertise matched only by their ability to educate and encourage.

Thank you also to the following for the support shown me on the release of Remember Texas, the first book in this series: Anna Horton, Darla McLeod, Adina Dunn, Dublin Public Library, Patty Hirst, Dublin Thursday Club, Mary Yantis, Karen Wright, Dublin Historical Museum, De Leon Free Press, Jon Awbrey, Sarah Awbrey, Kay Hodges, Dublin Citizen, Best Value Dublin Pharmacy, Angelee Gibson, Kymbirlee Jeschke, Hamilton Herald-News, Hamilton Public Library, Picketville Chapter of the Daughters of the Republic of Texas, Dublin Rodeo Heritage Museum, Writing Sisters Mentoring Group, and author Tina Radcliffe. I wish I could name everyone who cheered me on in some way, but there is not enough room here. If you bought my first book, wrote a review, told a friend about it, hosted me on your blog, or even liked, shared, or commented on a social media post, I appreciate you more than I can say.

Author's note: One incident in *A Texas Promise* was inspired by a true story, but the story as written here is not how the situation was resolved in real life. Please see my website at lauraconnerkestner.com for more details on what really happened.

LAURA CONNER KESTNER

A TEXAS
Promise

CHAPTER ONE

Moccasin Rock, Texas
October 1891

ELIJAH CALHOUN DIDN'T know the woman wandering around Martin's Mercantile, but he knew she was in trouble.

There were scratches on her face and hands, her long brown hair was tangled, and her bare feet, peeking out from the hem of a dirty, threadbare calico dress, were filthy—as was the bunched-up blanket in her arms. But the vacant look in her eyes worried him most.

"Ma'am, my name's Eli. I'm the sheriff here in Moccasin Rock. Can I help you with something?"

She glanced at the badge pinned to his vest. At least she understood some of what he was saying. Then she turned away, made a soft crooning sound, and began looking over the merchandise on the shelves again.

"Are you searching for something in particular? If you don't see what you need, I bet Silas might have it in his storeroom out back. He's the owner here. He can help you." Eli stepped closer.

The woman didn't seem grateful for the personal attention. Her eyes widened and her arms tightened around the blanket as she took a few limping steps away from him.

Eli was trying to figure out another approach when Silas Martin's insistent whispers drew his attention from across the room. "She's not going to talk to you, I done told you that."

The woman's gaze swung toward Silas for a moment and then back to Eli, but there was no real awareness in her eyes.

Eli moved closer to the storekeeper and lowered his voice. "Has she ever been in here before?"

"Nope, never laid eyes on her until a little while ago."

"She hasn't said anything to you?"

Silas shook his head. "Not a word. She wandered in here, clutching that bundle of rags and humming, and then walked over to the shelves and started going through all the merchandise. I tried to find out what she wanted, told her I'd help her locate it, if she'd please leave everything alone. Look at her; she's dirtier than that old sow of Adger Wilson's that roams all over town."

Eli's jaw tightened. "No need to be unkind." He glanced at the woman again. "I think she's got some serious problems."

Silas's shiny bald head reddened and his big mustache quivered as his exasperation increased. "I'm aware of that, Eli, that's why you're here. She ain't acting right. Now do something. I'm sorry for her troubles, whatever they may be, but I need her to go. No respectable woman will want to come in and shop with her here."

It was all Eli could do to keep from snorting in disgust at that statement. The morning sun spilling in through the window facing Main Street clearly illuminated the general chaos of the place. There were barrels and crates stacked haphazardly, full to overflowing with merchandise that Silas hadn't managed to sort and place, and the shelves and counter were packed.

Silas seemed to follow Eli's train of thought as he reached out and straightened a stack of fabric. "I gotta lot of work to do. Get her outta here, Sheriff. That's all I'm asking."

Eli nodded. "Let me talk to her for a minute. It won't help the situation if I frighten her."

The woman had stopped wandering while they spoke, and now

picked up a bottle of Dr. Goode's Miracle Elixir off the shelf with her free hand. She studied it a moment, and then sat it down and began unwinding the blanket in her arms.

Eli waited until she was immersed in her task before easing his way closer and placing a gentle hand on her shoulder. The woman stiffened and tried to jerk away. He mimicked the soft crooning sounds she'd made until she relaxed. The odor of smoke tickled his nostrils. It was coming from the woman's dress, and not just the woodstove that Silas had fired up to ward off the autumn chill. *Where had she been?*

When he was confident she wouldn't panic, Eli reached for the blanket. "Ma'am, can I hold that for you while you open the medicine?

She looked directly at him then, and Eli caught his breath. Up close, her eyes were a golden brown color, and the prettiest he'd ever seen. But there were shadows under them and the scratches on her face were even worse than he'd realized.

The woman nodded, and it took a moment for Eli to remember what he'd asked her. He could still hear Silas grumbling in the background as she transferred the small bundle to his hands.

Eli realized immediately what he was holding. An icy dread filled him as he pulled open the blanket and looked inside. His stomach sank.

A newborn. The poor child had been wiped clean but not washed thoroughly, and the umbilical cord was still attached. The woman reached out and trailed a finger down the baby girl's cheeks with such gentleness that Eli's throat tightened.

He touched the cold little body—every bit as gently—then nearly dropped her when she squirmed, gave a weak cry, and drew in her bottom lip in a suckling motion.

Clutching her closer, Eli's gaze flew to Silas. "Go find Nathaniel, now! Tell him to get here as fast as he can. And bring Peg Harmon if you can find her."

The urgency of Eli's tone made Silas abandon his litany of complaints and slam out the door at a run, leaving the bell on top ringing furiously in his wake.

Nathaniel, Eli's younger brother, was barely out of medical school, but he was the only doctor that Moccasin Rock had at the moment. Peg Harmon had been delivering babies around the area for years. Eli didn't believe either of them could do a thing for the child—she was too tiny and too chilled to live—but her mother needed their help in a big way.

The woman reached for the baby now, confusion in her eyes when Eli didn't relinquish the bundle.

"I'll hold her," he said softly.

Shaking her head, she pulled at his arm and then pointed to the medicine bottle. Although she hadn't said a word, her plea was clear. *Help my baby.* Suddenly she stilled, swayed, and crumpled to the floor.

Clutching the child in one arm, Eli crouched beside her, and then let out a ragged breath when he realized she'd only fainted. "Everything will be all right," he whispered, hoping it was true. *Hurry, Nathaniel.*

Eli had only recently become a praying man and still felt a little awkward trying to talk to God, but he sent a prayer up now, swallowing around a lump in his throat to get the words out. The sum of it was, *Please, Lord, help me to help them.*

Settling down with his back to the counter, Eli hugged the infant to his chest and pulled his coat over her.

He didn't know the circumstances surrounding this baby girl's entry into the world, but the least he could do was offer her a little comfort and warmth on her way out.

Maggie Radford fought the hands that held her down, as she had so many times in the past few weeks. Now, as then, it did no good, and what little strength she had was soon depleted.

Someone asked her name and she stilled. It was an unfamiliar voice. She wanted to tell them who she was, and what had happened, but her throat was dry, and her cracked lips couldn't form the words.

Pain, like consciousness, came and went in waves. When a hand touched her shoulder she flinched, waiting for the blows to begin. Instead, the strange voice was back, offering soothing words that she couldn't quite make out.

Where was she? Where was the baby? Maggie finally opened her eyes. She didn't recognize the faces around her. Her eyes stung and her throat tightened, but she didn't cry. She wouldn't cry. He might be here, and he liked it when she showed fear.

Her eyelids fluttered shut, but she must have managed to say something, because the voice was back, assuring her that everything would be all right.

"I'm Dr. Nathaniel Calhoun," the man said, "and my friend Peg Harmon and I are going to take good care of you."

Maggie stilled as those words penetrated her mental fog. A sense of calm washed over her. She had escaped.

God had answered her prayers.

Gentle hands brushed her hair back from her face and patted her arm now. A woman's voice assured her that everything would be fine.

It wasn't her mother. Then she remembered. Her mother was dead, Papa was sick and Hollis Anderson was in charge of her life now. *Was he here?*

Maggie began to struggle again, but exhaustion finally claimed her. Sinking back, she surrendered to the darkness.

CHAPTER TWO

ELI PACED AROUND the reception area at the front of the doctor's office while Nathaniel and Peg tended to the woman and infant in another room. He'd overheard the occasional bits of conversation, and the baby crying at one point, then nothing. *Was she still alive?*

He'd knocked on the door once, but Peg Harmon had poked her head out and told him to sit a spell. He didn't want to sit, he wanted answers.

Widening his loop around the room, Eli continued to pace. He was surprised to see how tidy the place looked. When Doc Bacchus had announced earlier in the year that he was moving to Houston to live with his daughter, the old man had offered Nathaniel an opportunity to purchase his medical practice—building and all.

Nathaniel, who'd just arrived, jumped at the chance to take over the man's practice. Although Moccasin Rock was small, and payment for medical treatment often took the form of food or firewood, it was a start.

The building, a single-story board and batten structure, wasn't much to look at, but there was plenty of space—including sparsely-furnished living quarters in the back.

Since he'd taken over, Nathaniel had scrubbed the whole place and made some changes to the layout. The supplies and equipment

Doc had left behind, some of it nearly obsolete, had been cleaned and sorted, and the furniture refinished.

Eli grinned. Who knew his brother could be so organized? His grin faded when he spotted the diploma from The University of Virginia School of Medicine.

Nathaniel had propped the diploma, unframed, atop a stack of books on a shelf in the corner. Eli had not seen it before. He touched it with a sense of renewed awe. They had gone from little boys with no real hope of survival, to young men without a nickel to their name. Now, here was a piece of paper declaring that his brother was *Dr.* Nathaniel Calhoun.

Eli was mentally measuring the diploma for a frame when the door opened. He winced as Brody Flynn tripped over his own feet while crossing the threshold.

"Careful," Eli said softly.

Barely fourteen, the boy was tall and clumsy, and one of the kindest, gentlest souls Eli had ever run across. The kid ran errands and did odd jobs for nearly everyone in town, and seemed almost pathetically eager to please.

Stopping in front of Eli, Brody drew in a deep breath and delivered his message in a rush. "You got a wire, Sheriff. You're supposed to be on the lookout for a missing woman named Maggie Radford."

Eli felt a prickle of unease at that bit of news, but kept his expression blank. "Oh?"

Brody's hands trembled as he glanced at the paper he held. Obviously it was big news as far as he was concerned. "Yep, she escaped from the insane asylum over in Fair Haven."

Eli drew in a harsh breath. The boy was too wound-up to notice.

"You're supposed to lock her up if you see her," he added.

Lock her up? What about the baby? Mind whirling, Eli reached out for the telegram. "Thanks, Brody."

"Do you need my help with anything today?"

Eli hesitated. He didn't want the boy involved in whatever was going on here. "If you want, you can go on over to the jail and keep Deputy Bliss company, as long as it's all right with your folks."

"Sure thing, Sheriff." Brody wasn't looking him in the eyes now. *Had Mrs. Flynn grown weary of her son's obsession with the law?* Eli always kept careful watch over the boy, but he couldn't blame a mama for worrying.

Thankfully, except for one momentous bank robbery, the occasional gunfight, and more common saloon brawls, not much happened in Moccasin Rock. After a lifetime of knowing too much about all that, and worse, Eli was grateful.

As Brody headed for the front door, Eli called out to him. "Don't tell anyone else about this missing woman for the time being."

Brody nodded and hurried out the door, big boots pounding out an awkward rhythm on the board sidewalk as he half-ran toward the jail.

The door to the examination room opened behind Eli. He turned to see Peg motioning for him to enter. *Finally, some answers.* The first words out of her mouth left him with more questions.

"First of all, that's not her child," Peg said, stepping back and pointing to the baby she'd cleaned, swaddled and placed in an open cabinet drawer.

Eli came to a halt just inside the doorway. "What do you mean?"

"Exactly what I said. That woman did not give birth to that baby."

"Are you sure?"

Peg, an older woman with gray hair, piercing green eyes, and a no-nonsense attitude, didn't believe in wasting words. "Yes."

So who did the baby belong to?

"I wasn't expecting that," Eli admitted as he walked over to look at the sleeping infant. "Will the baby make it?"

"It doesn't look good," Nathaniel admitted. "But we're going to give it all we've got."

The baby's fists were clenched like a brawler. "Keep fighting,"

Eli whispered, and then turned toward the table where the woman laid, eyes closed.

Noticing the direction of Eli's gaze, Nathaniel assured him she was only sleeping. "I believe she's primarily suffering from exhaustion."

Crossing to a glass-fronted oak cabinet in one corner of the room, Nathaniel selected a large brown bottle from a row of similar containers, while Peg brought in a pan of water she'd heated on the woodstove in the kitchen. Eli noticed she'd also gone home at some point and gotten the woman a long, white cotton gown to replace the calico. That dirty rag of a dress was probably in the trash.

Nathaniel uncorked the bottle and poured some of the contents into the water, before soaking a piece of cloth, squeezing it out and washing the woman's face. He then raised the long, loose sleeves of the gown and ran the cloth up and down her arms. Eli was impressed with the delicate care he took. Nathaniel's big hands were gentle, and his brown eyes full of concern. And anger. *What was that about?*

A moment later Eli understood. A chill slid down his spine when he spotted the first bruise. The woman's thin arms were covered in them.

"Yes, she's been beaten," Nathaniel said before Eli could even respond. "Severely, and more than once."

Eli's head snapped up. "How do you know it was more than once?"

"Some of the bruises are older, others more recent." Nathaniel's voice was matter-of-fact, but Eli could tell he struggled to maintain his professional demeanor.

"Whoever did the beating was real careful like," Peg added. "There's no bruising on her face. All the marks were covered by her clothing."

With a deftness born of long practice, she placed a blanket over the lower half of the woman's body and then reached under and raised the hem of the gown so that a small portion of the ribs and abdomen were showing. "It ain't pretty," Peg said, pointing to the vivid blotches of purple and blue, and the fading green and yellow.

Eli's stomach churned. *Had this happened to her at the asylum?* He'd heard horror stories about some of those places, but he found it difficult to believe this kind of abuse would be allowed to happen at all, let alone more than once.

His gaze drifted from the bruises to her face. *So young.* He couldn't imagine her in a situation that resulted in these kinds of injuries. He glanced at her left hand. No wedding ring.

Some people couldn't afford them, of course, so it didn't mean for sure that she wasn't married. If she was, where was her husband? Did he beat her?

Eli averted his gaze while Nathaniel finished washing the woman, and turned back when his brother assured him she was covered up again.

Nathaniel then uncorked another of the brown bottles and began daubing some foul-smelling liquid onto the scratches and cuts. He started with her face. When the woman began moaning, Peg hurried forward to sooth her. "Poor dear," she murmured.

After applying medication to the scratches on her hands, Nathaniel moved to her feet, remarking on the fact that one of the scratches on her right foot seemed deeper than the others. When he touched it she flinched and cried out, but still didn't open her eyes. He bent to examine her foot more closely. "There's a thorn in here." He moved to a tray of instruments and selected a pair of tweezers.

Eli's concern and confusion grew by the minute. "Why was she outside without her shoes?"

"Maybe she was running from something worse than briars, brambles and thorns," Nathaniel said.

Eli grunted his agreement. "Did you get any idea about her mental condition since you brought her in?"

Nathaniel looked at him, brows raised. "No, she's mumbled a few words, but never really said anything." He finished with the tweezers, daubed medicine on the puncture wound and began wrapping a bandage around the foot.

Peg gently pulled a leaf from the woman's tangled hair while Eli tried to decide what to do next. He confided in Peg and Nathaniel about the wire he'd received.

Eyebrows drawn together, Peg moved closer to the woman. "You're not sending her back to Fair Haven." It wasn't a question. She was ready to fight him over this. It didn't bother Eli one bit; it looked like the woman needed someone on her side.

Eli shook his head. "Don't worry. I'm not doing anything until I find out what's going on. That means we have to keep her presence here a secret for now. Except for Silas, you're the only two who know about her. So keep it to yourselves. Since there was no mention of a baby in the message, I'm not positive this woman is the missing escapee."

He had a deep suspicion she was, though.

"The question now is what do I do with her?" Eli said.

He couldn't keep her at the jail or his house—not that he had much of one right now—for her reputation and his. And Nathaniel couldn't keep her here, for much the same reason.

That left Peg. "Is there any way you could take her and the baby to your place while I do a little checking on things? I'll pay you for their keep."

Peg smiled as she walked toward the drawer where the baby was nestled. "Sure, Eli, I can do that. Don't worry about paying anything. I'd planned on taking care of the baby anyway."

Picking the infant up, she swaddled her tighter. "I managed to get a little milk into her. I know a woman who's got a nursing bottle that she doesn't need any more. Her baby's weaned now. I'll go see if she'll let me borrow it."

"Thanks, Peg."

Nathaniel returned the medicine bottles to the cabinet. "I'll help Peg get them both over to her house as soon as we're done here.

The woman was obviously in pain when I touched her ribs earlier, so I want to wrap them. I don't think they're broken, but they may be cracked."

Eli nodded, glad Nathaniel and Peg knew what they needed to do…and wishing he did.

CHAPTER THREE

ELI HEADED STRAIGHT to the jail after leaving Nathaniel's office. He needed to talk to Deputy Bliss Walker before the deputy talked to anyone else.

The man's main goals in life seemed to consist of napping, drinking coffee, and talking. About everything. If he'd gotten wind of the woman's presence here in town, and mentioned her to anyone else, it could end up causing a world of hurt for her and the baby.

Eli entered the jail to find Bliss in his usual position—leaned back in a chair with his boots propped up on Eli's desk. And in his usual condition—asleep. No sign of Brody. The boy must be off running another errand.

After checking to make sure there was still coffee in the beat-up pot atop the wood stove, Eli nudged the old fellow awake.

"Open your eyes, Bliss, I need to talk to you."

Without moving at all, the man mumbled, "Use my ears for that, not my eyes."

Eli bit back a sigh. He'd inherited the deputy when he'd taken the sheriff's job, more than a year ago. He'd gotten used to both, although it had taken some time.

He gave the deputy another nudge. "Well, maybe you could do me a favor and use both. This is important."

"Shoulda said so." Dropping his feet to the floor, Bliss stretched, yawned, took the cup that Eli handed him and slowly began to sip from it. Most of the time, the man did everything at a snail's-pace, including talk, which proved downright excruciating. Yet Eli had also seen that lazy, lackadaisical demeanor change in the blink of an eye.

Despite his age, Bliss was a crack shot, could hold his own in a fight, and sat a horse like he was born to the saddle. But unless those skills were needed, the man didn't feel it necessary to exert any extra effort on day-to-day activities.

Eli waited until Bliss had swallowed about half the hot brew and his faded blue eyes were opened all the way, before telling him about the woman and the baby.

By the time Eli finished talking, the man was wide awake and sitting upright. Nothing except the grim set of his mouth and narrowed eyes gave away how upset he was.

Placing the cup on the desk, Bliss stared at him and blinked a couple of times. "What are we going to do to the fellow who beat her? And when can we do it?"

"I don't know."

Bliss eyed him with a certain wariness he'd never seen before.

"What's on your mind?" Eli asked.

The deputy lifted one shoulder in a half shrug. "Wondering if you being a church-going man, all of a sudden, is going to keep you from taking care of things around here."

Eli shook his head. "Nope. Being a church-goer may have changed me, but it hasn't changed my job. However, there are a few other things standing in my way. First off, I don't even know who it was that beat her."

Bliss ran a hand through his unruly gray hair. "Yeah, that does present a problem. What about her husband?"

"Don't know that she has one. But I'll be looking into every possibility."

Bliss gave him a brisk nod.

"The most important thing I can think of right now," Eli said, "is to keep her hidden, and safe, until we figure out what's going on. We best not talk to anyone else about her or the baby, at all." Eli added extra emphasis on the last two words, making sure he got his message across.

"Got it," Bliss said. "What about the babe? Will she make it?"

"I don't know. She sure is a tiny little thing."

"Has Nathaniel looked her over yet?"

"Yep."

Seemingly satisfied with that, Bliss relaxed back in the chair.

Before Eli could say anything else, the door opened and Brody hurried inside, crossing straight to the stove and spreading his hands out toward the heat. "That wind has got a bite to it."

"Sure does," Eli murmured, stepping around the boy to add another log to the fire.

"Ain't it early for it to dip down like this?"

Eli looked at Brody. This wasn't idle chitchat, the boy's tone held real concern. Did his family have what they needed for the winter? He'd best check on them at the first opportunity.

"It's only a spell," Bliss assured the boy. "It'll warm back up in a few days. I expect we'll even have us an Indian summer before old man winter gets here for good."

"Bliss is right," Eli said. "This is probably only temporary. It could warm up, quick."

"Good," Brody said with a little shiver. "I don't care for the cold."

Bliss snorted. "Cold? Why, son, this here don't even come close."

"It doesn't?"

"Nah. I remember a time when the temperature dropped so low that everything around here froze solid."

"Really?"

Bliss leaned forward, hands on his bony knees, settling in for a long story-telling session. "Yep, a blue norther whipped through one year. Froze the wells, the crick, even the coffee in the cups. That frigid wind whistled in through the cracks around every door and window in town, down chimneys and stove pipes, and wrapped solid round pert near everything."

The old man shivered as if experiencing it all anew. "Right then I hurried outside to get my horse and dog. Figgered I'd better move them into the house with me for the night. Anyways, there was this owl sitting on a limb of a live oak tree when I stepped outside. That owl hooted, and the hoot just hung there. The norther had froze that, too."

Eli groaned. *The old man was laying it on thick this time.*

Brody was enthralled, eyes wide as he listened.

"I didn't think too much about it at the time," Bliss drawled. "I was too busy dancing to pay it much mind."

Even Eli couldn't resist asking about that remark. "Dancing?"

"Yep. I was afraid if I didn't keep moving, my blood would freeze. So I danced a jig all that night."

Eli grinned at Brody's rapt expression.

"Well sir, I danced until the wee hours of the morning," Bliss said. "I finally fell down, plum tuckered out. The next day the sun was a-shining, so I went on about my work and tried to get that whole ordeal outta my mind."

"You're right," Brody said. "I guess it's not that cold yet."

Bliss held up a hand. "Wait a minute, I ain't done yet."

The boy shot a look at Eli and then turned his attention back to the old man. "Oh."

Before Bliss could continue, Jamie Wilson, another young boy who ran errands, pushed through the door. "Hey, Sheriff."

Eli returned the greeting, and waited while the boy greeted the deputy and Brody.

"What brings you in?" Eli asked.

"Looking for Brody. Silas Martin said he has work enough for both of us for the whole day, if we're interested."

Brody's eyes lit up. "He did?"

"Yep, for some reason he's all in a dither about getting his store sorted out. Said stuff's piled up."

While Brody talked with Jamie, Eli studied the two boys. Even though Brody was twice Jamie's size, he seemed less sure of himself, more timid. Both boys were hard workers, and sought out odd jobs at every opportunity, but Brody seemed almost…desperate.

At that moment Brody tugged on his shirt sleeves and it occurred to Eli that it wasn't a nervous gesture. They were too short. At least an inch of arm was showing. And the boy didn't have on a jacket.

Without being too obvious about it, Eli leaned back in his chair, and glanced at Brody's boots. Ragged and worn. Wouldn't surprise him to find out there were holes in them.

While the others talked, Eli walked to his living quarters at the back of the jail. His room wasn't much different than the cells, but it held a bigger cot, a chair, and more importantly, a door without bars.

Eli grabbed a jacket off the hook, returned to the front of the jail, and tossed it to Brody, all while trying to figure out what to say. The boy was proud. Whatever the family's problems might be, his folks were raising him right.

When Brody caught the jacket, and looked at him questioningly, Eli chose his words with care. "Since you're helping out around here so much, I need to see to it that you're properly outfitted."

Brody hesitated for a moment, then grinned and shoved his arms into the coat without a second prompting. "Thank you, Sheriff. Does this mean I get a gun?"

Visions of the boy tripping and accidently shooting himself flashed through Eli's mind. He shuddered. "Nope."

"What about a badge?"

Eli's reply was the same. "Nope."

"Okay, I'll be back to see if you need anything as soon as I'm done with Silas."

"Sounds good," Eli said.

Bliss had been observing everything in silence. As Brody turned to follow Jamie out the door, the old man spoke up. "Hey, wait a minute. You didn't let me finish my story about the big freeze."

"It's finished as far as I'm concerned," Eli mumbled.

Wielding an injured expression as easily as he did a gun, the old man declared, "I didn't get to the part where the hoot thawed out and scared me plum nearly to death."

Brody paused in the doorway, but Eli waved him on. "Don't worry, I imagine Bliss will still be telling this same story when you get back."

Bliss grumbled good-naturedly as both boys laughed.

As soon as the door closed behind them, the deputy's expression sobered. "There's something strange going on with that boy."

"I was thinking the same thing myself," Eli told him. "I'd better ride out and see his family. What can you tell me about the Flynns?"

Bliss shrugged. "Not much. Brody's said very little about his folks."

"You've never met them? I thought you knew everybody."

"I do know most folks, but I can't recollect that I've crossed paths with them yet. The way Brody talks they live way out in the sticks, and they've only been here a few months."

"Well maybe it's time we made an effort to get acquainted with them. I'll try to get out there soon." Eli stood and stretched. "I got some stuff I need to tend to. Keep your eyes and ears open. Let me know if you hear someone asking about a woman or baby."

"Will do. When will Caleb be back?"

"Some time in the next few days."

"Good, been kinda quiet since he's been gone."

"Yes, it has." Even though Eli hadn't known he had a second brother until a few months earlier, he'd gotten used to having Caleb Calhoun around pretty fast.

Caleb was a Texas Ranger who'd blown into town with outlaws on his mind, but had also managed to fall head-over-heels for a local girl, get married, and take off on his honeymoon in short order. It would be good to see him again.

"Plus," Bliss added, "wouldn't hurt to have another gun-hand in town."

He made the statement with a quiet intensity—unlike his usual drawling commentary—that caught Eli's attention.

"Do you know something I don't?" Eli asked.

"Course, I do," the old man snorted. "Been alive more'n twice as long. Bound to know things you don't."

Eli growled under his breath. "I mean, are you expecting some kind of trouble?"

The old man grinned—knowing full-well what Eli had meant—yet he still seemed uneasy. After a moment, he shrugged. "Just a feeling I've had for the last few days. Nothing I can put a name to, so don't let it vex you. Trouble comes and goes, may be time for the next round of it, I guess."

Eli nodded. Although he wouldn't lay claim to being vexed, he could admit to the same unease the deputy felt.

He wasn't sure what to expect, or when to expect it, but he suspected whatever "it" was, it was following close on the heels of a young woman named Maggie.

A gentle tugging on her hair pulled Maggie Radford from a deep slumber.

Seconds before she lashed out at whoever was beside her, soothing whispers penetrated her mind. "Everything's all right. I'm trying to get some of the tangles out."

Maggie's eyes were heavy but she managed to open them enough to see a gray-haired woman standing nearby. "Who are you?" Throat dry, the words came out in a harsh rasp.

"My name's Peggy Harmon. You can call me Peg." The woman

placed the hair brush on a small table next to the bed. "I imagine you could use a drink of water."

At Maggie's nod, the woman helped her raise up, then held a glass to her lips. Maggie drank greedily. "Easy," the woman said. "Don't want to make yourself sick."

Maggie managed a few more words as she was lowered gently to the pillow. "Baby all right?"

"She's asleep. I'm not going to lie to you, though. I'm not sure she's going to make it." The woman's words were spoken in a clipped tone, but there was compassion in her eyes. "Right now about all we can do is keep her fed and warm. I've gotten her to eat about an ounce, and she's snug in some little gowns I had on hand. Other than that, all we can do is keep praying for her."

Please, God. Maggie wasn't even sure what she was asking for at this point, beyond the baby's survival and safety, but she found a measure of peace in knowing that God understood.

The smell of freshly-baked bread wafted into the room, making her mouth water. How long had it been since she'd eaten? She couldn't remember.

"I've got some chicken broth and bread," Peg said, as if reading her thoughts. "It's not much, but that's probably best for now."

Maggie thought back to the slop they'd called stew at the asylum. Her stomach lurched in protest. Fresh bread and broth would seem like a feast in comparison.

Promising to be right back, the older woman left her alone. Within moments Maggie was fighting to stay awake. Despite her best effort, her head drooped as if her neck wasn't strong enough to support it.

Frustration and determination kept her eyes open. She couldn't waste time sleeping; there was too much to puzzle through. Was anyone searching for her? Where were her friends? She'd been at the asylum for several weeks; why hadn't anyone arrived to help her? Could she escape from here and make it home? Should she even try? Would she end up in the same situation again? Or perhaps even worse? *Please, God, help me.* Once again, she couldn't seem to form coherent thoughts or prayers.

Footsteps in the hall signaled the older woman's return with food, and Maggie realized how her prayer should be worded: *Thank you, God.*

She and the baby had something to eat, the bedding was clean, and the room was warm.

Those were all things she'd never take for granted again.

But she still couldn't control the worry that spiraled through her mind. Her father was being misled, controlled, and possibly even abused. And Maggie knew who was responsible.

What she didn't know, was how to stop it.

CHAPTER FOUR

THANKS TO A demanding, nervous-wreck of a tax-collector, Eli spent the rest of the day providing armed escort part of the way to Austin.

The tax man was a fidgety little fellow headed to the state capitol with a sizable deposit and a fear of being robbed. He wouldn't even consider taking the train because of hold-ups earlier in the year.

Even though the outlaws responsible were now dead, and it had been quiet for several months, Eli understood the man's fears. Yet he hated to leave Moccasin Rock even for a short while. The woman and child were never far from his thoughts as he and the man plodded along at a maddeningly sedate pace.

When he finally parted ways with the fellow, after handing him off to another lawman, Eli made it back to Moccasin Rock in record time. It was still too late to drop by Peg Harmon's house. The next morning he knocked on her door.

In response to a call to come on in, Eli removed his hat and stepped into the front room, a cheerfully cluttered space with simple furniture, an excessive number of knickknacks and crocheted doilies, and a huge fireplace. "We're in the first bedroom," Peg said.

He followed her voice to the next room off the hall and entered to find Peg placing a quilt over the patient, asleep on an old iron bedstead.

"How is she?" Eli whispered.

"She's been in and out," Peg said. "She ate a little broth and then dropped off again. She's mentioned the baby. It's obvious she's worried about her."

"I was going to ask about the little one myself."

"She's asleep in the kitchen, in a box by the stove."

"How's she doing?"

"I've gotten a little food into her, and she's resting well. That's what she and the young woman need the most. And prayer."

Eli nodded.

Peg looked at him. "Adger Wilson sent for me. His wife had a baby, and he's worried because she's feeling poorly. I figure Susana Wilson is plain tired but I told him I'd stop by and look her over."

Eli didn't even try to hide his astonishment. "The Wilsons had another baby?"

"Yes." Peg grabbed a satchel from atop the dresser, and headed toward the kitchen. "This makes number nine."

"Nine?"

"Yes." She turned to look at him over her shoulder. "It's not a crime to have that many kids, nor is it a sin."

"No, of course not."

Following her down the hall, Eli tried to decide whether he was appalled or amused at the Wilson's news. He spent a good portion of his time chasing the family's pigs, goats and mule off other people's property. Thankfully, they kept a better eye on their children.

He was brought out of his musings when Peg said, "Would you mind keeping an eye on the woman and baby while I'm gone? I won't be long. If I run into something that will take a while, I'll have one of the Wilson kids ask Nathaniel to come here."

Eli swallowed hard. He'd rather do about anything else, including provide armed escort for the tax collector again but he agreed to the request. Hopefully, both patients would continue to sleep until Peg got back.

Peg gathered the supplies she needed while Eli moved the baby, box and all, to a corner of the bedroom.

Careful not to wake her, he set the box on the floor. The little mouth twitched a few times, and the tiny eyelashes moved, but she settled back to sleep within a few moments. "Hang in there," he whispered.

After Peg left, he tossed his hat on a hook by the door, and settled into a nearby rocking chair.

His eyelids had begun to droop when the woman in the bed stirred. He glanced up to see those golden brown eyes, completely lucid, staring at him.

Eli introduced himself, hoping she'd do the same, but all she said was, "Where's the baby?"

He noticed she didn't say "my baby."

Straightening, Eli cleared his throat, but didn't get a chance to reply before the woman answered her own question with another one.

"She didn't make it, did she?"

Lips parted to answer, Eli paused. Keeping her in the dark for a while might shed more light on the situation—as long as she kept talking.

When her eyes filled with tears, and her full lips started trembling, he couldn't do it.

"What's your name, ma'am?"

"Maggie."

His heart sank at the confirmation of her identity. "The baby's still alive."

Maggie drew in a shaky breath and then rubbed at her eyes, hard, as if to obliterate even the suggestion she'd been about to cry. She glanced around the room. "Where is she?"

Eli pointed to the box. "She's sleeping. But we'll talk about her in a minute. Right now, I'd like to know a little more about you. Where did you come from? How did you get here?"

A hard knock on the front door brought an abrupt end to his

questions, and fear to Maggie's eyes. Grasping the quilt with both hands, she twisted it between her fingers. "There was a woman here earlier, where is she?"

Standing and starting towards the door, Eli paused near the foot of the bed. "That was Peg Harmon. She'll be back in a little while. Peg's a midwife around these parts and she's been taking care of the baby, keeping her fed."

The woman looked away. "I…I appreciate that. The poor little thing must've been starving since…since I haven't been available to feed her."

Odd way to put it. Did she want him to believe she was the baby's mother? Interesting. "Peg's mixed up something to feed her for the past two days," he said, "and the baby's holding on."

The woman's mouth dropped open. "Two days?"

"I guess it's only a day and a half. You showed up here yesterday morning, at Martin's Mercantile. Looking for medicine for the baby. Do you remember any of that?"

Brow furrowed, she shook her head. "No, the last thing I remember is…" She clamped her lips together, her face draining of color. The memories obviously weren't pleasant ones.

"The doctor said you were exhausted," Eli told her. "Your body sorta shut down. And, of course, there are your injuries. I'm sure those contributed to your collapse."

"Yes," she said, placing a hand to her ribs. He stared at her, willing her to confide in him, but another knock, more of a pounding this time, drew his attention.

"I guess I'd better see what that's all about." Eli paused. *Did she have the strength to run?* "You stay in here, and keep quiet," he said, deliberately making his voice more commanding.

She nodded, eyes huge in her pale face, but there was a spark of something in her expression that hadn't been there before. *Defiance?* He was curious, but Peg's caller was getting impatient.

The man at the door—short, stocky, dark hair parted in the middle—was a stranger to Eli.

"Mrs. Harmon isn't here," he told the man after a quick nod. "Leave a message and I'll make sure she gets it."

"I'm not looking for her," the man said, stepping through the door without an invitation. "You're the one I wanted to talk to, Sheriff. I stopped by the jailhouse first and no one was there, but a man on the street said he'd seen you coming in here."

Eli stifled his annoyance at the stranger's pushiness. "What can I do for you?"

"My name is Murphy Patterson," the man said, pulling his suit coat open, "and I'm—"

The open coat revealed a gun.

Eli's own Colt .45 was in his hand and under the stranger's chin before the man could finish his sentence.

Patterson gave a startled blink, and swallowed. "I mean you no harm, Sheriff. I was getting a cigar from my pocket. I'm a Pinkerton agent and I'm investigating a disappearance."

Eli stared long and hard at the man, then the gun and the silver, shield-shaped badge pinned to his vest before he lowered his weapon and slipped it back into the holster.

"What can I do for you?" His tone was calm, his expression purposefully blank. He offered no apologies.

"I'm trying to locate a woman, name of Maggie Radford. Seems she wandered off and her fiancé, Mr. Hollis Anderson, is concerned for her well-being."

Eli wasn't surprised to find out the man was looking for Maggie. He was surprised by the flicker of disappointment when he heard the word "fiancé." He'd only spoken a handful of words to the woman, and what little he knew about her wasn't promising. So why did he care?

None of his confusion was apparent in his response. "Is that so?"

"Yes, and Mr. Anderson is offering a reward for her safe return."

While Patterson talked, Eli made his way to the hall door to close it. He could at least spare Maggie the embarrassment of being discussed by strangers.

Since the door to the bedroom was ajar as well, Eli got a glimpse of Maggie's face…and it stopped him in his tracks. She thought he was coming to get her. Her eyes, wide and terror-filled, reminded him of an animal caught in a trap. She pulled the quilt up to her chin, and clutched it as if that fabric could ward off all the evils of the world.

Eli's chest tightened when she looked at him, shook her head and silently mouthed, "Please." He didn't need to hear her say it, he felt it. The desperation behind that one word was staggering, and he was startled by an overwhelming instinct to protect her.

Since the minute he'd agreed to serve as sheriff of Moccasin Rock, he had taken his responsibilities to its citizens seriously; but this was different. *He understood that sort of desperation.*

The woman closed her eyes and bowed her head. She was praying. Good. She was probably a whole lot better at it than he'd ever be.

He didn't want to alert the stranger to her presence, but with his back still to Patterson, Eli gave her a small smile of encouragement. Changing his mind about the door, he left it open a little, confident that the other man couldn't see her.

Turning back, Eli asked, "Is the woman ill?"

Patterson rolled the cigar between his thumb and forefinger. "You might say that. She's been institutionalized for the past few weeks, for rest and recuperation."

Rest and recuperation. Right.

"How did she manage to wander off from an institution?"

The detective seemed to choose his words carefully. "There was a fire at the insane asylum over in Fair Haven, and in the ensuing hysteria, Miss Radford disappeared. We want to find her, for her own safety's sake, but also for others. You see, there's a possibility she started the fire. She may be dangerous."

Patterson struck a match, held it to the end of the cigar, and drew in a breath—while Eli held his. She may have started a fire. That changed things. *Should he hand her over? Probably.*

After a moment—a moment filled with thoughts of ugly bruises and desperate pleas—he just couldn't do it. "Sorry," he told the man, "can't help you."

"Well, thanks anyway," Patterson said with a sigh. "If you do happen to run across her I'd appreciate it if you'd hold her here, and then contact me. I'm told her fiancé loves her dearly and he wants to get her the help she needs."

"It's quite a ways from Fair Haven to Moccasin Rock, at least on foot," Eli said. "I'm assuming that she didn't have access to transportation. What makes him think she made it this far?"

"She was on foot," Patterson confirmed, "but the area near the asylum, some of it heavily-wooded, has been searched thoroughly and there's no sign of her."

Striking out through the woods could explain the woman's cuts and scratches, not the rest of the damage.

"And in answer to your question," the man continued. "Mr. Anderson doesn't necessarily think she's here. He knows she could be anywhere. He's got people searching for her all over this part of the state."

Eli whistled softly. "That must be costing him a pretty penny."

Patterson shrugged. "From what I understand that's not a problem for him. Rich man. He's paying us well for the search, and, as I mentioned, there's an additional reward for whoever brings her in."

Accepting a reward went against the Pinkerton code, but Eli doubted if any of the men would turn it down. And it could be a powerful incentive to make them search more diligently...and do whatever it took to bring Maggie back. *What about the baby? Why was there no mention of her?*

"Did anyone die in the fire?" Eli asked.

"Yes, they found several bodies. It looks like some might have succumbed to smoke."

"You're sure none of them were this Radford woman?"

"Positive. There were a few patients, but not her. Except for the doctor running the place, the staff made it out fine. Although it was a close call for some of them."

Patterson turned around as he reached the door. "I forgot to mention, Miss Radford is five feet, four inches tall, and a little on the thin side. She's got brown eyes, and long brown hair. I'm not sure how she was dressed when she left there."

Eli closed the door behind the Pinkerton agent. "She was dressed in rags and covered in bruises," he said softly. *And somebody's going to pay for that.*

But first, he had to figure out who was responsible.

CHAPTER FIVE

MAGGIE WAITED, HEART pounding. She hadn't heard the last part of the men's conversation, but she didn't figure it was any better than the rest of it.

She was in trouble. She was grateful the sheriff had denied seeing her, but would he arrest her now that he knew about the fire? Waves of nausea hit as she thought about those who died. *And she was responsible for at least one of those deaths.*

The sheriff entered the room. A tall, broad-shouldered, powerfully built man with dark hair and dark eyes, and the most forbidding expression she'd ever seen.

He lowered himself into the rocking chair, his big frame filling it completely. "Did you hear everything that man said?"

Maggie swallowed hard. "Most of it. Thank you for not handing me over to him. I can't go back there." *Was there even a "there" to go back to?*

The sheriff didn't say anything, and Maggie bit her lip to keep from blurting out the whole story. But she couldn't tell him. It wasn't only herself she had to think about now. If he arrested her, what would happen to the baby? She couldn't risk it.

"Did you start the fire?" the sheriff asked.

Maggie shook her head. She could tell him that much. "No. But I'm fairly certain I know who did." Closing her eyes, she fought the memory of the screams echoing up and down the hall. "There was a patient there, Mabel, who'd been committed because she set fire to her home and killed her husband."

The sheriff's gaze sharpened. "Do you think she was trying to kill everyone in the asylum?"

"No, she was creating a diversion. So I could get the...get my baby out of there. We didn't belong there."

His eyebrows rose. "The baby was born in the asylum?"

"Yes. I wasn't sure what Mabel had planned, but when all the commotion began I wrapped the baby up in the first thing I found and ran as fast and far as I could."

The sheriff studied her thoughtfully. "The baby isn't very old. You must've been weak from childbirth. I'm surprised that you had the strength to run."

Maggie drew in a shaky breath. *Careful now.* "That's true. But when you're terrified—when there's fire all around—you'd be surprised at what you can find the strength to do."

"You have a lot of cuts and scratches, and you even had a thorn in your foot. How did all that happen?"

"The people at the asylum took my shoes." At his startled look she explained. "I'm not crazy, or mentally disturbed in any way. I did not belong there. When no one would listen to me, I tried to escape, over and over again. To stop me from trying, they took my shoes and..." Mortified and angry all over again, she waved a hand. "Never mind, let's just say I had no shoes. When the fire broke out, I rushed from the back of the building and straight toward the woods. Even though my feet were hurting after a few steps, I kept moving."

"Who hit you?"

She hated to keep evading the truth, but what else could she do. "I...I don't remember." *If she told him the truth, the sheriff might try to track the man down.* She couldn't let that happen.

"How did you make it all the way to Moccasin Rock?"

At least Maggie didn't need to feign confusion about that. "I'm not sure. I didn't plan on coming here. I heard men shouting as I ran, and I thought they were coming after me. There are outbuildings all over the grounds, and I tried to get to one and hide. I didn't have a plan, I didn't even have any hope at that point. I kept moving and praying."

She cleared her throat, forcing herself to speak in a quiet, measured tone.

"There was a wagon behind one of the buildings. No sign of the driver. I climbed up in the back and pulled several burlap bags over us. I uncovered the baby's face. She was so still and quiet, and I was breathing so loudly that I couldn't hear if she was or not." Maggie's voice broke. "That's the last clear memory I have."

"So you don't remember arriving here? Or going into the mercantile?"

"No. I do remember a man saying he was a doctor and telling me that everything would be okay."

"My brother, Nathaniel. Now, tell me about the baby."

She jerked as if he'd shot at her, and took a deep breath to gather her composure. "What is there to tell?" Her tone was as casual as she could make it. "She's a newborn. Her name is Lucinda."

He glanced at her left hand. Maggie placed her right hand over it, but it was too late. He'd seen that she had no ring.

"Are you married?" he asked softly.

"I'm a widow," she said, and then mentally begged forgiveness for lying yet again.

"I'm sorry to hear that. When did your husband die?"

Maggie ducked her head. "It's been a while."

"If you don't mind my asking, how did he die?"

"From illness."

The sheriff made another soft murmur of condolence. "So how did you end up in the asylum?"

Despite Maggie's efforts to remain calm, bitterness crept into her tone. "Hollis Anderson, a friend of my father's, convinced him that I should be institutionalized."

The sheriff leaned forward, brow furrowed. "Your father? What does he have to do with all this?"

"My husband and I lived with my father."

"Where?"

Maggie hesitated. Trying to navigate her way through this web of deception was taking its toll. With a start, she realized she didn't need to lie about everything. "Fai..Fair Haven."

"What about your mother?"

A familiar ache settled in Maggie's chest. Once again, a question she could answer honestly. "She died a few years ago."

The sheriff ran a hand across his jaw. "Let me get this straight. Your husband died. Someone else proposed to you. And your father had you committed, even though you were expecting a baby. Then the asylum caught fire, and you escaped, with your child."

Maggie nodded. *Goodness, it sounded so bizarre when laid out like that. It had sounded better in her head.*

The sheriff continued, "And this Hollis Anderson, your fiancé, is so concerned that he has people combing the countryside for you."

"That man is not my fiancé!"

At the sheriff's startled reaction, Maggie groaned. She *had* to control her temper. No matter how badly she wanted to throw a fit about the injustice of it all, she couldn't be locked up again. *She wasn't sure she would survive next time.*

"That Pinkerton agent told me that you are betrothed to Hollis Anderson," he said, "and that you'd been placed in the asylum to rest."

Maggie's voice shook. "Both of those are lies. I didn't belong there, and I'm not betrothed. Although I'm sure that's what the agent was told. Hollis Anderson has somehow wormed his way into my father's good graces and has him believing all manner of things that are not true—including that he's a fine, upstanding citizen and would make a great husband for me."

"I'm not saying that you should marry someone you don't want to," the sheriff said, "but how do you know he's not a fine, upstanding citizen?"

The front door opening and closing, and footsteps in the hallway drew their attention. They both turned as Peg Harmon entered the room. She looked at Maggie, then the sheriff, and a troubled expression crossed her face.

The sheriff stood. "Hi, Peg. Everything go okay?"

"I was about to ask you the same thing."

"Everything's fine," he said. "Maggie and I have been talking about how she and her baby managed to escape a burning insane asylum."

Maggie tensed at the surprise on the woman's face. Was it her imagination, or did an odd look pass between Peg Harmon and the sheriff. Did they know this wasn't her child? *No. And they wouldn't as long as she kept her mouth shut.*

"Was Susana Wilson okay?" the sheriff asked.

"Yes," Peg said, "she's going to be fine. Adger's a worrywart when it comes to her. He's crazy about that woman."

While Peg chatted with the sheriff, Maggie's attention was drawn to the baby, or what she could see of her inside the box. Instead of the old blanket Maggie had grabbed on her way out of the asylum, the infant was wrapped in a small patchwork quilt.

Maggie glanced up to find the woman watching her. "It's good to see you awake and aware of your surroundings," Peg said. "Been praying for you and the little one, pretty steady."

"Thank you, ma'am. I'm grateful for the prayers, and for the care you've given us."

Peg nodded, and it appeared to Maggie as if the older woman was sizing her up. *Say something to alleviate their concern.* "I'm especially grateful to you for feeding Lucinda," Maggie said, "since I haven't been able to nurse her."

Vague but true.

Peg studied her a moment longer, then gave a brisk nod as if she'd reached some sort of conclusion. Taking the baby from the box, she unwrapped her from the quilt, and then offered her to Maggie—one hand under the infant's bottom, one supporting her neck and head.

Maggie's mind churned with a furious blend of fascination and fright. *Take the baby, or they'll know something's wrong.*

She held her hands out for the precious bundle, and was horrified when the baby immediately began to cry. Maggie tried to hand her back to Peg, but the older woman was already leaving the room. "I'll be back as quick as I can with a bottle."

The sheriff started to follow her out but Peg shooed him back. "Why don't you stick around for a minute. If that gal's head gets to spinning again and she gets weak, you'll be there to catch the little one."

With a short nod, he returned to the rocker, although he didn't appear any happier about the turn of events than Maggie did.

As the baby's cries escalated, so did Maggie's distress.

The sheriff watched both of them with an intensity that wasn't helping.

At some point, he would ask her what had happened *before* the fire. And she would have to tell him she didn't remember.

That was a lie. Not only did she remember, she doubted she'd ever forget.

∽

Eli looked at the door, willing Peg to hurry. The baby was still wailing away, and Maggie, though dry-eyed, seemed almost as distraught. She held the child stiffly and several inches from her body. Because of her ribs? Maybe. But she was also nervous.

She glanced up to see him watching her, and her color deepened. "This is my first child," she said. "I'm new to all this."

"I understand. It must be especially difficult since you've lost your husband. A lot of responsibility for a young woman alone."

She lowered her head. "Yes, it is."

Eli decided that whatever her current situation, Maggie Radford wasn't accustomed to lying. Nor was she good at it.

"You know," he said, "if you decide that she's more than you can handle, there's an orphanage over in Boone Springs. I can take her over there, if you'd like. They'll find her a good home."

Maggie's head snapped up. Instantly, and instinctively, she tightened her arms around the infant and glared at him.

"You will do no such thing," she hissed. "I'll learn what I need to know."

Eli acknowledged her declaration with a nod. "Do you see what happened there?"

Brow furrowed, she stared at him. "What do you mean?"

"When you held the baby more firmly and forgot to be all nervous about it, she relaxed." As if to prove his point, the baby made a soft snuffling sigh and stopped crying. "She's still hungry," Eli said, "but she isn't scared anymore."

Maggie stared at the baby in amazement, and then turned to him. "That was risky, Sheriff. What if I'd agreed to let you take her away?"

"It never occurred to me. You ran from a burning building through briars and brambles, barefoot, to keep her safe."

Maggie's eyes widened. "I did, didn't I?" She seemed more sure of herself.

Peg's return with a bottle brought fresh panic. Maggie tried again to hand the baby to the older woman.

"No," Peg said, with a shake of her head. "I'll help you, but you're going to be in charge of this. That's for your sake, as well as hers. The sooner you two get accustomed to each other, the easier it will be."

She showed Maggie how to hold the baby and the bottle, with Maggie mumbling things about it being her first child.

"It's all right," Peg said. "Every new mama has to learn."

At one point, Peg glanced at Eli, confusion in her eyes. He shrugged. He had no idea why the woman was pretending the baby was hers. But he intended to find out.

Turning her attention back to Maggie, Peg said, "Give her a little bit for now, and afterwards you'll need to put her on your shoulder and pat her back gently." Each word was spoken softly. Gradually Maggie relaxed.

Eli watched the scene unfold, curiously moved when the baby latched onto the bottle, drawing nourishment with a strength that surprised him. And when Maggie looked up with tears in her eyes and smiled at him, Eli's heart turned over.

Swallowing hard, he shot to his feet. "I'd best be on my way," he told Peg. "I'll be back soon. Miss Radford and I still have some things to talk about." He directed his next remark to Maggie. "Whatever you do, don't leave this house."

Maggie's expression took on that defiant look again. "But I need—"

He cut her off. "You need to stay safe. And since you can't remember who hurt you, how can you possibly protect yourself. Unless you suddenly remember."

Shaking her head, Maggie dropped her gaze to the baby.

"Well then, stay put. I'll be back as soon as I can."

"Thanks for sticking around today," Peg said.

"Yes, thank you, Sheriff," Maggie said. "For everything." But she still had that look in her eyes. She didn't like being told what to do. *Too bad.*

Eli nodded to them, grabbed his hat and left the house nearly at a run.

What happened back there when she'd smiled at him? He slapped his hat on his head and headed for the jail. *Nothing, that's what.*

His heart had been closed up and sealed off behind a wall for years.

It would take more than a woman's wobbly smile and a baby's soft sighs to break through it.

CHAPTER SIX

"THERE ARE SOME clothes in that trunk," Peg said. "Feel free to use whatever you like. I keep what I need in my bedroom."

Maggie raised the lid, surprised to find a stack of men's shirts, trousers and even a couple of hats inside.

She glanced at Peg in time to see an odd look pass over her face. *Grief. Pain.* Maggie dropped the lid closed.

Peg sighed. "Wrong trunk. Those things belonged to my husband. He's gone now."

"I'm sorry," Maggie began, but Peg stopped her with a wave of her hand.

"I can't fret over the past and neither should you. We both have to carry on."

"Yes, ma'am." Maggie wasn't sure what the woman was referring to, but she did see the wisdom of her words.

"The clothes I was talking about must be in the front room," Peg said. "There's a flat-topped trunk in there against the north wall. I've got it covered with doilies and knick-knacks to pretty up the place. Move all that over to the side table and see if there's anything you can use inside."

"Thank you."

Peg looked at the trunk again and then shoved it against the wall. "And if you should need anything in this, even if it's only for rags, feel free to take it."

No matter what the woman said about not living in the past, she was hanging on to more than her husband's old clothes. Should she ask Peg about his death? Would it help to talk about it? *Or make things worse?*

Before Maggie could decide, Peg brushed her hands together and left the room.

As Maggie made her way to the front of the house, the sound of rattling pots and pans drifted out from the kitchen. Since Peg Harmon was occupied, Maggie took the opportunity to study the woman's home.

As Peg mentioned, she'd prettied the place up with crocheted items and little figurines of animals, birds, even people—some made of glass or china, others wooden and hand-carved. *What an odd assortment.*

The floor was fashioned from wide wood planks, painted a dark brown, and softened by the addition of a large braided rug. Everything was spotless. There was a sofa in the room, and two chairs. A photograph in an oval frame hung above the fireplace. An elderly couple. Peg's parents she supposed.

Finding the trunk, Maggie moved the figurines and doily aside, lifted the creaky lid and searched through the garments. Everything was old, some faded, others patched, but all were clean, and about the right size. She selected several items that would work until she could get home to her own wardrobe.

After repacking the rest, she took the things she'd selected to the bedroom, where Peg was holding the baby again.

"I have a pot of venison stew on the stove," Peg said, "and I thought while it was cooking I would see if you wanted to learn more about caring for the baby."

As Maggie watched Lucinda's little arms and legs flailing about, a fresh wave of anxiety descended on her. Along with a bone-deep weariness.

Peg glanced up just as Maggie grabbed the bedpost for support. The woman's expression softened. "Why don't you sit a spell." She nodded in the direction of the bed. "Or maybe you should lay down for a while."

"I think I will sleep if it's okay."

"Why land's sake, of course it's okay." Wrapping the baby up, Peg took her and left the room.

Maggie was asleep within minutes of her head hitting the pillow. When she opened her eyes again, the sun's position in the window told her she'd slept at length.

"Do you feel up to taking a bath?" Peg asked from the doorway. "I'll drag the tub in from the back porch and start heating water if you'd like. Or would you rather eat first? I'm sure you're starving for some real food by now."

Maggie smiled. "I am hungry, but the bath sounds like heaven on earth."

At the asylum, she'd used a bucket of cold water, a rag, and a bar of soap she'd taken from a supply closet. She'd complained about the conditions, but only once, because that had prompted the woman in charge to pour the water over her head.

Now, as Peg put pots of water on to heat, Maggie glanced around the kitchen. She wasn't home yet, but this place was a vast improvement over where she'd spent the last few weeks. It was cozy, warm and clean. A round table stood in the center of the room, surrounded by plain ladder back chairs, with a lamp in the center, on yet another doily, and a well-worn Bible beside it.

The cupboard had been painted a soft yellow, and was filled with various plates and bowls, while pots and pans hung from a rack. Crocks, baskets and more knickknacks lined a shelf.

When the hot water was added to the tub, and then cold, Peg reached into a small basket and brought out a bar of soap with a strong odor and odd color. "That's all I have right now," she said. "But it'll get you clean. I'll leave you to your privacy. If you need me, just holler."

Even though the tub was small, Maggie longed to linger in the warm water. Instead, she made short work of the bath. She was disrupting the woman's life. She didn't want to inconvenience her anymore than necessary.

Drying with the towel Peg left, Maggie rewrapped her ribs as best she could, and then slipped on a plain cotton dress. Silk had never felt as good as the clean cloth against clean skin. In the bedroom she brushed her hair, checked on the baby, and then returned to the kitchen to see that the tub had already been emptied. Peg was stirring something on the stove.

"Can I help you with anything?" Maggie asked.

The woman glanced up in surprise. "Sure. If you start to feeling poorly though, be sure and speak up. Can't have you losing ground."

While Maggie sliced bread and set out the butter, Peg dished up the stew. Maggie found herself enjoying the experience more than she would ever have imagined. The older woman was pleasant company and the food delicious.

Maggie's attention was drawn to a small wooden carving on the shelf—a woman holding a baby.

Peg noticed the direction of Maggie's gaze. "A lot of the small figurines and the needlework pieces you see around the house have been given to me in lieu of payment. So was the soap, the stove wood, and most of the food in the pantry. Even this venison."

"Oh." *How did the woman survive?*

"A midwife doesn't make much in a town the size of Moccasin Rock," Peg said. The words were spoken matter-of-factly, not a smidgen of self-pity. "But God has never let me starve." She glanced down at her hips, and then back at Maggie. "Not even close."

Since Peg was tall and willowy, Maggie smiled at that comment. "So you don't charge for your services?"

"I do, but it wouldn't do any good to come up with a certain amount of money. People pay what they can, how they can and when they can."

"That must make it difficult to budget and plan."

"I'm fortunate that my husband made arrangements for me. I get a small check every few months. I can always count on that."

"Good."

"As long as I'm able, I'll keep doing what needs to be done." Suddenly the woman looked almost shy. "I was wondering something."

Oh, oh. Maggie suspected that the woman was curious about her situation, and she couldn't blame her. After all, she'd opened her door to a stranger, one with a baby, and they both needed caring for. Maggie longed to tell her everything. But she couldn't.

"Is Maggie short for Margaret? Peg is. Do we share the same name?"

Maggie relaxed. "No, it's short for Magnolia."

"That's beautiful," Peg said.

Maggie had never thought so, but somehow it made her feel closer to her mother now. "It was my Mama's choice. Her family was originally from Georgia. She's gone now."

"I'm sorry. I know you miss her, especially as a new mother yourself."

"More than I can say," Maggie admitted.

Peg asked a couple of more questions, but they were general in nature, and not prying or intrusive. Maggie relaxed more and more as the evening wore on. After they finished eating, she helped clean the kitchen and then followed Peg back to the bedroom.

The older woman went over everything she might need to know about tending the baby during the night—including how to change diapers.

"If you run into trouble, holler for me," Peg said. "I want you to learn to care for the little one, but you might need to take a few baby steps yourself."

Even with all Peg's encouragement and instruction, the night was a long one for Maggie. The baby slept fitfully, and Maggie even more so. Each time she dozed off, she'd awake with a start, plagued by a combination of memories and dreams, confused for a moment about where she was.

Eventually she lit a lamp, which pushed back the darkness but not the memories. She finally drifted into an uneasy sleep, only to dream herself back to the dark, damp room at the asylum.

The coldness, the hunger, the fear—things she wouldn't let herself dwell on awake—were real again. Even the grating sound the key made as it turned in the lock, the creak of the door as it opened, and the stealthy footsteps of the guard.

Awaking with a gasp, Maggie drew in great gulps of air as she gripped the covers with stiff fingers, every muscle tense.

It was only a nightmare.

She stared at the ceiling, but even wide awake, it wasn't just the wavering shadows cast by the flickering lamplight that she saw. It was the mean-eyed stare of the guard, the hollow-eyed faces of the asylum residents, and the wild-eyed fear of those who had any sense left. The resigned faces of the women who worked there.

Some of the patients had truly been disturbed, even deranged, while others were probably in situations much like hers. None of them deserved the treatment they'd received.

Maggie remembered the triumph in the guard's eyes when he'd finally reduced her to tears. Well, no more, she'd told herself that night. No more crying.

And she would also not show weakness here. She wanted to trust the sheriff and the midwife. *But were they what they seemed?*

Peg Harmon, probably so. But what about Elijah Calhoun? Maggie thought back over their conversation. What all had she told him?

Sleep crept up on her, and she drifted into dreams again. Only this time, it wasn't the asylum she visited.

It was home she dreamt of, and her father—tall and thin, his brown hair graying at the temples. She saw him smoking his pipe in the drawing room, then sitting behind his desk frowning down at a stack of papers, and smiling at her from across the dining table.

Maggie awoke with tears streaming down her face. The dream of home had accomplished what the asylum nightmares hadn't, and she gave in to the tears. She jumped when a tiny cry penetrated her despair.

The baby. She reached the makeshift crib at about the same time that Lucinda began kicking her little feet. Maggie lifted her out and placed her on the end of the bed, trying to remember all the older woman had told her.

With shaking hands she changed the flannel, then rewrapped the baby in a dry blanket and took her to the kitchen. It took several minutes to get a bottle warmed, and Maggie, remembering what the sheriff had said, held the baby close to her body as she paced around the room.

She murmured soothing words, and hummed a little tune that she didn't even recognize. *Where had that come from?* Was it something her mother sang to her? Again, tears sprang to her eyes. But she wasn't only grieving for her mother. What happened to her father? Why had he let Hollis Anderson send her away? Why hadn't he tried to help her? Tears flowed freely now.

"Oh, well," she whispered to the baby. "There's no one to see us, is there sweet girl? We might as well have a good cry."

As the baby nursed, Maggie dried her eyes against the sleeve of her borrowed gown, and made her plans. She needed to figure out a way to get to Fair Haven as soon as possible, and find out what was going on with her father.

But how could she get there without being seen or recognized?

Balancing the baby on one arm, Maggie felt almost an expert in childcare as she returned to the bedroom. That notion fled her mind when she couldn't get Lucinda back to sleep. Rubbing the baby's tummy, and then her back, all while humming and walking, didn't work at all.

She jumped when Peg spoke from the doorway. "Having trouble?"

"Yes," Maggie admitted, "and I'm not sure why. I tried everything you told me. She's still fussing. I can't figure out what I'm doing wrong."

Peg gave her a tired smile. "I should have told you that sometimes it doesn't matter what you do, a baby's gonna cry. There's no absolute foolproof method of childrearing."

"Oh." Maggie hadn't meant for all her defeat to be expressed in that one word, but that's how it emerged.

Peg held out her hands. "How about I take her for a few hours? Can't promise any better results, but you never know."

"Thank you," Maggie said. "I'm afraid she'll get sick if she keeps on this way."

After she heard the door to Peg's room close, Maggie tried to sleep again, but it was no use. She finally rose, tugged the trunk away from the wall and eased the lid up. Grabbing a pair of trousers and a shirt, she tossed them on the bed.

She froze when a thud broke the silence. *Something had fallen to the floor.* Maggie held her breath, waiting for Peg to return.

When no sound came from the other room, she exhaled. Kneeling down, she searched every inch of the rug, running her hand as far under the bed as she could reach. The stretching caused her ribs to hurt, so she straightened and tried it from another angle. Even after going over the room twice, Maggie couldn't locate what she'd dropped.

She finally gave up and returned to the trunk. She would look again when it was daylight.

In addition to the garments she'd selected, Maggie found a slouchy old hat and a corduroy jacket. How long had Peg's husband been gone? Judging from the cut of the cloth and the colors and patterns, it had been a while. It was all much too big, but she would make it work.

Maggie didn't mind looking like an unstylish old man. She did not want to look like a desperate young woman.

Unfortunately, that's what she was.

CHAPTER SEVEN

THE SOUND OF breaking glass brought Elijah Calhoun out of a sound sleep. He was on his feet in seconds, alert and on guard. It was a trait he'd developed as a young boy. A method of survival at the time, it still served him well.

He was spending the night at the jail because he didn't want to be too far away if something happened. Bliss had told him earlier that he had something he needed to "tend to" and would be gone for a couple of days.

The old man had taken off several other times. The first time, Eli had asked him where he was headed. Bliss had clammed up and acted all mysterious about his plans.

Eli hadn't really known him, and hadn't really cared. He understood if Bliss didn't want to work with an untried lawman, and in truth, he'd never expected to see the man again. He was surprised when Bliss showed back up a few days later—never letting on about where he'd been or what he'd done.

Eli was curious, but since he had plenty of his own secrets, he didn't pry. *Would Bliss come back this time?* He hoped so. Eli had come to like and appreciate the man.

Thanks to the light of a full moon, it only took a moment for Eli to locate the source of the noise. The large window at Martin's Mercantile was laying in jagged pieces on the boardwalk, along with a child's chair that had been hanging on a nail inside the store earlier in the day. There were also several women's shoes, and a whole bolt of some kind of frilly white fabric.

Eli dodged as a small vase sailed through what was left of the glass in the window frame. *What in the world was going on?* Making his way to the front door—which appeared to have been jimmied—he stepped through.

The two men inside didn't even seem to notice him. Nor were they trying to hide, or keep their voices down. They appeared to be all liquored up and…shopping.

Eli was trying to figure out what was happening when Big John, the owner and bartender at Finley's Saloon, stepped inside.

"What's going on here?" Eli asked.

John shrugged. "Not sure, but I know how it started. Over poker. There were five of them to start with. It seemed a peaceable enough game, everybody having a good time. Eventually three of them lost their money and wandered on out. That left these two. All of a sudden, the bigger fellow yells out, 'You done took all my money. My wife's gonna kill me.'"

Big John shook his head. "I was laughing at first, then the second fellow declared he was going to help him out. I thought he was going to give him some of his money back—which would have been a first—but instead, he stood up, said, 'Follow me' and headed over here."

"I'm surprised they could even walk," Eli said, staring at the men who were swaying and staggering while pawing through the merchandise. He didn't recognize either one of them.

"I didn't realize how drunk they were 'til all this started. I normally cut them off before it gets to this. But the place was packed, has been for weeks. Lots of extra folks around town."

The same thing had kept Eli busy.

"Out of curiosity, I followed them," John said. "Before I even knew what he had in mind the smaller fellow picked up a rock and busted out the glass. I grabbed him, but he's a fighter. Took several minutes to subdue him, and in the meantime the bigger one had managed to get the front door open and stepped inside."

"Tossing a rock through the window from outside explains why there's broken glass in here," Eli said, "but how did so much glass get on the boardwalk?"

"Apparently, the tall man found something he wanted to give his wife as a gift, but instead of carrying it out the door, the idiot tried to throw it through the hole in the window. He missed and what was left of the glass shattered everywhere. I had finally got a good hold on the other fellow, but the glass breaking caught me off guard and he slipped loose. Instead of running, he came back in here and started…"

John seemed at a loss for words, so Eli supplied the missing one. "Shopping."

John scratched his head. "Yeah, so it seems. Of course, they ain't paying for anything. Don't think Silas will be too pleased."

"Nope."

They looked up when one of the burglars hollered, "This'll do," as he grabbed onto a roll of ribbon and started clumsily unrolling it and wrapping it around his hand.

"What about a hankie?" the other man asked. "Women love hankies."

"Then get me three or four," the first man hiccupped.

"We'd better stop them," Eli said, "before they destroy anything else."

"I was headed out to get you when you showed up."

Eli grabbed one of the punch drunk gamblers, while John got the other. As he'd said, the smaller, wiry man was combative, and Eli was going to help when the barkeep waved him off. "Tend to that one, this is getting personal."

Eli laughed. "Do you know who he is?"

"Not really," John grunted as he wrestled the man to the floor. "He came in with some drovers that are camped out near the Brazos."

"Ah." This one was probably staying out there, too.

They had both men under control by the time Silas Martin came down the stairs from his living quarters. Eli had seen the man sleep through sermons in church, but how in the world he'd slept through this racket was anybody's guess.

Rubbing a hand over his bald head, Silas looked like he was torn between crying and cussing as he surveyed the mess. "What happened?"

Eli had handcuffed the fighter, and then used some of the ribbon to tie the other one's wrists together. It was more for show than anything.

Big John filled the storekeeper in while Eli began gathering the items from the boardwalk.

The next hour was spent listening to Silas rant and rave, and threaten to kill the two drunks personally.

By the time Eli got Silas calmed down, and the other two to jail, it was nearing dawn. The fight had gone out of the drover. He fell onto the cot, sound asleep within minutes.

Being arrested had brought a measure of sobriety to the other one—the one who'd worried so much about his wife's reaction to the loss of his money.

Studying him, Eli could see that he was younger than he'd first thought; probably early-twenties. He was tall, lanky, with brown hair a little long. Instead of being dressed like the cowboy, he was wearing a tweed suit that had seen better days, and a bow tie. *Who was he?*

The man was sitting on the edge of the cot, head in hands. Every now and then he'd let out a deep broken sigh.

After making a pot of coffee, Eli filled a cup and tapped on the bars to get the man's attention.

Anxious eyes were raised to meet his.

"Thought you might could use a little fortifying," Eli said.

The man stood and accepted it gratefully, then perched on the edge of the cot and took a sip. "Thank you."

"You and your friend part of that cattle outfit that's camped out by the river?"

"He is. I'm not. And we're not friends. I've never laid eyes on him before tonight."

"So what caused y'all to team up and rob a place then?"

The man groaned. "It wasn't like that at all, Sheriff. This is all a misunderstanding."

"What's your name?"

"Walter Miller."

"Where are you from?"

"Originally from Tennessee, but most recently from Blairsville."

"That in East Texas?"

The man nodded.

"Are you part of the bridge crew," Eli said, "or the surveyors?"

"No, sir. Neither one."

"What are you doing here?"

The man took a deep breath. "I'm the new teacher."

"Teacher?" Eli let out a low whistle. "They may not let you keep the job after this."

Eli had heard that the former teacher had up and quit right before the new term was to start, leaving the Moccasin Rock children without an instructor. The board of education had put notices in newspapers throughout the state. Apparently one had reached this young man.

"You mentioned a wife," Eli said. "I'm surprised they'd hire you on, most times they want unmarrieds."

"Therein lies the problem," Walter said.

"What happened?"

"The salary is small, but it came with housing. Unfortunately, all that meant is a room at the superintendent's house. When I mentioned that I had a wife and daughter, he told me I could keep the job, but I'd have to find somewhere else to live."

"Not making enough money for that?"

"Not much, but it was still doable. Since we'd sold most everything we owned when we left Blairsville, we had some money with us. I figured I would pick up a little work on the side, and my wife, D…Dovie, is real good with needlework. We're willing to work hard. Figured maybe God would provide the opportunity to do so. So I rented a house."

Eli noticed the way he'd stumbled over his wife's name.

"Why don't you tell me what's really going on?"

"The landlady, a Mrs. Dunlop, doubled the rent, *after* she saw my family. I told her I was married and had a child, and she was all right with that. I had planned on keeping them out of sight until I had a chance to explain. Then we moved in. We didn't have much with us—our clothes and dishes, a couple trunks, and a bedstead. My little girl, Ruthie, had been running in and out of the house, so I didn't see Mrs. Dunlop until she was already standing in the kitchen. She stood there with this horrified look on her face. It turned to anger."

Anger? "What was she angry about?"

"She didn't come right out and say it, but she was looking at my wife, Dovie. Actually, her name is Little Dove."

Oh. Eli had encountered Mrs. Dunlop several times in the past year. She had a tendency to want everything to go her way. She was whip-thin, sour looking, and didn't suffer fools lightly. She was also a judgmental fuss pot. Eli believed that Mrs. Dunlop wanted other people to go to heaven, she just didn't want to have anything to do with them while here on earth.

"So what does this have to do with you wrecking the mercantile?" he asked.

"It sounds crazier now than it did at the time, but I was looking for a present for my wife. That other fellow had the bright idea that a trinket of some sort would make up for me losing our money." He groaned and rubbed his forehead. "What was I thinking?"

"I understand the shoes, frilly fabric, and hankies and such that you tossed outside, but why the little chair?"

"Couldn't go home without something for my daughter," he said. "In my mind that was going to make it all better. I am such an idiot."

"Drunk people do dumb things," Eli said.

"The only reason I got in the game was that I was trying to turn what little money I had into more. I was desperate."

Eli topped off his coffee cup. "Gambling when you're desperate tops the list of dumb things."

"I know that…I knew that," Walter said. "I'm not sure what happened."

He seemed so defeated.

"Well, obviously you're a bright fellow," Eli said, "or you wouldn't be a teacher. You'll figure a way out of all this."

"Teaching was what my Pappy wanted for me. I wanted to make him proud. I doubt if he would be right now. I've got to figure out what to do. The lady gave me two weeks to come up with more money, or get out—which is what she's really wanting."

"For now, try to get some rest. We can revisit all this later."

"How long will I be in here?"

Eli studied him. "I haven't decided yet." He was leaning towards letting the man go after a day in jail. After all, he couldn't make the repairs to the store while he was incarcerated. No need to let him know that yet.

Walter handed Eli the cup, then gripped the bars. "I made a huge error in judgment and I'm fully prepared to pay for it, but is there any way you could get a message to my wife?"

Eli didn't want the man's family to worry. "Where can I find her?"

It turned out the house they'd rented was next door to Peg's place.

"Dovie is very cautious, in fact, she's downright scared of most white people," Walter said, "and for good reason. So it might take some coaxing to get her to open the door. Tell her that Walter said you're a John Alan."

"What does that mean?"

"It's the name of an old man who helped us leave Tennessee. He was a good friend, to anyone in need. Dovie thought the world of him. It's come to be synonymous for anyone we can trust."

"All right, I'll tell her."

Eli made his way to the house, a simple little structure about half the size of Peg Harmon's. He tapped on the door and it opened a crack.

"Mrs. Miller? I'm Sheriff Elijah Calhoun. I'm here with a message from your husband Walter."

A young woman—with long black hair in a single braid over her shoulder—opened the door wider—but the frightened face staring out was not welcoming.

"Walter will be home tomorrow. I'll let him explain where he's been. And he asked me to tell you that I'm a John Alan. He said you would know what that means."

Her worried expression eased. Still, she didn't say anything, merely nodded and closed the door.

Eli turned his collar up, then blew into his cupped hands. The breeze from earlier had whipped around and was blowing in from the north now. Despite what Bliss had said, it did feel downright chilly for October. Again, his thoughts turned to Maggie Radford and the baby. He was glad they'd made it to safety before the temperatures dropped.

Although he'd certainly seen people in worse condition, had been one of those people, there was something about the two of them that tugged at him as nothing had in a long time. Who had hurt her? Eli didn't believe for a minute that she couldn't remember. So why wouldn't she tell him about it? Hopefully she would come to trust him soon.

Eli realized he'd stopped in front of Peg's house. The sky was beginning to lighten, and the dried up grass along the edge of the yard was covered in a fine coating of frost. Smoke curled above the chimney.

He drew in a deep breath, tucked his hands under his arms, and stood there a moment. *Why?* He'd passed Peg's house many times and never felt a pull the way he did now.

He was brought from his reverie when a movement drew his attention. A man in baggy clothes, hat pulled low, was coming from the back of the house, creeping along the side, headed straight toward him.

CHAPTER EIGHT

ELI DREW HIS Colt and slipped forward. He halted at the corner of the house and holstered his gun.

It was Maggie Radford. She was looking back over her shoulder, and ran headlong into him. He reached out to steady her.

"Going somewhere, Miss Radford?"

She pressed a hand to her mouth, stifling a gasp. Letting it fall, she gave him a disgruntled look. "Sheriff, you scared me."

"You'll live," Eli said. "You could've been in serious trouble if someone else had spotted you first." He looked her up and down. "What's that you're wearing?"

Maggie tugged the hat down lower. "These belonged to Peg's late husband. I'm borrowing them. I know better than to let myself be seen. A disguise seemed like the best solution."

"Where would you get such a crazy idea?"

"I read about it in a book."

"A book?"

"Yes. I'm an avid reader. I remembered a similar situation in one of my favorite novels."

"What?"

Her eyes narrowed. "You're not one of those men who think that reading is a waste of time for a woman, are you?"

He hadn't even opened his mouth to reply before she was talking again. "Surely you weren't expecting me to sit around and wait for you to solve all my problems."

"Yes, that's exactly what I was expecting. I told you to stay put."

She took a step back, as if suddenly wary of him. "Don't tell me you're one of those men who think that women, as well as children, should be seen and not heard. That a woman is incapable of using the brains that God gave her. Are you that type of man?"

Good grief, he hadn't said any of that. "Not at all. But I happen to know best in this particular situation. I have experience, strength, and the law on my side. Are you the type of woman who has a problem with that?"

She tilted her head, jaw clenched.

Eli crossed his arms, waiting for her response. Apparently she had none.

"Where were you going?" he finally asked.

"I…" She seemed to be searching for a plausible explanation.

Deciding that might take awhile, Eli changed his question. "Where's the baby?"

Her shoulders relaxed as she glanced at the house. Obviously that was something she didn't mind answering. "I couldn't get her to sleep last night, so Peg took her into her room a few hours ago. They're both still resting."

As if that explanation opened up a new possibility for her early morning excursion, she began speaking in a rush. "I was on my way to the general store to get some things for Lucinda now." She moved to step around him. "So if you'll excuse me."

He blocked her path. "Does Peg know you're leaving?"

She stammered a bit before answering, "Well…of course she does."

"Nice try," he said. "But I don't believe you."

Maggie pinned him with a stare, opened her mouth, and then abruptly snapped it closed. Tears sprang to her eyes. She wiped them away with an angry swipe of her hand. Just like the first time, she seemed determined not to cry.

"How about telling me the truth," he said softly.

She sighed. "The truth is I want to go home."

Compassion filled Eli. How many times in his life had he wished for the very same thing? Even when there'd been no home left.

"I understand," he said. "Your whole life's been turned upside down. The comforts of home can be a strong pull. It can make you throw caution to the wind, do anything. But you need to let me find out what happened at the asylum first; for your own sake, as well as the baby's. Or did you change your mind about raising her on your own? Is that why you're trying to leave without her?"

Maggie shook her head. "No, absolutely not. I wasn't abandoning my baby; I was coming back for her. I promise." She straightened her shoulders. "In fact, I'll fight anybody who tries to take her away from me."

She crossed her arms, mirroring his posture.

This lady was going to drive him crazy. Yet Eli couldn't help but be fascinated by her.

She looked absolutely ridiculous in that outfit, was probably still in pain, and was definitely in over her head, yet she wasn't giving in or giving up. That caused that strange little reaction in his heart again. *Admiration, that's all it was.* He'd feel the same no matter who was fighting this hard for survival.

Eli realized that she was speaking again.

"Although I would love nothing more than to sleep in my own bed," she said, "and wear my own clothing, and cook in my own kitchen, that's not why I want to go home."

Maggie pushed the hat back and looked him in the eyes. "It's my father. I'm worried about him. I have to see to his welfare. There's no one else to do it. I don't trust Hollis Anderson. If he's still influencing my father's decisions, there's no telling what will happen. Hollis could end up putting Papa away somewhere, and I might not ever see him again. I have to take care of him."

"That's admirable," Eli said, and meant it. "But no matter what your intentions are, it's not safe for you to be out."

Before she could object, he made an offer that surprised them both. "How about I go check on your father? And you stay here."

"I appreciate your offer to help, Sheriff, but I want to see my father with my own eyes. I'm going home."

Eli let out a frustrated sigh, took his hat off and ran his fingers through his hair. "Not if I lock you up, you won't."

"You would really do that?" There was such fire in her eyes that the quiver in her voice took him by surprise.

He gentled his tone. "No, I won't, at least for now. But don't push me. I understand your concern for your father, but you are my concern."

She glared at him, and Eli stifled the urge to simply pick her up and haul her into the house.

"Look," he said, "I'll take Nathaniel with me, so he can check your father over physically. But you must stay here. There's no telling what could happen if you were spotted by Anderson, or one of those Pinkerton agents he's hired."

At the reminder that there was more than one person searching for her, Maggie seemed to wilt a little.

"All right," she sighed. "I don't mean to sound ungrateful. I'm just overwhelmed. I truly appreciate the offer to check on my father. And for everything you've already done."

She pulled the hat from her head and turned toward the back of the house; her long hair spilling down around her shoulders. "Besides, I'm already tired of looking like a boy."

"It's going to take more than those clothes to make you look like a boy," he mumbled.

She looked back at him. "What?"

"Nothing. Get on inside. I'll be back as soon as I can and let you know what I found."

"Thank you."

"You're welcome. And Miss Radford?"

"Yes?"

"I'll have some questions when I get back. I expect you to provide the answers."

She gave him a brisk nod, but this time there was more than defiance in her expression. There was fear. *Why wouldn't she tell him the truth?*

CHAPTER NINE

ELI WAS SURPRISED to find Bliss sitting in front of the desk when he returned to the jail.

Brody was curled up in front of the stove, sleeping soundly. *Why?*

"When did he get here?" Eli whispered.

"He was here when I came in," Bliss said.

"When did you get here?"

"Little bit ago. Where you been?"

Eli was tempted to fling the question right back at him, but now wasn't the time. "Couple fellows got into some trouble at Finley's that eventually spilled over into Martin's Mercantile. Broke the big window glass out and tore the place up some."

Bliss glanced toward the cells. "I noticed we had company. What are you gonna do with them?"

Eli shrugged. "Neither one seems like the usual brand of troublemaker, so I hate to see them wind up in serious trouble." *Lord knows he'd been given some second chances.* "And they're ready to make good on the damage. Old Silas, once he woke up, lit into them pretty good. They're even going to do the repair work themselves. At least that's what they were promising when we hauled them in here. Going to be some real sorry fellows when they wake up later today, probably going to feel like a horse stomped them. They're fortunate that it isn't worse. Silas was acting like he wanted to lynch them on the spot."

"That's exactly what woulda happened back in the old days," Bliss muttered. "And they'd had to pay for their own rope."

Eli laughed as he took off his coat and tossed it on a hook. The sound woke Brody. The boy sat up, yawned, and rubbed his eyes, then did a double-take when he saw them both staring at him. "Hey Sheriff, Deputy Bliss."

"Brody, what are you doing here?"

An odd expression crossed the boy's face. *Guilt?*

"I took out real early this morning, before daylight." He gave Eli a sheepish grin. "Reckon it was a mite too early. Came in to talk to you, wasn't nobody here. Decided to wait, and then couldn't keep my eyes open."

Something about the whole thing didn't ring true.

"Is everything okay, Brody? At home I mean. How are your folks doing?"

The boy averted his gaze, and rose awkwardly to his feet. "Everything's fine."

"Did you wake them up and tell them you were coming here?"

"No...but believe me, they know where I am." He'd started his sentence hesitantly, but he finished strong. Brody was telling the truth about that much.

"Did you eat before you left home?"

"No sir, I was in a hurry. But I'm fine." Eli wasn't buying that. The boy had come in sometime after he left, and before Bliss arrived. *Why?*

He noted once again that Brody was scrawny. Well, until he could get out there to see what the Flynns needed, he could at least feed their boy. He was shooting up like a weed, but it wasn't a healthy look.

"Run on over to Bony Joe's and have some breakfast," Eli said. "Tell him I said to put it on my tab."

Brody opened his mouth, but Eli cut him off. "On second thought, I'll go with you." *Maybe the kid didn't want to eat alone.* "You do enough work here to earn a meal every now and then. I'll feel like I'm cheating you if you don't take it. I'm sure you wouldn't want me to feel like a dishonest man."

Brody looked horrified at the thought. "No, sir."

"Then let's go and eat. I want to talk to you anyway. I have a job in mind for you."

"Thank you, Sheriff."

Forty minutes later, they'd finished a meal of eggs, bacon, fried potatoes, biscuits and gravy, with coffee for Eli and milk for Brody, when Bliss ambled in.

"Everything okay?" Eli asked.

"Those fellows are awake, reckon we oughta feed them."

Eli agreed, and went back to the kitchen to place two more breakfast orders with Joe. When he returned, Bliss was sitting at the table, telling Brody more about the big freeze he remembered.

Bliss paused long enough to look up at Eli. "That Mrs. Dunlop came by the jail and said that one of those animals of Adger Wilson's ran right into her bakery. She declared she's gonna shoot them next time."

"She didn't see who was sleeping in the cells, did she?"

"No. She barely stuck her head in the door. Why?"

"She's dealing some grief to one of those men I arrested," Eli said. "I don't want her to know that he's in trouble. Try to shoo her out if she comes back in."

"I doubt if she'll be back today, said she was catching the train to Fair Haven, buying some supplies. But she said she expected you to go talk to Adger, or she'd be talking to the town council about you not doing your job."

Eli sighed. "Which animal was it this time? Never mind, it doesn't matter."

"Good, cause I can't rightly recall if it was the pig, the goat or the mule," Bliss said. "She was carrying on so much that I closed my ears."

They both knew it could easily have been one of half-dozen different animals. The Wilsons had cows, pigs, mules, chickens, goats, dogs, cats, and one old swayback horse, and not a single one was penned, confined or supervised in more than the most desultory manner. They also had a whole passel of children. There were nine of them now, Eli reminded himself. *Nine.* At least they kept better track of the kids.

Leaving Bliss in charge of feeding the prisoners, Eli walked on to the Wilson place at the edge of town. He stood there a moment. The house hadn't seen a lick of paint in years, the windows were missing a few panes, and the porch sagged on one end. And yet the children—running, laughing and playing—were obviously happy. According to Nathaniel, they were all remarkably healthy.

Eli spotted Adger leaving a ramshackle barn, leading a milk cow at the end of a frayed rope.

"Howdy, Sheriff."

Eli got right to the point. "Adger, you've got to do something about these animals. They're scaring the young and old alike, and generally making a nuisance of themselves."

Adger, a thin, good-natured man of indeterminable age, turned an engaging smile his way. "Tell truth, Sheriff, I haven't had time to build any pens."

"Make time," Eli snapped.

The man gave him a bewildered look. "I'm busy from sun-up to sun-down as it is. What in the world am I supposed to give up?"

Eli dodged as a handful of kids ran past him, shouting and screaming. *He could think of at least one thing Adger could cut back on.*

He realized he'd lost Adger's attention, and followed the man's gaze to the doorway of the old house. Susana Wilson stood there, a baby in her arms.

Adger grinned at her and winked. Eli was amazed to see the

woman actually blush as she returned the smile. Susana then turned to Eli.

"Would you care for some coffee, Sheriff?"

He tipped his hat. "No, ma'am. I guess I'd better get on back to the jail. Thank you, though."

Turning to Adger, Eli made one last effort. "Please try to keep the animals confined as best you can."

"Sure thing, Sheriff."

As Eli headed for the road he was intercepted by one of the younger Wilson children, a tow-headed boy wearing a pair of pants that were too small, a shirt that had enough room for another sibling or two, one sock, and a pair of worn shoes that had obviously been handed down from an older brother.

"Sheriff, I'd like a minute of your time please."

The boy's demeanor was so at odds with his bedraggled appearance and surroundings that Eli struggled not to smile. He crouched down and gave the boy his undivided attention. "What's on your mind, little man?"

"Will you tell Miss Peg not to be coming out here anymore?"

Eli rocked back a little. "Do you mind telling me why?"

"Every time she comes here, she leaves a baby. There's not room for another one."

Eli wasn't sure he'd heard right. "What?"

The boy swiped at his nose with a sleeve of the once white shirt. "She's the only one who could be bringing them. We don't have much other company dropping by. Sometimes, Miss Peg comes and talks to Ma awhile, and don't leave a baby. But plenty of times she does."

The boy bent down to pull up the sock. "I've tried getting a look in that bag she carries, to see how many babies are in there, but she won't let it out of her sight. I'm not sure where she gets them, but she needs to find some other place to leave the next one. I figured

Ma or Pa would tell her to leave off, but they keep smiling and thankin' her when she leaves."

Eli covered a grin by rubbing his hand across his mouth. "You think Peg Harmon is bringing babies out here?"

The kid looked at him with suspicion. "That's what my big brother said. Can you think of any other way they're getting here?"

Eli cleared his throat. "No, can't say as I do. Tell you what, I will have a word with Peg. Maybe she can just come visit your mother from time-to-time for a while."

Still all business, the boy nodded. "Preciate it." He wasn't allowed time for anything else as one of his older brothers stuck his head out the barn door and hollered, "C'mon, squirt. You got chores to do."

The boy loped off, joined by two other siblings before he reached the barn. Several of the kids looked exactly like Adger, and Eli had a fleeting thought of a smaller version of a Calhoun. He couldn't help but smile.

He'd made it to the road when he suddenly stopped still. *Where had that thought come from?*

Considering his own childhood, and his way of life, he'd long ago given up thoughts of having a family of his own. Even though he was building a house, he'd always pictured himself living there alone.

In fact, he'd pretty much blocked out any notice of children. Now suddenly it seemed that kids were everywhere. Maggie Radford's baby, Brody, and the Wilson children.

Eli realized what was happening.

He had to get that woman's problem solved and get her out of here.

Chapter Ten

MAGGIE PUSHED OPEN the back screen door and stepped onto the porch. Drawing in a deep breath, she leaned against the porch rail enjoying the sunshine and crisp air.

She'd gotten Lucinda to take two ounces from the bottle before falling asleep. Peg said it was a good sign. Encouraged, Maggie had cleaned the kitchen and cooked enough food for the day, after convincing Peg that she would prefer to help instead of convalescing. As long as she moved carefully, her ribs didn't hurt as much as they once had.

Still, Maggie was restless. She adjusted the shawl that Peg had given her, pulling it tighter over her shoulders. She had safety, at least for now, but no peace of mind. Although her thoughts were clearer than they had been in weeks, she was still not…home.

How long had she been here? She didn't even know what day it was. Neither Elijah Calhoun nor Peg Harmon kept regular hours. Like physicians, a sheriff and a midwife responded at a moment's notice when called on by those in need.

It struck Maggie that she was one of those people. *Thank you, Lord, for bringing me here.*

Although her gratitude was genuine, her unease and discontent soon occupied her mind again. She was used to coming and going as she pleased. Now her world was reduced to an unfamiliar house at the edge of a small town. And she didn't really know these people.

Eli Calhoun had threatened to lock her up, for real, if she tried to leave again. She was lucky he even let her go outside to use the privy—which was the only thing she could see from the back of Peg's house, besides a dense thicket of woods.

She wasn't going to get anywhere by being obstinate with the man. From now on, Maggie was going to do her best to convince him that she could be trusted. Hopefully it wouldn't take long. She needed to go home. In addition to her father, she had important things to tend to, including the annual Society Sisters Community Charity event to arrange. There was an important planning meeting that she couldn't miss.

Sighing, Maggie took another look around. According to Peg, her house was the last one on the south end of town. There was no discernible trail through the woods, but there was the occasional break in the trees. Some had lost their leaves, but the cedar and live oak trees were green. If she and the baby were going to be confined somewhere, this was better than many places.

There was a neighbor immediately to the north, and from her vantage point on the porch Maggie could see a small yard, and a portion of the eaves and roof.

The melodic toll of church bells brought a fresh rush of homesickness to Maggie. *It must be Sunday.* She tilted her head trying to determine how close the church was. Would she be able to hear them sing? She had no idea what the Moccasin Rock church looked like, so she closed her eyes and pictured instead the beautiful old rock church at Fair Haven. The place her family had attended for years.

She and her father always sat in the same spot—on the right hand side of the aisle, second pew from the front.

Maggie's eyes popped open at a rustling sound and she caught a glimpse of a little dark-haired girl in the yard next door. The child was talking to a rag doll in a singsong voice, kicking leaves as she walked, followed by a little white dog. Charmed, Maggie stepped forward, then halted when she recalled the sheriff's caution about not being seen, by anyone.

Better safe than sorry, she thought, contenting herself with listening to the girl's happy chatter. *What would Lucinda look like at that age?* The thought sobered her. She was responsible for the care and upbringing of another human. A helpless one. And she couldn't even seem to help herself these days.

A voice called out from the house next door, in halting English. Maggie didn't recognize the accent. "Ruthie, come inside, it's getting colder."

"But Mama, I'm showing my baby and Ollie how to sing."

"I've made fresh bread," her mother said.

That did the trick. Maggie smiled as the girl scurried inside, talking to her doll and the dog the whole time.

With the girl gone, Maggie ventured forth into the yard. She'd gotten nearly to the back, bending to look at some red berries on a wildly-overgrown hedge row, when she heard a grunt, then a high-pitched squeal.

From the corner of her eye she saw a flash of movement, but before she could form a coherent thought someone grabbed her upper arms and dragged her backwards.

Maggie kicked and thrashed out at her captor and was dropped immediately. Landing on her bottom in the leaves, she looked up into the face of the man towering over her.

"I'm so sorry, Miss Radford."

Maggie scooted backwards, alarm coursing through her. "Who are you? How do you know my name?"

"I'm Brody Flynn. Sheriff Calhoun told me about you. I'm sorry for scaring you, but that sow of Adger Wilson's was about to run you over." He pointed toward the biggest pig Maggie had ever seen, one that was currently headed around the house and toward the road.

It took a few moments for Maggie to catch her breath, and

another few before she realized that despite his size, Brody was only a young boy. *And he'd been sent to watch over her.*

Standing, she straightened her dress and shook leaves from the shawl. "Are you supposed to be guarding me?"

The boy stammered a few times. "I…I don't know as I'd rightly call it that. I don't have a gun or anything. But the sheriff said I was to run for the deputy if any strangers showed up here or if…" His voice trailed off.

"Or if I tried to leave?" Maggie snapped.

He ducked his head. "Yes, ma'am."

Remorse filled her. No matter how frustrated she was with her current lot in life, none of it was this boy's doings. "Why don't you come on in and have some cake? I just made one."

He glanced at the house, and then back at her. "I'm not sure if I should, I'm supposed to be watching the place."

"Aren't you supposed to be watching me? Seems like you could do that better if you're sitting right beside me."

The boy smiled at her. "Yes, ma'am. I believe you're right about that."

When he was seated at the table with a glass of milk and a large piece of cake, Maggie picked up the baby and joined him. The boy was eating fast, like he was starving to death. She wasn't so much worried about his table manners as she was his health.

"Slow down, you're going to make yourself sick."

He paused, color filling his face. "It sure is good."

She handed him a napkin. "Thank you. How old are you, Brody?"

"I've turned fourteen." He said it with a hint of wariness.

Maggie's curiosity was piqued.

"How long have you lived in Moccasin Rock?"

"Since I was thirteen."

Due to the vagueness of his reply, that could mean anything

from a few days to a year. *It was a simple enough question, why did he seem so uncomfortable?*

Maggie tried asking a few more questions, and though Brody answered each one, politely, he never offered any additional information. And he was choosing his words carefully. Since she'd been doing much the same thing recently, Maggie was more aware of it than she normally would've been.

She tried a different tact. "So tell me about Moccasin Rock."

"Don't guess I know much. Just a town like any other."

"Then tell me about Sheriff Calhoun."

Brody's face lit up.

Maggie smiled, glad the boy had swallowed his last bite of cake as words spilled from his mouth.

"He's the nicest man I know."

"Is that right?"

"Yes, ma'am. He never hollers at me. Always has a kind word. And he lets me hang around the jail and help him. He won't let me use a gun yet, though."

"A gun? Why I should hope not. Don't your folks worry about you spending time at the jail?"

He glanced away. "They're okay with it."

Or maybe they weren't.

"It's not dangerous," the boy said. "Folks say that when Sheriff Calhoun came here everything got better."

She refilled his glass with milk. "Why's that?"

"Because he shot some bank robbers—but that was before he was the sheriff."

Maggie set the pitcher down with a thump. "He what?"

"Sheriff Calhoun stopped a robbery at the bank here, but he didn't live here yet. I heard Mr. Martin—he owns the mercantile—telling somebody that Eli Calhoun had stepped off the train at the same time that some robbers were holding up the bank. Mr. Martin said that Eli walked right up to them. Like he wasn't afraid to die. Killed them both."

"But he wasn't the sheriff yet?"

"No, ma'am."

"What was he doing in Moccasin Rock?"

Brody shrugged. "Don't know. Folks think he was passing through. Silas said he looked "worse for the wear" at the time, but his gun-hand was steady. Silas said the town's other sheriff was killed in that robbery, and Eli was offered the job. They didn't know much about him, but they knew he wasn't a coward."

As Brody talked, his enthusiasm increased, telling her in great detail about an outlaw that Eli had shot down in the street during the summer. But when she asked about his own family, he clammed up.

"Thank you for the cake, Miss Radford. It was about the best thing I've eaten in a long time. I guess I'd better get on back outside. If Sheriff Calhoun passes by I don't want him thinking I deserted my post."

"If he asks, I'll tell him you took very good care of me," she said. "And please, call me Maggie."

Color rose in his cheeks as he smiled. "Thank you, Miss Maggie." He glanced at the baby again.

"Would you like to hold her?" Maggie asked.

Brody's eyes widened as he backed toward the door. "Oh, no. Thank you, though."

Maggie smiled down at the baby in her arms as the boy hurried down the back steps.

"I'm sure he didn't mean anything personal by that, Lucinda."

What an unusual boy.

Then her thoughts returned to Eli Calhoun.

A man—and not a lawman—who was that good with a gun.

Maggie shivered at all that implied.

CHAPTER ELEVEN

ELI FOLLOWED NATHANIEL up the steps of the huge, two-story brick house that was home to the Radford family. This is where Maggie lived? For some reason that bothered him, but he didn't have time to dwell on why.

Nathaniel knocked several times before the door opened. A thin man with black hair, prominent eyebrows, long sideburns and a frosty expression greeted them with less than enthusiasm.

Eli recognized him from Maggie's description. Hollis Anderson.

"Sorry for the delay, we're currently understaffed." The man gave them a sweeping glance. "How may I help you...gentlemen?"

The deliberate pause before the word gentlemen amused Eli. If Anderson was trying to intimidate or insult them, he would have to do better than that. Eli didn't care one bit what this dolt thought of them. Then he realized the man had said *we're* understaffed.

Maggie hadn't mentioned that Anderson was living here. Did she know?

"I'm here to see Mr. Nelson Radford," Nathaniel said.

The other man's gaze sharpened. "In regards to what? Who are you?"

Nathaniel pointed to the leather satchel in his hand. "I'm Dr. Nathaniel Calhoun, and this is my brother, Elijah Calhoun, the sheriff of Moccasin Rock."

A flicker of surprise crossed Anderson's face. "What do you want to see Mr. Radford about?"

"I recently acquired the practice of Dr. Bacchus over in Moccasin Rock," Nathaniel said, "and a few of the patients I'm supposed to check-in with on a regular basis live in Fair Haven. I'm here to give Mr. Radford a routine checkup."

Eli was impressed with how well Nathaniel handled the request. Everything he'd said had been the truth. He hadn't actually said that Mr. Radford was one of the patients.

Anderson's gaze shifted back and forth between the Calhouns before lingering on Eli's badge, and then the Colt .45. "Do you always bring an armed guard with you for patient visits?" he asked Nathaniel.

Eli could tell that Nathaniel's smile was forced, but he doubted if anyone else would notice. "No, my brother had business here in town as well."

Hollis Anderson then leveled a look at Eli. "Aren't you out of your jurisdiction?"

Eli nodded. "Yep. My business here in town is personal." *And it was.*

Nathaniel drew Hollis Anderson's attention again. "Are you a relative of Mr. Radford? Shall I feel free to discuss any medical concerns with you?"

The subtle reference to Anderson's control seemed to please the man. He straightened his collar. "Yes, I'm Nelson Radford's future son-in-law." He motioned them inside.

Eli's fists clenched. If Maggie was telling the truth, this man was at best a liar, and at worst he was the one who'd beaten her.

As Anderson seemed to consider Nathaniel's request, Eli almost wished the man would take a swing at them. Eli wanted, badly, to beat him senseless.

And the strength of that desire surprised him. He'd been in

control of his feelings for years, at all times. Emotion was dangerous—it could get you killed.

Hollis Anderson was still deliberating, or at least enjoying
making them wait in the entryway, when another man stepped into
the hall from an adjoining room and beckoned to Hollis. Eli studied
the new man. He was too young to be Maggie's father.

"Excuse me a moment," Hollis said, before joining the other
man. The two of them held a hushed conversation before Hollis
suddenly cursed and smacked his hand down on the banister.

Something had made Hollis Anderson angry, which brought
satisfaction to Eli. Still scowling, Anderson looked at them.

"You can go on up," he said, pointing to Nathaniel, "but you
stay here, Sheriff." He then resumed his conversation.

While Hollis and the other man continued to speak in urgent
tones, and Nathaniel made his way upstairs, Eli took the opportunity
to peek into the room to his right. It was well-appointed, luxuri-
ous even, with heavy wallpaper, lush textures, fancy rugs and gold
wall sconces.

Since Hollis was still engrossed in his conversation, Eli eased
over to the other side of the wide hall, and got a glimpse of a dining
room with massive chandeliers and a table nearly as long as his cabin.
There was a huge hutch filled with gold-trimmed plates, white with
delicate pink and green blossoms. There was also gold-rimmed glass
ware. Crystal? Most likely. He was sure that the drawers underneath
were filled with costly silver. This is what Maggie was accustomed to.

Most of the time Eli used a beat-up graniteware plate and a
Mason jar to drink from. Unless he was outside, then he used a
hollowed-out gourd dipper.

Eli had seen houses like this, even been inside some of them.
He could never imagine living this way. He stepped back into the
hall in time to overhear the men talking.

"Well tell them to keep looking," Hollis said. "She has to be
out there somewhere."

They were talking about Maggie. Eli waited until the other man was gone before addressing Hollis. "Sorry, couldn't help but overhear about the missing woman. A Pinkerton agent stopped in Moccasin Rock and told me about it. Sad, terrible situation. Have you had any luck yet?"

Scowling, Hollis shook his head. "Not a bit. I can't imagine where she's disappeared to."

"Lots of countryside. If she made it to the train she could be in Fort Worth, or anywhere by now."

"True. When I find her, I'm never letting her out of my sight again. The poor girl's not in any condition to take care of herself."

A chill swept over Eli. He knew Maggie Radford was lying to him about something, maybe everything, yet for some reason he trusted her more than this man. But he still needed information. He was getting ready to dig for more, when Nathaniel started down the stairs.

Nathaniel reported to Hollis Anderson that Nelson Radford seemed to be fine, and then he and Hollis shook hands. It was all Eli could do not to visibly cringe. He hated having to pretend to like this man. Even if he hadn't dealt the blows to Maggie himself, Hollis was responsible.

At the thought of the bruises on Maggie's body, it took all Eli's control not to pull back his fist and hit Hollis right in the middle of his smug face before they left.

Once outside he waited until they'd reached the street before questioning his brother. "So what was Mr. Radford like?"

"He seems like a nice man, and, except for being a little on the frail side, he appears to be in good health, physically and mentally."

"I have to wonder how nice he is if he agreed to placing his daughter in a lunatic asylum."

"I know," Nathaniel agreed. "It is confusing. While we were talking, I asked about his family, and he talked about his daughter. His only child. The man's expression softened, and he spoke of her with pride. I'm not sure he knew exactly where Maggie was being kept."

"Did you ask him about Hollis?"

"I did, and his answers indicated that Hollis is not holding him here against his will. He said Hollis is his friend, and is looking after him while his daughter is recuperating from a nervous condition. And he was adamant about the fact that she will be marrying the man."

"That means that at least for the time being we can't raise a ruckus about Anderson being here," Eli grumbled. "I don't want to draw any attention to us, or Moccasin Rock, until we can figure out what to do. It sounds like both men are of like mind, and right now that could be dangerous for Maggie."

Nathaniel agreed. "So what did you find out while I was up there?"

"Only that Hollis Anderson and his hired men still don't have any idea where Maggie's disappeared to."

"That's at least some good news."

"True. Now we have to figure out *what* she's hiding, before they figure out *where* she's hiding."

CHAPTER TWELVE

BEFORE LEAVING TOWN, Eli and Nathaniel stopped for dinner at a little café near the railroad depot. The food was good, and the servings generous. Eli stopped eating and started listening when the men at the next table began talking about the fire at the asylum.

He caught Nathaniel's attention and motioned for him to listen.

"I'm heading back out there after I eat," one man said.

"They still cleaning up?"

"Yep, hopefully be finished soon. And no nasty surprises like the last time."

"That your first dead body?"

"No, just a horrible place. Bad things happened out there. Don't feel right."

His dining companion laughed. "You're not superstitious, are you?"

"Before I can answer that, you'll have to tell me what it means," the other man said.

The Calhouns both smiled, then Eli whispered to Nathaniel, "While we're here, you want to take a look around at the asylum?"

"Why not," Nathaniel said.

They paid for their meals and hurried out, so they could be waiting when the other men left. It was only a few minutes before one of them did.

"We overheard you talking about heading out to the asylum," Eli said. "Was wondering if we could hitch a ride with you."

The man—who said his name was Cap—didn't seem interested until Eli mentioned they'd pay. "Okay, I'll take you, but you'll have to find your own way back," he said. "I got work to do out there, don't know how long it'll take."

"No problem."

Nathaniel hopped in the back of the wagon, so Eli took a seat beside the driver. "I heard you saying it was a horrible place. What did you mean?"

The man gave him an uneasy look. "People dying, crazy women running loose. Heard that some of them were murderers, and at least one of them escaped. I want to get done and get outta there."

Cap was sweating, which, considering the temperature, seemed strange. Eli shifted in the seat, and glanced over to see the man staring at his badge.

Shaking now, Cap pulled on the reins, trying to stop the wagon. He was about to make a run for it.

Eli grabbed his arm. "Just tell me what's going on. I'm not here to arrest you."

"I don't know how that girl got in my wagon," he blurted. "I was supposed to meet up with some man in Moccasin Rock, and bring back a load of corn for the patients here. I got there early and was going to grab something to eat first. I parked in the alley. That's when I saw that dead girl. I swear, I didn't kill her."

It finally dawned on Eli that the man was talking about Maggie. "Why didn't you go for help?"

"I was afraid that everyone would think I killed her."

"So what did you do?"

"After I ordered my meal—which I couldn't even eat cause my belly was churning—I decided to get rid of the body. I planned to leave her somewhere, and then hightail it out of there."

"What happened?"

Cap looked at him, wild-eyed. "She was gone when I got back. I was so spooked I just ran. Not sure what happened, but I did not kill that woman. You got to believe me."

"I do," Eli said, relieved they'd had this little talk where no one would overhear. "That's all I wanted to know. Since you've been so helpful, and even though it probably means you left here while the asylum was still burning instead of sticking around to help, I won't tell anyone else about your involvement. As long as you don't go around talking about it. Deal?"

The man nodded at him eagerly, grabbed the reins, and set the wagon in motion again.

It didn't take long to reach their destination. From the corner of his eye Eli saw the driver set the brake, jump down and take off. Probably never to be seen again. Eli didn't care; his attention had been captured by the Fair Haven Lunatic Asylum.

It was an eerie, almost unbelievable sight.

It had obviously been a showplace at one time—three stories of dark red brick, steeply-pitched roofs, at least five chimneys, massive porticos, and a wrought iron fence with fancy little curlicues running along the top. But it wasn't a showplace now. There were busted windows and missing shingles. Bars had been installed on the windows of the ground floor, but none on the top. *No one could escape from up there.* A broken hinge on the gate had left it hanging.

Only part of the place was burned. The way Maggie had talked, Eli had expected to see charred ruins. Of course, in the dark of night, from the inside, it must've seemed like the whole world was on fire.

One of the men milling around outside the place turned to stare at them, coming forward when Eli and Nathaniel stepped down from the wagon.

"I'm Sheriff Shiloh Clark," the man said. "What can I do for you fellows?"

Eli told him their names, but before he could come up with an appropriate, but vague, reason for being there, his brother did.

"I'm treating a patient who was held here briefly," Nathaniel said. "I was in town on another matter, and heard folks talking about what happened out here. Out of curiosity decided to stop by."

"It seemed too strange to be true," Eli added.

"Yeah, it's strange all right," Shiloh Clark said, "but unfortunately, it's true."

"I've never seen anything quite like this place," Eli admitted. "Mind if we take a look inside?"

"Can't wander around," Shiloh said. "But I don't mind showing you the front room."

Eli followed the sheriff up the steps and inside, where signs of the original grandeur were still evident—expensive woods, marble floors, vaulted ceilings, and a fire place big enough for a full-grown man to stand up in. A wide staircase in the center of the room swept off into two separate staircases when it reached the second floor—one curving to the left, the other to the right. Nothing was burned, but there was smoke damage.

"What's the story on this place?" Nathaniel asked.

Sheriff Clark tilted his hat back. "It was built by a man back east for his wife and daughters in the 70s."

"This must have cost a fortune," Eli said. "In materials alone. There wasn't much of anything in this area back then, let alone a place to find marble and mahogany. How did he even get it all here?"

"Believe it or not, he had materials shipped in to Galveston, from all over the world, and then freighted in from there by ox and wagon. Took him years. I've heard that several times the wagon trains were attacked by Indians. And they had to deal with outlaws. There was bloodshed over this monstrosity from the very beginning."

Awed, Eli continued studying the structure. "I guess my question is *why* would he build here? Nothing personal, but Fair Haven doesn't seem like a logical location, especially then."

Shiloh Clark shrugged. "I don't understand it either. Some people called him an eccentric. Seems to me he was just crazy. He'd made his fortune and grown bored. He was convinced there was untapped wealth to be had in this part of Texas. I sure ain't seen none of it."

Eli stood in front of the floor-to-ceiling windows overlooking the cedar covered hills. "How long did they live here?"

"Never did. The man finally convinced his wife to come and see it, thinking she'd fall in love. She didn't. His girls were nearly grown by then, and they didn't want to live here either. He took them back into town and the whole family was gone the next day. Nobody seems to know what happened to the man after that. This place was empty and a nuisance for years. There was a caretaker, but he was always calling on us to help run people out of here."

"So how did it become an asylum?" Eli asked.

A troubled expression crossed Clark's face. "A few years ago a man by the name of Manson Mitchell showed up and said he was buying this place and was going to fix it up. To be honest, we didn't really know what was going on out here until we heard about the fire."

"Somebody had to know," Eli said, "for there to be patients out here."

"We knew it was an asylum. We didn't know about the experiments."

A chill crept up Eli's spine. "What kind of experiments?"

Shiloh took off his hat, tapping it against his leg as he ran a hand through his hair. "I don't really understand it all, but it wasn't good. We found some strange looking contraptions in the basement—more than the usual straps, chains and things. He'd even set up an operating room. Dr. Mitchell was either doing surgeries on these women, or planning it. There were boxes of files in one of the unburned rooms. I don't know anything about medicine, and don't want to, but even I could tell that some of it seemed more like torture than cure. "

He led them to the front door. "I don't like to talk ill of the dead," Shiloh added, "but I'm glad the fellow died here. Course, there were some innocent folks who died too."

Outside, Eli craned his neck to get a better view of the upper floors. A bird flew out through one of the broken window panes and he thought of Maggie trapped here.

It would be disturbing enough to walk into a place like this under your own power, but to be hauled inside against your will, when you were in your right mind, was unthinkable. Even the women who genuinely needed help, didn't need this kind.

"I still don't know exactly what all happened out here," Shiloh said. "But there's a girl that hasn't been accounted for. I suspect she holds the key. Her family is searching for her. When they find her, I plan to get some answers."

Maggie was running out of time. And where did the baby fit in? Not one person had mentioned her.

Chapter Thirteen

MAGGIE GREETED ELI with a hesitant smile and hopeful eyes when he stopped at Peg's just before noon the next day.

"Do you have news of my father?"

"Yes, Nathaniel was able to see him. He seems to be physically frail, but of sound mind."

Her smile brightened. "That's wonderful. Please, tell me all about it. Do you mind if we talk in the kitchen?"

"Not at all. I also have some questions for you, since we didn't get much of a chance to talk yet."

Maggie's smile slipped a little, but she led him to the back of the house without further comment.

She waved him toward one of the kitchen chairs, while she hurried straight to the stove. Eli was surprised to see her doing so well. She hadn't actually given birth he reminded himself, but still he was impressed.

Her hair was tangle free, brushed smooth and shiny, and pulled back with a yellow ribbon. The scratches on her face were starting to heal. Dressed in a faded yellow and white gingham dress, one of Peg's he supposed, she had on thick socks, but no shoes.

She sure looked prettier in Peg's dress than she had the late Mr. Harmon's clothing.

The baby was sleeping in a box on a chair. Eli stood and stepped closer. She too, looked a lot better.

He glanced up to see Maggie watching him.

"How's she doing?" he asked.

Maggie smiled. "Peg thinks she's going to be all right."

"I'm glad to hear that," Eli said.

While Maggie used a fork to turn pieces of chicken sizzling in a cast iron skillet, he filled her in on the visit to Fair Haven. He'd only gotten as far as saying that Hollis Anderson opened the front door and let them in when she turned to him with surprise that quickly turned to anger.

"Are you saying that Hollis has taken up residence in my home?"

"It sure looked that way," Eli said.

"There's nothing I can do about that, yet," she said. "But Lord willing, that man will be out of our lives soon. So did you actually get to see my father?"

"I didn't," Eli said. "Anderson would only allow Nathaniel to go up. But he assured me that your father was in good shape. Now, I have a few questions for you."

She bit her lip and turned back to the stove. "Can it wait until after we eat? You're welcome to stay. There's plenty."

Eli's stomach protested as he opened his mouth to decline the invitation. The smell of the chicken, mashed potatoes, greens and cornbread was making it awfully hard to turn the offer down. But was it the food that made him want to stay? He needed to tread carefully here.

"Sheriff?"

Eli blinked when he realized he'd been staring at her.

"Will you stay for dinner?"

Eli couldn't think of a polite way to refuse the invitation; perhaps because he really didn't want to. "You sure you have enough? Don't want to intrude."

"Oh, yes. There's plenty."

She thrust a bowl of mashed potatoes into his hands and asked him to place it on the table just as Peg Harmon walked in.

"Hey, Sheriff," Peg said with a smile. "You figure on staying?"

"Yes, ma'am. If it's all right with you."

"Sure it is. Have a seat."

Within a few minutes they had all the food on the table. He waited until the women were seated before he pulled up a chair. He didn't really feel comfortable saying grace, and was relieved when Peg did.

"How are things in the sheriffing business?" Peg asked as she scooped up some mashed potatoes for his plate.

Maggie added a couple of pieces of chicken, and the other food while Eli answered. "About like always. Long stretches of nothing at all, then everything happens at once."

"I guess that's the way it is with about everything," Peg said. "Same with me."

Eli had known Peg Harmon for a year, but really didn't know much about her, except that she was a widow. Nathaniel worked with her a lot, but it was the first time Eli had ever spent any time in her company. She'd always seemed brusque and no nonsense. He was surprised to find her pleasant company.

And Maggie, well, she pretty much talked nonstop after Peg got quiet. And although the younger woman's voice was soft and pleasant, there was a desperate edge to it that saddened Eli.

She was either trying to distract herself from thoughts of the coming conversation, or distract him. She talked about the weather, the train service to Fair Haven, even her favorite foods. He couldn't make himself bring up the questions about the asylum or the baby...yet.

"This is an excellent meal," Peg said to Maggie. "Where did you learn to cook like this?"

"I'm curious myself," Eli admitted. "Even though Hollis Anderson mentioned being understaffed, it looks like y'all had plenty of help there."

Maggie waved a hand. "We do. But my father only ever liked my mother's cooking. I learned at her side. When she died, I began preparing food for him. We had servants for everything else. My father was good at making money. My mother was good at making my father happy. She spoiled him, pure and simple."

Considering what Maggie had said when he caught her trying to escape, Eli couldn't resist asking her another question. "Do you think it was wrong of her to devote her time to your father?"

Maggie's expression softened. "No. The devotion was mutual. My father adored my mother. I don't recall him ever saying a cross word to her. He told me once that he considered it a privilege to provide for her."

When the baby fussed, Maggie left the table to prepare a bottle, but she didn't stop talking.

When Peg finished eating, she offered to put the baby to bed in the other room.

Once she left, Maggie sat back down at the table. "What is it you wanted to talk about, Sheriff?"

"Please, call me Eli."

She nodded.

"I'd like to start by sorting out some of the lies you've been telling me," he said.

Maggie stiffened and drew herself up like she was ready to fight him.

Eli kept his voice low and even. "I need the truth, Maggie, or I'm never going to be able to help you. You understand?"

She stared at him for several long seconds before an expression of resignation settled on her face. "What do you want to know?"

"Have you ever been married?"

She glanced down at her hands. "No."

"What about the baby?"

Face filling with color, Maggie shrugged. "It's a story as old as time, do I really need to go into detail?"

So she still wasn't willing to tell him the whole truth. "Are you engaged?"

Maggie lifted her head and those golden brown eyes stared straight into his. "No. I told you the truth about that. Hollis Anderson is not my fiancé."

"Why is he telling everyone that he is?"

"My father is encouraging him. I don't know why, except maybe Papa is desperate to see me taken care of before he dies. He worries about what will happen to me. He's afraid I'll die a spinster."

Eli didn't believe there was any possibility of that happening. "How old are you?"

"Twenty-three."

"My, my. You are in your dotage."

Maggie smiled, but it didn't reach her eyes. She surprised him with a question of her own. "How old are you?"

Eli answered without a second thought. "Thirty-one, for a few more months."

"Do you have a wife? Children?"

"No, I…" He stopped. *Maggie was trying to distract him. And doing a fine job.* "Let's stick to the matter at hand for now."

"All right."

"So I understand now why Hollis Anderson is claiming to be your fiancé. Why did he have you committed?"

That question brought back a spark of outrage. "Because he could! He wanted to show me that he will be in charge of me. That he can make my life as miserable as he wishes."

"I hate to keep repeating myself, but why?"

"I embarrassed him. Also, even though he's a wealthy man in his own right, I think he believes if he can control me now, he'll have no trouble controlling my inheritance."

"This is about money?" *He should've known.*

"Yes. Papa's made no secret of the fact that he's leaving everything to me."

"Even if Hollis is interested in financial gain, what makes you think he doesn't love you?"

Maggie immediately launched into a long list of reasons, including the fact that he acted completely different when her father wasn't around.

"How did he convince your father to go along with placing you in the asylum?"

Maggie glanced away. "Papa happened to come into the kitchen moments after Hollis Anderson placed his hands on my arms and shook me."

"He shook you?"

"Yes. And his fingers were biting into my arms. I…I may have reacted a bit strongly."

"Strongly? Like how?"

She exhaled deeply. "I hit Hollis in the head with a cast iron skillet."

Eli ducked his head to hide a grin.

"You have to understand," Maggie rushed on, "at the time I felt like I was fighting for my life. I realize now that I would've been much better off remaining calm until he was gone, and then talking everything over with my father."

Maggie twisted her napkin, then untwisted it and smoothed it out. "I wish I could live that day over," she admitted. "The tighter he held me, the more I panicked. Hollis managed to convince Papa that I was close to breaking down and needed to rest. That I'd be better off somewhere that knew how to care for me. Papa signed some papers, and in short order I was sedated and committed to the Fair Haven Lunatic Asylum. I doubt if my father knew where I was being sent. I wasn't aware the place existed until I was confined there."

Eli worked to keep his expression blank. He didn't want her to know how upset he was until he'd heard the whole story. He wished now he had punched Hollis Anderson in the face. Especially after learning what the asylum doctor might have been planning. *Did she know about that?*

"The Fair Haven sheriff told us they found some sort of contraptions and notes that made it seem like the doctor planned to do medical experiments on the patients out there. Did you endure anything like that?"

Her face turned ashen. "No," she breathed. "How awful."

"How long were you there?"

"Several weeks. I tried to escape a few times, so they made it increasingly difficult for me. As I mentioned before, they took my shoes. Then they took my clothes away at night, so I wouldn't try anything. They'd give me a dress in the morning. Not my own clothing, but I was grateful."

"Have you remembered anything about how you made it to Moccasin Rock?"

She shook her head.

"I think I might have an answer," Eli said, telling her about the man named Cap.

"I'm so grateful that he left the wagon where he did," Maggie said. "I can't imagine what could have happened if I'd climbed out of there anywhere else."

She'd touched her ribs again, probably without realizing it.

"Maggie, who beat you?"

She drew in a shaky breath. "One of the guards. There were several male guards, patrolling outside. Inside there were women working there. To be honest, I'm not sure if they were nurses or not. If so, they hadn't had much training. They were negligent, but they weren't violent."

Maggie pressed her fingers to her eyes. When she lowered her hands, the bleakness in her expression hit him like a punch to the gut.

"One night, one of the male guards came into the room and yanked me up from the cot by my hair. At first, he just slapped me a few times. The second time he came in, it got worse. Even when it seemed unbearable to me, he reminded me that he was pulling his punches. That he could kill me without ever breaking a sweat. Everyone there called him Tiny. He wasn't."

Eli felt anger tightening like a coil inside. "Didn't anyone working there come to help?"

"No. In all fairness, they seemed overwhelmed at times. Almost scared. After the first beating, they let me keep the dress to cover the bruises. I think they were afraid of being blamed. Or maybe they were afraid the same thing would happen to them."

"This guard, did he…" Eli was trying to determine the most delicate way to phrase his question. He didn't want to add to her misery by embarrassing her. But she understood the question without him voicing it.

"No, he didn't. I was terrified that he would, and he even admitted he wanted to, but he told me that Hollis had warned him that I'd better still be…pure, when I returned home."

Maggie brushed back her hair with a trembling hand. "The beatings were merely a form of persuasion," she said.

Eli's fists clenched. He wanted to find that guard and dispense a little frontier justice. He was also intrigued by the fact that she seemed to have forgotten she was supposed to have been in an advanced stage of pregnancy at that time. *Not exactly the definition of pure.*

Why wasn't she telling him the whole truth? But he didn't say anything about the obvious contradiction. If he could keep her talking, he'd have the full story soon enough. "What was the guard trying to persuade you to do?"

"He said that Hollis instructed him to do whatever it took to make me return home and marry him. And I had to sign some papers."

Eli blinked a couple of times. "Papers?"

"Yes. I had to agree, in writing, that I'd turn over my trust fund to Hollis when we marry, and I had to pretend to care for him. My affection had to seem sincere."

Obviously she was right about the money, but the second part was confusing. "I don't understand."

"It's not difficult at all, sheriff. Not only does Hollis want control of my future finances, he wants me to grovel. In public. You see, I rejected his proposal in front of several prominent people. They were attending a dinner in our home. In Hollis's opinion I had to pay for that. He wanted me to see how easy it would be to control me, whenever, and however, he wants. That way, I'd be the perfect little submissive wife."

Why hadn't she attacked the man with something worse than a frying pan? "Doesn't the Bible say something about submissive wives?"

So far, all his questions had produced fearful or evasive responses, but that idle question was like throwing a match into dry timberland.

"A man is supposed to love his wife the way Christ loves the Church," Maggie snapped. "Violently shaking me, intimidating me and having me committed to an asylum does not seem the sort of thing a loving husband would do."

"No, it doesn't," Eli murmured.

"Even if I felt Hollis had any real affection for me, I wouldn't have tolerated that," Maggie said. "I will not be dictated to, abused or oppressed, by any man. Although I strive to live peaceably with everyone, I answer only to God and my father. Until such time as I'm married, and then I will also submit to my husband."

She paused, then raised a hand and started in again as if he'd been arguing with her. "As long as his dictates are biblical, I prefer to be a helpmeet to my future husband, not a servant or a possession."

Good grief. Eli had a feeling this wasn't the first time Maggie Radford had given this speech. Probably sent more than one suitor running scared. No wonder her father was worried. And yet it didn't scare Eli, at all. In fact, he was mesmerized by her passionate response; even more so as her brown eyes flashed and her skin took on a lovely shade of pink again.

Shaking his head, Eli drew himself up and got back to business. He'd seen men mesmerized by a lot of things, including snakes. None of it ended well.

"So you see why I have to get home to my father," she said.

"I can see why you want to, and why you feel the need. But what if you're arrested for starting the fire? Sheriff Clark expressed an interest in finding you. It's too risky."

"Why can't you go with me to Fair Haven? Together we could talk to my father and try to get him to see what's happening. You're a lawman. Maybe that'll make a difference."

"I have no authority there," he said.

She leaned back in her chair and crossed her arms. "Then I have no choice but to go alone. I'll have to take my chances."

Eli groaned. "You're the most exasperating female I have ever run across, and that's saying something." His tone gentled. "Then again, if you weren't strong, I don't suppose you could have survived these past few weeks."

Her expression and posture relaxed a little. "I'm not trying to be difficult, Sheriff. I'm desperate."

"I understand," Eli said. "Give me a little time to sort this all out. I really am trying to help you, and keep you safe."

"I know, and I appreciate it." She stood, as if their conversation was over. "Would you like some cake before you go?"

Well, that was subtle. "No, thank you," he said. "Sure enjoyed dinner, though."

"Glad you liked it." Maggie gathered plates from the table, then scraped them and placed them in a round graniteware pan before filling a kettle at the pump and placing it on the stove. "I forgot to heat the water for the dishes."

She then gathered the cups and glasses from the table; relaxed, smiling, still talking, but with less desperation now.

It was a scene of domestic tranquility that Eli had never experienced. Even though it was only temporary, he let himself soak it all in—the warmth of the room, the beauty of the woman, the flow of gentle conversation.

Eli hated to end it. But he had no choice.

Maggie was facing away from him, when he said, "Before I go, why don't you tell me the truth about the baby? Who's her mother?"

The cup she held slipped from her fingers, shattering as it hit the floor.

Chapter Fourteen

WITH SHAKING HANDS Maggie picked up the bigger pieces of the shattered cup.

He knew. She should've been prepared. She should have known he'd figure it out. Drying her shaky hands on her apron, Maggie tried to decide what to tell him.

Eli leapt up to help. He finished sweeping up the smaller pieces and sat back down at the table. He didn't say anything, just kept those coffee brown eyes leveled at her. Waiting for the truth.

Mind spinning, Maggie opened her mouth to lie again, but she couldn't do it.

Pulling out a chair, she sat down across from him. *Please Lord, help me make him understand.*

"Her mother's name was Lucy Gray," Maggie said softly. "She was only sixteen, and a patient at the asylum. Everyone there called her Little Lucy."

He frowned. "I didn't realize there was anyone there that young. Was Lucy insane?"

"No, in some ways, her situation was similar to mine. She'd been placed there unjustly. As a young girl she'd gone to work as kitchen help for a wealthy family. The baby's father was her employer's son."

"The son didn't want to marry her?"

"It wasn't that. According to Lucy, the young man loved her.

When he learned about the baby he asked her to marry him. He was older than Lucy, but from what I gathered, he wasn't much more than a boy himself."

"I noticed you referring to the mother in the past tense, what happened to her?"

"She died right after Lucinda was born."

Eli's brows drew together. "I'm sorry to hear that. I need you to tell me everything you remember about this girl. What did she look like?"

"She was small, had reddish blonde hair, and a birthmark beneath her right eye."

"So what happened that night?"

Clearing her throat, Maggie told him how it had all unfolded, or at least what she could tell him. "The day before the fire, Lucy went into labor. One of the women who worked there told me the physician who was running the asylum had requested my assistance. I was to report to his office immediately."

"Had he made that request before?"

"No, and I admitted that I didn't understand why he wanted my help. I had no medical training or experience. The doctor explained that Lucy had been asking for me. And that she'd been screaming for hours. For a while, Lucy and I had been in the same room. Then they moved her to the other side of the building. Unfortunately, the doctor didn't want my *help*, he wanted me to handle everything. He was leaving. An important appointment, he said. I decided he picked me because he knew there was nothing wrong with me. And Lucy and I had formed a friendship."

"He couldn't have gone far," Eli said. "His body was found in the rubble."

Maggie shivered. "Right before he left, the doctor finally admitted that Lucy was having difficulties, and that she would probably die. He said there wasn't anything I could do except to keep her quiet"—Maggie's voice broke—"until it was over."

"Keep her quiet?"

"Yes, according to him, some of the patients were reacting poorly to her screaming. I don't think they were upset about the noise—there was always screaming there—I think they were upset because Lucy was suffering and no one was helping her."

"What about the baby? Wasn't the doctor concerned about her?"

Maggie shook her head. "He said she would be dead soon, too. He told me to place "it" in a bag, and to not move anything out of that room." A thought struck her. "Do you think he planned to use their bodies for his research or experiments?"

The sheriff's expression tightened. "It's possible."

Nausea hit Maggie. She squeezed her eyes shut, gripping the edge of the table until the room stopped spinning. When she opened them again, the Sheriff was standing beside her.

"You okay?"

"I'm fine," Maggie said. "Please sit down. I don't think I can go through this again. Let's get it over with."

He took a seat across from her, but he still seemed concerned. "When you feel up to it, tell me what happened next."

"I told the doctor I would take care of Lucy, but I couldn't do it alone, that I needed help. So he let Mabel go with me."

Eli interrupted her. "Was she…" he cleared his throat. "Did that woman need to be there?"

"In my opinion nobody needed to be there," Maggie said. "But if you're asking was she insane, yes, I believe so. As I told you before, I think she was responsible for the fire. She was a big woman, scary looking, but she was gentle when it came to Little Lucy. She told me that Lucy reminded her of the daughter she'd lost years ago."

Eli nodded, and motioned for her to continue.

"Mabel was furious when she found out that the doctor didn't plan on delivering the baby himself. She said she was going to create a distraction so I could get Lucy out of there and get her help."

Maggie had started off intending to deliver a brief summary

of the night, but she found herself reliving each moment, in vivid detail. And yet she was only able to vocalize bits and pieces of the horror. She realized her voice had dropped when Eli leaned in closer.

"There was only weak lighting, and it was so cold. And there was so much blood. There was blood everywhere."

The sheriff's gaze was trained on her hands now, and Maggie realized she was wringing them in a scrubbing motion. She placed her hands in her lap.

"Mabel left, and I never saw her again. The fire started not long afterwards. Lucy was dying right before my eyes. She begged me to take the baby out of the asylum and find a home for her. She didn't want her child to spend even one day in that awful place. The last words I said to her were that I would take Lucinda and raise her as my own. She smiled at me and whispered thank you. That innocent baby was the only good and decent thing to come out of this ordeal, Sheriff." Maggie clenched her fists. "I will fight for her."

"I understand that, but there's one other consideration. What about the baby's father? You said Lucy was working for a wealthy family. Where did they live?"

"All…all I know is that the baby's father is dead."

He continued to question her, and Maggie answered each question, but she couldn't answer them fully.

"Why do I get the feeling you're still holding something back?"

She shook her head, unsure how to answer that.

Eli rubbed his temples. "All right. I've got things to do around town. I'll be back to check on you soon."

"Thank you, Eli. You sure you wouldn't like a piece of cake before you go?"

He pushed back his chair. "No, I'd better get on back to the jail. But thanks."

Maggie had one other question for him. "Does Peg know? About the baby, I mean?"

"Yes, and Nathaniel."

She pressed her hands to her face. "I'm so sorry about this, and embarrassed—"

A knock on the front door stopped her. Eli motioned for her to remain in the kitchen and headed for the front.

Maggie relaxed when she heard him say, "Come on in." It was someone he trusted.

"Came to check on my patients," Dr. Nathaniel said, as he stepped into the kitchen ahead of Eli.

They all knew it wasn't her baby, and yet they were treating her with kindness and respect. Grateful, but still embarrassed, Maggie said, "We're both doing well, doctor. Thank you for the fine care you gave us."

He nodded, and then went straight to the box to look at the baby. "You're welcome, but it was mostly Peg. And please, call me Nathaniel."

"I'm grateful to both of you."

While he looked the baby over, with Eli hovering nearby, Maggie studied the two brothers, noticing their similarities—dark hair, brown eyes, firm jaw line. But there were also differences. Eli wore denim pants, light gray shirt and black vest. And a long black coat—a duster—over it all.

Nathaniel also wore a dark vest, and light-colored shirt, but he'd paired it with dark trousers. Nathaniel was clean shaven, and Eli had a day's stubble. The main difference was there was no gun on Nathaniel's hip.

The doctor glanced up to see her staring. "Don't fret. The baby is doing remarkably well."

"Thank you for checking," Maggie said. "Would you like something to eat? I have a cake ready to slice."

He didn't even hesitate. "Sounds good."

Maggie was surprised when the sheriff pulled out a chair next to his brother and sat down again, too.

"I guess maybe I'll take that cake after all," Eli said.

She sliced another piece and set it before him, her casual smile belying her turmoil. *Why was he staying?* She'd told him everything that had happened that night.

Well, almost everything.

CHAPTER FIFTEEN

ELI AND NATHANIEL were waiting at the depot for the returning newlyweds. Eli knew the minute Caleb stepped off the train that he had some big news.

The youngest Calhoun brother strived hard for a steely lawman look, and it worked—most of the time, with most people. But Eli could read him almost as easily as he did his other brother.

Despite their vastly different childhoods, and not even knowing of each other's existence until a few months ago, there'd been an almost instant bond between him and Caleb. Once they'd gotten past a few punches.

"So what's got you lit up like you swallowed a lantern?" Eli asked him now.

Caleb grinned. "I don't know how you do that, but yes, I do have some news." He paused and drew in a deep breath, managing to convey both elation and a little alarm. "You're looking at a soon-to-be Papa."

Eli's reaction was a blend of genuine happiness for Caleb and a surprising stab of envy.

The happiness quickly took top place. He slapped Caleb on the back. "Congratulations, Papa."

"Thanks. Abby insisted that I not make a big fuss," Caleb grumbled. "She's as happy about the news as I am, but she seems to think that a quiet announcement once we get back to her family's boarding house will suffice."

They all three glanced in the direction of Abby, who was surrounded by her own family, and smiled at the sudden burst of excited exclamations and a flurry of hugs.

"I think maybe she went ahead and told them," Nathaniel said.

"Looks like they're as happy as we are for y'all."

"So what did your bride think of New York?" Eli asked.

"She loved it, but not as much as she loves Moccasin Rock." Caleb looked around him. "I was surprised to discover I missed this little town, too. So what's been going on since I left?"

"They've begun construction on the bridge to Boone Springs," Eli told him. "They're almost through with the hotel, and the surveyors are working on the site for the new courthouse."

"Which means lots of folks in town," Nathaniel said.

Eli wanted to ask Caleb for his opinion about the situation with Maggie Radford, but first there was one other bit of news he wanted to share. Before he could get the words out, Nathaniel beat him to it. "We started going to church right after you left. Got saved and baptized."

Caleb's expression softened. "I'm glad to hear that. Real glad."

As Caleb and Nathaniel talked, Eli reflected on how strange life could be. When an old gun-toting evangelist had preached a revival during the summer, it had changed several lives, including Eli's, even though he hadn't attended even once.

He wished he could tell Caleb how he felt, how grateful he was to both him and the old preacher, but it was difficult to put into words all that had gone into making such a decision.

"I sure am sorry I wasn't here for the baptism," Caleb said. "Wouldn't have minded seeing you guys dunked in the Brazos."

"Thought about waiting," Eli admitted. "But Pastor Wilkie warned us that the river was getting awfully cold, and that we might have to wait until next spring. Didn't want to wait for months, and didn't want to catch my death either."

Caleb laughed. "Can't say I blame you. So, no trouble while I was gone?"

Eli's hesitation was brief, yet Caleb picked up on it. "Something wrong?"

"In a way," Eli said, "but it's not something I want to get into out here. Can you come by the jail when you get a chance?"

Caleb's gaze sharpened. "Let me say hello to everyone, then I'll head that way. Abby and I are staying with her folks at the boarding house until we get our housing situation figured out. I plan to build us a place as soon as possible."

"I know of one vacant house you might consider in the meantime," Eli said.

Nathaniel also threw in a suggestion or two, and then they watched as Caleb made his way to the Hortons. The welcome he received was just as enthusiastic as Abby's had been. *Apparently everyone was glad to have him back in town.*

Although Eli had no doubt that he could handle whatever trouble was coming, he had to admit it felt good to have someone to back him up.

In less than an hour, Caleb was sitting in front of the stove at the jailhouse. He glanced around. "Where's Bliss?"

"Who knows," Eli said. "Did you need him?"

"No, wanted to say hi. Abby and I saw him in Weatherford, leaving a bank. I hollered at him, but I guess he didn't hear me. Kept walking."

"You sure it was Bliss?" *What was the old man doing there?*

"Yep. Now what's on your mind?"

Eli told him about Maggie Radford's unusual arrival, and everything he'd learned since then. He'd already filled Nathaniel in on her confession about the baby.

Caleb let out a low whistle. "That's some story. What do you need from me?"

"I think she remembers more than she's letting on," Eli said. "I was hoping that you'd talk to her, in the guise of investigating the fire. See if you can learn anything new."

Caleb glanced at Nathaniel, who nodded his head in agreement. "She's definitely holding something back."

Putting his hands behind his head, Caleb leaned back in the chair and studied Eli. "You're the one who intimidates everyone, why can't you get her to talk?"

"That's just it," Eli said. "I don't want to intimidate or scare her. She's been through too much."

Caleb looked at him with an odd expression. "I see."

"You see what?" Eli growled.

Caleb shrugged.

"Look," Eli said, "I would feel this way about anyone who'd been through what she has. I'd rather not add to her misery by badgering, if we could get the same information through charm and sweet talk. And let's face it, you're the one that people find so charming."

Caleb glowered at him, obviously not thrilled by that statement, which gave Eli at least a little satisfaction.

"Okay," Caleb said, "what do you need, specifically?"

"When Maggie finally admitted the baby wasn't hers, she was still in a great deal of turmoil about something. I want to know what."

Shrugging, Caleb said, "After everything she went through, maybe her fear and mistrust is going to linger for a while."

"That's true." Eli knew how hard it was to forget some things. "But what if the baby's mother didn't really die?"

Neither Caleb nor Nathaniel had an answer to that.

"And even if she did," Eli continued, "what about the baby's grandparents? Lucy was an orphan, but the baby's father has family somewhere. What if they want her?"

"You've got a point," Nathaniel said. "Did Maggie tell you who they were?"

Eli shook his head. "No. All she would tell me is that Lucy said they were horrible people. Maybe she'll tell Caleb who they are."

Caleb reached for his coffee, drained the last of it, and placed the cup on the desk. "Why don't we make sure the mother did die in the fire, and then go on from there?"

"Nathaniel and I went by the asylum in Fair Haven, or what's left of it." Eli said. "I also talked to the Claiborne County Sheriff, Shiloh Clark, about the bodies they'd recovered. I couldn't ask too many questions, and no specifics, or he would've wondered why. According to Clark, one woman had family to claim her, but several were buried at the Fair Haven cemetery in unmarked graves."

"What happened to the patients who survived?" Caleb asked.

"Sheriff Clark said they loaded them up and took them to a facility in Cartersville." Eli knew in his heart that he needed to visit that asylum, and yet he still hated having to do it.

"I feel like a heel, doing this behind Maggie's back," he admitted, "and I can't even imagine having to take that baby from her, but…" His words trailed off.

"You have a responsibility to do the right thing," Nathaniel said softly.

Eli nodded.

"If you want to check that place out," Caleb said, "I'll go with you."

"I appreciate it," Eli said. "Having a Texas Ranger along is never a bad idea." Eli looked at his other brother. "Do you want to go?"

"I'd best stay here," Nathaniel said. "Got several patients that need tending to."

"I understand. Do you mind checking on things at Peg's if you get a chance?"

"Don't worry," Nathaniel said, "I'll look in on Maggie and the baby."

"Thanks," Eli said. "I'm not sure exactly what I'm worried about. I have an uneasy feeling about all this."

And that unease was only growing stronger.

CHAPTER SIXTEEN

ELI AND CALEB left early the next morning, taking a train to the Cartersville asylum, a rambling structure that had once been part of an old Army fort.

It in no way resembled the place where Maggie had been held, but when they pushed through the iron gates and entered the front door there was definitely a sense of gloom.

They were greeted by a formidable looking woman wearing a long black dress with a full-length white apron on top. There was a huge ring of keys attached to the wide leather belt at her waist. *Is this the kind of woman that Maggie had seen?* Eli also wasn't sure if the woman was a guard or nurse. But he could understand how helpless Maggie must have felt.

After Eli explained that he was there on behalf of a Fair Haven patient's family member, which baby Lucinda truly was, the physician in charge invited them into his office and answered their questions. Working from what little he'd learned from Maggie, Eli gave the man Little Lucy's description, full name and age, and what little he knew about her mental condition.

The doctor countered with the same information about the patients who'd been transferred to his facility. None of them seemed like a match.

"Because of the fire, it was all a rather hurried affair," the man admitted. "And I'm not sure how accurate any of it is. We do have some young women, though. I normally try to sort the patients by those who were born with some sort of mental defect, and those who've developed some sort of mental or emotional derangement. For now, all the transfers have been grouped together."

The disorganization didn't help reassure Eli that Lucy Gray wasn't there. And he really wanted to know. "Is there a way we could actually see the patients?"

The doctor studied him a moment. "I don't normally let anyone into the wards. However, since you're here in an official capacity I will make an exception. As long as you're prepared for what you might encounter."

Eli had started to stand, but he sat back down. "Such as what?"

"Anything," the man said bluntly. "Some of these women are in a near comatose condition, while others are combative. Many of them are dangerous. Some of the inmates are chained, because they're a danger to others."

Leading them out of his office and down a corridor that branched off into two long hallways, the doctor explained that the men were housed in separate quarters.

After a few steps down the first hall, Eli wished he'd not asked for the personal tour. Caleb's steps also slowed. The doors resembled cell doors, barred and narrow. Eli knew that in most asylums people were referred to as inmates, and he could see why.

While the doctor was able to clinically assess the situation it was startling for Eli, and he suspected for Caleb, to see women in various stages of emotional and even physical distress. Some of the cells—and Eli could think of them no other way—held multiple inmates, and others only one or two. Some of the women were jeering and calling out to them and others were staring into space. Not all of them were dressed. It wasn't for his sake that he wanted to leave. It was for theirs.

Eli glanced at the doctor. "Sometimes their clothing is taken," the man explained, "for a variety of reasons. Sometimes they undress themselves."

From the corner of his eye Eli saw a woman reach through the bars, trying to grab Caleb. She was wearing a baggy, shapeless dress that dragged the floor. Her arms were stick thin, her face gaunt, and her gray hair was clipped close to her head. She was babbling away to Caleb, seeming to plead with him, while his brother tried to soothe her and back away at the same time.

Eli shook his head. People instinctively liked Caleb, even with a badge pinned to his vest. And yet people seemed scared of Eli, even without the badge. Of course, he was responsible for that. There'd been times in life that a hostile expression and harsh demeanor were all that kept him alive. *That and his speed with a gun.*

Eli hung back, aware of the agitated murmur of those around him, his attention on Caleb. No telling what these people had been through, maybe at the hands of the law. He didn't want to upset them more. He'd let Caleb handle everything.

Even though Eli was listening to the doctor, he realized the woman was now saying something about a baby to Caleb. *Baby?* Had she been in the fire and managed to get away? Did she know anything about what had happened to Lucy Gray and her child that night?

Eli started toward the woman, but she suddenly pushed back from Caleb and stumbled away. Crawling on to a cot, she turned to face the wall.

Caleb walked away from the cell, shaking his head, compassion in his eyes.

"What was she telling you?" Eli asked.

"I don't really know for sure," Caleb said. "She was crying and jabbering about her baby, and then sorta collapsed. The last thing I heard was her mumbling some nursery rhyme or poem."

Eli turned to the doctor. "Has she said anything else about a baby since she was transferred?"

The doctor adjusted his glasses. "Even if she had, I doubt it's relevant to your search. That's not one of the Fair Haven patients. It's a sad story. Some soldiers found her tied to a tree years ago. She was broken, physically and mentally, and wasn't expected to live. Said she'd been left there by Indians. But she made a remarkable recovery. She even helps out here. Most of the time, you'd never know that anything was wrong with her. Every now and then, though, something will set her off."

They left the asylum a short time later. Although Eli was disturbed by what he'd seen, none of it had anything to do with Maggie Radford or Lucinda's mother. It looked like Lucy Gray had died. Now Eli had to eliminate the grandparents as possible guardians.

"When we get back to Moccasin Rock, will you talk to Maggie?" he asked Caleb. "See what you can discover?"

"Sure," Caleb said. "I can't promise I'll have any better luck than you did."

"I know. But I can't let it go."

It wasn't that Eli wanted to take the child away from Maggie. Just the opposite. He wanted her to be able to keep Lucinda.

But not if the baby rightfully belonged to someone else.

✍

Maggie stared at the ranger, trying hard not to fidget. She would tell him everything she'd told Eli. Then again, that really wasn't everything.

Not that she was happy about it. Hiding the truth wasn't something she was accustomed to, and now she'd lied to not one, but two, lawmen.

Caleb Calhoun had introduced himself as the sheriff's brother, but she would've known he was related to Eli and Nathaniel without being told. Even though this man had green eyes, and the other two had brown, there was a strong family resemblance.

"So you went to the asylum in Cartersville. What did you learn?"

"Not much," he admitted. "Can you describe the baby's mother to me?"

"Yes, of course. Like I told the sheriff, she was small, reddish-blonde hair, a birthmark beneath her right eye. Was there anyone like that there?"

Maggie waited, praying that there had been, but she knew in her heart that she'd seen the life draining from Lucy's eyes.

"No," the ranger said. He then gave physical descriptions of the women he'd seen. None of them seemed familiar, but their situation certainly did.

"It's all so sad," Maggie said.

"It is," Caleb agreed, "but, at least from what I saw, most of them needed some kind of help. Although I admit it is hard to tell. There was one woman who seemed perfectly sane one moment, then suddenly started shrieking and reaching for me, and babbling about her baby. After a few moments, she stopped talking, stumbled off and started saying some little poem over and over again."

Her baby? Maybe Lucy had survived. Maggie leaned forward. "What did she look like?"

Caleb swallowed a sip of coffee. "Short, skinny, with gray hair that was chopped off."

"Poor soul. I don't recognize her from the description. She might have been kept in some other part of the building I was in."

Shaking his head, Caleb said, "Sorry for the confusion. I was saying that it was difficult to know who truly needed help. According to the guards, that woman has been there for years. They said she'd been found in the woods somewhere, tied to a tree. She'd been left there by Indians. As I was walking away, she was huddled up in a corner humming some tune, and mumbling something about wind pudding and rabbit tracks."

Compassion welled up in Maggie. "Wind pudding and rabbit tracks? That probably means something to her, but no one will ever know what. How tragic."

"Yes," Caleb agreed. "Now, can you tell me more about the women who were at the asylum in Fair Haven?"

Maggie told him what she remembered about Mabel and how the woman had offered to create a distraction, and what little she recalled about the others.

She knew this is what Eli had wanted, for her to talk freely, and she didn't see any harm in giving them what information she could. Without giving them too much. Gradually the conversation shifted to the subject of Lucinda's father.

"I don't know much about him," Maggie said. "I'm sorry I can't help you there."

Caleb placed the pencil on the table. "Maggie, this isn't about helping me. It's about the baby. I'm sure you want to do what's best for her."

"I really do." Maggie said, throat tight.

"Then will you tell me about the father's family?"

Guilt settled in on Maggie, as well as resignation. "His name was Anthony Chadwick, and I know that because Lucy called him by his full name every time she talked about him. Always with awe in her voice. Even after everything she'd been through, she was still amazed that *the* Anthony Chadwick had even noticed her. She said he came from a wealthy family in Fort Worth."

"How did she meet this man?"

"Lucy was a maid in the Chadwick home."

Writing all that down, Caleb nodded for her to continue.

"When her employers discovered what they referred to as 'her situation' they demanded that Lucy leave. Not only that, they laid the blame for everything at her feet…sure beyond a shadow of a doubt that their son wouldn't have been involved in anything… unseemly." Maggie couldn't control the derision in her tone, remembering how devastated and alone that Lucy had been.

"So she was put out of the home," Caleb said, "but how did she end up in the asylum?"

"She wasn't put out, at first," Maggie said. "The son stood up to his parents, told them he was the responsible party and that he planned to marry Lucy. I never did know all the details about what happened next, because Lucy couldn't tell it without crying, but the baby's father died before the wedding. Somehow he fell from his horse and broke his neck. After the funeral his parents wasted no time disposing of their problem. They said that having Little Lucy committed was the most compassionate thing they could think of. After all, they couldn't put her out into the world in her shameful condition."

"What about Lucy's family? Couldn't they have come to her aid?"

"She was an orphan. So you see, I'm all this baby has now."

Caleb didn't argue with her, but Maggie could see that he wasn't entirely convinced either. She tried to look at the situation from his point of view. *He didn't know her.* For all he knew it could be a fabrication. She didn't want to make things difficult for him or the sheriff, but she wasn't willing to risk Lucinda's well-being. Little Lucy had been sick with worry about how horrible the Chadwicks were. She had been frightened of them. And scared for her baby. So was Maggie.

While he was making notes about their conversation, Maggie asked several questions of Caleb, including how long he'd been a ranger, and if he enjoyed the work—and he graciously answered.

"So interesting that you and your brother are both lawmen," she said. "Was it something y'all wanted to do from an early age?"

Caleb Calhoun stared at her over his coffee cup.

Uh, oh. This man didn't seem as intimidating as his oldest brother, but he was every bit as sharp. He knew she was digging for information.

"I'm not sure how much you know about our family situation," Caleb said, "but I wasn't aware that I even had brothers until recently."

Maggie felt the heat rise in her face. "I didn't know that."

"We had the same father, but different mothers. We didn't meet up until earlier this year."

Even though Maggie found that intriguing, she was really more interested in discovering all she could about Eli Calhoun's past. If the man hadn't been a lawman long, how did he acquire the speed and proficiency with a weapon?

"Eli came here over a year ago," Caleb said, "and Nathaniel ended up here about six months later. I met them both over the summer."

"That's fascinating," Maggie murmured. "Wonder how long Eli's been a lawman. I hear he's awfully good with a gun."

Again, Caleb Calhoun gave her that appraising look. "You should ask Eli these questions yourself."

"Yes, of cou…course," Maggie stuttered.

"I'm assuming that you've heard that Eli shot and killed some outlaws that were robbing the bank," Caleb said. "I can tell you that it's true."

He provided few details, but everything he told her matched what Brody had said.

"And yes," Caleb added, "he's fast with a gun. Fastest I've ever seen. He's a good man, good brother and a good sheriff. I trust him with my life."

The comment was pointed. She needed to trust Eli, too.

Ranger Calhoun left a short time later, and Maggie remained at the table. She hadn't learned everything she'd wanted to know, but she felt a little better about her situation.

She too, would trust Eli Calhoun with her life.

She had no choice.

Chapter Seventeen

ELI HEADED FOR the depot as the train whistle sounded in the distance. News of some big-wig politician's last minute decision to stop in Moccasin Rock had spread like wildfire and the crowd had been building at a steady pace for the past hour.

But that was always the way. Whether it was a revival, a baptism, a funeral or a carnival, anything out of the ordinary brought folks out in droves.

Eli hadn't attended a revival yet, though he supposed he would the next time one was held, but he'd been to plenty of the other events, including a few political rallies—which was more than enough.

Obviously, not all folks felt that way. It looked like everyone in Moccasin Rock was here. Except for Maggie and Caleb. *How was their discussion going?* He hoped Caleb had better luck than he had.

Eli reached down and plucked a little freckle-faced boy from the railroad tracks just before the train chugged into view. Eli handed the boy to his harried-looking mother.

"Much obliged, Sheriff."

"You're welcome."

Despite the shriek of the whistle and the deafening rattle, people pressed closer, some with hands over their ears, as the train shuddered and screeched to a stop. As the smoke cleared and the last car—draped with flags, banners and bunting—came into view, a small band began playing a rousing patriotic tune. Eli stared at them in astonishment. He hadn't even known Moccasin Rock had a band.

People surged toward the back of the train as several men, all nattily dressed and waving to the crowd, stepped out onto the platform of the last car.

An eager young man with a wide grin and big ears began introducing the illustrious visiting speaker, describing his business experience, his impeccable character, and good old-fashioned horse-sense. "Ladies and gentlemen, it is with great pleasure that I introduce you to J. L. Slidell, the next senator for the great state of Texas."

Eli stifled a yawn as the crowd broke out in wild applause. He doubted if most of these folks had ever even heard of Slidell. He hadn't.

Glancing once at the man of the hour—black suit, red vest, black hat—Eli gently, but firmly, began moving people back again.

He was facing away from the train when the first words left the politician's mouth. "Hello, folks. So kind of you to join me today."

Eli stopped moving. Unable, unwilling, to believe what he was hearing. *It couldn't be.*

Pushing his way deep into the crowd, Eli stopped, turned and reluctantly faced a piece of his past. *Jasper.*

His stomach lurched as the man glanced in his direction. Heart pounding, Eli stepped back even deeper into the crowd, tilting his hat down to cover his face.

He won't remember you. You've changed too much. Strangely, Jasper had hardly changed at all. The blond hair was now silver, but he had that same old easy laugh and carefree grin.

Bliss made his way through the cheering throng. "If you squeezed all the hot air out of that fellow there wouldn't be nothing left."

"I would like to squeeze the life out of him," Eli said, realizing that his tone hadn't matched the carefree jesting of his deputy's when the old man's eyes narrowed.

"Something I should know?"

"No, everything's okay." No sense involving Bliss in whatever was going to happen. And something was going to happen. For a moment he'd been that scared kid again, but only for a moment. *Where was Nathaniel?* Eli had to warn him. Pushing past people he headed toward his brother's office. Nathaniel had just stepped out, coat in hand.

Eli wasted no time on a greeting. "Jasper's here."

Nathaniel froze, his eyes revealing the same horror that Eli had felt when he heard the man's voice.

Then Nathaniel visibly pulled himself together and put on his coat. "Where?"

"At the train station. He's the politician that everybody's in such a dither over."

Nathaniel's mouth dropped open. "Jasper is J.L. Slidell?"

"I had no idea," Eli admitted. "I don't guess I ever remembered hearing his last name back then."

"Me either." They listened to the roar of the crowd. "What do you want to do?" Nathaniel asked.

"I want to beat him to a bloody pulp," Eli said.

Nathaniel nodded. "What are we going to do?"

"I'm going to beat him to a bloody pulp."

Nathaniel kept that steady gaze leveled at him. He didn't say anything else; he didn't need to.

"That man shot someone," Eli said. "And somehow or other he needs to pay for what he did."

"Agreed. And he especially needs to *not* win this election. If there's anything more terrifying than the thought of Jasper as an evil private citizen, it's the thought of him with power and clout. But we can't run up and attack him. For numerous reasons."

Nathaniel was right.

In silence, they returned to the depot and watched from the edges of the crowd. People were pressing forward to get a better look at the man of the hour, some even trying to touch him. As if he was a hero. It was disturbing.

"We have to do something," Nathaniel muttered.

"I know," Eli said. "But he's surrounded by people. I don't recognize most of them, so I'm assuming they're traveling with him. I wasn't even aware he was still alive, let alone that he'd gone into politics. We need to know everything there is before we make a move."

"One person we might ask is the publisher of the *Gazette*," Nathaniel said. "Newspaper folk usually know what's going on."

"Couldn't hurt," Eli agreed. They looked around, hoping to catch a glimpse of Luther Tillman, but saw only his young reporter.

Together they approached the newspaper office, just down the road.

"Surprised you aren't over at the train station," Tillman said when they walked in.

"Was about to say the same to you," Eli said.

The publisher waved a hand. "I heard Slidell's speech a few weeks ago in another town. Nothing new. I did send my reporter to cover this one, though. If there's anything particularly newsworthy, he'll let me know. So what can I do for you?"

"Maybe nothing," Eli admitted. "I was thinking while I was standing out there listening to Slidell, that I don't know much about the man's past at all. There's such a big crowd to see him that he must be doing something right. Figured you might have some information about him."

Tillman's gaze was shrewd. "Slidell's a businessman from San Angelo. He's owned, or been a partner in, more than half a dozen businesses. Very successful. But a good portion of his wealth comes from his wife's people."

"His wife? I don't think I've heard anything about his family."

"He's married to a woman named Maria Gaetti, owner of Benedetto Boots. They have three children."

Luther was bent over the typesetting tray and didn't see the incredulous looks that Eli and Nathaniel shared.

It was the last thing they'd expected to learn, but it was exactly what they needed to stop Jasper Slidell.

∽

"Hello, Jasper."

The man leaving Bony Joe's café, cigar in hand, seemed surprised by the too-familiar greeting from the unfamiliar face.

But he retained his slick politician's smile as Eli and Nathaniel blocked his path.

"Good afternoon, gentlemen." Jasper reached into his coat pocket, removed a flyer, and pressed it into Eli's hand. His practiced smile slipped a little when Eli opened his fingers and let the paper drop.

"Do you have a problem, Sheriff?"

"No," Eli said, "but you do."

Frowning, J.L. Slidell looked around him.

"If you're looking for your friends, they're at the station master's office," Nathaniel said. "They got a message to meet you there. That'll give us a few minutes to talk."

"Talk about what?"

The man had no idea who they were. "You don't remember us, do you?"

"Of course he doesn't," Nathaniel said. "The last time he saw us we were kids."

"You're correct," the man said, "I don't know you. And you seem to have me confused with someone else." His gaze shifted from Eli to Nathaniel and back again. Eli knew the instant he remembered.

"Unfortunately for you, we're not kids anymore, Jasper."

A look of fear flickered across the man's face—a mere flash, gone in an instant—before he regained control. Pulling himself up straighter, he gave them that same old lazy smile. "Well, well, it appears that you two survived after all. I would've been willing to bet that you died before you hit puberty."

"I wouldn't have given much for your chances of survival either," Eli said. "The night we left you were in quite a predicament."

Jasper's expression tightened. "Yes, thanks to you, I was. Luckily, I'm a better talker than I am a gambler."

Up close, the lines on their old benefactor's face were more pronounced, and the hair was a little thinner, but it was still the same old Jasper.

"It's been a delight catching up with you boys," he said, "but it's getting late. What do you want?"

"I wonder how the citizens of Texas will feel when they hear about your past," Nathaniel said.

Jasper shrugged. "Doubt if it will matter one bit. People understand youthful indiscretions."

"First of all, it's not like you were a kid," Eli said. "And even though it's true some people won't blink an eye about you running brothels back in your younger days, they may feel differently about you trying to kill someone."

Nathaniel's eyes narrowed. "Yes, Jasper. That's a different story. I think they'll find that particularly interesting. The authorities might not be able to get a conviction after all these years, or even take it to trial, but I have a feeling it will make a difference to the voters."

"Especially to Maria," Eli said softly.

Jasper jerked back as if he'd hit him. "I should've come after you that night," he snapped. Pulling himself together he gave them another smile. "You'll never be able to prove a thing. Who's going to believe you? You were nobodies then, and you're nobodies now. You'll be making enemies of some powerful people if you even try to sully my reputation."

Jasper was probably right, but Eli wasn't about to let him walk away. "I'll take my chances."

With a dramatic sigh, Jasper said, "Is it money you're after? Are you boys strapped for cash?"

Eli grinned and staggered back. "You wound me," he said. Then he sobered. "Not that it'd be the first time for that either. We don't want a thing from you. Except a couple of promises."

Jasper's voice took on an edge. "Promises of what?"

"That you'll quit this race, and that you'll never run for public office again."

Jasper's eyes narrowed. "I don't think you realize who you're trying to intimidate, boys. Don't you understand I could have you eliminated in a heartbeat? Nobody would ever suspect a thing. I have some very powerful friends."

"We understand that fully," Eli said. "That's why we made arrangements—with some powerful friends of our own—before we spoke to you. If anything happens to us, a world of hurt is going to come crashing down on you."

Although Eli had dashed off a letter and arranged for its delivery to Caleb if anything should happen to them, he was making every-thing sound more threatening than it was. He *had* to stop Jasper Slidell from running for office. Otherwise, Eli wasn't sure what he would do.

Jasper's lips curled into a sneer. "There'll always be people like me. You can't stop them all."

"Then I guess I'll have to settle for stopping you," Eli said softly.

Throwing down his cigar, the man ground it under his heel, never breaking eye-contact with Eli.

The message was clear. He could do the same thing to the Cal-houn boys any time he wanted.

CHAPTER EIGHTEEN

MAGGIE DIDN'T HAVE much time to brood or worry over her conversation with Caleb Calhoun.

After he left, Brody Flynn knocked on the back door. He'd been by several times since their first conversation, a little more relaxed with each visit.

The boy still seemed intrigued by the baby, and still reluctant to get closer.

This time, as soon as he sat down Maggie thrust Lucinda into his arms, giving him no chance to refuse.

"Do you mind holding her?" Maggie said. "I need to get the wash in off the line. She'll need fresh bedding and diapers soon."

The look of fear on Brody's face was almost comical. "I might drop her," he said.

Maggie shook her head. "You'll do no such thing. Keep her in the crook of your arm, and don't let her head bob around."

Since Maggie had recently been on the receiving end of the same instructions, it felt good to be the one passing them along.

Brody still seemed hesitant, so she played her best card. "Sheriff Calhoun held her."

"Really?"

Knowing that his hero had done something made him at least

willing to try. The boy settled back in the chair, cradling the baby with such a look of trepidation that Maggie couldn't hide her smile.

"Thank you for your help, Brody." She pointed to a plate on the table. "And for helping me, you can take that whole batch of cookies with you."

He was smiling when she left.

It took only a few minutes to gather the laundry and put everything in the basket. As Maggie made her way up the back steps, she was startled to see someone brush past her and into the kitchen. The little girl next door. And following her was the puppy.

"Hello. You're Ruthie, right?"

The girl nodded. Clutching a rag doll in one arm, her dark brown eyes surveyed the room in wide-eyed appraisal. Her gaze lingered on Brody and the baby, and then narrowed in on the cookies. The dog, a mutt of some sort, was sniffing around the room, tail wagging.

"What's your puppy's name?" Maggie asked.

The girl smiled. "Ollie."

"Ollie is a beautiful dog."

Brody looked at the little girl and then at Maggie, while the girl looked at the baby. Catching Brody's eye, Maggie shrugged.

"I'm going to put these things away," Maggie told Brody. "Won't be gone but a minute. You okay to hold Lucinda a little longer?"

"Sure," Brody said, with a certain amount of swagger now.

Maggie figured it would be an altogether different story if the baby began to cry. Smiling she hurried from the room, and glanced down to see Ruthie tagging along beside her.

In the bedroom, the girl watched silently as Maggie removed the clothes from the basket, folded a few items, and placed them in the wardrobe. She added others to a stack to iron later. Maggie tried several times to get a conversation going, but the girl spoke mostly in monosyllabic replies.

At one point Maggie thought Ruthie left, then realized she'd moved to the other side of the bed, and was now looking at everything on top of the dresser. Then she bent down and stared at the rug. *Curious child.*

As they were leaving the room, Ruthie pointed to Maggie's crocheted slippers.

"What's those?"

"These are my shoes," Maggie told her. "At least for now. I don't have my real shoes with me."

The girl followed Maggie back to the kitchen. Again, her gaze lingered on the cookies. Maggie's heart warmed when Brody reached out and snagged a couple and handed them to her.

Ruthie was staring at him with an expression of awe when a worried voice sounded from next door. "Ruthie? Where are you?"

With treat in hand, and the dog on her heels, the girl disappeared as suddenly as she'd arrived.

After Brody finished off several cookies, he left, too, saying he was making deliveries for Silas Martin that afternoon. As she'd promised, Maggie wrapped up the remaining cookies in a napkin for him to take.

Maggie fed the baby and put her down for a nap, and then sat down at the table to peel potatoes. A soft tap at the back door had her on her feet again, wiping her hands on her apron. Maggie cracked the door open. It was the little girl again, holding a pair of beautiful, beaded moccasins. She handed them to Maggie.

"What are these for?"

Ruthy pointed to Maggie's feet. "My mother said to give them to you."

Truly delighted, Maggie thanked the girl, who nodded and promptly disappeared again.

Maggie was still standing there marveling over a stranger's kindness, when Peg entered the kitchen. She was followed by a young woman carrying a couple of brown paper packages.

"Maggie, this is Abigail Calhoun, Caleb's wife and Eli and

Nathaniel's new sister-in-law," Peg said, then seemed at a loss as how to finish the introduction.

Placing the moccasins on a chair, Maggie smiled. "My name is Maggie. I'm a guest of Peg's. It's nice to meet you, Abigail."

Blue eyes sparkling, the other woman smiled. "Please, call me Abby." Setting the packages down on the clean side of the table, she tugged off her gorgeous fur-trimmed, sateen lined coat, and then her suede gloves—a soft cranberry color—and placed them in the coat pockets, before laying it across the back of one of the kitchen chairs. She was chattering away the whole time.

Maggie wasn't quite sure what to think of the woman. Although she was expensively clad, she was completely at ease among the kitchen clutter. Peg seemed to be well-acquainted with the young woman. But Maggie wasn't comfortable, and apparently it showed.

"Please don't be concerned," Abby said. "Caleb told me about your current situation."

Maggie was relieved, but also curious. *Exactly what had Caleb said?*

Thankfully, Maggie hadn't told him everything. *What would a Texas Ranger do if he knew she was responsible for a man's death?* Maggie had asked God for forgiveness, but she couldn't speak of it to anyone else. She might be put away somewhere worse than the asylum.

"Please, sit a spell," Peg said to their guest. "Would you like a cup of tea? Or coffee?"

"Nothing for me," Abby said. "I won't be long. I wanted to drop off a few things for Maggie. Caleb said that it's not safe for her to return home at the moment."

Abby then opened the larger package and took out several dresses. "I hope you're not offended," she said to Maggie. "They're not new, but they haven't been worn much. And I think they'll fit you."

"I'm not offended at all," Maggie said, taking one of the lovely garments and holding it in front of her. "I'm grateful." *Another person who didn't know her had stepped up to help.*

Peg left the room, saying she had things to tend to, and Maggie sat down across the table from Abby.

Handing Maggie the smaller package, Abby said, "These, however, are new." Maggie opened it to discover a hairbrush, comb, toothbrush, tooth cleaning powder, hair pins, and a bar of scented soap. Things that she'd taken for granted her entire life, and never would again. She had adjusted to a lot, but not to using a rag to clean her teeth.

Maggie stared at the other woman in astonishment. "How thoughtful of you. I will pay you for these as soon as I'm able."

Abby waved a hand. "Please, don't worry about it. I stopped by the mercantile and tried to think of what I would need if I'd had to leave home with nothing."

"I can't tell you how much I appreciate this," Maggie said. Beyond that, she really didn't want to say much else. She hated to lie to this woman, and yet if they talked for very long, she would have to. Abby's cheerful, easy manner soon won her over.

Maggie poured tea for the two of them, while Abby talked. Maggie learned a little more about the Calhoun brothers, including the fact that Eli was building a house on some land just outside of town, near the Brazos River, and that Caleb had purchased land there also. Abby's face lit up as she talked about her recent trip to New York and about her happiness at being home again.

At one point Abby leaned forward. "I'm expecting a baby in the spring."

"Oh, that's wonderful," Maggie said. Moments later, when Lucinda's cries sounded from the bedroom, Maggie invited Abby to see the baby.

Abby jumped at the chance, and as she held Lucinda and fed her, it was obvious she was already more comfortable with the baby than Maggie had been. "I was eleven when my little brother was born," Abby explained.

Maggie enjoyed their time together so much that her guilt continued to grow. When all this was resolved she would come back to find all the Calhouns, and apologize in person.

After Abby left, reluctantly placing a sleeping Lucinda in the box, Maggie returned to her cooking, fixing a pot of potato soup and cornbread.

By the time Peg led a young red-haired man into the kitchen, Maggie was actually beginning to tire. But the minute he introduced himself, she rallied.

"Ma'am, my name is Wilkie Brown. I'm the pastor of the Moccasin Rock Church."

"Oh, it's so nice to meet you," Maggie said.

Peg excused herself so that the two of them could talk.

"Sheriff Calhoun mentioned to me that you were a guest of Mrs. Harmon's," Wilkie said, "and due to circumstances not of your own making, you can't attend church for the time being."

Maggie was touched by Eli's thoughtfulness. "Yes, unfortunately, that's true. And I miss it so much."

Waiting until she was seated, the man lowered himself onto one of the chairs. "I was wondering if you might like me to pray with you. Or perhaps a scripture reading? The sheriff thought it might bring you comfort."

"Both would be wonderful."

What followed was the most peaceful hour that Maggie had spent since she'd been taken from her home. The preacher read from the twenty-third Psalm and then several other passages, some of her choosing, and some of his, before bowing his head and praying with her, and for her.

Later that evening, Eli dropped by, knocking softly on the back door.

Peg had gone to bed early, and the baby was asleep, but Maggie was awake and working in the kitchen.

"I saw the light back here," Eli said. "Wanted to drop this off." He reached down for something on the porch. A cradle.

"Oh my, where did you find that?" Maggie said as he brought it inside.

"I made it."

She stared at him in surprise. "It's beautiful. I'm so grateful."

He nodded and moved to the stove, hands outstretched to warm them up. "How are y'all getting along?"

Maggie knelt beside the cradle, running a hand along the side, then touching it gently to start it rocking. "It was a day filled with visitors and surprises."

Concern flashed across his face.

"All good," she said. "Thank you for sending your pastor to talk to me. It meant a great deal."

"Oh." Eli looked at his boots, then at the stove, and then past her, before looking at her. "I'm new to the church-going thing," he admitted, "but I figured it might be important for someone who was used to it."

Curious, she stared at him. "How did you know I was missing church?"

"I didn't really, but I've seen you praying a couple of times."

The man was even more observant than she'd first thought. She found that comforting and concerning at the same time.

"I know about two of your visitors," Eli said. "Thank you for talking to Caleb."

"Did he tell you about Lucinda's grandparents?"

"Yes."

Despair hit Maggie anew. "Eli, I'm begging you, please think long and hard before you contact them. They're not good people."

He seemed to give her plea thoughtful consideration, but made no promises. "I'll let you know what I decide. Who else did you see?"

She told him about Abby, Ruthie and Brody.

"I'm not surprised about Abby," Eli said. "She's a sweet girl and comes from a good family. Haven't met Ruthie yet, but I've met her Pa. Seems like a nice fellow."

"Tell me about Brody," Maggie said.

"He's a great kid. His family lives way back in the woods; and from what I understand, they rarely venture into town."

"What are his parents like?"

Eli shrugged, turning around in front of the stove. "Brody's hinted from time-to-time that his folks aren't much on visitors so I've tried to stay away. I'm planning on going out to see them soon, though."

"So you've never met them?"

"I've sent messages with Brody but apparently they're real skittish. Might have some sort of secret they're hiding, I guess. People like their privacy. Brody's a good boy, even has good manners. That tells me a lot about his folks. He's being raised right."

The baby started fussing before Maggie could question him further, and Eli left. But Brody and the Flynn family stayed on her mind long after the baby was quiet.

Maggie was still wide awake when Lucinda began crying again from her new bed. The sound didn't bring the fear it once did. "Well, hello there sweet baby," she crooned. "Let's see how fast Mama can get you dry and fed."

Maggie stopped and then smiled. It was the first time she'd referred to herself as "Mama." It felt right.

In the kitchen, with the lamp light creating shadows on the wall, and the wood in the stove crackling, Maggie settled down in a chair and cuddled the baby close. Her eyes had begun to droop when a noise sent a prickle of unease through her.

It was the creaking of wood, such as footsteps on a floor, but it hadn't come from the direction of the hall. It was coming from the back porch.

Maybe it was Eli. It wouldn't surprise her to find that the sheriff checked on them during the night, yet this felt different.

Reaching out with a trembling hand, she doused the lantern. Darkness descended on the room, except for the light from the stove.

Grateful that the baby was now sleeping and soundless in her arms, Maggie stood and crept toward the window.

Lifting the curtain a bit with one finger, she peered out into the darkness. She couldn't see a thing.

Then she heard it. Another furtive movement. The barest whisper of sound. Then came the unmistakable ping of someone bumping into the wash tub.

"Who is it?" she called, heart pounding.

Seconds passed, each feeling like an eternity, before Ruthie's dog began barking, startling Maggie and waking the baby.

"Shhh," she whispered to the startled baby. "It was only a dog we heard."

Then a thought occurred. What had the dog been barking at?

Chapter Nineteen

"I'M GOING STIR-CRAZY, Eli. I've been cooped up here for two weeks. I've cleaned every inch of Peg's house. The poor baby has been cleaned as thoroughly and as often, and she's tired of hearing me sing lullabies. Peg has her now. Can't I please go for a walk? I promise I'll be careful."

Despite her fright of several nights ago, Maggie had convinced herself that it was definitely the puppy that had bumped into the washtub. She'd simply worked herself into a case of nervous hysteria because of her dread of Hollis Anderson.

Eli didn't say anything, and Maggie had almost given up hope when he said, "How would you like to go fishing?"

"I would love it...I think."

"Have you never caught a fish?"

She shook her head. "No."

"Time you did. Put on those men's clothes again and we'll go. Not only will you get some fresh air, but if the fish are biting we'll have a good lunch."

Maggie would much rather have worn a dress, but she readily donned the trousers and shirt and hurried to where Eli waited in the kitchen.

He smiled when he saw her, then shook his head a little. Leaving by the back door, he led her directly into the woods where they were swallowed up by thickets and brush.

For a moment, Maggie's thoughts flashed back to her terrifying flight from the asylum and her breath caught in her throat. But she reminded herself that no one was chasing her this time.

In fact, Eli was patiently holding back limbs and branches so that she could pass through easily. She took a couple of deep breaths and pushed the bad memories from her mind.

"There are people set up in tents in that direction," Eli said, "so we need to go this way."

Maggie nodded, not really noticing which way he pointed, her attention captured by a chattering squirrel that jumped from one tree-top to the next. She smiled. Obviously the critter wasn't pleased to have company.

After they'd been walking awhile, Eli pointed off to the west. "I'm building a house about a half mile down that way," he said.

Curious, Maggie hoped he would suggest stopping by there, but he pressed on. Apparently he was more excited about fishing than she was. Standing on the banks of the Brazos River a little later, Maggie still didn't know if she'd enjoy fishing, but she could say that she loved being outside.

The sky was a brilliant blue and there was only the slightest breeze. It had been cold several days ago, now the temperature was perfect. The weather wasn't the only thing that Maggie was aware of, though. She was captivated by the way the sunlight played over Eli's dark hair, the way it reflected in his eyes. He'd rolled his shirt sleeves up, and the muscles in his forearm rippled when he used a knife to cut a willow branch to make her a fishing pole.

After tying a string to the stick, and a hook to the string, Eli used a smaller stick to dig around in the damp earth.

"What are you doing?"

"Looking for bait." Pulling a fat, wriggling worm from the dirt, he held it up.

Smiling, Maggie wrinkled her nose. "I don't know that I could eat something that's last meal was a worm," she teased.

He returned the smile, but his eyes were shadowed. "You'd be surprised what you can do if you get hungry enough."

Maggie wanted him to expand on that, but he stuck the willow branch in her hand and helped guide her to the perfect spot. "This area of the Brazos truly is beautiful," she said.

Eli agreed. "One of my favorite places. There's an old legend that says it was the Spanish friars that named this river. Supposedly, after a rather miraculous escape from marauding Indians, they declared it to be Los Brazos de Dios—which, if I recall correctly, means the arms of God. Through the years everything but the word Brazos, which means arms, was dropped."

"I love that," Maggie said.

"Me, too. To be fair, there are other accounts of how it came to be called the Brazos; but that's my favorite."

"I'm surprised you didn't decide to build your house closer to the river," Maggie said.

"I didn't dare. It is beautiful, but it's also deadly at certain times of the year. This placid little place can be a raging torrent after a few days of rain."

Maggie settled down on the bank, amazed at the freedom of movement the trousers allowed. "So you can build a house, catch fish with a stick, make a cradle, shoot a gun, and probably lots of other things I don't know about. How did you learn to be so resourceful?" *She was most curious about the gun.*

"I grew up without my folks," Eli said simply. "Learned to do a lot of things, and learned *not* to do a lot of things. Sometimes the hard way."

Oh dear. "I'm sorry. How old were you when they…passed?"

"Well, that's a little complicated."

"How so?"

"Mama died first, but we had her a little longer than we had Daddy."

"I don't understand."

"Daddy left one day, and while he was gone, Mama died when our cabin caught fire."

"Oh, Eli, I'm so sorry."

He acknowledged her sympathy with a nod.

"How long was your father gone?"

"He never came back. Or so we thought at the time."

Maggie was confused, and admitted it.

"So were we, until recently," Eli said. "We thought he had abandoned us. But we found out that wasn't the case."

"You tracked him down?"

"No. But when Caleb hit town this summer, I knew at first glance we had to be kin. And given his age—younger than me and Nathaniel—I realized Daddy had started another family."

She was about to tell him that Caleb had shared a little of the story with her, when he started talking again.

"I was stunned, and Caleb was every bit as surprised to find us. He was here on business, working on putting away an outlaw gang."

"I heard about that. It was big news in Fair Haven."

"According to Caleb, when Daddy returned for us all those years ago, he was told that we died in the fire with Mama. He later remarried."

Maggie gasped. "Why would someone do that?"

"I've wondered that myself. The old man who took us in, Mr. Pedlam, might have been worried that Daddy would kill him if he found out that we'd run from there…and why. That's the only thing I can figure out."

"Why did you run away?"

Eli's expression was suddenly so grim that Maggie was sorry she'd asked.

"Nathaniel started crying the first night we were with the old man. So much of that time is a blur, but I'll never forget that. We were little, our parents were gone. Our whole world was gone. We were scared. We weren't carrying on or anything, just crying. Laying on the floor in front of the fireplace. Unfortunately, that man wasn't having any of it. He'd been drinking out of a jug all evening."

Maggie closed her eyes against what was coming, her heart hurting for the little boys they'd been.

"With no warning at all, he staggered over and kicked Nathaniel in the stomach, told him to stop that squalling. Said he was going to make men out of us. Of course, that only made Nathaniel cry harder. So the man grabbed a leather strap, and started beating on him. When I tried to stop him, he turned on me. He finally got tired and stopped. We waited until he was passed out and we left."

"So the man told your father that y'all had died. And you never knew he'd even returned."

Eli nodded. "We thought Daddy had left us for good. Then Caleb told us that Daddy had heard a rumor that we might still be alive, and that he'd spent years looking for us...right up until he died. We had no idea."

"I can't imagine how that hurt," Maggie said.

"Yeah. But at least the waiting and wondering was over. I went looking for that old man after I was grown," Eli confessed. "Luckily for him, and maybe me, he was already dead."

"So where were you in between that time?"

"We wandered all over the place," Eli said. "To be honest, I don't know how we're even still alive. We were on a barge that capsized, I was bitten by a snake, Nathaniel was bitten by a dog, we nearly starved a time or two, and...well, you get the picture."

Yes, she did. And what a tragic picture it was.

"We met some good folks, and some bad folks, and learned that there were people out there even worse than Mr. Pedlam."

A fish tugging on the line distracted him, and Maggie was grateful. She wanted to learn more about Elijah Calhoun, but not if it made him miserable in the telling. She'd be leaving soon, and might never see the man again. Why bring him unnecessary pain?

The rest of their time at the river passed pleasantly, but too quickly. Maggie didn't get a fish, but she didn't mind. Eli caught four and told her he'd clean them if she would cook them. She agreed.

As they walked toward Peg's house, Maggie's thoughts drifted to Eli's story; such a horrible string of events for boys so young. She knew from experience that it was difficult to lose a parent at any age, but doubly so for children who lost both parents so young.

What if something happened to her father, and she never got to see him again? The thought made her physically ill. She had to convince Eli to let her go to Fair Haven before it was too late.

When he stopped and held a tree branch out of the way, she broached the subject again. "Since this outfit was enough of a disguise to go fishing in, maybe I could get away with wearing it to Fair Haven. If I could get to my father without anyone recognizing me, I could convince him to let me come home."

He was already shaking his head before she finished talking. "Not a good idea," Eli said. He was just getting in to a list of whys, when a shot rang out through the woods.

In lightning fast moves that seemed unreal, Eli dropped the stringer of fish, pulled the gun from his hip with one hand and pushed Maggie to the ground with the other.

She lay there, heart pounding. Was someone aiming at her? Or at him?

After a moment they heard a rustling sound in the underbrush, somewhere between them and the house. Helping her up, Eli motioned her behind another tree.

"I'm going to look around," he leaned in and whispered. "Stay here."

He didn't need to tell her twice. A moment later when a doe bounded by, relief filled Maggie.

Eli returned with gun in hand and a concerned look on his face.

"Did you see that deer?" Maggie said. "It was only a hunter."

"Maybe." But he didn't seem convinced. Eli looked around for several more minutes before holstering his gun.

"What are you thinking?"

"I don't know. Seems odd that's all." He then added something about the sound of the gun and the angle of the shot being wrong. She hadn't noticed.

"If not a hunter, who could it be?"

"What if it was Hollis Anderson?"

Despite the fact that she despised Hollis, Maggie had a hard time wrapping her mind around that notion. "I can't imagine him doing this."

"If he already has your father under his control, and he wants to make you pay, this could be the next step. Hollis is living in your house. Maybe he's setting himself up to be a son, instead of a son-in-law. He arranged for someone to beat you. What makes you think he wouldn't kill you if it would help him get what he's really after?"

Maggie had no answer to that.

CHAPTER TWENTY

MAGGIE COULDN'T BELIEVE her ears. "Do you mean it? I can go to Fair Haven? Why did you change your mind?"

"That shot in the woods got me to thinking about how truly vulnerable you are. No matter how much I want to, I can't watch you every minute. Your best bet is to get your father to come around to your way of thinking, for him to boot Hollis Anderson out of your house, out of your life."

"I couldn't agree more," Maggie said. "And I'm sure I can get him to listen to reason."

Eli held up a hand in caution. "There are a few conditions."

Maggie scurried around the kitchen, pouring hot water from the kettle to the dishpan, clearing the breakfast dishes, wiping down the table top and sideboard as Eli listed the stipulations on her accompanying him to Fair Haven.

"First, as you suggested, you have to wear some of those clothes that belonged to Peg's husband."

Maggie nodded. "Whatever it takes."

"Secondly, when we get there, you don't march up to the front door and demand to see your father."

That she had a problem with. "I have to. If I could only tell him what's happened to me, then I could convince him that Hollis

Anderson is trying to pull the wool over his eyes. That even if we don't know for sure what the man's doing, he's up to something."

"I agree. Like I said, that's why you're going. But my brothers and I have talked it over, and your approaching the house directly is too dangerous."

"So what am I to do?"

Pulling a chair out, Eli sat down and over the next few minutes presented a carefully thought-out plan that involved distraction, subterfuge and stealth. Then he summed it up in one sentence.

"So, Nathaniel and I will distract Hollis Anderson and any of his friends, while you sneak inside to see your father. They've seen me and Nathaniel before, so it won't seem too suspicious for us to show up there again."

Relieved that she'd be able to go at all, Maggie nodded, and they discussed a few more details. Eli suddenly grew silent, a somber expression on his face.

"What's wrong?" she asked.

"Maggie, I know you love your father, but are you sure you can trust him? Sometimes emotion can cloud a person's judgment."

Trying to prove how unemotional she could be, Maggie spoke in quiet, measured tones. "I trust my father completely. He is a kind, gentle man who has always wanted the best for me. Not once, in my entire life, have I felt threatened by him. No fear. If you can keep Hollis out of my way, then I'm sure I can make him see reason."

Eli didn't question her further. "Okay. Peg's agreed to watch the baby, and Caleb will help Bliss keep an eye on everything here. I'll be back in about an hour and we'll head out."

He stopped at the door. "Can you fix us up something to eat? Not a good idea to stop anywhere."

"Of course."

After gathering enough food to feed the four of them, including thick slices of ham and bread, and some tea cakes she'd prepared, Maggie hurried to the bedroom and dug through the trunk. Between the fishing, and then hitting the dirt when the shots were fired, the other clothes were dirty. She'd planned on laundering them today. But it could wait. This trip was far more important.

At the bottom of the stack she found a buckskin coat with fringe along the sleeves and around the hem at the bottom. She fingered the soft leather, still supple. It was in remarkably good shape.

After selecting a pair of trousers from the trunk, she rolled the legs up and pinned them in place. Since the weather had shifted yet again, the chill in the air had her donning both a flannel shirt and the buckskin jacket. It swallowed her up, but she adjusted the sleeves as best she could.

She hurried from the bedroom and into the front room where Peg was rocking the baby. The older woman was smiling and making a crooning sound as she cuddled the infant, but when she glanced up, the look she gave Maggie was tearful.

"Peg, is everything okay? Are you feeling poorly? I can take Lucinda with me."

The woman ran a work-worn hand across her eyes. "Everything is fine. You run on now. I enjoy the chance to hold a baby whenever I can."

Maggie wasn't convinced, but Peg didn't offer any further comment, and Eli's arrival meant it was time to go.

She met him at the door. He looked her over once, sighed and then shook his head. "Try to stay as low in the wagon as you can," he said.

Outside, Maggie greeted Nathaniel and Brody with a wave, but didn't say anything for fear of being overheard. Her voice did not match her appearance.

The back of the wagon was loaded with barrels, boxes and full burlap bags.

"What is all this?" Maggie whispered.

"Some are things we may need, and you'll be able to rest against the bags when you want to. It won't be a comfortable ride, but we can't take the train. Too risky. And I'm afraid you'd be more notice-able up front."

"I understand," Maggie said. "Whatever it takes. I'm tougher than I look."

"Nathaniel and I will be riding up front, and you and Brody will be in the back, hopefully looking like two young boys. Sorry about that."

"Don't be. I understand what needs to be done. Despite what you may have decided about me, I am a perfectly reasonable person, Sheriff."

They stared at each other a moment before Eli gave her a brisk nod, and helped her climb in.

"I need to stop by the jail and get a rifle," Eli said after everyone was situated.

"Are you expecting trouble?" Maggie asked.

"Not expecting it, but I believe in being prepared for anything."

Guiding the wagon to a stop near the front of the building, Eli cautioned Maggie about keeping her hat pulled low and her head down. "I'll be back in a minute."

As he approached the jail door, an older man with a badge stepped through and out onto the boardwalk. He opened his mouth to say something to Eli, and then froze, staring at Maggie wide-eyed.

Maggie smiled at him, but when his expression didn't change she glanced over her shoulder. Perhaps he was looking at someone else. No, at this early hour there was almost no one stirring, and definitely nothing unusual.

Eli seemed confused, too. "What's wrong?" he asked the deputy.

With a shake of his head, the old man muttered, "Nothing."

Eli looked back and forth between the deputy and Maggie. "Do you know Miss Radford?"

"Nope, can't say that I do." The man then stepped past Eli and greeted Maggie. "Howdy, ma'am."

"Keep your voice down," Eli hissed.

"I'm Bliss Walker," the man said, a little quieter. "I've heard about what happened to you, and I'm glad to see you looking so perky."

Maggie smiled. She wasn't sure why he'd reacted so strangely, but he seemed like a nice enough man.

As Eli stepped inside for the rifle, the old man stood next to the wagon, making idle talk with Nathaniel and Brody. More than once his gaze strayed to Maggie. It would've made her uncomfortable, but she didn't get the feeling that there was anything dangerous or improper in his behavior. Just strange.

Eli returned, stowed the rifle under the seat, and then gave a few last minute instructions to the deputy.

After the older man went back inside, Eli turned to Maggie. "Bliss said he didn't know you, but I was wondering if you recognized him."

"No. Why?"

"Just curious. I've never seen the man speechless before. Seemed odd."

Once they were under way, Maggie enjoyed the scenery as they traveled along the well-worn road over the rolling tree-covered hills.

In the spring, this was an incredible sight—with wildflowers and cactus in abundance. But even in the late fall and winter, it was something special.

Maggie had seen other areas of Texas—ranging from the deep piney woods, to the coastal region, and areas further west. Each had something special about it, and plenty of folks to sing its praises. But to Maggie, this part of Texas was the most beautiful of them all.

Although she and Brody talked a good bit, mostly about the landscape and occasional wildlife they spotted, eventually the boy fell asleep against one of the burlap bags. Maggie was content to breathe in the fresh air and feel the sunshine on her face. But as they drew nearer to Fair Haven, the more nervous she got.

What if she couldn't sway her father? Despite what she'd told

Eli, she wasn't certain of her success. Her father had changed in the past few months. He'd worn a frown more oft of late. Maggie had assumed it was from missing her mother.

She sat up straighter as they crested a hill and headed down in to Fair Haven proper. It seemed like she'd been gone forever. The streets were filled with carriages, buggies, wagons and carts; men, women and children hurrying along the boardwalk. The sight was familiar, and oh so dear.

Maggie was so focused on soaking in the sights and sounds, that at first she thought she'd dreamed up the image of her dearest friend. She blinked. No, this was real. Avalee Quinn was walking down Main Street and headed around the corner near the bank.

She watched as the woman crossed and turned onto the less congested side street. When Nathaniel slowed to allow another team of horses to turn first, Maggie jumped from the wagon, sprinted toward Avalee, grabbed her arm and tugged her toward the alley.

In her excitement, Maggie hadn't considered the possibility that her friend wouldn't recognize her in her new disguise. She figured it out when Avalee swung her purse, hitting her hard across the head.

"Ouch." Maggie put her hands up to shield her face.

"Unhand me this instant, you miscreant," Avalee screeched. She swung the purse again, and then kicked Maggie in the shin. "Help! Somebody help me!"

Hopping around on one leg, Maggie hissed, "Avalee, stop! No, don't scream!"

The blows ceased as suddenly as they'd begun. Maggie peeped through her fingers. Eli had grabbed Avalee and was holding her up off her feet, one hand across her mouth.

Avalee was kicking and struggling, and Eli was growling and glowering, obviously unsure what to do with this threat to Maggie's safety.

"Eli, it's all right. She's my friend."

Avalee's eyes rounded in surprise as she stilled. Eli removed his hand from her mouth. "Maggie?" she whispered. "Is that you?"

"Yes. That's what I was trying to tell you."

"Oh, Maggie, I've missed you." Still squirming, Avalee added, "Put me down this instant, you big ox." Then she looked up at Eli, drew in a breath and stopped struggling. "Oh, my."

There was something about the look on Avalee's face that Maggie didn't care for. The speed with which Eli released the woman made her feel better.

On her feet again, Avalee straightened her bonnet and continued to stare at Eli.

Eli gave Maggie a questioning look. "Who is this?"

"This is Avalee Quinn. We've been friends since childhood."

Eli straightened his own hat. Avalee had nearly knocked it off in the struggle. "I thought our deal was that you wouldn't let anyone get a good look at you," he said. "You don't know who all Anderson has under his thumb."

Now that Eli didn't have his arms wrapped around Avalee, Maggie was feeling sentimental about her old friend again. "Believe me; she would never cause me harm."

Maggie and bubbly little Avalee had sat side-by-side on the first day of school. They'd shared a slate and their lunches. Maggie's mother had filled her lunch bucket with sandwiches and fruit. Avalee had brought boiled eggs and two cookies. They'd split their bounty and became fast friends that day.

"Where have you been?" Avalee squealed now.

Maggie crossed her arms. "I was drugged, shackled and placed into a mental asylum."

Avalee stared at her for a moment before tears sprang to her eyes. "You're serious."

"Yes."

Eli had been hovering, but the genuine shock and horror on Avalee's face was obvious. If he'd had any doubt about whether

Avalee was truly Maggie's friend, that look should have erased it. He returned to the wagon, and left them to their conversation.

"Oh, Maggie, I'm so sorry," Avalee whispered.

"Why didn't anyone come looking for me?"

"I did," Avalee insisted. "I went to your house. I was worried when you didn't show up for the Society Sisters meeting. But that stuffy friend of your father's, Hollis Anderson, told me that you'd gone on a shopping spree to New Orleans. He said y'all were getting married."

Her words brought renewed anger to Maggie. "Hollis lied."

"I thought it was strange that you missed the meeting," Avalee said. "And that you didn't invite me to go with you, or even say goodbye. I decided you must have been in a big hurry." She made a little sniffling sound. "To tell the truth, I was hurt. I didn't even know that my dearest friend was getting married."

Maggie hugged her. "I'm not. And I didn't go shopping. I had no idea that Hollis was saying things like that."

"There were other ladies around town who were concerned," Avalee said. "Several even telephoned your father. He said the same thing that Hollis did. Why would your father lie? What is going on here?"

A wagon pulling in from the other end of the alley had Eli returning to Maggie's side. Several men exited the back door of one of the largest buildings and began unloading crates. One of the men looked at Avalee with an appreciative smile.

"We need to get a move on," Eli said. "Too many people here. We can't take any chances."

Avalee gave him a dimpled smile. "Maggie, you didn't introduce me to your friend."

Ignoring Avalee, Eli shot Maggie a look of warning.

Although Maggie knew full well she could trust her old friend with her life, she understood the sheriff's concern. If Hollis had managed to convince her father, her own flesh and blood, to go along with his schemes, there was no telling what he could do.

"He's a friend of mine," Maggie told her. "That's all I can say for now. He's on my side. I escaped the asylum and I'm perfectly safe. I'll explain everything as soon as I can."

"But, Maggie…"

"I've got to go, but no matter what Hollis Anderson says or does, don't believe him, and whatever you do, please don't tell him you saw me today."

"I won't," Avalee promised. "When will I see you again?"

"If everything works out like I'm hoping, I will be home for good soon. If not, I will figure out a way to send word."

Avalee nodded. "I'll be praying for you."

"Thank you," Maggie said, giving Avalee another hug. "I can't wait for life to get back to normal."

Yet even as she said the words, Maggie had the strangest feeling that normal might never be the same.

CHAPTER TWENTY-ONE

ELI TENSED AS they rounded a corner near the Radford house. Nathaniel held the reins, and Eli was watching Maggie over his shoulder. She was looking with longing at the grand structure from under the brim of her hat. *Be patient, Maggie.*

The plan was to pass the place once, looking it over to see if anyone was outside, and then leave the wagon on the next block and return on foot. That way they could each approach the house separately, and from different directions.

Suddenly Maggie's head snapped up and she gasped.

"Get down," he hissed, before tracking her gaze to the front porch where a man sat in a chair with a blanket wrapped around his shoulders.

The gasp she'd given should've been warning enough for Eli, but before he could stop her Maggie jumped from the wagon and bolted toward the house—dashing in front of a fancy carriage with a pair of matching black horses, narrowly missing being run down in the street. After what she'd pulled earlier, he should've been prepared.

By the time the carriage and the irate driver had passed, Maggie had neared the edge of the lawn. Eli couldn't call out to her for fear of alerting someone inside the house. He jumped from the seat and dashed after her, praying he could reach her in time.

Didn't she understand the risk? If Hollis Anderson caught her she could disappear again. And this time there might be nothing that Eli could do to help. His heart stopped when the front door opened. *No.*

He made a last desperate lunge for her, but Maggie halted so suddenly that he nearly plowed her over. Grabbing her upper arms, Eli jerked her backwards and down behind some shrubbery just as two men stepped through the front door.

One of the men was Hollis Anderson. Eli didn't recognize the other fellow. But he was grateful for their rather spirited conversation. Otherwise they would've seen Maggie. Eli pulled her further away until they were out of the men's sight. As soon as he caught his breath, he intended on giving her the griping out of a lifetime.

But he never got the chance. Maggie stared up at him, eyes huge, all color gone from her face.

"It's him," she whispered.

"Your father?" *Had his appearance changed so much that it frightened her?*

Maggie shook her head.

Eli glanced in the direction of the house. "You knew Hollis Anderson was staying here, right?"

"Not him. The other man. The one Hollis is talking to. I thought he was dead. I thought I killed him."

"Killed him?"

"Yes, that's one of the guards from the asylum. He's Tiny, the one who beat me. When the fire broke out and I made a run for it, he grabbed me." Her words tumbled out in a whispered rush.

"What made you think you'd killed him?"

She gulped. "I hit him in the head with a fireplace poker. He was pulling me away from everyone else. I had to get away…from him and the fire. I knew Lucinda was probably in worse danger than I was, even though the blanket protected her some. I picked up the poker with my free hand and hit him as hard as I could. I left him there, and I ran." She looked at him with a tortured expression. "I left him to die."

"Is that the secret you've been keeping from me?"

She nodded, still trembling.

"Didn't you hear the Pinkerton agent say that except for the doctor all the staff and employees made it out alive?" Eli said.

"No, but I wish I had. I'm so glad I didn't kill him. I've seen his face in my dreams. He must have come to and crawled out on his own."

Eli put his arm around her. "It's okay, you made the right decision. Even if it would've turned out differently, you did the right thing. You had to get the baby out." He swallowed hard thinking about what could have happened. "*You* had to get out of there."

"But I left him to die."

"It's okay," he soothed. "We can talk about it later. We need to leave."

She pushed back from him, a look of devastation on her face. "I didn't get a chance to talk to my father."

"It's too dangerous right now, Maggie. Remember, I have no authority here. And I don't know who Hollis might have on his side. We can try again, soon."

Still visibly shaken and disappointed, Maggie made an effort to pull herself together. "Okay. Where are Nathaniel and Brody?"

"Hopefully, they're waiting around the corner." With a firm grip on her arm, Eli led her away from the house. Her sorrowful expression hurt him, but it didn't sway him.

They found the wagon waiting on the next block. Eli hoisted Maggie up into the back, and climbed in after her.

"Everything okay?" Nathaniel asked.

"Yep, but it was a close call," Eli said. "We're going to scratch this attempt and get on back to Moccasin Rock. We can try again another day."

Nathaniel nodded.

"Brody, why don't you sit up front," Eli said. "I need to talk to Miss Radford."

While Brody clambered over the seat, Eli murmured for Maggie to keep her head down. Then he leaned back against a burlap bag, pulled his hat low over his face, looking, he hoped, like a man about to catch a little shuteye as the wagon rumbled along toward the edge of town.

Under the brim of his hat Eli couldn't see much of Maggie, but he could see she was trembling. Without changing his position, and keeping a distance between them for any curious town folk they passed, he reached out and took one of her hands in his.

She gripped it and held on as if he'd pulled her from a raging river. No words were exchanged.

As soon as they cleared town, Eli sat up straighter. Glancing over his shoulder at Nathaniel and Brody, who were deep in discussion about the day's events, Eli moved closer to Maggie.

This was the nearest thing to privacy they would have until they reached Moccasin Rock. He didn't want to wait until then to say what was on his mind.

Maggie tilted her hat back and looked up at him.

Eli leaned in, and then hesitated. *What if she didn't trust him after this?*

He had long ago stopped caring what people thought of him. In fact, he'd still been a kid when he realized that some people would look down on him simply because he was poor, hungry and dirty most of the time. Even if none of that had been his choice.

He and Nathaniel had been called every name in the book. It had taken him time to realize that said more about the name-callers than it did him and his brother. *So why was he so worried about Maggie's reaction?* He'd have to sort it out later.

CHAPTER TWENTY-TWO

"MAGGIE, I UNDERSTAND what you're going through," Eli said, "I've been there."

Her golden brown eyes were troubled. "You have?"

"Yes. As I told you before, I know how it feels to be on the receiving end of abuse. To be smaller, weaker than the other guy."

"That's difficult to believe," she said, looking him up and down.

"It's true. Remember when we were fishing and I told you about some of the things that Nathaniel and I went through? And how we met a man who was worse than Mr. Pedlam?"

"Yes."

"Well, I was talking about a man named Jasper. We were still young when we ended up in San Angelo, scared to death." Even though he'd never told anyone about that time in their lives, Eli found himself telling her everything. "Nathaniel had lost weight, he wasn't eating, wasn't sleeping. When Jasper offered to take us in, I was wary. We'd been through so much in the few years since we'd fled from that old man's house near Taylor's Crossing. As I mentioned, we'd had some close calls."

"Yes, it seems a miracle that y'all survived."

"I suppose it was," Eli admitted. "Anyway, Jasper didn't hit us, which was a big improvement over some of the places we'd stayed. I was so relieved that we weren't dodging flying fists, that I mistook lack of violence for kindness. He wasn't a kind man. In fact, he was the definition of evil."

"So why did he let y'all stay?"

"He said we could run errands for him. He owned several businesses at the time, although I didn't really understand what they were, at first. They weren't the sort of places kids should be living."

"What were they?"

"Brothels, saloons."

Her eyes widened. "Oh."

"I made deliveries for Jasper and his friends—sometimes large amounts of cash, sometimes alcohol, sometimes worse. I was young, but I could drive a team of horses and a wagon. Boys grow up fast in that kind of environment. I often hauled drunks away from the place. One of Jasper's men would load them in the wagon, and I would take them to the edge of town and roll them out. And I left them there, like I was told. At least once it was a dead man that I dumped off. He'd died in a fight. I suspected Jasper had a hand in that, too."

Eli swallowed hard. "I didn't just leave him, though. Before I left, I took that man's gun. In my mind I justified it by saying he didn't need it anymore. But I did. I stole from a dead man."

"Oh, Eli."

"I practiced with that gun every spare minute I had. I watched men who were fast draws, and I learned how to emulate them. I also became cold, distant. Men like that seemed to live longer."

So far, Maggie's eyes were filled with compassion, not judgment. But he had to tell her all of it.

"Jasper kept us around because I didn't talk to anyone, and was cheap labor for him. He paid us in food and gave us a place to sleep. I honestly thought heaven couldn't be any finer at the time. I gradually realized what all was going on there, but I was beyond caring. Until something happened that still haunts me."

"What?" she breathed.

Eli paused, glancing over his shoulder to make sure the others were still engrossed in their own conversation. "One night Jasper told me to take a message to someone who owed him money. I recognized the name right away. Mr. Gaetti was an Italian man who ran a shoe shop. He was a nice old fellow. He'd borrowed money from Jasper right after he got there from Italy. He was having trouble paying it back. Mr. Gaetti refused to go see Jasper, he was scared of him. In fact, the old man got to where he'd hardly leave his shop at all."

Eli paused. At some point in the past few minutes he'd begun rubbing his thumb across Maggie's hand.

He glanced at her, but she seemed to be waiting patiently for him to finish his story. Either she hadn't noticed his touch, or she didn't mind. He hoped it was the latter.

"Jasper instructed me to make Nathaniel lay down in the alley and cry, and I was supposed to go knock on Mr. Gaetti's back door and beg him for help. When I worried aloud about what would happen to the old man, Jasper told me to do as he said and fake Nathaniel's injury, or he'd give him a real one."

Eli's voice dropped. "It was the first time he'd ever threatened either one of us. The lack of bluster, the quietness with which he said it, made it all the more deadly. To add a little weight to his threat, Jasper took hold of my arm and twisted it behind me, hard enough that I thought I'd pass out."

A chill swept over Eli, remembering the look in Jasper's eyes. The man hadn't lost his temper and lashed out in a moment of anger. He had calmly, casually, tried to break a child's arm.

"When he let go of me, I fell," Eli said. "I was literally shaking in my boots. I hated that feeling, and if I'd been on my own I would have taken off right then. But I had Nathaniel to think about. He'd gained weight—for the first time ever there was plenty of food available. And he was sleeping through the night again. So I did as I was told."

Maggie's eyes held compassion as she squeezed his hand.

"I knew that Jasper was going to beat Mr. Gaetti. I didn't have to fake the tears that were running down my face when I banged on that back door and the old man answered. In fact, I was crying so hard that I couldn't say anything. I pointed to Nathaniel. He was lying in the alley, as he'd been ordered to do. Mr. Gaetti rushed toward him. He hadn't made it three feet when Jasper stepped out of the shadows and shot him."

Maggie gasped.

"The old man never saw it coming, and neither did we. Nathaniel scrambled up and began screaming. Mr. Gaetti's daughter, Maria, ran outside, crying hysterically. She was older than us, but I don't think she was full-grown yet. She was a beautiful girl. Jasper rushed toward her, told her that he'd witnessed the whole thing. He said some ruffian had tried to break in through the back door of their shop and then had shot her father. Jasper said he tried to stop him."

"That was beyond despicable," Maggie snapped.

"It was, but that was Jasper. Don't forget, I had a hand in it, too. I lured the old man outside."

Brow furrowed, Maggie shook her head. "You were only a child. You didn't know what he had planned."

"No, but I knew something bad was going to happen. I felt like such a coward." He squeezed his eyes shut for a moment, but the images were still there. "Jasper told Maria he'd help take care of her father, then he told us to get on back to his place. We did. The old man was still laying there in the dirt."

"Did he die?"

"No, but he was crippled for life. I didn't know that for a long time. He's gone now, of course."

"So you've relived that night over and over again," Maggie said.

"Yes. Why hadn't I stood up to Jasper? I wanted to hit him, kick him. Tell him exactly what I thought of him. But I left there in silence, same as Nathaniel. Inside, I felt as if I'd aged instantly. Like I was older than Mr. Gaetti. I felt so helpless."

"So you went on living with him?"

Eli nodded. "For a while. He'd warned us not to say anything to anybody, and not to leave. He threatened to do to us what he had to Mr. Gaetti. But the resentment and hatred kept building in me. Then one night I saw a way to escape—and to see that Jasper was punished at the same time. It wouldn't be punishment for what he did to Mr. Gaetti, but it was better than nothing."

She raised her brows. "How did you manage that?"

"Jasper had been in a poker game for several hours. For once, it wasn't going his way. There were two other men at the table who were better than him, or maybe they were cheating. Whatever was happening, Jasper was losing big."

"How did he take it?"

"Not well. I don't remember all the details—a lot has happened in the years since then—but all of a sudden Jasper had his hands up. One of the biggest, meanest-looking men I've ever seen was holding a gun on him."

"I bet it was difficult to feel any sympathy," Maggie said.

"Oh, I didn't. Jasper yelled my name and I hurried forward to see what he wanted. He told me to go upstairs and get some money. He told me exactly where it was. The man who was holding the gun on him was making enough threats that I knew it was going to be bad news for Jasper if I didn't follow his orders."

Eli leveled a look at Maggie. "I didn't care if the other man killed him. In fact, I hoped he would. I took Nathaniel that night and we ran as fast and far as we could go, looking over our shoulders for months. We'd been lost and scared before, but we had become almost feral by that point. We trusted no one. It would have been easier to find a place for one of us, but neither of us wanted to leave the other. So we kept on running."

"I can't even imagine how difficult and lonely that kind of life had to be."

No, a girl like Maggie probably couldn't imagine. And Eli liked it that way. "Like I said, I practiced with that gun for hours at a time."

"And you became very proficient."

"You could say that. I got older and replaced it with a better one. People paid attention to me. I used to think that I was a better talker with a six-shooter in my hand. Eventually I realized that the gun made other people better listeners."

"It's certainly an attention-getter," Maggie agreed.

"I never wanted to hurt anybody with it. I only wanted to be able to defend myself and Nathaniel."

"That's understandable. So where did y'all go when you left?"

"Everywhere. In some places we found work, and some places only shelter. We scrounged food where we could. And we never, ever let our guard down. If it turned out badly, we always managed to get away."

She pondered that in silence for a moment. "Did the other gambler kill Jasper that night?"

"You know, I wondered that for years. Then I saw him the other day, and he was alive and well."

"The other day? I don't understand."

"Jasper showed up in Moccasin Rock."

Maggie's eyes widened. "He finally caught up with y'all?"

"No, it wasn't like that. He was as surprised to see me and Nathaniel as we were to see him." Eli told her about Jasper's political ambitions.

Maggie gasped. "The man you knew as Jasper is J.L. Slidell? I've heard of him. He's the owner of Benedetto Boots."

"That's him," Eli said. "That boot company began as Benedetto Gaetti's shoe shop. His daughter Maria inherited it. Jasper married her. I'm not sure how much of the success story belongs to her.

Jasper's a bad man, but a good businessman. Apparently Maria never found out what he did."

"I certainly hope Mr. Slidell doesn't win that race. I can't imagine how ruthless he'll be with some political power behind him."

"Don't worry, Nathaniel and I did our best to talk him out of it." Thinking back to all those hours practicing with a gun, and the target he'd secretly been hoping for, Eli was amazed that talking was all he'd done when Jasper showed up.

"Even though I want him to pay for what he did, I didn't draw on him," Eli admitted. "I'm not sure why."

"Maybe it was simply maturity."

"I don't know about that. I still wanted to beat him within an inch of his life."

Maggie nodded. "I can't say that I blame you for that. But I'm glad, for your sake, that you didn't."

"I may not be seeking vengeance, but I'm still interested in justice," Eli said. "What he did, what he's capable of, just eats at me. It's unsettling to think that kind of evil's in the world. But it is."

She glanced down a minute, and then back into his eyes. "I understand that more than you know. I didn't tell you everything that guard said to me the night of the fire."

"Oh?"

"He saw the baby in my arms. Even though I had Lucinda's face covered against the smoke, he figured it out. He smiled at me—a smile that gave me cold chills—and said that I could either come with him without a struggle, and he'd make sure I got out of there alive, or he would drag me with him." Her voice broke, "and he threatened the baby."

Fighting to keep his expression from revealing his fury, Eli squeezed her hand again.

"At the time, my instincts told me to fight and run," Maggie said. "Now that I've had time to think about it, I believe it was the right decision. I doubt that he would've taken me out of there, even if I'd done everything he said. I very much suspect that my body would've been found in the fire."

She was right. And Eli realized he wasn't over his desire for vengeance after all.

Not when he thought about a man that threatened babies and beat on women.

CHAPTER TWENTY-THREE

"WE SHOULD BE home in less than an hour," Eli called out. He had joined Nathaniel on the driver's seat after they'd stop to eat their supper, and Brody was once again Maggie's traveling companion.

The boy was chattering away, but it was difficult for her to concentrate on what he was saying. Her mind was still filled with Eli's story. What a sad life these two men had lived.

The crack of splintering wood rang out, scattering her thoughts and pitching her and Brody sideways.

Something had broken on one of the wagon wheels at the back.

"Whoa," Eli soothed the spooked horses as he fought for control. "Easy now."

Maggie gripped the side of the wagon, but didn't say anything. Brody was silent, too, but once Eli had the team under control and had stopped the wagon, the boy had plenty of questions.

It started with "what happened" and continued on through "what now." Brody didn't seem scared, only interested.

After making sure that everyone was unhurt, Eli answered the boy's questions about the cracked wheel. Maggie was impressed with his patience. Only Brody's "What do we do now?" seemed to give Eli pause.

"I'd rather get on home tonight," Eli said. "I'm sure Peg will be looking for you, Maggie, and Brody your family will be worried."

The boy waved away his concern. "It's okay, Sheriff. They know I'm safe with you."

"Thanks, Brody." Eli looked around. "I really don't want all of us walking either. I'm trying to decide whether to get y'all settled for awhile and go on alone or make camp here. I might be able to fix the wheel."

Eli conferred quietly with Nathaniel, then reached up and helped Maggie down. "We can at least make y'all more comfortable while we're figuring it out."

"Thank you," Maggie said. "It will be nice to stretch my legs."

As Maggie walked around, Eli removed several boxes in the back of the wagon, which held everything from bedrolls to a coffee pot and lantern.

"Are we going to need all this?"

"Haven't decided whether to stay or not, but it's best to lighten the load as much as possible while we're working on it. This is standard for me. As I mentioned before, I always believe in being prepared for anything."

"You should see how much he can pack on a horse," Nathaniel said.

"He's one to talk. You should see all he carries in that doctor bag he has."

The two men teased each other for a minute, and Maggie suspected that their childhood was responsible for many of their cautious ways and habits.

After removing most everything from the wagon and unhitching the horses, Eli handed Maggie a blanket to wrap around her shoulders, then again turned his attention to the damaged wagon wheel.

Even after listening to his and Nathaniel's discussion, Maggie wasn't sure what they planned to do. The best she could figure out, Eli was going to attach some sort of skid to the broken wheel that would allow it to be dragged, even as the other three wheels turned. It was something he'd seen an old settler do years ago.

The temperatures continued to drop as they discussed it. Thankfully, they'd stopped in an area where cedars and live oak trees provided a natural barrier of sorts from the elements.

Shivering, Maggie stepped away from the activity around the wagon, taking shelter under a big live oak. Sitting with her back against the tree trunk, she pulled the blanket tighter.

The creaking of the tree branches, the sound of male voices, and the warmth of the blanket had lulled her into almost a sleepy state when she was suddenly pulled up, jerked a distance away from the tree and pressed against a broad chest.

Eli's voice was a soft whisper, but there was an urgency to it. "Maggie, don't move."

Instinctively, she whispered too. "Why?"

"Just trust me."

"I do," she said, meaning it sincerely.

He suddenly pressed his left arm around her, but instead of circling her waist, the arm was against her head, covering one of her ears and pressing the other ear against his chest. She couldn't hear anything but the rapid beat of his heart.

Maggie's own heart raced out of control. *She shouldn't have let him hold her hand...but it had felt so good.*

She pulled back a little. "Eli...you seem to have a mistaken idea about me. I'm not that kind of woman."

Eli's arm dropped slightly, and his tone was bewildered. "What?"

"I said, I'm not that kind of... oh well, perhaps one kiss wouldn't hurt."

She had a quick glimpse of his thunderstruck expression before his arm flew up again and covered her head and ear, jerking her against his chest. She had no time to respond before a shot split the night.

Maggie realized, when something fell from the tree and landed with a thud nearby, that Eli had been protecting her, not making advances.

Giving her a wondering look, he released her. "You okay?"

Knees weak, Maggie managed to say, "Yes, I'm fine. Thank you," before she sank straight down to the ground in a little heap. Eli looked almost as startled as he had when she'd offered to kiss him. Grabbing the blanket she'd dropped, he placed it around her, clumsily patted her on the shoulder, and left.

The next few minutes were a blur of activity as all three of the males examined, and exclaimed over, the animal that had been crouched in the tree directly over Maggie's head.

Again, it was a time where Eli answered Brody's questions.

"What is it?" the boy asked.

"A panther," Eli said. "Some people call them mountain lions. Either one is correct."

Nathaniel whistled. "Look at the claws on that thing. I can't even imagine what that could've done to one of us."

Maggie closed her eyes, and her mind, against the image that produced. *Thank you, Lord, for your protection.*

Even though they tried to include her in the conversation, Maggie couldn't do more than murmur and nod. Even after they'd dragged the carcass away, she was still shaking.

"She may be getting too cold, or she could be suffering from shock," she heard Nathaniel say.

"I'm fine, everyone," she assured them. "Just a little unsteady." *And embarrassed.*

Eli spoke up. "Perfectly natural and understandable." He then went into a crazy story about a close encounter he'd had with a bobcat once, and within a few minutes both Brody and Nathaniel were discussing their own wild animal experiences.

He was trying to divert everyone's attention. Although Maggie was grateful, she still couldn't look him in the face. But she did look over her shoulder at every sound, worried about another panther.

Maggie was rearranging the blanket for the third time, when Eli crouched down beside her.

"Got a minute?" he whispered.

"Sure."

"We need to talk."

He tugged on her hand, pulling her up and over to the far side of the wagon. He led her to a crate and motioned for her to sit, then did the same, shifting a little so they were side-by-side and face-to-face.

"I'm sorry about the misunderstanding earlier," he said. "I was afraid if I took time to explain what was happening that thing was going to pounce. They're not uncommon out here, but they will usually high-tail it away from that much noise."

Crossing her arms in an effort to control her shivering, Maggie nodded. "I understand. *Now.* I'm just embarrassed about... you know."

Eli gave her a little smile. "I should probably come up with something real sensible to say here. Something that would make you feel better. But I never have been a smooth talker."

She waved a hand. "Oh, that's okay. I'll recover." *Eventually.*

He glanced down at his hands, and then up into her eyes, his expression no longer teasing. "Just so you know, you weren't wrong," he said.

"About what?"

"About one kiss not hurting anything." Placing his hands on her arms, slowly, giving her every opportunity to back away, he pulled her into his arms and lowered his head to hers.

Maggie felt strangely light-headed and breathless. Just before their lips met, she whispered, "You said you aren't married, but is there a girl out there who's planning to be Mrs. Eli Calhoun?" *There was no way a man this attractive had gone through life unattached.*

Eli pulled back, obviously surprised by the question. He appeared to give it thoughtful consideration. "No, although I thought I was in love once."

"Is she no longer a part of your life?"

"It was years ago."

"What happened?"

"Long story, so I won't go into detail, but it started with me and Nathaniel getting arrested and ended with us going our separate ways. After he married the girl I thought I loved."

Whoa. There were so many things that captured her interest in that brief statement that Maggie wasn't sure where to start. "Arrested? For what?"

"For vagrancy. We'd fallen asleep while waiting to board a ship at Galveston."

"Where were you going?"

"The ship was headed to New Orleans, and from there we weren't sure where we were going. Trying to find something better. We'd grown since we'd left Jasper, beyond boyhood, although not considered men by most people. We'd held down steady jobs when we could find them, but they weren't enough to make a living. Getting arrested was one of the lowest points of my life. When they pulled us in front of the judge, I was terrified. I figured we were too old to be sent to an orphanage, and I'd heard tales of people being sent to poor houses or work farms, and even being sold into slavery."

How had the Calhoun brothers even survived?

"The judge turned out to be a good, decent man. He and his wife were an older couple with one daughter, a beautiful girl named Tessa. Nathaniel and I both fell in love with her at first sight. But she had eyes only for Nathaniel."

Maggie didn't understand that statement at all. Nathaniel was a good-looking man, as was Caleb, but they weren't...Elijah. She puzzled over that for a moment, and then tried to understand the brief stab of jealousy she felt at Eli's expression. Whatever he was remembering about this Tessa girl, they were fond memories. He'd stopped talking, and Maggie could tell that he was a million miles away.

"So what happened?" she asked.

"Nathaniel and Tessa married, both too young as I look back on it now. I'm surprised that the judge and his wife even allowed it. I hit the road not long afterward."

When did you realize you didn't love her? "Where did you go?"

"I drifted for a long time, doing everything from building railroad, to herding cattle, bounty hunting, logging, and, for awhile, I was a hired gun. That was the most lucrative, but also the most unsettling. I was at a low point in my life when I ended up in Moccasin Rock. I'd missed Nathaniel through those years, but I knew he was happy and that gave me some comfort. I realized not long after I left that I hadn't really loved Tessa. After a lifetime of running in and out of some of the worst places known to man, she was just so sweet and innocent that it was only logical to be drawn to her. But Nathaniel did love her. And she loved him."

Maggie struggled with an urge to bombard Eli with questions about the paragon of virtue who had captured his youthful eye.

She glanced in the direction of Nathaniel. "He hasn't mentioned having a wife."

"She died."

Eli didn't seem to hear Maggie's indrawn breath. "Oh, I'm so sorry."

The sound of a horse's hooves claimed their attention.

Eli stood, their conversation forgotten as Deputy Bliss Walker rode into view.

"When you didn't show up, I figured you might have trouble," the old man drawled.

"You figured exactly right," Eli said. "And you got here in time to give us a hand."

It seemed like no time at all before the three men got the wagon ready to roll. Or drag and roll. Either way, it worked, and they were finally on their way home.

Eli and Nathaniel were talking together in the front, and Brody was hanging over the side of the wagon telling the old deputy about the panther.

Maggie tried to sort out her tangled emotions—disappointment over her father, worry over what to do next…and regret that she'd stopped Elijah Calhoun from kissing her.

If he ever tried again, she wouldn't.

CHAPTER TWENTY-FOUR

MAGGIE SHOOK HER head as she watched Brody eat a bowl of chicken and dumplings with as much enthusiasm as he had the cake the first day she'd met him. For someone so thin, the boy sure had an appetite.

But it wasn't only the cooking he enjoyed—he seemed to thrive on Maggie and Peg's attention and interest. He'd been dropping by nearly every day since their trip to Fair Haven the previous week. But every time the conversation drifted to anything personal, Brody clammed up.

With the boy so relaxed now, Maggie was determined to discover more about his family, even if it took all afternoon. It didn't take nearly that long.

"Is that one of your favorite foods?" she asked.

Mouth full, Brody merely nodded. After swallowing, he said, "Yes, ma'am. Mama used to make dumplings just like this."

The moment Maggie noticed he'd referred to his mother in the past tense Brody froze with the spoon halfway to his mouth. Apparently he'd realized it too.

"What happened to your mother, Brody?"

He placed the spoon in the bowl and pushed it all back, appetite gone. "She died."

"Oh, Brody, I'm so sorry. How long has it been?"

Brody glanced away. "Don't remember exactly."

"So it's only you and your father now?"

He looked at her then, and the depths of despair in his eyes hit her like a physical blow. "No. My father's dead, too. It's only me."

What? "You live in a house in the woods all by yourself?"

"There is no house."

Maggie stared at him in confusion. "I don't understand. Brody, where do you actually live?"

"Nowhere."

"Nowhere? How can that possibly be?"

He shrugged. "There's plenty of places to sleep, and plenty of food to be had. I make do. There's money to be had if you're willing to work for it."

"Your parents are both dead? Why didn't you tell anyone? How long has it been?"

"About six months, best I can recall. Kinda hard to keep track of the days sometimes."

"Why didn't you ask for help?" Maggie said. "I haven't been in Moccasin Rock for long, but I know there are people here who would help you."

"That's true," he said. "But I wasn't sure if I might be sent to an orphanage. I figured it was best not to tell anyone."

Lucinda started crying, and Maggie was glad to have something to occupy her attention as she struggled to gain control of her emotions. If she reacted the wrong way, the boy would stop talking.

Baby in her arms, she returned to the table. "Brody, how did you come to be in Moccasin Rock? Is your family from here?"

"No. We were living in Huntsville when Mama took sick, and then passed away. It was only me and Daddy then. He was real worried when he took the fever, too. He gave me all the money that he had, almost twenty dollars, and told me to take the train to Fort Worth and use the rest for food and what I would need. Said he had friends there. That maybe they'd help me. Daddy told me

I'd have to work hard, prove that I'd be useful to have around. He went over and over with me the ways I could make myself useful. So they'd never want to let me go."

"Didn't they want you?"

"It wasn't that. I never could find them. I found the street where they were supposed to be living, but somebody else was there. They said the other folks had moved on, and nobody knew where they'd gone."

"What did you do?"

"I couldn't go back to Huntsville. Our landlady had helped me get my ticket and pack my things. She was selling her house, and moving back east, somewhere that I'd never heard of. She told me how sorry she was that I had to go."

Maggie listened to the rest of his story with growing dismay. It was all as tragic as the beginning. She moved Lucinda, asleep now, back to her cradle.

"When I couldn't find my father's friends, I went back to the train station," Brody said. "I wasn't sure where I should go. Then I decided to return to Huntsville anyway. Even if I didn't have a place to stay, I knew the streets, and a few people. I bought a ticket, then boarded and fell asleep. When I woke up, there was a man going through my pockets. When I tried to stop him, he told me it would be better to lose my money than my life. There wasn't much money left anyway, I didn't figure it was worth dying for."

"Oh, Brody."

"When the train stopped here in Moccasin Rock, there was a family near the depot with a wagonload of kids, and I sorta blended in with them that day. When they moved on, I stayed here."

Her throat tight, Maggie struggled with what to do or say. She wanted to wrap her arms around the boy, but she knew it would embarrass him. She contented herself with patting his hand.

"I fell asleep that night behind the train depot," he said. "When I woke up, I tried to remember everything Daddy had said about making myself useful. I offered to carry things for people, I ran errands. I worked hard. Some folks would give me a few coins, some didn't."

Maggie had a sudden vision of Brody eating the cake she'd offered that first day. He hadn't been hungry for sweets. He'd been plain hungry. "So what happened when you didn't have money?"

"A few times I stole some food, and then when I started making friends it got better. My friend Jamie Wilson shared with me. And the Sheriff did, too."

Maggie and Brody both turned when Eli stepped through the door. *How long had he been standing there?* Long enough.

Her heart twisted at the look on Brody's face as he stared at Eli. Sadness. Dismay. His hero now knew the truth about him.

Color flooded the boy's face, and his hands shook. "Sheriff, I paid folks back as best I could," he blurted. "Sometimes it wasn't the same food I'd taken, but I've always left something in return, or worked for them and wouldn't take money."

Eli shook his head. "Brody, I'm so sorry," he said softly.

The boy's eyes widened. "Why are you sorry? Everyone here has been so nice to me, but especially you. In fact, other people started being nicer to me when you did."

"But I should have known."

Maggie suspected that the shock and sorrow in Eli's eyes was a mirror of her own.

"Why?" Brody asked. "I did my best to make sure you didn't know. I'm the one who should be sorry."

"So you have no home, no relatives, at all?" The bewilderment in Eli's voice made Maggie's eyes sting.

Brody dropped his gaze. "No, but I've made do."

"What about schooling?"

"I can read and write," Brody said. "I've had plenty."

He sounded so much like a typical boy that Maggie wanted to smile.

"There may still be some things you could benefit from knowing," Eli said. "I could talk to the new school teacher, and see about getting you caught up."

Brody didn't seem thrilled by the thought, but he nodded.

"What about church?" Maggie added.

Brody shrugged. "I go sometimes."

"I don't remember seeing you there," Eli said. "Although to be honest, I only recently started going."

"Sometimes I stand outside and listen," Brody admitted. "I figured someone would catch on if I was by myself every Sunday. Even if I can't hear everything, it reminds me of my folks. Especially the hymns."

Maggie couldn't take it anymore. Standing, she walked around to Brody's side of the table, leaned down and wrapped her arms around the boy.

Obviously startled, Brody relaxed after a moment and returned the hug, shoulders shaking as he began to cry. *How long had it been since anyone had hugged him?*

Maggie struggled with her own tears as she watched Eli looking at the boy.

The sheriff opened his mouth several times before speaking. Maggie could see him choosing his words carefully, trying, she suspected, not to hurt Brody's pride. "You're welcome to come home with me. To stay. If you want to, I mean. I'm not going to force you."

Brody turned eager eyes to Eli, but his tone sounded uncertain. "I don't want to put you out none."

"You won't be putting me out, at all. I don't have much, I live in an old cabin for now. I'm building a house, though. What I have is yours, from this moment on."

The boy smiled, but he still seemed uncertain what to say. The sheriff didn't appear to be doing much better. When an awkward silence descended on the room, Maggie got another bowl from the cupboard and dished up some chicken and dumplings for Eli. Maybe things would be easier if they could visit over a bite to eat.

It worked. Within a few minutes, the two of them were behaving like they normally did, talking about everything from fishing to the plans for the new courthouse. Eventually though, the meal was done.

"I promised Silas I would help him this afternoon," Brody said, smiling at Eli in a way that broke Maggie's heart all over again. Eager and hopeful, but wary.

"You go on and do what you need to do," Eli said. "A man should always keep his word. We'll talk later."

As the boy headed to the door, Eli added, "Brody, find me before nightfall. I don't want you sleeping outside."

"Yes, sir."

After he'd gone, Maggie said, "I think he wants to live with you. He's worried about being a burden."

"Yeah," Eli said, "but it's more than that. I went through the exact same thing. That's why I can't believe I didn't catch on to what was happening right in front of my eyes."

"Why do you think he's hesitating?"

"You learn not to get your hopes up. There are good-hearted, kind people of all walks of life. And there are cruel people just looking for someone to hurt or something to destroy. The faster you learn to sort them out, the better chance you have of surviving."

In Maggie's opinion Eli's concern bordered on cynicism, but then he'd lived a completely different life than she had. He'd been even younger than Brody when he'd lost his parents, and had been alone far longer. It had left a mark on him.

"I don't think there's anything wrong with going in to a situation hoping for the best, believing the best of people," Eli said. "But when you've been knocked down over and over again, it does make it harder to trust folks."

"I understand," Maggie said softly. "I think Brody trusts you, though."

"I do, too. But when you've been in a situation like he's in, it makes you cautious. Even good people have a way of dying, or disappearing on you. When I was a kid, I got to where I'd hold something back, didn't get too close. To tell you the truth, I'm still that way." He suddenly clammed up.

What had he been about to say?

"Brody needs some time," Eli said. "I'll be waiting when he comes around."

Maggie walked over and hugged him. "You're a good man, Elijah Calhoun."

She turned away and started toward the stove. Eli grabbed her by the apron strings, tugged and twirled her into his arms.

Heart skipping, Maggie stared into those brown eyes. She recognized that look. Eli wanted to kiss her. And this time she wasn't stopping him.

They both froze at the sound of hurried footsteps. When the knob on the back door turned, Maggie stepped away.

Eli gave her a rueful smile when Brody burst inside, then turned his attention to the boy.

"Something wrong?"

"You said to tell you if I saw any strangers nosing around."

Eli sobered instantly. "Yes?"

"When I stepped around the side of the house, there was a man near the front. He had a hat on so I didn't get a good look at his face, but I don't ever remember seeing him before. Not even in that group out by the river."

"I'll be back," Eli told Maggie. "Lock the door behind me."

She did, and had cleared the table, washed the dishes, and swept the floor before he returned.

"I searched the area near the house," Eli said, "and a good ways into the woods at the back. Didn't see anyone. I'm going to have a look around town now. I also want to check out those tents down by the river. There are so many strangers around that it's making this more difficult than it normally would be. I'll let you know if I find anybody."

After he left again, Maggie resumed her work, yet she couldn't help worrying about Eli and Brody.

She hadn't known either of them a few weeks ago, and yet they'd both become very dear to her. How strange it was to think she might return home soon and never see them again.

The thought of that made her eyes sting again.

CHAPTER TWENTY-FIVE

ELI SPENT MORE than an hour talking to everyone camped out down by the river.

Even though some of them seemed secretive and standoffish, from what he could tell it was the usual reaction that some folks had to a badge.

He didn't take it personal, and he didn't assume that everyone who reacted that way was a criminal. Some folks just wanted to mind their own business and wanted other folks to do the same. Unless they broke the law, Eli had no problem with that.

Back in town he made the rounds, talking to every business owner and even citizens on the street.

The only one with anything unusual to report was Eagan Smith at the livery stable. "A fellow came in earlier, asking about my horses."

"That seems reasonable," Eli said, "unless you've suddenly switched to renting out camels or something."

Eagan laughed heartily, black eyes flashing. The man was one of Eli's favorite people in Moccasin Rock. He knew horses and guns—two things that were vital to Eli's way of life—and he was quick to offer advice about either one.

"No camels," Eagan said. "The reason I found it strange is that this man asked exactly how many horses and mules I had available, and then asked about every wagon, buggy, and even cart. Then he wanted to know how much it would cost to rent everything I had."

That was different. "What did he look like?"

Eagan described a man that didn't sound familiar at all—stocky, red complexion, with a gap between his front teeth.

At Nathaniel's office, Eli discovered he'd also had a stranger stop by. "A man came in wanting to know if anyone seeking medical attention had come in lately."

"What did you tell him?"

Nathaniel grinned. "I told him that most everybody that came in here was seeking medical attention."

"Good point."

"He never asked specifically about Maggie, but he kept asking questions, including if I'd treated anyone for burns lately. Several times he looked down the hall, like he was trying to see if anybody else was here."

The questioning of Eagan was strange, but nothing alarming. The questions posed to Nathaniel, on the other hand, put Eli on edge.

"How did you answer that?"

"I told him no burns," Nathaniel said. "I said there'd been a lot of people in and out of Moccasin Rock lately, and a good many found their way into my office. No one stood out in my mind."

"Good. What did this man look like?"

"Hefty, ruddy skin tone." Nathaniel didn't remember if the man had a gap in his front teeth, but he did recall a scar on his chin. "Looks like he'd been stitched up at some point."

Were Nathaniel and Eagan describing the same man?

"Let me know if he shows up again," Eli said. "And try to get some information about him this time. Even a name would help."

"Sure thing."

Troubled, Eli searched the town again, but he also took the time to berate himself along the way.

He was losing control of his life, and he didn't like it one bit. His worry over Maggie and Lucinda went beyond his normal concern for folks in trouble.

Getting this involved in someone else's life was dangerous. It was something he'd vowed years ago to never let happen again. And now he couldn't keep them out of his mind.

So many other questions kept gnawing at him, but there were no easy answers.

How could he not have known what was going on with Brody? How fast could he get his house finished? What had possessed him to tell Maggie Radford so much about his past?

Eli had talked more since he'd met Maggie than he had in his whole life. He cringed thinking about their trip back from Fair Haven. Had he let her get a word in edgewise? *Good grief, he was turning into Bliss!* Hopefully he at least talked faster than the old man.

And what should he do about Lucinda? Were her grandparents looking for her? He'd tried not to think about it. Should he go see them?

And what about the kiss that he'd almost shared with Maggie? He wanted it more than he'd wanted anything in a long time. Her words kept coming back to torture him. *One kiss wouldn't hurt.* Would it? Could he walk away after one? Would he want to walk away?

Taking his hat off, Eli ran a hand through his hair. Now that he knew who'd beat Maggie, what would he do about it?

That was the only question with an easy answer. Sighing, he slapped his hat back on his head and turned his horse towards town. He couldn't do that. Yet.

"So you still miss your mother?" Brody's tone was casual, but Eli knew the answer was important to the boy.

"Yep. It gets easier, though. You still miss them, but it doesn't hurt as bad when they cross your mind. You're able to remember the good times, and it makes you smile."

Handing a two-by-four to the boy, Eli waited while he tossed it onto a rapidly growing pile of boards destined to be the window frames of his new home.

He'd invited Brody to go with him to pick up a wagon load of lumber at the sawmill in Boone Springs and help him unload it at his new place. He'd told the boy about his own parents' deaths, part of it anyway, and encouraged him to talk.

But Brody wasn't talking as much as usual. However he was listening.

Brody reached for another board. "Your mother was pretty special, huh?"

"Yes, she was," Eli said. "No matter how bad things got, Mama always figured out a way to make us laugh. Like when we tried to trap rabbits to eat and didn't catch one. We'd ask Mama what we were going to have for supper, she'd say, 'I guess we'll have to get by on wind pudding and rabbit tracks tonight, boys.'"

Brody, brow furrowed, tilted his head to the side. "I don't understand. How did you eat something like that?"

Eli laughed. "We didn't. Mama was…whimsical. I guess that's what you'd call it. She would say the most unusual things, and always made us smile. Sometimes she'd say we'd get by on a prayer and a promise. According to her, prayer was the right thing in any situation, and a Texas promise was better than any other kind."

Where was all this coming from? How strange that Eli could suddenly remember so much about his mother. Was it because he was letting himself remember? For years he'd tried to block it all out of his mind.

"I'm not sure what whimsical means," Brody said, "but she sounds nice."

Eli nodded. "Nice fits her, too. Mama loved poetry, songs, and even nursery rhymes. I don't really remember any of them. Seems like there was one about blackbirds baked in a pie."

Brody grimaced. "That doesn't sound good."

Chuckling, Eli pulled off his coat, tossed it over a fence post, and rolled up his sleeves. "No, it doesn't. About as good as rabbit tracks, I guess."

Smiling, Brody took the next board from him and added it to the stack, while Eli recalled other memories.

Mama must have been worried sick while she waited for Daddy to come home. Scared out of her mind at times. There'd been peaceful Indians in the area, but there'd also been Comanche raids. And yet Mama had never let them see her fear. As he thought back on it now, he could see her eyes trained toward the road. Waiting and watching for her husband. They were both gone forever shortly after that.

Eli hadn't lied to Brody. It did get easier, but sometimes, even as a full-grown man, the thought of his folks brought a peculiar, empty ache to his chest. Brody's pain had to be fresher, more intense.

"So what did y'all really eat?"

Brody's voice pulled him back from the past. Eli shrugged. "Most times we had beans. Sometimes cornbread. Whatever wild greens Mama could gather. Sometimes berries, plums and pecans. And like I said, if we could snare them, we'd have rabbits."

"Your papa died, too?"

Eli kept his answer simple. "Yes, he's gone, too."

"Just like mine," Brody said.

"Yep." Eli tugged off his gloves and shoved them in his back pocket. "Why don't we take a break? A drink of water sounds good."

Eli brought up the pail from the bottom of the well, and handed Brody the gourd dipper so he could have the first drink.

After the boy finished, he swiped a hand across his mouth. "My mama knew some interesting things, too."

"She did?"

"Yes. She told me one time that a dove will fall to the ground and limp around dragging her wing, even if she's not really hurt."

Eli knew that, but he wanted to encourage the boy to keep talking. "Why would she do that?"

"To distract people from her nest, to keep them from getting too close."

"That's right smart of the mother," Eli said. "Nature's remarkable if you take the time to notice what's happening around you."

They talked a little about their fathers, and Eli was grateful that the bitterness he'd once felt for Amos Calhoun was gone. He felt sympathy for his father now that he understood that he hadn't intended to leave his family for good.

They worked in silence for awhile, then Brody said, "I guess I will hang around. If you're sure you don't mind."

"Don't mind one bit. I welcome the company."

"I'll work hard, Sheriff. I'll earn my keep."

Eli looked at him. "Brody, I don't mind having your help because that's what folks do. Friends and family help each other out. You don't have to *earn* anything. I want you to understand that. It'll be like it is when Nathaniel, Caleb and I give each other a hand. I don't want to be your boss. I want to be your family."

Brody seemed pleased, and a little shy and uncertain, but the wary look was gone.

"And that means that I'm going to get you some clothes and boots," Eli said. "Nothing fancy," he added when Brody opened his mouth.

After a softly-spoken thank you, Brody said, "Does this mean I can't help around the jail anymore?"

"You're still welcome there any time. And if you want to, you can still work for others in town. But I'll buy you the things you need."

The boy's expression cleared.

"I do expect one thing from you," Eli said.

"What's that?"

"The truth. Always. I understand why you lied to me and why you felt it was necessary, but it's not necessary anymore."

Brody ducked his head. "Yes, sir."

"I'm curious about something," Eli said. "In the past, when I've asked you if your parents knew where you were, you always seemed so sincere when you told me yes."

The boy glanced away again. "I might've been misleading you, but I wasn't out-and-out lying. I've had plenty of churching, and my mother read the Bible to me all the time. I know they're in Heaven." He swiped at his eyes, but his voice stayed steady. "I figured they knew everything that was going on with me, Sheriff."

Throat tight, he patted the boy on the back. "Why don't you call me Eli?"

Brody flashed him a grin. "Yes, sir. Eli."

"Let's wash up, and then we'll stop by the mercantile and get you something to wear."

The boy's expression brightened. "Can I have a badge?"

"Nope."

"A gun?"

"Nope."

Eli realized with a start that this very scene might be played out a hundred more times before Brody was full grown.

What if he didn't do the right thing by the boy? At some point, soon, Brody would need to learn how to shoot, and ride a horse, and how to talk to girls. Eli felt more than competent at the first two, but wasn't sure if he'd ever feel comfortable with the third.

Please God, let me do right by him.

CHAPTER TWENTY-SIX

AS USUAL, MAGGIE stepped further back into the kitchen at the knock on the front door. Although her heart no longer pounded at every noise outside, she was still cautious. Eli had stopped by to tell her about his talk with Brody, but now the visitor had interrupted them.

As she heard Eli open the front door, there was also a tap at the back door.

Thinking it was Brody, Maggie smiled and opened it.

Her smile faded when Hollis Anderson stepped into the room. "Hello, Maggie."

Heart in her throat, Maggie stepped back and grabbed a cast iron skillet as he stepped closer.

Anderson's eyes widened, but he addressed her in a soothing tone. "Now, now, dear, let's not do anything we'll regret."

"I won't regret it one bit," Maggie snapped. "And don't you call me dear."

"You don't mean that, love."

"That's strange," Eli said, stepping back into the room from the hall. "There was no one at the front d…" His words trailed off as he caught sight of Hollis.

From the corner of her eye, Maggie saw Eli draw the Colt from his hip with a speed that astonished her. But when several other men—including the Fair Haven sheriff—entered the room from the back porch and stood behind Anderson, Eli lowered the gun.

Maggie recognized several of the men. Unfortunately, they were friends of her father's, not hers, so appealing to them for help wouldn't do any good. *This can't be happening.*

Eli also seemed to recognize the sheriff. "What's this all about, Sheriff Clark?"

Hollis Anderson spoke up first. Nodding his head in Maggie's direction, his gaze remained fixed on Eli. "You've got something that belongs to me. I've come to take her back."

Maggie bristled. "I do not belong to you, or anyone else."

Hollis smiled. "I guess I was being a bit premature. You're only promised to me, at this point. But it's only a matter of time."

"I am not promised to you," Maggie said between clenched teeth. "I will not marry you." She was startled to feel Eli's hand on her back. The warmth of it steadied her.

"I've gone to a lot of time and effort to find you, sweetheart," Hollis said. "Detective Patterson here has been looking for weeks."

Patterson. The name of the Pinkerton agent who'd shown up looking for her that first day. Hysteria bubbled up inside Maggie.

"I wish you'd been more honest with me, when we were out at that asylum," Shiloh Clark said to Eli. "You didn't let on that your interest was personal."

Eli nodded. "Yes, it was personal. Still is. And Mr. Anderson coming here has been a mistake. I don't want to fight about it, or even talk about it. You see, Miss Radford is marrying me."

Stunned silence and opened-mouth amazement met his announcement. Realizing that she was one of those with their mouth gaping, Maggie snapped it shut.

Forcing a smile to her face, she peeked at Eli from under her lashes. His expression was steely as he eyed Hollis, but his fingers were gentle as they tightened around her waist and pulled her closer.

Grumbling erupted among the men who stood with Anderson.

"I thought you said Maggie Radford was being held here against her will," Shiloh Clark said to him.

"Let me have a few minutes alone with her," Hollis Anderson said. "I'm sure we can get this all straightened out."

Maggie tightened her grip on the skillet handle. "There's nothing to straighten out. I'm not going back to Fair Haven with you. I'm staying here with Mrs. Harmon, so I can be near my fi...fiancé."

"She's right," Eli said. "What's to straighten out? Maggie and I are getting married." He turned to look at her, "As soon as possible, right sweetheart?"

Maggie blinked. His expression had softened, and even though she knew he was only saying the words to protect her, her heart was behaving most peculiarly. "Yes, that's right."

Shiloh pushed past Hollis Anderson and stepped up to Maggie. "Can we talk somewhere? Alone?" He glared at both Eli and Hollis, daring either one of them to interfere.

Maggie placed the skillet on the table. "Of course, let's go into the front room."

As soon as they shut the hall door, the sheriff got straight to the point. "Are you here against your will?"

"Absolutely not."

"Is there any truth to anything that Hollis Anderson is saying?"

"No, not a bit."

"So what is going on?"

"For some reason Hollis decided several months ago that he was going to marry me, whether I wanted to or not. I didn't want to then, and I still don't. Unfortunately, my father not only agreed to Mr. Anderson's request, he insisted that I accept."

Sheriff Clark's expression tightened. "Am I going to have trouble with your father over this?"

Maggie stifled her frustration. "I don't see why you would. I'm old enough to make my own decisions."

The man sighed. "How old are you?"

"Twenty-three."

"And you don't object to Sheriff Calhoun's attention?"

Heat filled her face. "Not at all."

He leveled a hard look at her, one that Maggie was sure had worked on many a criminal. "Young lady, did you have anything to do with that fire at the asylum?"

"No, sir." Now that Maggie knew that the guard who'd beaten her was alive and well, she shared everything with the Fair Haven sheriff. Well, almost everything. He didn't ask about the baby, and she didn't volunteer any information.

Apparently her explanation about Mabel and the woman's history of arson satisfied him.

"All right," he said. "I probably won't ever know exactly what happened out there, but I'm ready to put this whole thing behind me."

"Me, too," Maggie said.

"But I'll tell you the truth, Miss Radford, I don't like this situation with Hollis Anderson one bit. For whatever reason, he's fit to be tied about all this. If I were you, I would stay outta his way for awhile."

"Don't worry," Maggie said, "I intend to do just that. Thankfully, I've made friends in Moccasin Rock. As I said, they've invited me to stay here while I try to sort it all out."

Sheriff Clark stared at her a few moments, then gave a brisk nod and motioned her back toward the door.

When they entered the kitchen, Maggie smiled at Eli and assured him that everything was fine and the others would be leaving, without her. But she couldn't quell a flicker of fear when Hollis Anderson pinned her with a cold stare.

Hollis waited until everyone else had left before saying, "You will regret this."

Eli stepped forward and held the door open, waving Hollis

toward it. "You lay one finger on Maggie, or cause her grief in any way, and you'll be the one who's sorry."

The quiet tone, the absolute confidence Eli's words implied, sent a shiver down Maggie's spine. Based on Hollis's expression, he too seemed to realize it was more a promise than a threat. He left without another word.

There was silence after the sound of footsteps faded. Despite the fact that she trusted Eli to watch over her, Maggie couldn't help but worry about what would happen once Hollis was back in Fair Haven.

"Do you think he'll take it out on my father?"

"I don't think so," Eli said, "but I'll keep an eye on the situation."

She nodded, then they stood there, looking everywhere but at each other.

"I appreciate you saying what you did," Maggie finally said. "It certainly set Hollis back."

Eli cleared his throat. "Yeah, sorry to catch you by surprise like that."

"It was no less surprising than my first betrothal."

"Well, hopefully this one will help you, instead of making your life miserable."

"I'm truly grateful," Maggie said, "but what do you think Hollis will do when he discovers that we've deceived him?"

"No reason he should find out for now," Eli said. "We can pretend to be engaged for as long as it takes to make sure you're safe." He spoke the words casually, but his gaze was sharp as he waited for her reaction.

Maggie took a deep breath, amazed at the sudden turn of events. "How do we proceed from here?"

Eli didn't have any ready answers to that. Maggie made a fresh pot of coffee and they sat at the table and discussed it.

"We'll need to tell Nathaniel, Peg and Caleb what's really going on," Eli said.

Maggie agreed. "That's true. They've all been so good to me; I can't imagine lying to them."

Eli snorted. "You sure didn't have any trouble lying to me."

"That's not true," she said softly, "it was one of the most difficult things I've ever done."

He held her gaze a moment. "I understand. But I hope you won't feel it necessary to do it again."

"I won't."

Suddenly Eli frowned. "Hey, you don't plan on hitting me in the head with a frying pan, do you?"

Fighting a grin, Maggie shrugged. "That's not the sort of thing one plans, Sheriff."

His answering smile, perhaps the first full one she'd seen, took her breath away.

"I'll consider myself forewarned," he said. "I've slept with one eye open many a time."

Flustered by this lighter, teasing side of the sheriff, Maggie had trouble concentrating on their discussion. The man's smile was nearly as lethal as the gun on his hip—at least to the female heart.

"Since we don't want to lie, how about I court you," Eli said. "If we're seen together, with me being attentive, everybody in Moccasin Rock will have us married off in no time anyway."

"I suppose you're right," Maggie said. "People have a way of jumping to conclusions. We probably won't even need to nudge them."

"Right. To tell you the truth, I was worried about Peg's reputation with me coming in and out of here so often," Eli said.

Maggie pushed a plate of cookies toward Eli, and refilled his coffee cup. "I hadn't thought of that."

"I mentioned it," he said, "and told her I was sorry if it caused her any problems."

"What did she say?"

"I'm not sure. She was laughing so hard that I couldn't understand a word. Then she said, 'Thanks, Sheriff,' and left the room."

Maggie couldn't help but laugh herself. "That sounds like Peg."

Eli polished off a cookie in three bites then brushed off his hands. "Back to our courtship. The more people talk about us, the faster it'll get back to Fair Haven and Hollis Anderson. He's the one who needs to believe that it's all going forward."

"That makes sense. I would prefer to tell your pastor the truth. And mine, if I could figure out a way to get word to him."

"All right, we should be able to arrange for that."

Maggie did have a few concerns. "What do we say if anyone asks how we met?" She wasn't worried about her reputation, only her and Lucinda's safety. But she was embarrassed by the condition she'd been in when she arrived.

He shrugged. "We can say you were visiting Moccasin Rock, and we met at Martin's Mercantile and that I've hardly let you out of my sight since then."

That was truthful enough. "How do I explain Lucinda?"

"For the time being, probably best not to offer any explanation at all," he said. "No one has mentioned her, which I've wondered about myself. Did anyone even realize she'd been born?"

"I suppose only the doctor, the guard and some of the patients. There's a possibility that the few who knew are dead. Except for the guard."

Hoping this wouldn't lead to a discussion about Lucinda's grandparents, Maggie changed the subject. "So where should we make our first public appearance together?"

"We could always go out for a walk today, and then I could accompany you to church on Sunday."

Maggie loved the idea of getting to go to church. "Let me see if Peg minds watching the baby while we're gone today."

The woman in question entered the room in time to hear her name. "I don't mind at all," Peg said, "but where are y'all going?"

Eli explained everything, while Maggie removed her apron, thanked Peg and left to freshen up.

It only took a few minutes to brush her hair and then twist it in a bun at the back of her head. Staring at herself in the dresser mirror, she ran a finger across the remaining scratch that marred her face. It might leave a permanent scar. But considering the kind of scars she could've had, she thanked God once again for his mercies.

Leaving the house with Eli, Maggie felt a few jitters regarding what they were about to do, but those soon disappeared, replaced by pure elation at being out of the house.

Her happiness was replaced by frustration when Eli stopped before they reached the main street and turned to her.

"Maggie, stick close to me while we're out like this. And let me do the talking."

Although she didn't say anything, her expression must've revealed her vexation.

Eli looked her in the eyes. "I'm not trying to order you around for the fun of it. It's for your safety, for my safety, and for others. There are a lot of strangers in town right now. I don't want to cause a problem for some innocent person."

"Problem?"

"Yeah, like shooting someone who accidently bumps into you."

Oh. Hopefully Eli was exaggerating, yet she could see the wisdom in his cautious ways. But she didn't have to like it. "That's a perfectly logical explanation," she said, "and I understand. But I get the feeling that you'd prefer if I agreed with everything you said without hesitation."

"That's not true. I prefer to be around opinionated, strong-willed people. It makes discussions more lively and interesting. I particularly enjoy..." Eli hesitated, his gaze dropping to her mouth for a moment, "...arguing with a sassy woman."

He turned and resumed his unhurried pace, casually studying the area, while Maggie's feet were unsteady now as she tripped along beside him. She was not ready for the conversation to end. "Which sassy women have you been arguing with?"

He stopped and smiled. "That, my dear pretend fiancé, is none of your business."

Mumbling under her breath, Maggie placed her hand on the arm he offered as they stepped upon the boardwalk. "Okay," she agreed, "I'll stay close. But why can't I do the talking? Do you honestly think I can't handle this?"

He considered that for a moment, then relented. "You're right. You will probably do a better job at it than I would. But we—both of us—have to pull together for this to work."

"I agree."

He placed his hand over hers where it rested on his arm. "And to tell you the truth, that's how I feel about a real relationship, too."

Maggie was once again caught off guard. Just when she thought she had this man figured out, he managed to surprise her.

CHAPTER TWENTY-SEVEN

ELI BIT BACK a smile at the expression on Silas Martin's face when Maggie walked right up to him with a huge smile on her face and held out her hand, palm down, fingers curled slightly—in that peculiar way that ladies had.

"Mr. Martin, I understand that I owe you my deepest gratitude."

Silas looked like he was about to swallow his tobacco. "You do?"

"Yes, I've been told that it was you who fetched the sheriff when I was in dire straits, and that it was you who went for the doctor and midwife."

Silas ran a hand over his bald head. "Well, umm, I only did what any responsible citizen would do."

"Nevertheless," Maggie said, "it was you who came to my rescue. The world would be a better place if there were more people like you."

Silas's head had reddened to match the handkerchief hanging from his back pocket. Eli almost felt sorry for him.

Catching Maggie's eye, Eli said, "We have a few more stops to make, darling."

"Oh, yes. Thank you for the reminder…dear."

After one astonished glance in Eli's direction, Silas returned his attention to Maggie who was asking about some of his yard goods, and complimenting him on the appearance of the store in general.

For the next few minutes, Maggie talked and smiled a lot, and Silas nodded and blushed a lot, while Eli leaned against the counter, thoroughly enjoying himself. Maggie was good at this. He should never have doubted her.

Eli was distracted by the sight of Walter Miller stepping out of the back room with a hammer in hand.

The man waved at him, and Eli headed his way. "You about to get finished with the repairs?"

"I already did, but then Mr. Martin hired me to build him a display area. I sure am grateful for the money. I need to find another place to live, and now I have to find another job."

"Why?"

"The school board met and then sent word that they're going to use someone else."

"I'm sorry," Eli said. "I didn't tell a soul about what happened."

"Thanks, Sheriff. I think it had more to do with my wife and daughter than it did anything else."

"What makes you say that?"

"Mrs. Dunlop's husband is one of the school board members."

Poor Walter couldn't catch a break. First the other fellow Eli had arrested disappeared the first day he had let them out to work, and now this. At least the drover had left his poker winnings to help pay for the repairs. It still left Walter to do all the work. So, no housing, and now no long term income.

"Let me see what I can do," Eli said. "With all the building going on around here, there's gotta be work somewhere."

"Much obliged, Sheriff."

Walter walked over to the north wall and Eli trailed after him to look at the new display case.

"This is quality work," Eli said.

Walter shrugged the compliment off. "Mr. Martin seems to like it okay."

"I dabble a little in woodworking," Eli said, "and I know a good job when I see one."

Smiling, Walter admitted that he loved carpentry work. "I've always enjoyed doing this. Like I said before, my Pappy was the one who wanted me to be a teacher. This is something I do because I love it."

"It'd be nice if you could make money doing something you love," Eli said.

"A fellow can dream," Walter agreed.

After leaving the mercantile, Maggie and Eli made brief stops at several other places, including Bony Joe's restaurant and the post office. Most people in town made a stop in one or the other every day, so it didn't take long to meet a few of the Moccasin Rock citizenry.

At the hotel, Eli talked to the owner and discovered that they were in need of help on the interior work.

"I've got plenty of laborers," the man said. "What I'm lacking is skilled labor."

"I know just the man for you," Eli said. "His name is Walter Miller. Go on over to Martin's Mercantile and look at the display case he's building. Tell him I sent you."

"I'll do it right now," the owner said.

Eli and Maggie's last stop was at the newspaper office.

As soon as they entered the door, Luther pulled his ink-stained apron off and laid it aside. Eli had never seen the man do that before.

"To what do I owe this honor?" Luther asked.

"Miss Radford is new to Moccasin Rock," Eli said, "and a guest of Peg Harmon's. I wanted to introduce her to a few people."

"Is that right? Well, it's a delight to meet you, Miss Radford. Where are you from?"

Eli began to second guess his decision to make the newspaper office one of his stops when Luther's first question was followed by a string of others. Eli should've known that a newsman would be curious.

He breathed easier when he noticed that Maggie had somehow shifted the attention back to Luther. She was asking him where he'd been born, how long he'd lived in Moccasin Rock, how long he'd been in the newspaper business. She'd done the same thing to him a time or two. This was more fun.

To make sure that the visit accomplished their goal, Eli smiled at Maggie and winked—then wondered if that was a good idea when she went wide-eyed and mute. She'd been doing great, and now she seemed to be floundering for something to say. Eli never would figure women out. They left not long afterwards.

Before they returned to Peg's house, Eli took Maggie to see his house, or what there was of it. Her reaction was positive—the site, the view, even the simple design seemed to meet with her approval. She truly was a sweet woman, Eli decided, although she might've had a few concerns had their engagement been a real one.

By the time Sunday rolled around, Eli was pretty sure that everyone in town had heard about him and Maggie Radford, including Murphy Patterson. If the Pinkerton man was still watching and reporting back to Hollis, he'd have plenty to report this time. Sitting with Maggie at church should remove any last doubts about their rumored courtship.

Stepping up on Peg's front porch just as the church bells began to chime, Eli tugged on his collar, smoothed his hair down with the palm of his hand, and then knocked on the door. He was surprised by the way his stomach was flip-flopping around. *Whose idiotic idea was this anyway?*

Oh, it was his.

Although Eli had attended church services recently, he was only now getting to where he was comfortable. He liked to slip in late, sit in the back seat, and then slip out again as soon as the final amen rang out.

It wasn't that he was unfriendly, or disliked the congregation. He'd just gotten accustomed to keeping to himself through the years.

He was second-guessing the whole plan when Maggie opened the door.

All other thoughts flew from his mind.

Eli had been certain she was one of the prettiest women in Texas already—even in rags, buckskin, or borrowed trousers—but Maggie all dressed up was something special indeed.

Her dress was a soft golden-pinkish color. He'd seen that exact shade on a fish fin once—a sun perch if he remembered correctly. The dress was simple, no fussy ruffles, lace or yards of excess fabric. It probably had some fancy name, both the color and the style, but all Eli knew was that it was a stunning combination. She wasn't wearing a hat. Her beautiful hair was piled up in swirls on the top of her head.

She smiled at him. "How do I look?"

Lovely. Beautiful. Should he mention the fish? "You look nice," he settled for saying.

"Thank you. You look nice yourself," she said, and Eli was glad he'd gone to the barbershop the day before. He'd also shaved this morning and slapped on some smell-good stuff he'd borrowed from Caleb.

Peg had agreed to keep the baby at home, so he and Maggie headed to the church. They arrived while the congregation was still gathering. By unspoken agreement they sat with Nathaniel and Brody in the pew behind Caleb and Abby, and Abby's family.

When the words to the first hymn rang out, Eli relaxed. In some way that he couldn't explain, it felt right—all of it.

He only mouthed the words to the song—aware that his singing sounded a lot like a stepped-on toad frog—but he loved hearing those around him sing.

"Have you been to Jesus for the cleansing power?
Are you washed in the blood of the Lamb?

Are you fully trusting in His grace this hour?
Are you washed in the blood of the Lamb?"

As always, Pastor Wilkie Brown's sermon held Eli's interest. He spoke about trust, and faith, reading from the sixth chapter of Matthew. "Take therefore no thought for the morrow: for the morrow shall take thought for the things of itself." *Don't worry about tomorrow.* That made sense. But something else tugged at Eli's mind, and he couldn't figure out what. He quit puzzling over it when Pastor Wilkie moved on to the next scripture.

After the service, he waited while Abby introduced Maggie to several people, including the Horton Boarding House residents.

Outside, Abby pulled Maggie along with her when another woman excitedly motioned for them. "Come see what my husband bought me," she called.

As they all exclaimed over the new Singer sewing machine in the back of a wagon, picked up earlier at the train station, Eli kept his gaze on Maggie. Even though this was all a plan to keep her safe, she seemed to truly be enjoying herself among the people of Moccasin Rock. He wished he'd thought of it sooner.

Caleb and Nathaniel wandered over to join him. "So what part of the courting ritual are y'all observing this afternoon?" Caleb asked.

Eli's head snapped up. "What do you mean? We've already walked around town together."

Caleb grinned, thoroughly enjoying Eli's discomfort. "You want this to seem real, right?"

"Yeah." Eli had never courted a respectable girl. He had no idea what else to do. It seemed like there was a lot of parlor-sitting involved; often under the watchful eye of a Papa. That wasn't going to work.

"Luckily for you," Caleb added, "most people don't do much on Sundays except go to church. But tomorrow you could…"

Eli cut him off. "No, I've got plans."

"What kind of plans?" Nathaniel asked.

"Nothing I want to talk about," Eli said.

What he had to do, he needed to do alone. After several more questions that met with the same response, both his brothers gave up. That was good, because Eli was enjoying watching Maggie again. Perhaps a little too much, he cautioned himself. He needed to tread carefully here, and not for his own sake. Eli didn't want to mislead her. Even in the past, he'd never misled or lied to a woman.

Although he and Maggie had been thrown together for the time being, their lives—past, present and future—couldn't be more different. He had nothing to offer a woman like her. *The woman read books. For fun!* Eli had learned to read and write enough to get by, but that was about it. Nope, there was absolutely no future for them.

Maggie looked up at that moment and gave him a dazzling smile. Despite everything he'd just told himself, Eli's heart tripped over itself.

Relax, she's pretending. That's all it is. Her motivation is safety, not love.

CHAPTER TWENTY-EIGHT

THE NEXT MORNING, after making sure that Bliss could keep an eye on things in Moccasin Rock, Eli removed his badge and laid it on the desk.

Despite the old man's persistent questioning, Eli wouldn't tell him what his plans were. "I'll be back before night fall," he said. "That's all you need to know." He wasn't telling the deputy or anyone else what he had in mind.

Eli wasn't sure what to do yet about Hollis Anderson, or even how to help Maggie long-term, but there was one person he could deal with.

The man called Tiny. And he would do it alone.

Unfortunately, Caleb was waiting outside as Eli left the jail.

The knowing little grin on his youngest brother's face put him on guard. Eli nodded at him, but didn't say anything.

"Where you headed?" Caleb asked.

Eli pushed past him. "Out."

Caleb's grin widened. "Need help with anything?"

"Sure," Eli said over his shoulder. "If you want to give Bliss a hand around here, that'd be great."

"I think I'd rather go with you," Caleb said, striding along beside him.

Eli stopped and turned. "Why?"

"To make sure you don't get yourself into trouble over in Fair Haven."

He knew. "I should never have told you about what that guard did to Maggie," Eli grumbled. "Or that I had something important to tend to today."

"Yeah, you're not that hard to figure," Caleb said.

"Then unfigure me," Eli snapped. "I don't need any help. I'll be fine."

"Probably so," Caleb agreed. "I believe I'll go along for the fun of it."

Eli struggled with his frustration as the train whistle sounded in the distance. "Okay, but only if you accompany me as my brother, not a lawman."

Caleb's grin slipped a little. "Not sure I can promise that, especially if you plan on breaking any laws."

"I'm not *planning* any such thing. I only want to have a talk with the man. Don't interfere."

Caleb nodded, but made no promises. Eli realized it was the best he was going to get. Despite his brother's repeated attempts to get information as they traveled, Eli wouldn't tell him anything. Eventually, the youngest Calhoun quit asking, but he made several comments about taking the high road, and doing the right thing. Eli yawned and closed his eyes.

After arriving in Fair Haven, it took less than an hour to locate the man who'd done Hollis Anderson's dirty work. Tiny was leaving the barber shop, all freshly shaved and spiffed up.

As Eli stepped toward him, his brother motioned for him to stop. "Is that the man you've been calling Tiny?" Caleb whispered.

At Eli's nod, Caleb said, "Well hold up a minute. I recognize him. I may need to talk to him, too."

Eli eyed the man. Big, about a head taller than him, with a long face, deep-set eyes, thick dark brows, and a crooked nose that had been broken at least once. "He wanted for something?"

"Yep. A whole string of somethings. He's got half-a-dozen aliases."
Eli thought about asking for details, then decided it didn't
matter. As long as he had his chance to talk to the man first, he
didn't care what Caleb did.

While they stood there, talking, the guard kept walking. *They
were going to lose him.* Without being obvious about it, Eli and Caleb
followed along. The man's pace increased. Although he hadn't turned
to look at them, Eli was sure he was aware of their presence.

"He's spotted us," Eli told Caleb, glancing over in time to see
his brother move his jacket aside to uncover his badge.

Just then Tiny lunged through the swinging doors of a saloon.

"I'm going in after him," Caleb said, "you go around to the alley."

Eli took off before his brother even finished talking. He rounded
the corner in time to see the man walk out the saloon's back door
with a smirk on his face.

Drawing his gun, Eli pointed it at him. "Hello, Tiny."

Smirk gone, the man slowly raised his hands.

"That was easier than I thought it would be," Caleb said, stepping through the same door into the alley. "Looking forward to
telling my captain that you're in custody." He slipped handcuffs on
the man.

Gun still in hand, Eli struggled to control his frustration as he
drew closer.

The prisoner didn't seem to notice. His attention had been captured by the cuffs. "You got the wrong man," Tiny said. "You got
me confused with somebody else."

Caleb laughed. "Yeah, I'm sure there are a dozen others who look
exactly like you. Besides, you don't even know yet what I'm arresting
you for. How can you be sure you didn't do it?"

"Before you get too far along in this process," Eli said to Caleb,
"let me remind you that I'm the one who came here looking for the
man. He and I have some unfinished business to tend to."

Tiny stopped talking to Caleb and turned his attention to Eli.

"What business?"

"I want to talk to you about your time at the asylum."

The man's eyes widened. "Hey, I didn't start that fire. One of them crazies did." He jerked around to plead with Caleb. "Seriously. I had nothing to do with it."

"I believe you," Eli said, "but it's not the fire I want to talk about."

The man's gaze swung back to Eli. "What then?"

"I want to talk about Maggie Radford."

Tiny stilled, expression wary. "Never heard of her."

"Eli, what are you wanting to do?" his brother asked.

Eli shrugged. He couldn't kill the man. *Could he?* No. He knew what Pastor Wilkie Brown would say, and probably even Maggie, "Vengeance is mine sayeth the Lord."

But Eli's finger itched on the trigger and the churning in his stomach wouldn't allow for the man to just waltz off to jail.

Eli wasn't sure if he wanted to talk to the man or stomp a hole in him. Whatever he did, he wasn't doing it in front of Caleb.

Holstering his weapon, Eli saw the flash of relief and a moment's triumph in the guard's eyes.

"I need a word with the prisoner," Eli told Caleb. "Alone."

Caleb shook his head. "Afraid not."

Eli glared at him. "I want you to leave. Now," he added between clenched teeth.

"Sorry, not happening. This man's in my custody."

At Eli's growl, Caleb tried to explain. "You stopped me from making a similar mistake a few months ago, and I intend to repay the favor."

"That was all kinds of different," Eli said. He held out his hand. "C'mon, give me the key to the cuffs."

Caleb's brows rose. "Well, that's different. If you insist on *talking* to the man I'm a little more comfortable knowing it's a fair talk."

That stung. "Did you really think I'd have a talk with a hand-cuffed man?"

"No," Caleb admitted.

"Then give me the key and make yourself scarce."

The man in custody had been glancing back and forth between Eli and Caleb, brow furrowed. "Talk to me?" He looked at Caleb. "You're not going to leave me here with him are you? He doesn't plan on talking!"

Ignoring him, Caleb pitched Eli the key. Tiny let loose a string of cuss words that turned the air blue.

"Don't let him get away, and don't kill him," Caleb said.

"Don't worry."

Then Caleb added, "As you know, I haven't been a church-going man for long, but it seems to me that there's a verse in the Bible that says something like, "Vengeance is mine sayeth the Lord."

Eli groaned. "Not you, too."

"What?"

"Nothing," Eli grumbled. "As you well know, I've been a church-going man for even less time than you, but I reckon what you say is true. Yet I'm recalling another verse: "The Lord works in mysterious ways."

Caleb grinned at him. "I don't think that's even in the Bible."

Eli shrugged, but he didn't back down. This man was going to think twice before he ever picked on anybody less than half his size again.

Caleb sighed. "I wish you'd reconsider."

"And I wish you'd get outta here."

"I'm going," Caleb said.

As soon as his brother was out of sight Eli unlocked the cuffs and let them fall.

"You really mean to give me a fair fight?" Tiny asked.

"I meant what I—" A fist landing on Eli's mouth interrupted his statement.

Eli stepped back, spit blood, and then grinned. "I deserve that, for being so stupid." Before the other man could respond, Eli shoved him against the back of the saloon, then leaned in and whispered, "But Maggie didn't deserve it. This is for her." Eli hit him in the gut, then pulled the man up by the collar and slammed a fist into his face.

"And that's also for Maggie," he said, "and the times you left bruises where no one could see them. I want people to see what I've done to you."

Despite his massive size Tiny was a surprisingly agile opponent, and his answering blow left Eli reeling. After that, everything was a blur of fists on flesh, grunts and groans coming from his own throat, the smell of blood, and a ringing in his ears. Eli didn't know how many punches he'd landed, or even how many he'd thrown. But he knew he was losing.

Until the guard said, "I shoulda done what I really wanted to do to that girl. That might've made this all worthwhile."

Maybe it was the blood dripping into his eyes from the cut on his brow, but a red haze was all Eli saw. With a renewed intensity fueled by rage, Eli deliberately set about stomping a hole in the man.

Tiny was on the ground when Eli heard his brother call his name, but it wasn't until a gun was cocked that he stilled.

Glancing over the man's prone figure, Eli eyed the Remington 44-40 that Caleb had leveled at him.

"I'm gonna need you to step away."

Struggling to catch his breath, Eli opened his mouth to argue.

"Sure would hate to shoot my own brother," Caleb drawled.

Eli froze. Not because he held any fear of the youngest Calhoun firing at him—he knew better. But because it was the same words he'd said to Caleb the first time they'd met.

Stepping back, Eli used the tail end of his shirt to wipe sweat and blood from his face, struggling to catch his breath.

"I thought I was supposed to be the reckless Calhoun," Caleb said. "I've come to admire that steely resolve and reserved demeanor. What happened there, man?"

Eli shook his head. "I thought about what he'd done to Maggie and I lost it. I didn't kill him, did I? I didn't mean to."

Caleb snorted. "Good to know. Fortunately for you, he's still alive, if not exactly well."

They both helped get the man on his feet, and then Caleb slipped the cuffs back on. "I'll take him to the Fair Haven jail and send word to Captain Parnell where to find him."

Eli picked his hat up from the ground and slapped it against his thigh to remove the dirt. "I'll help you."

"No, I think it's better if you stay out of the way," Caleb said. "See if you can't clean yourself up a little, you're a mess. I'll meet you at the train station."

As Eli waited at the depot, he found himself regretful for losing his temper. He'd fought many men in his life, but never had he lost control like that. That kind of thing was dangerous.

What was happening to him?

CHAPTER TWENTY-NINE

MAGGIE'S STEPS SLOWED as she approached the front room. The door was open just enough for her to catch the sound of a low pitched voice. She stopped. She didn't know who all was in there, but one of them was Elijah Calhoun. *Were they talking about her?*

Peg had been the only one at home when Maggie had gone out back to hang the laundry. She didn't hear any sound from the woman now. Only Eli's voice.

In case he was talking to the Pinkerton agent again, Maggie lingered in the hall, head tilted, trying to make out what was being said. After several moments, she was even more confused. Eli's tone of voice sounded as it usually did, quiet and confident, but the words themselves weren't making any sense.

Then she heard one sentence clearly. "You're a fortunate little girl to have Maggie Radford on your side."

She smiled. Eli was talking to the baby. Unlike most people, he was using his regular voice.

"A little girl needs a mother to watch over her," he continued. "So does a little boy for that matter. Eventually, you'll be all grown-up and running your own house. And as long as you've listened to Maggie, I wouldn't be a bit surprised by what you manage to accomplish. You'll be strong, that's for sure."

Since the door was partially open, Maggie peered through before announcing her presence. Eli was sitting in a chair by the fireplace, holding the baby. The infant's hand was wrapped around one of his fingers. The contrast of the white, unblemished skin against the rough, darker skin, held her spellbound.

"I don't know who your papa will be," Eli said, again in a conversational tone, "but I imagine you'll have one someday after y'all get back to Fair Haven. And if he doesn't treat you right, I'll come and kick his…" He paused. "Let's just say he'll straighten right up when I'm done with him."

Maggie blinked against unexpected tears. There was so much more to this man than she'd first suspected. She'd placed her hand on the door, ready to push it open, when he spoke again. And this time, he did it in a soft, singsong voice, as he recited a nursery rhyme to Lucinda. The baby made a little sighing sound.

"Did you like that?" he asked. "I know more of them. My mama used to sing to me and my brother. And she told us stories. So many stories. She read the Bible to us every day, telling us about Daniel and the lion's den, and Noah, and Jonah."

He adjusted the blanket around the baby, pulling her a little closer. "And Mama also told us about the early days of Texas and the Alamo, Goliad and San Jacinto. It didn't mean much then, but it does now. I don't remember everything she said. Just bits and pieces. She would tell us to hold our heads up high, always, because we were sons of patriots and kings." He laughed softly. "And I think there were some scalawags, rascals and outlaws in the family, too. Course, Mama liked to say they came from Daddy's side."

Maggie smiled. He was once again talking to the baby as he would Peg or her.

"And Mama was a good cook—even if sometimes all we had to eat was wind pudding and rabbit tracks."

Maggie shook her head. *Wind pudding and rabbit tracks.* How odd. The second time she'd heard the words since she'd been here. She pushed through the door to mention it to him, and then stopped.

Her heart twisted as she got a look at his battered and bruised face. "Oh Eli," she breathed.

He glanced away, not meeting her eyes. "Hello, Maggie. I brought a message for Peg. She was needed out at the Baker place. I told her I'd watch the baby until you came inside."

Maggie couldn't believe he was acting as if nothing was wrong. "Eli, what happened to you?"

"Nothing. I'm fine." He laid the baby down in her cradle and tried to brush past Maggie, but she tugged on his sleeve.

"Elijah? Please?"

He stopped, but still wouldn't meet her eyes. "I ran into something," he mumbled.

"Must've been something pretty solid to do that kind of damage."

He seemed to be struggling with what to tell her. Suddenly she knew.

"That guard, Tiny. Did he do this?"

Eli nodded.

Maggie let out a breath. "Let me guess. He's in even worse shape than you."

Eli grinned, or tried to. His lip was split, so the crooked smile he gave her made her cringe.

He looked away again. "Sorry sight, huh?"

"No, not at all." Maggie placed her hand on his arm. "It's still a very handsome face."

Eli's startled gaze flew to hers. "You're not going to gripe at me for what happened?"

"No. Especially since I'm really not sure what did happen. I suspect you wanted to settle a score for me, so I'm going to say thank you."

Mouth open, he stared at her.

"Thank you for caring, Eli. But please, don't ever do anything like that again." She dropped her hand and turned toward the door. He grabbed at her fingers, tugging her back.

"Maggie, no matter what I promise or how good my intentions,

I'll have more encounters like this. I went looking for this fight, and I probably shouldn't have, but trouble finds me often enough. I'm the sheriff. For some people, that's all it takes for them to want to fight me."

She nodded. "I believe that."

"As I mentioned to you before, I found out the hard way that there are bad people out there. I avoided trouble if at all possible then, and I'll do that now. But other people—innocent folks—depend on me to step between them and the bad guys."

"I know you'll have to do what needs doing," Maggie said. "But this didn't need doing, that's all I'm saying."

"I considered walking away," he admitted. "Pastor Wilkie said being good doesn't get you to heaven, repenting of your sins and accepting Jesus as your Savior does. But he also said being saved should make you *want* to do better. Be better. Said something about being a new man in Christ. And I really do want that. Eventually, I think I might be able to turn the other cheek."

His expression grew more sober. "But that's only when it's me involved. I don't think I'll ever be able to stand around when someone else is being abused. Whether I'm wearing a badge, or not."

"I know." Maggie was trying to decide what else to say when they heard the back door fly open.

Eli grabbed for his gun, while Maggie scooped up the baby, each bracing for a confrontation. Then they looked at each other in confusion. It was little feet headed their way.

A moment later Ruthie burst into the room, tears trickling down her face. "Come quick," she said. "The mean lady is making my Daddy mad, and my Mama cry."

⋞

Eli waited long enough for Maggie to throw another blanket around Lucinda. Peg Harmon walked up as they were leaving.

"Where's everybody going?"

"Ruthie's house," Maggie said. "Something has her upset."

"Poor thing. Here, let me have the baby while you go check on her," Peg said.

Hurrying outside, they heard a commotion from next door, and entered to a scene just as Ruthie had described.

Dovie was crying, Walter looked ready to explode, and Mrs. Dunlop, obviously the "mean lady" in this instance, was standing with her hands on her hips.

"What's going on?" Eli said.

Mrs. Dunlop gaped at him. "Goodness gracious. What's happened to your face?"

"Nothing worth repeating. Now tell me what's happening here."

"Very well," Mrs. Dunlop said. "I've asked these people, nicely, to please vacate these premises. They refuse to comply. Now do something about it."

Maggie stared at the woman, brow furrowed. "Why are you asking them to leave?"

Mrs. Dunlop's expression grew even frostier. "Who are you? I saw you in church, but I don't believe I received an introduction."

"My name is Maggie. I'm a friend of Peg Harmon, and I'm a guest in her home. Who are you?"

"I'm Myrtle Dunlop. I own the bakery in town. My husband George is a member of the board of education." The woman sniffed. "He's a very important man."

"How nice for you," Maggie murmured.

Eli lowered his head to hide a smile. He wasn't sure how she'd done it, but Maggie had just insulted Mrs. Dunlop.

Maggie turned to Walter and Dovie. "Do you want to leave?"

"I'm not anxious to live in her house," Walter said, "but I don't have anything else lined up yet. We had an agreement, then she changed it. Doubled the rent. I've been trying to come up with the extra money, and I told her I almost have it—if she'd only give me a little more time."

"Do you have the amount she originally asked for?" Eli asked.

"Yes."

Maggie turned to Mrs. Dunlop. "So why did you ask them to leave?"

"It's only fair that I get what the house is really worth."

"If I give you the extra money will you let them stay?"

Immediately Walter started to object, but Eli held his hand up to stop him. He wanted to see where this was going.

Mrs. Dunlop couldn't quite meet Maggie's eyes now. Obviously she was still opposed to the Millers as tenants. "No, I will not."

"Do you have someone else ready to move in?"

"No."

Maggie's eyes narrowed. "Why don't you tell me the real reason you want them leave."

"All right, if you want me to spell it out, it's because she's a sava…"

Eli wasn't sure if the woman stopped talking because of his expression, or Maggie's—she was staring at Mrs. Dunlop as if she had grown horns.

"She's what?" Maggie said softly.

"You know," the woman hissed.

"One of God's children?"

"She's an Indian," Mrs. Dunlop sputtered.

Maggie drew in a deep breath, and Eli suspected she was trying to hold on to her temper. He glanced around the room for a frying pan.

"Mrs. Dunlop," Maggie said, "my first instinct is to tell you how ridiculous you're being, but I'm not going to do that."

"Well, I should hope not."

"You may have reason to mistrust or fear Indians," Maggie said. "I have no idea what you've been through. But I want to ask you one question. Has this particular Indian woman ever done anything to you?"

Mrs. Dunlop's mouth tightened. "No."

Eli waited, ready to lend his support to Maggie's efforts. There seemed to be no need.

She not only saw things logically; she was able to explain them that way.

Both Maggie and Mrs. Dunlop were still talking. Eli realized he'd lost track of the conversation when he looked over to see Mrs. Dunlop with a tiny smile on her face. Or at least an attempt at a smile. Maybe she had a stomach ache. "Okay," Mrs. Dunlop said. "They can stay."

As Maggie, Dovie and the landlady went over the new arrangements Walter picked up some of their belongings from the back porch and returned them to the front of the house, a smiling Ruthie by his side. Eli picked up a trunk and followed.

"You okay with how everything worked out?" he asked Walter.

"More than okay," the young man said. Then he smiled. "Miss Maggie sure is something."

"Yes, she is."

Eli thought about how quiet and empty Moccasin Rock would be once Maggie and Lucinda went home.

Why was he working so hard to make sure that happened? She wanted to go, and it was the right thing to do.

Besides, he didn't know if he really wanted her to stay…or if he wanted her to go.

Could his life get any more confusing?

For over a year Eli had lived in the same town as Abby Horton, and except for noting how pretty she was, never gave her a second thought. Then Caleb came to town, saw the same woman, and fell head over heels.

What was that "something" that drew you to a person? It was more than physical, of that Eli was certain.

But that was about all he was certain of these days.

Chapter Thirty

ELI WOKE IN the middle of the night, troubled, for no specific reason he could determine. Glancing around the cabin he saw nothing unusual, nothing out of place.

Brody? Even as he wondered, he heard the boy sigh and turn over on his bed in the loft. There appeared to be nothing wrong.

So what woke him? He'd gone to sleep easily enough. For a few days after his fight in Fair Haven he'd had trouble sleeping, thanks to multiple bruises, contusions and some other big words that Nathaniel had used.

His brother had fixed him up, bandaged his ribs, and determined that his nose wasn't broken. So far, Eli had been able to deflect, distract or ignore questions from others.

He had dreaded running into Bliss, figuring the old man would be as concerned as Maggie and his brothers about what happened to him. But once Bliss had done the double-take Eli expected, the man looked like he was trying not to grin. Eli had asked him what was so funny.

"You are," Bliss said. "As long as the other fellow got a dose of his own medicine."

"He did."

"Good. Was it the man who beat on Maggie?"

"Yep."

Bliss sat up straighter. "Did you kill him?"

"No. But he's in jail. Probably be there a long time."

The man nodded and settled back in his chair. "Good enough."

Now, Eli stared at the ceiling, letting his mind wander. He needed to hurry and get the house finished. He had spent the summer months clearing cactus, mesquite and cedar trees from the land, selling some of the cedar posts, and saving others for future use. Then had come digging and hauling limestone for the exterior walls. Eli was glad he'd pushed on with it. He and Brody couldn't stay in this cabin forever.

As was often the case these days, it took only a few minutes for his mind to work its way around to Maggie Radford. And the baby. That's when it hit him. He'd been dreaming about Lucinda's grandparents. They had come for her, and it had devastated Maggie.

Eli shook his head, trying to clear the image of Maggie's tear-streaked face. As much as he hated to do it, he had to go see the Chadwicks.

He rearranged his pillow and turned over.

According to what Maggie told Caleb, they were horrible people. What if it wasn't true? Everything Maggie knew about them had come from Lucy. What if she'd been wrong? Or what if the girl had been deceiving Maggie on purpose, out of revenge?

Eli didn't want to do it, but he had to go see them. If they came for the child years from now, it would hurt even worse.

According to Caleb, the family lived in Fort Worth. Eli didn't have a street address, but he had a name and neighborhood, Castle Hills, so it shouldn't be too difficult to track them down.

He wasn't sure what he would say once he got there, but he wasn't going to rest easy until he did. For Maggie and Lucinda's sake.

Eli caught the first train out the next morning. He didn't tell anyone where he was going, but he did ask Nathaniel to keep an eye on Brody. Even though the boy had survived on his own for months, Eli didn't want him to ever have to again.

Once the train reached Fort Worth, the first person he saw was able to give him directions to the Chadwick estate. *Estate?*

He understood as soon as he saw the place. The house was a fine one, even grander than Maggie Radford's. In fact, it was a mansion.

If these people were to take the baby, she would never want for a thing. Maggie could also provide for her, Eli reminded himself. And money was definitely not the most important thing when it came to happiness.

The door was opened by a round little man with a British accent and a stiff mustache—covering, no doubt—a stiff upper lip. If he was an indication of what the Chadwicks were like, Eli was dreading the next few minutes even more.

But when the couple was seated across from him a short time later, they were not what he'd expected at all. Instead of the cold, elegant older people he'd imagined, they were warm and friendly, and probably only in their early forties. The wife had a peaches and cream complexion, and striking blond hair held in place by diamond studded combs. Mr. Chadwick was darker, with sandy blond hair. Despite their obvious curiosity about his visit, they were gracious and hospitable.

As much as it pained Eli to admit it to himself, the baby would probably be better off here.

Both Prentice and Dorothy Chadwick wore smiles as they invited Eli to sit down. The smiles faded as soon as he mentioned their son Anthony.

Rising to his feet, Prentice Chadwick motioned to the door. "If that's the only thing you wanted to see us about, then I'd like for you to leave."

Eli stood, but he didn't leave. He couldn't.

"Our son Anthony passed away in a tragic accident," Mrs. Chadwick said quietly.

"I'm sorry for your loss," Eli said. "But I think there's something you should know. It concerns your grandchild."

Dorothy Chadwick, who'd started to stand, gave a little cry and collapsed back into her chair.

Her husband regarded Eli silently for several seconds. "Let me save you some time, Sheriff. After I heard about the fire at the asylum, I made some discreet inquiries and learned that the girl who'd made those egregious claims against my son had died in the blaze. So if you're here to get money from me to support some other child you can forget it."

"The girl did die," Eli said, "but not until after the baby was born."

"What?"

"The baby survived. Your grandchild is alive and well."

"Let's get one thing straight," Mr. Chadwick said, "my eldest son, Jerome, and his wife, Sara, will present me with my first grandchild two months from now. That will be the only one to bear the Chadwick name. You can trot pathetic little servant girls through here from now until Christmas, each with a babe in arms, and I will tell you the same thing. I only have one grandchild."

Anger rolled through Eli in waves. He wanted to grab this disgusting excuse for a human being by the collar and tell him he wasn't good enough to raise Lucy's baby. Instead, he said, "Are you willing to put that in writing?"

The man's brows lifted in surprise.

"There's someone interested in raising the baby as their own."

Chadwick shrugged. "If you'll join me in my office, we'll get this settled now. But only if you understand that the child will never receive one penny of Chadwick money."

Eli nodded.

The man never even glanced in the direction of his wife. Eli did. He waited for a moment before following her husband, giving Mrs. Chadwick an opportunity to object. She said nothing.

Prentice Chadwick was talking on one of those new-fangled

telephones when Eli entered the office, demanding that his attorney drop everything and appear at once.

Fifteen minutes later a nervous little man rushed in with a leather satchel under one arm and his hat in the other. He was followed by two other men in much the same state.

They didn't even look at Eli, and he was glad. He didn't want to associate with them, and he didn't want to be here one second longer than need be.

Eli listened with disgust and disbelief, as the solicitor and Mr. Chadwick drafted a document signing over any interest in an unnamed child, *possible* issue of Anthony Chadwick, born at the Fair Haven Lunatic Asylum to Lucy Gray, in exchange for no money changing hands, and no use of the Chadwick name.

At one point, Prentice muttered something about nobody being able to prove the baby's parentage anyway.

"Don't you even want to know who's going to raise the baby?" Eli asked.

"No, I have no interest in the matter whatsoever."

The whole transaction was completed within the hour and Eli left Prentice Chadwick's office hoping he'd never lay eyes on the man again.

Eli was outside on the porch when Mrs. Chadwick slipped through the front door behind him. After one nervous glance over her shoulder, she looked at Eli and whispered, "Was it a boy or girl?"

"A little girl."

Her eyes filled with tears. "A girl. Oh my. Is she okay?"

"Yes, ma'am." Feeling sick all over again, Eli braced himself for the worst. "Do you have any qualms about what your husband is doing?"

"In the long run it's for the best." She pressed a handkerchief to her eyes. "After all, what would I say to my friends? I could never live with the shame of a grandchild born to a servant girl."

A mixture of relief and revulsion hit Eli. This woman was every bit as vile as her husband.

"I only wanted to make sure she was all right," Mrs. Chadwick said.

"She's perfectly fine, and in the best possible hands." Eli meant that with all his heart.

His mind and conscience was clear as he headed home, even though he worried about Maggie's reaction. Would she be angry with him for interfering? Or would she be glad that the situation was resolved? *Probably a little of both.*

He intended on going straight to Peg's house from the train station, but Bliss was waiting for him with a troubled expression.

"What's wrong?"

"There's a kid missing," Bliss said.

Fear hit Eli like a blow. Had someone shown up and taken Lucinda while he was in Fort Worth? Had Hollis Anderson figured out a way to get to Maggie through the baby?

Before he could ask, Bliss said, "She's the daughter of one of those fellows you locked up for breaking into the mercantile."

Ruthie.

CHAPTER THIRTY-ONE

MAGGIE SHIVERED, MORE from dread than the cold. Even inside the schoolhouse, the baying of hounds could be heard from a distance, along with muffled shouts of the searchers calling Ruthie's name. *Please be with her, Lord. Keep her safe. Guide those looking for her.* Tears stung Maggie's eyes as she picked up a coffee pot and made her way around the room; holding the pot high overhead as she pushed through the crowd.

People came in to report on areas they'd searched, and warm up for a few minutes, drink a quick cup of coffee and head back out.

Maggie recognized many of the faces from around town—including the owners of the store, the livery stable, and the newspaper—having met some of them on her walks with Eli, and others in church. Still, she'd had to beg Eli to let her help. He was concerned about Hollis Anderson grabbing her. He'd finally relented when she promised not to leave the schoolhouse on her own.

Maggie's hopeful gaze swung toward the door as it opened, as did all others. It was the owner of the local eatery bringing in more food. Both Bony Joe and Mrs. Dunlop had been generous with their offerings, although Myrtle Dunlop had made a big show of taking food directly to Dovie.

Maggie wasn't sure who the woman was trying to impress with her gesture. Maybe just herself. She'd seemed genuinely stunned by Maggie's comments about her un-Christian behavior. And there was no doubt that the food was appreciated and needed. It wasn't up to her to guess at Mrs. Dunlop's intentions. Dovie didn't seem to notice anyway. She stared at the door, eyes huge, and seemed to sag a little more with each negative shake of the head from searchers.

As several of those inside fastened their coats, tightened scarves, and pulled on hats in preparation of returning to the search, another team came inside to warm up. Maggie filled cups and mugs and thrust them into eager hands.

"Would you like some coffee?" she said to one man who had his back to her. "Or something to eat?"

Caleb Calhoun turned, his face lighting in recognition when he saw her. "Yes, to the coffee," he said.

A lanky young man with blond hair and brown eyes stood beside Caleb, hands stretched toward the stove. Maggie pointed to the coffee pot. "How about you?" she asked.

The man gave her a shy smile. "Sure, thanks."

"Maggie, this is my friend, Henry Barnett," Caleb said, before glancing around the room. "And that's his wife, Jenna, over there beside my wife, Abby."

There was something about the way Caleb's expression softened when he said the name Abby that tugged at Maggie's heart. She yearned to bring that look to a man's face someday.

Although Eli had looked at her lovingly recently, she mustn't forget that he was pretending. And she didn't want Hollis Anderson looking at her with any kind of expression.

"I met Abby," Maggie said. "She was kind enough to bring me some clothing and other things I needed."

"Good," Caleb said. "If there's anything else you need, please don't hesitate to ask."

"I sure do appreciate it."

The door opened again, and all eyes turned. It was the deputy, Bliss. He shook his head at their unasked question.

Maggie took him some coffee.

"Would you like some food?" she asked.

"No, I'm headed back out in a minute."

Maggie's gaze was drawn again to Dovie, huddled in a corner, nearly folded in on herself. The distraught mother had tried more than once to join the search, but Walter was worried that something would happen to her.

The door opened again, and Maggie got a glimpse of several men gathered together near the front of the school, Eli among them. He hadn't been in yet.

Taking the coffee pot with her, she grabbed a few empty cups and stepped outside, gasping as the cold bit into her. Abby Calhoun followed her out with more coffee and cups. Another group of men had returned, and both women filled cups as fast as they could, Maggie's eyes repeatedly drawn to the lanterns and torches flickering across the countryside. *Please Lord, let them find her.*

Maggie's gaze landed on Eli. She took a cup of coffee to him. Her hand brushed his, and it was like ice. She couldn't imagine what little Ruthie was going through.

"Any word at all?" she whispered to him.

He wrapped his hands around the cup, and took a sip of the hot brew before shaking his head. "No, and the longer this takes, the worse it looks." His voice was hoarse from shouting, and she leaned in to hear him.

He took another sip, but before he could say anything else, a man hurried toward him from the wooded area between the river and the school. *Walter Miller.*

"We haven't found her yet," Eli said. "I came in to check with the others, I'm headed back out now."

Walter ran a hand over his eyes, lips quivering. "It's not looking good, is it Sheriff?"

Eli glanced down at the ground, then patted the man on the back. "Don't you give up. We're not. Keep looking, keep praying."

"I will. Thank you, Sheriff. I'm going inside to talk to Dovie for a minute. Then I'm heading out again."

Eli turned to another man who'd walked up. "You see anything out there, Adger?"

Maggie didn't know the man, but she knew the name. This was the man with all the children, and the livestock that escaped to roam the town. Despite the animal escapades, most everyone had referred to the man fondly, and she'd gotten the impression that he was normally a cheerful sort of fellow. Not now.

"Not a glimpse of her," Adger said. "Where could she be?"

"I don't know. We've got people looking in every direction." Eli paused, a sweeping gaze taking in the man's shivering, weary countenance. "Adger, why don't you go on home. I'm sure your family needs you."

The man gave a decisive shake of his head. "No, sir. That little girl is their only child. Their only baby. I've got nine kids, and I can't stand the thought of losing even one of them. I can't imagine what they must be going through."

"Why don't you at least go inside and get warmed up," Eli said. He looked down, and Maggie realized a young boy had joined them. Adger gave the boy's shoulder a squeeze. "Jamie, you best get on home. Your mother probably needs your help."

The boy seemed disappointed, but all he said was, "Sure, Pa," before heading toward the road.

He'd made it several feet when the sound of someone yelling brought him to a halt. Everyone turned toward the noise. There'd been shouting all night, but there was something different about this.

There was urgency in this man's words, but also…excitement. It was still several seconds before Maggie could make out what he was saying.

"We found her! She's okay."

Dr. Nathaniel Calhoun rushed into the school yard. He'd taken off his coat and had it wrapped around a small bundle in his arms as he ran. Several men ran along beside him, smiling and laughing.

Everyone outside gathered around them, cheering, and people from inside dashed out. Within seconds Ruthie was in her father's arms, and her mother was attempting to hug them both.

"Ruthie, where have you been?" Walter said.

The little girl shivered and clung to him. "I was lost. I was scared. He told me not to cry."

Walter smiled at Nathaniel. "Thank you, Doctor."

Nathaniel shook his head as Ruthie answered more of her father's questions.

"I was chasing Ollie," she said, "and I was lost. I couldn't find my pup, and I couldn't find home." She looked around. "He told me to run down this road as fast as I could, and it would take me to the schoolhouse. He was going to get Ollie for me."

Everybody turned to Nathaniel. "It wasn't me. I'm not sure who she's talking about. She was walking alone when I spotted her."

The little girl closed her eyes and laid her head on Walter's shoulder.

"Who helped you, honey?" her father asked.

"It was the big man," she whispered.

"Where is he?" Walter asked. "Do you see him here?"

The girl glanced around, shook her head, and then broke into sobs again. "And I don't see Ollie. I thought I heard him following me, but now he's not here. Daddy, please find him for me."

A frantic yapping sound had every eye turning as a bedraggled pup rushed up to the school. He was wet and muddy, and shaking as badly as Ruthie.

As the little girl squealed in excitement, someone scooped the pup up, while someone else rang the school bell, calling all the searchers in. As they returned, women held on to their husbands and sons, grateful for their safe return on a night that could have ended so tragically.

Again, Walter asked his daughter to point out her rescuer, but all she said was, "He's not here."

Just as Maggie stepped up beside Eli, they both realized who was missing. "Brody," he whispered.

Maggie turned to Ruthie. "Did Brody help you? The one who shared his cookies with you at Peg's house?"

The girl nodded, eyes drooping as she snuggled into her father's embrace. "He's nice. He told me not to cry, to follow the road to the school, that he'd get Ollie and be right behind me."

Everyone exchanged bewildered glances. The little girl and the dog were safe. Where was their rescuer?

Eli spoke quietly with Caleb and Nathaniel, and then turned to Maggie. "We're going to look for Brody. Something feels wrong."

Maggie felt it, too. "Can I help you search?"

"Thanks, but I'd feel better knowing you're home with Peg." Eli turned around, as if looking for someone else. Spotting Henry Barnett, he motioned for him to come closer.

"Henry, will you make sure Miss Radford makes it back to Peg Harmon's?"

There was no hesitation. "Sure."

"I don't know if you're aware of her situation," Eli said, "and I don't have time to explain, just don't let her out of your sight until she gets inside the house."

"Don't worry," Henry said. "I'll take care of her."

"Thank you. We're headed out to look for Brody. If he was drenched and cold, he might've gone straight to the cabin to dry off."

Although he said it matter-of-factly, Eli's expression belied his casual tone.

Maggie watched the three of them head out, sending up prayers once again for the searchers, and this time for Brody.

"Hey, wait up, Sheriff," Walter Miller said. He then led his wife toward Henry. "Do you mind seeing my family home, too? We live next door to Peg Harmon."

"I'd be glad to," Henry said.

Walter helped Dovie, and the dog, into the back of the wagon, and then gave Ruthie a kiss on the forehead before handing her up to his wife. He called out to Eli. "Tell me where you want me to search. I want to help."

"Me too," Adger said. Although the man wanted his son to return home, the boy begged to go along.

"Brody is my friend," Jamie said, "I should be helping."

"Okay, son."

Several other men announced that they were heading back out, including Bliss.

Henry Barnett ended up with a wagonload of women and kids to see home.

Sitting in the back next to Dovie and a sleeping Ruthie, Maggie pulled her shawl tighter, and stared up at the moon.

Brody had a better chance of surviving than little Ruthie on a night like this, but her heart was heavy.

No matter how resourceful he was, Brody was still a kid.

CHAPTER THIRTY-TWO

DESPITE HER BEST intentions, Maggie dozed off in front of the fire not long after returning to Peg's. Lucinda was asleep nearby.

Maggie awoke with a start when Peg touched her shoulder. One look at the older woman's expression and Maggie's stomach sank.

"Did they find Brody?"

Peg nodded, her eyes brimming. "Yes."

"Is he alive?" Maggie whispered.

"Barely, according to Caleb. Eli asked him to stop by and let us know. They've taken him to Nathaniel's office, and Eli doesn't want to leave the boy."

Fear pushed Maggie to her feet. "What happened?"

"Caleb said they found him laying in a shallow part of one of the creeks off the Brazos. Thankfully, he wasn't fully submerged, and he was laying face up. Nathaniel thinks he hit his head on a rock, probably tripped on something. Bad wound, but the cold water kept him from bleeding to death."

It didn't need to be said that icy water could cause problems, too.

"I'll watch over the baby if you want to go see him," Peg said.

Without even thinking about it, Maggie gave the woman a hug on her way out. "I honestly don't know what Lucinda and I would've done without you these past few weeks." After a surprised look, Peg smiled and then shooed Maggie on her way.

The town was still quiet when Maggie reached Nathaniel's office. The front door was locked. Going around to the back, she tapped on the door that led to the doctor's living quarters. There was no response to her knock. She opened the door a crack to reveal a kitchen that was neat and tidy, if a bit sparse.

"Hello," she called. "It's me, Maggie."

"We're down the hall," Nathaniel said.

She found him in the examination room, bent over Brody. The boy was as white as the sheet that was draped over him and shivering uncontrollably.

"I need to get him warmed up," Nathaniel said. "Then I'm going to stitch his head. After that, I'll need to tend to his ankle. I don't think it's broken, just a bad sprain."

Maggie didn't see Eli until he stepped from the shadows, and stared at the bed. He nodded at her, not saying anything. He was dry-eyed, but wore such a look of agony that it made her own eyes burn.

Nathaniel was now hurrying around the room gathering supplies. "Eli," he said, "I need more wood for the fire. Might have to cut some."

Eli wrenched his gaze from Brody and left the room without saying a word.

"I need the firewood," Nathaniel told Maggie. "More importantly Eli needs to keep busy."

"I understand," she said. "Is there anything I can do?"

"Yes, will you put some water on to boil, and then go back to Peg's and see if she has some spare blankets or quilts? As fast as you can."

"Of course."

The next few hours passed in a blur of images that Maggie prayed weren't the last memories she would have of Brody Flynn— piling blankets on him and rubbing his cold hands, holding a lantern high, and at the right angle for Nathaniel to stitch the back of the boy's head, and the moment when the adults in the room looked like they wanted to cry when Brody called out for his mama and daddy.

Maggie gripped his hand tighter, telling him over and over again that everything would be okay.

Despite the laudanum that Nathaniel administered, the boy whimpered—sweat on his brow and tears on his cheeks.

Nathaniel was also sweating by the time he was finished and the boy was resting comfortably. "Hopefully, Brody will sleep for awhile. I'll know more in a few hours. You two can go on and get some rest."

Eli refused to leave, and Maggie stayed as long as she could, but Lucinda needed her.

Back at Peg's house Maggie fed and bathed the baby, got some sleep and then prepared a meal. With Peg's permission, she made enough for Eli and Nathaniel, too.

The woman insisted on helping, and Maggie marveled again at what a caring, generous person she was when she had so little in life.

"What's wrong?" Peg said, glancing up to catch Maggie watching her.

"Nothing. I was thinking that when I first got here, I was so worried about getting home in time for my Society Sisters Community Charity meeting. And how disappointed I was when I didn't."

"Oh, I'm sorry you missed it."

"I'm not," Maggie admitted. "They did all right without me, and I learned more here."

Peg's brows rose. "Like what?"

"What love for your fellow man really looks like."

Obviously perplexed, Peg opened her mouth and then closed it again.

"I've attended lectures and conferences on poverty," Maggie said, "since I was old enough to tag along with my mother. Mama took the Bible verse to heart that says, to whom much is given, much is required."

Peg stirred the potatoes sizzling in the skillet. "That's commendable. So what's got you so down in the mouth?"

"I realize that I don't know how to really help anyone. I wasn't able to do a thing for Lucy. You might have been able to save her."

"First of all, I've had years of experience," Peg said. "And from what you've told me, I'm not sure anyone could've helped her."

"Still, I wish I could've done more. I'm not sure I've really ever made a difference to anyone."

"What do the Society Sisters do?"

"Mostly fundraising efforts."

"There's nothing wrong with helping folks in whatever way you're able," Peg said. "I wouldn't have a clue how to raise money. I bet you're good at it."

Maggie shrugged. "I'm not as good as some of my friends." She looked at Peg. "What if the only person I was helping was me? I always felt good later."

"That's nonsense," Peg said. "There have to be folks who give money, and help get money from others. Just as those who have nothing but time to offer—those who are willing to get their hands dirty in the name of Jesus—are doing their part."

"Maybe so," Maggie said. "But I have a feeling I've missed many an opportunity to be a true blessing to others."

Peg grabbed a small towel from a hook on the side of the cupboard and wiped her hands.

"If that's how you truly feel, then be watchful for the next opportunity. Just do what you can, when you can. Most of us won't ever get a chance to do something for others on a grand scale, but we can do a little here and there. If enough people do that, it all adds up."

≪ↄ

Maggie stepped inside in time to see Eli, expression grim, pin a star-shaped badge to the boy's shirt.

"Is he...?" She couldn't even finish the question.

"He's alive," Eli said, "but he's got a rattling sound in his chest, and wheezing when he breathes, and some other stuff I don't even understand. Nathaniel said it doesn't look good."

It seemed the most natural thing in the world to go to Eli. There was no pretense involved. Maggie placed her arms around him, unsure if it was the right move until he returned the embrace so tightly that she could barely breathe.

They stood together for several minutes, with Maggie whispering words of comfort.

Eli was silent except for one word. "Why?"

Only a one word question, but Maggie had no answer. "I don't understand why bad things, horrible things, happen to people who've been through so much, those who've done the best they can. It's difficult to understand. God doesn't say we won't ever have any trials, what He does say is that he'll be there with us, every step of the way. And he says we'll understand more, someday. In 1 Corinthians, it says: *For now we see through a glass, darkly; but then face to face: now I know in part; but then shall I know even as also I am known.* Pray, Eli."

"I am," he assured her.

"I'm not saying that God will answer our prayers the way we want him to," Maggie added, remembering the death of her own mother. *Oh, how she had prayed for Mama to get better.*

Brody moaned in his sleep, drawing them closer to his bedside.

"I've been worried about all the things I needed to teach him," Eli said, swallowing hard, "and I may never get a chance to do any of it. I let him down."

"No, what you did was make him happy. Even if he doesn't make it—and I'm not saying that he won't—you made a difference in his life. Just as you have others."

He shrugged. "Lots of people would do the same."

"Maybe, but it seems to me that God has placed you directly

in the path of people who needed *you.* In addition to Brody, you've helped me and Lucinda, and Walter Miller, and I'm sure there are literally countless others."

He frowned. "I just help out when I can."

"It seems you and Peg have that figured out, but some of us are just now catching on. Don't discount what you do, Eli." Maggie then told him what Peg had said earlier. "Those things you've done, 'just helping out' have been life-changing for others."

He seemed to be considering that, but he also seemed about to drop from fatigue.

"How long has it been since you slept?" Maggie said. "Shouldn't you get some rest?"

"No. I'm not going anywhere." Eli lowered his voice. "Brody lived alone too long. He's not going to die alone."

His simple declaration broke Maggie's heart. "I know Nathaniel's a good doctor, but God's in charge. And I believe he still performs miracles. Keep praying, Eli."

CHAPTER THIRTY-THREE

ELI WOKE WHEN his head lolled to one side. Where was he? He bolted upright when memories of the past few days came flooding back—the search, the horror of seeing Brody in the water, how desperate he'd felt while Nathaniel was working on him.

Had it been enough to save the boy? Eli had fallen asleep in the chair by the bed praying that it was.

He watched now as Brody's chest moved up and down easily with each breath. He wasn't struggling like he had been. And maybe it was only hope at work, but the boy's color seemed better.

"I think he's going to make it." The voice was low and laced with exhaustion.

Eli glanced over his shoulder. Nathaniel looked in worse shape than the patient, but he'd been rock steady all during the crisis. The little brother he'd worried so much about was now strong and competent, and an excellent physician.

"Why don't you get some rest now?" Eli said. "I'll stay with Brody."

Nathaniel yawned. "I think I will. Come get me if you need me."

He only slept two hours. When he returned he seemed refreshed and wide awake, and insisted that Eli go and rest.

After arguing for several minutes, Nathaniel said, "At least go get a bath and something to eat."

Eli was already shaking his head when he heard the boy mumble, "I'm fine, Eli. Everybody knows you're supposed to do what the doctor tells you."

Relief hit Eli with a wallop. He sank down on the side of the bed, unable to speak for a moment. "I think fine might be overstating it a bit," he finally said, "but it sure is good to hear you talking."

Brody's eyes cracked open. "What happened to me?"

"You were helping search for little Ruthie Miller, and found her," Eli said. "Then you must've slipped and hit your head on a rock. We found you floating in one of the creeks out by the Brazos."

"I didn't slip," Brody murmured, already half asleep again.

"You didn't?" Eli said it in a teasing tone. The boy's next words wiped every bit of humor away.

"Somebody pushed me."

Rising to his feet, Eli waited to see what else Brody would say, but in the next breath he was sleeping again.

"Go on, get out of here for awhile," Nathaniel said. "It's likely that the laudanum had him dreaming and imagining things. Not unusual."

"All right. I'll be back soon."

Eli left out the front door, stopping by the jail for a change of clothing, and then heading on to the barber shop. He could get a bath and shave there without going all the way out to the cabin.

Just as Eli reached the barbershop door, the *Gazette* publisher hailed him from across the street. "Hey Sheriff, wait up a minute."

"Hello, Luther."

"I'm not sure if you and your brother found all the information you needed about J.L. Slidell," Luther Tillman said, "but I got a bulletin in for this week's edition that I thought you might find interesting."

Eli hadn't told this man why they were interested in the politician, and Jasper wasn't high on his list of priorities right now. "What's that?"

"Slidell has dropped out of the senate race."

Tillman had Eli's attention now. "Why?"

"No explanation. Just announced that he'd decided not to pursue public office, and that he's stepping aside. He wishes his opponent the best of luck."

"That is interesting," Eli said. "Thanks for letting me know."

Tillman had taken a few steps away when he turned back. "Strangely, Slidell came into the office that day he was here, asking as many questions about you and your brother, as you did about him. Is there anything you can tell me about that?"

"Nope. Not sure what he was after." Jasper must've been trying to decide if they had any connections powerful enough to back up their threats about bringing trouble down on him.

Tillman nodded, and returned to his office. Eli entered the barbershop with a lighter step than he'd had in days. Brody was on the mend. Jasper was out of the senate race. And that was good news for everyone in Texas.

Maybe Maggie was right. Perhaps doing the right thing when you could, even if it was only one small thing, could make a difference.

After the bath, he walked over to the jailhouse to change into different boots. No one was there, not even Bliss. Even though he hadn't intended to, Eli fell asleep on the cot, waking up when a wagon rumbled down the alley.

He hurried back to Nathaniel's to find a whole passel of people gathered around Brody's bed—Maggie and the baby, Caleb, Peg, Walter, Dovie and even little Ruthie were there.

Nathaniel looked at him over the heads of the visitors. "The Miller family heard that Brody's on the mend. They came to express their gratitude."

Caleb smiled. "I just stopped by to see how he's doing. Glad to find him awake." Peg and Maggie acknowledged the same.

"I can't thank you enough for what you did," Walter said to Brody, while his wife softly added her own appreciation.

Brody turned several shades of red. "Aw, anybody woulda done the same," he mumbled.

"Maybe so," Walter said, "but I'm grateful for what *you* did. Anytime you need a favor, anything, don't hesitate to ask."

The boy's discomfort was obvious, so Eli drew Walter's attention to the tin star on Brody's nightshirt. "He received a little promotion while he was recovering."

At Walter's low whistle of admiration, Eli hastened to assure him it wouldn't involve any actual confrontations with outlaws. "He's only to wear it at home, for now. It'll be a few years before he can pin it on for good." Even as he reassured the other man, Eli was reassuring himself.

Ruthie stepped closer to the bed, smiling shyly at Brody. Pulling her hand from her pocket, she held up a silver badge. "I have a star, too."

The smiles and conversation of the adults turned to confusion and silence.

"That's a Texas Ranger badge," Eli said softly. He glanced up at Ruthie's parents. They seemed as bewildered as everyone else.

Eli held out a hand to the girl. "Do you mind if I hold it?"

She placed the badge on his palm without comment.

Turning it over, Eli examined it closely and then looked at the only other lawman in the room.

"It's not mine," Caleb said. "Doesn't belong to anyone I know. Some rangers don't even wear badges, we're not required to. Others commission their own. Sometimes someone will have a badge made and present it to a ranger personally, in appreciation. I had mine made by a jeweler in Austin."

"This is excellent craft work," Eli said.

"How strange," Maggie murmured, while Nathaniel took a turn looking at it.

Walter's brow was furrowed. "Ruthie, where did you find the star?"

The child yawned, and pointed to Peg Harmon. "At her house."

CHAPTER THIRTY-FOUR

AS EVERY EYE turned her way, Peg Harmon dropped into the chair by Brody's bed. Leaning her head back, she appeared to have aged several years in a matter of moments.

Eli placed a hand on her shoulder, and Nathaniel hurried to her other side.

"Peg, is everything okay?" Nathaniel asked.

"Yes. I just haven't seen that in years."

Eli held the badge up. "This is yours?"

"My husband's."

"I had no idea," Eli said. From the expressions of the others in the room, it was clear he wasn't the only one.

"I thought I'd misplaced it," Peg said softly. "I can't imagine how Ruthie found it."

Maggie spoke up. "That may be my fault. I think it fell out of the clothing that you offered me that first night. When I took one of the shirts out of the trunk, I heard a sound, like something hitting the rug. I never could figure out what it was. Later, Ruthie followed me in there. I should have kept searching. I'm so sorry."

Peg waved the apology away, then closed her eyes again.

Walter caught Eli's attention and gestured toward the door. "We're going to take Ruthie home."

After they left, Eli wasn't sure what to do. Peg was sitting there, rocking back and forth, eyes closed again. The rest of them exchanged uneasy glances. Nathaniel searched through a cabinet and withdrew a bottle of medicine. But even he seemed unsure of how to act.

Maggie moved forward. "Peg, is there anything I can get you?"

"No, I'm okay. Just brought back a lot of memories."

Eli wondered if he and Caleb should slip out and let Maggie or Nathaniel handle this. But leaving without acknowledging Peg's loss, even if it happened years ago, wasn't the right thing. Asking a bunch of questions didn't seem appropriate either. While he was trying to decide what to do, Peg started talking.

"Ever heard of two rangers named Blue and Reuben?"

"Of course," Eli said, as those around nodded. "Everybody has. Those men were legends even among other lawmen."

"That's true," Caleb said. "I've heard stories about them many times. Two of the toughest men ever to wear a badge. They battled outlaws, Indians and renegades."

"Blue Harmon was my husband."

Again, astonishment greeted her words.

"Didn't he die rescuing a baby?" Nathaniel asked.

Peg looked grief-stricken all over again. "Yes. It's one of the strangest tales to come out of the early days in Texas. One summer, a band of Indians stopped at a farm house belonging to the O'Brien family—some of the first settlers in the area."

"Did they hurt them?" Brody asked.

"No, they were friendly, but at first the family was terrified. The Indians merely looked them over and left. They came several more times, and eventually the settlers grew accustomed to the sight. In fact, sometimes they would exchange small gifts. And Mrs. O'Brien fed them a time or two. Then one day she'd gone down to the spring for water, and when she came back her child was gone. She'd left the infant in a basket on the hearth. That spot was now occupied by an Indian baby."

Maggie's eyes widened. "My goodness. How strange."

Peg nodded. "The mother ran to the field where her husband was plowing, and they took the Indian baby and went running to their nearest neighbor's house. Blue and Reuben were already in the area, chasing after some outlaws. When they heard about the abduction they took the Indian baby, told the O'Briens to go home and wait, and they took out after the Indians. It didn't take them long to find them. They were camped on a creek just a few miles away. The whole bunch of them were gathered around the little O'Brien baby."

"I'm surprised they stayed so close," Nathaniel said.

"They didn't expect any trouble," Peg said, voice shaky. "They were shocked that they were being accused of stealing a baby. They'd left a fair trade in their opinion. Blue was able to negotiate an exchange. The Indians were a little disgruntled that their gift was being rejected, but they were peaceable enough about it."

Nathaniel brought Peg a glass of water, and asked if she needed a dose of the medicine.

She shook her head. "Reuben and Blue left the Indian camp, going slow because Blue was carrying the O'Brien baby. They were in a good mood—looking forward to getting the little one back with her parents. The outlaws they'd been trailing suddenly came up out of a gulley. Ambushed them. Blue jumped from his horse and rolled, still cradling the baby, keeping her sheltered. He was shot in the back before he ever had a chance to draw his gun."

Maggie tightened her grip on Lucinda. "Did they hit the baby?"

"No, she made it all right, just a few scratches. Blue only lived for a few minutes."

"I'm sorry, Peg." Eli spoke the words, wishing he knew what else to say.

She nodded, and then continued. "Reuben was also shot. Even wounded he returned fire and killed two of their ambushers—all while trying to protect Blue and the baby. The other outlaws scattered and were captured later."

"Whatever happened to him?" Eli wondered aloud. "Heard he just disappeared."

"That's what I heard, too," Caleb said. "Everybody said he stuck around long enough for Blue Harmon's funeral, and then dropped outta sight. Some people say he moved away from Texas. Others say he's been dead for years."

"I've always been curious," Eli admitted.

"Why don't you ask him yourself," Peg said. "There he is."

Everybody turned to stare at the doorway. Bliss had just stepped in from the hall. He cast an anxious look toward Brody. "What's the matter? Something wrong with the boy?"

"No, Brody's fine," Eli said. "In fact, Nathaniel said he's going to make a full recovery."

"Well, that's good news. So, why are you looking so strange?"

Eli held up the badge.

All the color left the old man's face. Sagging against the door frame, he shot a look at Peg as if she'd betrayed him.

⤚

Spinning on his boot heel, Bliss moved back up the hall, faster than his normal amble.

Everybody started talking at once. Eli didn't stick around to see what would come of it. He took off after Bliss, catching up with him on the boardwalk out front.

"Hey, wait a minute."

The old man didn't slow down. "Ain't got a minute."

"Where you headed?"

"Outta here."

"Why?"

Bliss started across the road to the jail. "Cause I don't wanna talk about what happened back then, and I don't intend to. Hasn't mattered to a living soul in years."

"Sure it matters, Bliss. Y'all were he—"

The old man spun around in the middle of the street. "Don't you dare say the word hero to me. Blue was, but I let down the person who trusted me most."

"How did you let him down?"

Bliss turned his back on Eli and marched on across to the jail. "Blue's dead, isn't he? If I'd come up with a plan, or been faster or smarter, he might still be alive." He stormed in to the jail and tried to shut the door behind him. Eli pushed through.

"You can't think like that," Eli said. *Second guessing yourself could drive a person crazy. And it didn't accomplish anything.*

"Sure I can," Bliss said. "That's what happened. Actually I let two people down that day."

"Two?"

"The last thing Peg said to me every time we left out of here was, 'Take care of him.' Do you know the last thing that Blue Harmon said to me before he died?"

"No."

"He said take care of them."

"Them?"

"Peg was expecting their first baby."

"Peg has a child?"

"She lost the babe the day Blue was buried. A little boy."

Bliss sank down into a chair as if his legs had given out on him. "I tried to do what Blue asked. Peg wouldn't take a thing from me. She was grieving. But she was more angry than anything. She couldn't figure out why a man like Blue was snatched by death. He had a wife, and a young 'un on the way. He was a good person, through and through. Peg didn't say it out loud, but I knew she was wondering why somebody like me was allowed to live."

"Bliss, come on, you can't believe that."

The old man shrugged. "It's true. I had no answer for her. I left Moccasin Rock."

"Why did you come back?"

"My promise to Blue nagged at me. Thankfully, everybody here had already lost interest in the story about the O'Brien baby. I was just Bliss again, Barnes and Minnie Walker's boy. I'd never been known by that name in the Rangers. Just here. When new people came they didn't know who I was, or care. Finally, nobody talked about it anymore. That suited me fine."

Eli realized he'd never seen Peg and Bliss together in the same room. Or even the same building. Until today. "What about Peg?" he asked. "Did you two ever make peace?"

Bliss shook his head. "I tried, Eli. God knows I tried. Even later, when she'd had time to think about it, Peg wanted no help from me. She said it hurt her to talk about Blue, or even about what he wanted. She refused to take a dime from me. I offered her money over and over again."

Bliss started to say something else, and then clamped his mouth shut.

"So you two have lived here in the same town, all these years, without talking?"

The man sighed. "An occasional word in passing, nothing important. There was only one time when we had a longer talk. A young writer had come to town, doing a story about the early days of Texas, especially about the Texas Rangers. He wanted to find out what happened to Blue Harmon's widow, and the child they were expecting. And he also wanted to track down the other ranger. Thankfully, the few folks who remembered it all wouldn't tell him a thing. I hurried to Peg's house, and we both agreed not to talk. We would let the story die. Cause every time it was dredged up again, it brought back memories so powerful it pained her. We vowed never to speak of it again. And we didn't. Until now."

He looked at Eli with confusion in his eyes. "What made her show y'all the badge?"

"Walter Miller's little girl had it in her pocket. She's been stopping in at Peg's place to visit. Must've picked it up at some point."

Bliss blinked a few times, then closed his eyes.

Eli understood not wanting to dwell on what had happened, all the loss and pain. He also knew that talking to Maggie about his past had made him feel better. He didn't want to force the old man to relive anything he didn't want to, but he would provide an opening, just in case.

"So what was Blue Harmon like?" he asked.

Bliss took his hat off and leaned back. "You heard men described as larger than life? That fit Blue like nothing else ever did. He wasn't as big as you, size wise. He just…lived. I never met a man before, or since, who could wring as much out of life as he did. Even every day sorta things. No matter what situation we'd find ourselves in, Blue made it better."

Eli nodded.

"The men woulda followed him anywhere," Bliss said. "And women too, for that matter. But from the minute he laid eyes on Peg that man never looked at another female. Peg was beautiful. Still is. But back then, she had long, dark red hair. Heard somebody call it auburn. Whatever you call it, it was a sight. Blue was a goner the minute he set eyes on her. Told me he wanted a whole house full of red-headed babies."

Eli smiled, but kept his silence.

"And she loved him right back," Bliss said. "I admit I was envious of what they had. But I was also happy for them, if that makes any sense. I loved them both. They were my friends. Like to have killed me to lose them." He raised faded blue eyes to Eli. "That coat that Maggie was wearing the first time I saw her. That was Blue's. Set me back. Then I figured Peg must've give it to her."

That explained the strange reaction. "I'm sorry," Eli said, truly regretting anything that might've caused the old man more pain.

"You couldn't have known."

Bliss started in on another story about the bygone days, while

Eli got the coffee pot, filled a cup and passed it to the man. And let him talk.

"It's been hard to watch Peg struggle through the years," Bliss said later. "Midwives don't make much in a place like this, nobody does. Even when there's plenty of work, there's sometimes no money."

Yet somehow Peg survived. And Eli thought he knew how. "Nathaniel said she gets a check every few months. Some kind of pension that her husband had."

Bliss looked a little uneasy. "Could be."

"Caleb said he saw you leaving a bank in Weatherford."

Bliss knew instantly what he was talking about. Pushing to his feet he pointed at Eli. "You say one word to Peg and I'll lay you out flat."

He looked Eli up and down. "Even if it takes me a couple of tries, I'll do it."

Eli had no doubt that the old man would try. He nodded.

"I mean it," Bliss said. "If you tell Peg, I'll walk right outta here, for good this time. After I'm through with you."

"I won't tell her, if that's what you want," Eli agreed. "It's your secret for the telling, or for the keeping."

Maggie prepared a cup of tea for Peg, and then one for herself. They'd returned to the house in silence, and now, sitting at the kitchen table, Peg was sharing years of thoughts and memories.

Murmuring words of encouragement when it seemed appropriate, Maggie mostly listened. *Peg probably hadn't talked to a soul about this in years.*

The older woman told of the first time she'd seen Blue Harmon, the immediate connection, the courtship, their wedding and plans for the future.

"The having him then makes up for the hurting now," Peg said. "But there was a time I didn't think I'd survive it."

Maggie placed a hand over Peg's. "I'm so sorry."

Peg nodded, throat working as she battled tears.

"Was Blue his real name?" Maggie asked.

"No. His name was Joel James Harmon. He said his father wanted to call him J.J. but he had these deep blue eyes. A real unusual shade. Said his mother started calling him Blue. It just stuck." She took a sip of the tea. "Something similar happened to Bliss. As you heard earlier, his real name is Reuben, but his mother called him Bliss. Eventually everyone around here did, too."

Peg seemed lost in her thoughts for awhile, then suddenly began talking again. "Blue's buried here in Moccasin Rock, you know. He'd traveled all over Texas and Mexico, and fought battles and engaged in skirmishes from one end of the state to the other, and he died within a day's ride of home."

Reaching into her pocket, Peg pulled out a handkerchief and swiped at her eyes.

"They brought him home in an old wagon. The coffin was a wooden box they'd pieced together in a hurry. Every lawman in the area, as well as a good many of the peaceable Indians, rode along. There was no fancy funeral. Not that many people living here at the time. So a preacher said the words over his grave. But everyone that could be was there. Some people were there out of love, some out of respect, and some probably out of curiosity."

Maggie was unprepared for Peg's next statement.

"I lost the baby that night," she said softly. "It was a little boy."

"Oh, Peg."

The woman was miles away now, lost in her memories, and Maggie was struck anew by what a generous soul she was.

Peg had lost her husband, and her son, and yet she'd spent years trying to make sure that other women would experience the joy of cradling their infants in their arms.

Swallowing several times, Peg's voice had gone husky when she spoke again. "It was wrong of me to shut Bliss out the way I did. At the time all I felt was pain when I saw him. The man who came back wasn't the one I wanted. Nothing Bliss said or did would change that. I figured that he'd leave, but he stuck around. I also believed he'd gotten over it all years ago."

Peg raised sad eyes. "When I saw that look on his face today, I knew he wasn't over anything. He's still hurting too. I'm so sorry about that."

"I'm sure if there's anyone who could understand, it would be Bliss," Maggie said.

"Probably so." After a few moments, Peg started in reminiscing again about her husband.

Eventually, the older woman went off to bed, while Maggie remained at the table deep in thought. Peg would probably revisit many memories of her laughing, blue-eyed husband in the days to come, while Maggie's mind was suddenly filled with a brown-eyed man who seemed far too serious for his years; a man who carried much responsibility on his shoulders.

Maggie didn't know if anyone else would still remember Eli Calhoun years from now—like they did Blue Harmon—but she would.

CHAPTER THIRTY-FIVE

MAGGIE ENTERED DR. Nathaniel's office to find the front area empty and followed the sound of familiar voices toward the back.

Nathaniel had stopped by Peg's that morning, on his way to see another patient, to let them know that Brody was continuing to improve—to such a degree that he was now getting bored.

Eli was taking him home the next day, but Nathaniel had encouraged Maggie to visit Brody if she could. With Peg's blessings, she'd left Lucinda for a while in order to bring him his favorite cookies.

She entered the room to find Eli sitting in the rocker by Brody's bed, trying to get him to eat.

Maggie smiled, watching the two of them—Brody with a mulish expression, and Eli playfully coaxing. "C'mon, a little more oatmeal," Eli said. "You have to get your strength back."

"I will," Brody grumbled. "Seems to me that I'd have a better chance of doing that with some real food, though."

"Oatmeal is real food."

"Better than wind pudding and rabbit tracks, I guess, but not by much."

Maggie stared at Brody in surprise. *Rabbit tracks?* Was she the only person not familiar with that expression?

Eli laughed, which did Maggie's heart good. After so many hours of worry and waiting vigil at Brody's bedside, he looked nearly as young as the boy.

The laughter faded when he saw Maggie, replaced by a soft smile as he sat the bowl down and pushed to his feet. It was a smile of welcome that seemed to go beyond the mere hello he offered. Maggie wasn't sure exactly what it meant, but she wouldn't mind seeing it more often.

"Something wrong?" Eli asked.

She hadn't responded to his greeting. Maggie wasn't about to tell him what she'd been thinking. "Oh, nothing really. I've never heard that expression before, the rabbit tracks thing, and now I've heard it three times recently."

Eli's brows lifted. "Three times?"

"Yes, just now from Brody, and I heard you say it when you were talking to the baby."

Eli ducked his head. "Oh, you heard that, huh?"

Maggie couldn't help but tease a little. "Yes, and I would love to hear you sing the songs you remember from your childhood."

Raising his head, Eli grinned. "Not a chance."

Laughing, Maggie turned her attention to the patient. "How are you feeling?"

"I'm great," Brody said. "At least I will be when Eli lets me eat."

"You'll be eating real food by this evening," Eli assured him. To Maggie he said, "He's eager to get at some of the gifts that people brought him." He pointed to a corner table stacked with various breads, cakes and cookies.

"I can't believe so many people have been here to see me," Brody said, eyeing the heap of goodies. He seemed awed by the town's thoughtfulness.

That warmed Maggie's heart. "Goodness," she said, adding the cookies to the stack, "folks have been generous. You better take it slowly with all that."

Brody sighed heavily. "I am, Eli's seeing to it. At least he let me have a piece of candy."

"You'd be regretting it right about now if I'd let you tear into all that," Eli said. He turned to Maggie. "Silas even brought Brody a whole bag of licorice, peppermint sticks and lemon drops."

"You take some, Miss Maggie, there's plenty," Brody added. "Eli had one."

Eli raised his hands. "I didn't touch the licorice or lemon," he said, "although I was coaxed into having a peppermint."

Maggie laughed. "No thank you, Brody, maybe later."

Eli stretched and yawned. "When was the third time you heard someone talking about rabbit tracks?"

"Caleb said it."

Eli frowned. "Caleb?"

"Yes."

After a moment's thought, he shrugged. "Well, it's a thing my mother used to say. So I guess it makes sense that Daddy said it, too. Since Caleb had the same father, that's probably where he heard it."

"Maybe, however in this instance, he was talking about a woman he'd seen at the asylum in Cartersville."

Eli had picked up the bowl and offered more oatmeal to Brody, now he turned his attention to Maggie. "What woman?"

"Caleb didn't say a name. Just said that the woman had been crying to him about her baby, and then mumbled something about wind pudding and rabbit tracks."

At Eli's thoughtful look, she added. "Caleb didn't seem to think it unusual. I guess it's a common enough saying. After all, you and Brody both said it."

"Brody said it because I did."

The boy had been looking back and forth between them. "That's true," he told Maggie. "I'd never heard it before I met Eli."

Eli handed the bowl to Brody and turned toward the door. "I need to talk to Caleb," he muttered.

He stopped and looked back. "When I return, I want to hear that you've been eating like a bear waking from hibernation—real food first, then the sweets."

Brody said, "Yes, sir," and was smiling when Maggie hurried from the room after Eli. She caught up with him in Nathaniel's kitchen. "Eli, is something wrong?"

"I don't know," he admitted. "I guess I'm wondering if that woman might've known my mother. We're probably not the only family that used that little saying, but it's not exactly common."

Eli was always so in control, so absolutely sure of himself in any situation, that it was strange to see him so befuddled.

Maggie had about a hundred questions, but now wasn't the time. "Hopefully Caleb can help you."

"Thanks, Maggie."

To her utter astonishment, Eli reached out, pulled her close and kissed her before leaving.

Maggie was still staring at the closed door, hand to her mouth, when it suddenly popped open again. Eli stepped inside, eyes wide. "Did I…"

Lowering her hand, Maggie smiled. "Yes."

"Do I need to get a skillet for you?"

She laughed. "No. I didn't mind."

He gave her that full smile again—the one that did funny things to her stomach.

"Good to know. I've wanted to do that for a while. Couldn't decide on the right moment. I guess my mind settled it for me." He stepped closer, and placed a hand on her cheek. "I need to go on to Caleb's, but I hope you'll be agreeable to trying that again soon."

Heart hammering like a drum, Maggie nodded.

"Good." He stepped back and ran a hand through his hair. "Sorry to be so distracted. I can't get that rabbit tracks thing outta my mind. I don't know what to think. What a strange coincidence."

"Do you remember any of your mother's friends?"

"No. We didn't have any close neighbors or friends that I recall, except that one old man."

A thought occurred to Maggie. What if it wasn't someone who'd known Mrs. Calhoun? *What if it was her?* She didn't voice the question. "What do you remember about the day you last saw your mother?"

"Not much. The house was fully ablaze when Nathaniel and I got there, and Mama was nowhere to be seen. She'd been in the house when we left. We tried to get to her." He squeezed his eyes shut for a moment, anguished even after all these years.

But he was obviously thinking along the same lines Maggie had. "How could she have survived something like that?" Eli said. "And that neighbor of ours told us she was dead. I'm sure it's some weird coincidence, but I want to see if Caleb remembers anything else about the woman at the asylum."

"I'm sorry I didn't mention it sooner," Maggie said. "I meant to tell you the day I heard you talking to the baby. Then I got a look at the damage to your face, and I forgot all about it."

"A similar thing happened with me. I had something I'd planned on telling you the night Ruthie went missing."

"You did? What?"

Eli hesitated a moment before he spoke. "I went to see Lucinda's grandparents."

Even as the anxiety and denial built in Maggie, he was speaking again. "Don't worry. She's yours. I'll explain it all later. I was afraid that someday they could come and claim her." His voice dropped as he cupped her chin and looked into her eyes. "I was trying to do right, by everybody, and I didn't want to see any more misery in those beautiful eyes."

Before she could think of anything to say, he murmured goodbye, opened the door, and left.

From the doorway she watched as he walked right in front of

a horse and rider, apologized to both of them, and then passed by several of Adger Wilson's animals with only a nod.

Poor man. He really was in a distracted state. Could his mother somehow have survived the fire? And if it were her, how had she ended up in the asylum? How long had she been there?

Maggie shuddered at the thought. She had only been confined for a few weeks, and it had changed her. How bad would it be if you'd spent years there?

✧

Eli found Caleb finishing dinner at the Horton Boarding House. After greeting everyone, Eli declined an invitation to stay for dessert and told Caleb he'd wait on the front porch.

With an increasing sense of urgency that didn't make a bit of sense in his own mind, Eli waited for his youngest brother to join him. It was only a few minutes later.

"You need help?" Caleb asked as he settled down in the porch swing facing the chair.

"No, just curious about something."

"What's that?"

"Maggie happened to mention that you'd heard a woman at the Cartersville asylum talking about wind pudding and rabbit tracks."

"Yeah, that was a sad one," Caleb said. "It was that woman who was trying to grab on to me. One minute she seemed almost normal, then the next she went all to pieces. Why are you asking? Is it important?"

"I don't know," Eli admitted. "Can you tell me exactly what she said?"

"Maybe not exactly, but as best I can remember, she was talking about her baby."

"Her baby?"

"Yep, when I walked up, she said something about her baby, and then she reached through the bars. To be honest, I didn't give it much thought then. Now that I'm recalling it, she was looking at me with the strangest expression."

Eli tensed. "Like what?"

"She looked disappointed. She was mumbling something under her breath."

"Disappointed?"

"Yes, that's how it seemed. Like I'd let her down. Then she walked away."

"And that's when she said something about wind pudding and rabbit tracks?"

Caleb nodded. "She was mumbling those exact words. Sure didn't make sense. But considering where we were, I didn't find it too odd."

Thoughts were tumbling around in Eli's head. He couldn't get a firm grasp on any of them. "Do you remember what she said about the baby?"

"Sorry, I didn't hear most of it. The only part I heard was, "my baby's eyes are brown."

A chill ran down Eli's spine as his fragmented thoughts suddenly snapped together. He looked at Caleb's face, so like his own.

"Maybe she thought she recognized you," Eli said softly, "because you look like me and Nathaniel. Like she remembered my father looking. Maybe she was saying that her babies—both of them—had brown eyes."

Caleb stared at him in astonishment. "Are you saying you think that was your mother?"

"I don't know what I'm saying." Eli pushed to his feet and started pacing back and forth across the porch. "I need to find out more about that woman."

"I thought your mother died in a fire."

"She did." Eli shook his head. "I mean, I thought she did. But what if she didn't? I'm going to Cartersville. I'd better see if Nathaniel wants to go."

"Do you want me to keep an eye on things here while you're gone?"

"Yeah, thanks." Eli was almost out of the yard when he stopped. "Did the woman say what her name was? Or do you recall hearing anybody say it?"

"No. What's your mother's name?" Caleb asked.

"Cordelia."

"Do you recall any of the names the doctor said that day?"

"It seems like I remember him naming off Maude or Myrtle, maybe Bess. Nothing that could be confused with Cordelia."

Eli turned to see Nathaniel coming through the gate into the Horton's yard.

"When I got back to the office Maggie was sitting with Brody," Nathaniel said. "She mentioned you might want to talk to me. What's going on?"

As Eli filled him in, Nathaniel was as stunned by the whole turn of events as he was, and as reluctant to get his hopes up. Thankfully, he was also as determined to go check it out.

Nathaniel stared at Eli, brow furrowed. "If by some miracle it is Mama, do you realize what kind of shape she might be in?"

"Yes. And there's even a better chance that it's not her at all. It's like pinning our hopes on something as substantial as rabbit tracks and wind pudding."

But he wouldn't let himself dwell on that.

CHAPTER THIRTY-SIX

ELI AND NATHANIEL pushed their way past the startled porter, murmuring apologies as they left the train station platform at a near run, hurrying toward the asylum at the edge of town. They'd left Moccasin Rock calmly enough, but the closer they got to Cartersville, the more anxious they'd become. Now everything—the wagons and carriages, the people walking in the streets and on the boardwalk, seemed to be moving at a snail's pace.

Finally, they reached the iron gates, mercifully unlocked, and pushed their way through.

Plowing through the front doors, they were met by a sour-faced woman. She was outfitted like the other women Eli remembered from the first visit, right down to the ring of keys attached to the wide leather belt at her waist.

"I'm the nurse in charge here. What do you want?" the woman demanded.

As both Calhouns started to explain, she held up a hand. "Can't hear neither of you if both of you are talking."

What she said made perfect sense, but Eli felt as if he would explode while waiting for Nathaniel to explain. He spoke quietly and calmly, while Eli fought the urge to run up and down the halls screaming their mother's name. *Would she even remember her own name?* That thought brought another wave of troubling thoughts. What if she didn't?

Whatever Nathaniel told the woman worked. She motioned them to follow her as she started down one of the long corridors.

"I'm not sure the patient you're looking for is still here," she said. "They took several women to Austin due to the overcrowding." She looked at Eli. "If the doctor let you in once before then I doubt he'd mind if you checked again." Eli hadn't heard Nathaniel mention his and Caleb's previous visit, but was grateful that he had.

Heart pounding, Eli barely heard and didn't acknowledge the comments and taunts from behind the bars, or even the anguished cries—but he searched the faces. After all these years, would he recognize her? If he remembered correctly, the woman who'd talked to Caleb was in one of the last cells.

"This place is more like a prison than a hospital," Nathaniel said.

Eli increased his pace. "Part of an old fort. I heard they're building a new facility further out from town."

They'd neared the end of the hallway. *Where was she?* As they reached the last cell, he noticed there was one woman who hadn't moved to the door to look at them. Wearing a baggy dress, she lay on a cot, facing in the opposite direction. She appeared to be a tiny, birdlike woman, like he'd seen talking to Caleb.

Could it be her? In his memories Mama was hale and hearty. Of course she wouldn't be after all these years.

Standing in front of the bars, Eli called her name. No response. His heart sank...until he noticed the woman had stilled. "Cordelia Calhoun," he called again. Still nothing.

Gripping the iron bars until his knuckles turned white, Eli leaned forward and softly said, "What are we having for supper tonight, Mama?"

At that, the woman rolled over facing them, but still she didn't speak. Her brown eyes were fixed on Eli as if she was hypnotized, until Nathaniel stepped into view.

"I imagine we'll have wind pudding" Nathaniel said. "I can't remember what goes with it. Do you?"

Eli gripped the bars tighter. *Please, Mama.*

The woman spoke then, only a whisper, but it reverberated through Eli's head. The words were unmistakable. "We'll have rabbit tracks, boys."

"Ma…" Nathaniel's voice broke.

Throat so tight he could barely speak, Eli turned to the woman with the keys. "Open the door."

"I can't do that," she said, looking at him as if he'd taken leave of his senses.

"Please."

The woman inside the cell was on her feet now and moving slowly toward the bars. "My babies," she whispered, tears streaming down her face. "Am I dreaming?"

Eli's gaze swung back and forth between the two women. "Please, open the door."

"No, sir," the guard said. "I'm not about to lose my job."

Eli drew his gun. "Open this door, right now, or so help me, I will blow the lock off."

The guard stepped back from his fury.

Nathaniel intervened, placing his hand on Eli's arm. "Put that gun away," he said, before addressing his next remarks to the woman with the keys. "Where's the doctor?"

She flashed an angry glance at Eli, before grudgingly answering. "He should be in his office."

"Get him," Eli snapped. He added, "Please," when Nathaniel gave him a pointed look.

The woman shuffled off, muttering something about folks who think they're better than everybody else.

Eli turned his attention back to his mother. She was sagging a little, like she could drop any moment. *Please God, don't let anything happen to her. Not now.* "Hang on, Mama, we're going to get you out of here."

As they waited, Eli kept repeating his plea to God over and

over again, unable to say more. He turned at the sound of footsteps behind him.

It was the same man he'd met on his previous visit, and at first the doctor's welcome was friendly. But as soon as Eli said he wanted to take one of the patient's away, the man's expression tightened.

"I can't let her walk out of here," the doctor said. Although Eli and Nathaniel tried to explain what had happened, they didn't really know enough about the circumstances to present a valid argument. And, understandably, that seemed to bother the doctor.

"I admit that I'm not sure what happened to her," Eli said, "or how she got here. However, I am sure she's my mother. And she is *not* spending another night in this place."

Again, Nathaniel placed a hand on Eli's arm. Even though Eli normally admired his brother's calm temperament, right now it was aggravating him no end. But Nathaniel suddenly surprised him.

"If you don't let her go," Nathaniel said softly, "then you can look forward to having the two of us camped outside this cell. And if you try to forcibly remove us, we will call in every favor we've ever been offered. You may be surprised how many people feel they owe a lawman and a physician."

Eli was impressed by Nathaniel's bluff, until he realized he might not be bluffing. He had no idea what his brother had done, or who he'd known, in the years they'd been separated.

About to throw in his own threats, Eli noticed the change in the doctor's expression. "You're a physician?"

Nathaniel nodded. "Yes."

"Why didn't you say so? I can release her to you."

Eli's knees went weak with relief.

After several moments of inquiry regarding Nathaniel's credentials, the doctor motioned for the nurse to unlock the door. "Dr. Calhoun, you'll need to stop by my office and sign some papers before you leave. Remember, you two are fully responsible for whatever happens from here on out."

"Not a problem," Nathaniel assured him. He turned and followed the doctor, and then stopped as Eli emerged from the cell carrying their mother. "Just a minute," Nathaniel said.

Retracing his steps, Nathaniel reached out and placed a hand against his mother's head. Tears filled Eli's eyes, as he saw them course down his brother's face.

"I'm so sorry, Mama," Nathaniel whispered. "We didn't know."

∿

Long before the train reached Moccasin Rock, Cordelia Calhoun was asleep on the seat across from Eli and Nathaniel.

When news had spread that she was going home, one of the nurses, a kinder one, had found a dress and a bonnet for her to wear. "They're not much to look at," she said, "but they're decent."

Cordelia walked out of the asylum between her sons, head high. Only the tightening of her hand on Eli's arm had given any indication of how scared she was.

At the train station she'd been frightened of the crowd, and even the train. *Had she ever seen one before?*

After they'd boarded, she'd relaxed a little, and then dozed off about the time Eli realized that he didn't know what needed to happen next.

Part of him wanted to never let her out of his sight. But this was a woman he didn't really know anymore. And she didn't know him. He doubted if she'd had any problems when she'd been committed. What about now?

Would she wake up scared? Would she try to escape? How had she been treated? How did she even get to the asylum to start with?

He and Nathaniel discussed it quietly, noticing after several moments that their mother was listening to every word. Her eyes were wide open as she regarded them.

Voice quivering, she said, "You're not going to leave me somewhere, are you?"

They both froze, staring at her.

"No, we'd never do that," Nathaniel said.

"You're safe," Eli assured her, "we're not about to let you go." After a moment he said, "Do you really remember us, Mama?"

She stared at him, eyes searching his face, and Eli's heart sank.

Then she gave him a tired smile. "You're Elijah Travis Calhoun and Nathaniel Houston Calhoun. The last time I saw you, you were little boys. Now, you're the spittin' image of your father. And I missed it all."

At the mention of Amos Calhoun, Eli shot a look at Nathaniel. They still hadn't told her about their father. Before he could fret over how to tell her, she took the decision out of his hands.

"Amos is dead, isn't he?"

Startled, Eli nodded. "Yes, Mama, he is. How did you know?"

"Because he would've come for me, if he could've."

"So would we," Eli said. "But we all believed you were dead."

Her eyes rounded in surprise. "Why did you think that?"

"That's what the old man who lived down the road told us."

Her fingers clenched the armrest. "Mr. Pedlam?"

"Yes," Eli said. "When the cabin caught fire, and we couldn't get to you, we ran to his house. He told us to stay inside, and that he'd go check it out. He came back later and told us that Indians had set fire to the place and that you were gone. And we were going to live with him."

"Oh, no," she whispered. "No. The Indians did start the fire, but that man was the one responsible for me being gone."

Eli stiffened. "What do you mean?"

"I ran when the Indians got there, going in the opposite direction of the creek in case they heard me. I wanted to draw them away from the two of you. When I heard them leaving, I crawled out and crept back to the house. It was burning. They'd ripped open the pillows, there were feathers everywhere. They'd even poured out the molasses. What they hadn't destroyed, they'd carried off. Mr. Pedlam found me crying. Instead of helping, he attacked me. Then when the Indians came back—drawn by my screams—that old man gave me to them. Like I was his to give."

Her face took on an anguished expression. "I can't believe that he took everything from me. And that he raised you two."

"He didn't," Eli hastened to assure her. "We left not long afterwards. We didn't like him. We never saw him again." *Thankfully, that old man was dead. Eli wasn't sure he could've kept from killing him.*

"You left?" his mother said. "Where did you go? Who took you in?"

"We can talk about that later, Mama. Please, try to get some sleep."

She dozed again, finally, but even in her sleep, she seemed heartbroken. Eli didn't know exactly when they would talk about the lost years. He did know that she would never, ever hear most of what had happened to him and Nathaniel.

Maggie Radford, Lucinda in her arms, was waiting for them at the station. The telegraph office in Cartersville was right next to the train depot. Eli had sent a telegram to Caleb, asking him to tell Maggie what had happened. Now, the first words out of Maggie's mouth were music to Eli's ears.

"Peg Harmon asked me to offer you her hospitality, ma'am. She had someplace else she needed to be. She wanted me to assure you that she knows both of your sons, and holds them in the highest regard. She would be delighted for you to stay with her."

His mother shot a scared look at him, which Maggie, mercifully, seemed to interpret. "I know things are a bit unsettled," Maggie said, "and I'm a stranger to you. You don't have to make any decisions now. Perhaps you'd all like to join us for supper."

"That sounds good to me," Eli said. "Is that okay with you, Mama?"

His mother nodded, hesitantly.

Please, Lord, help me know what to do.

Chapter Thirty-Seven

MAGGIE WAS UP at first light the next morning. She stoked the fire in the stove, and after feeding Lucinda, she began making biscuits. She wanted to have a hot breakfast waiting for Mrs. Calhoun.

Despite Maggie's best efforts, the meal they'd all shared the night before had been awkward. It had obviously been years since Cordelia Calhoun had sat at a table with others, and her nervousness and anxiety had spread to her sons.

Although it was clear that Eli and Nathaniel were thrilled to have their mother again, it was also obvious that none of them knew how to act, or what to say.

Maggie, probably more than any other in the room, had understood what Mrs. Calhoun had become accustomed to. Even she wondered exactly how much the woman had suffered.

Trying to think of safe topics of discussion through the course of the meal was difficult. Talking about Lucinda or Brody only served as a reminder of all that Mrs. Calhoun had missed with her own children, as did talking about what was going on in the world.

Despite the stilted conversation, Cordelia Calhoun held herself with dignity, and when Maggie placed the meal on the table, the older woman had reached out a hand to each of her sons, and bowed her head. Whatever else she'd forgotten through the years, she'd remembered some of the things that were important to her.

And Mrs. Calhoun wasn't the only woman that impressed Maggie. Once again, Peg Harmon had stepped up. She'd returned from seeing a patient about halfway through the meal, and had breezed into the kitchen, inviting Cordelia to stay and telling her how much she'd enjoy having someone closer to her own age to visit with. Cordelia had thanked her and accepted the offer, but was still ill at ease. Hopefully, today would go better.

Maggie reached for a towel and wiped her hands when a knock sounded at the back door. She opened it to find Eli standing there, hat in hand.

"Good morning," he said.

Glad that she'd brushed her hair and dressed for the day, Maggie motioned him in. "Good morning."

She waved him toward a chair, but he remained standing. "Can't stay but a minute. I just wanted to thank you for everything you did for Mama last night. I think it will get easier, with time. Don't you?"

"Yes," Maggie said sincerely, "and you're welcome."

"Have you seen her this morning?"

"No, I'm the only one up right now," she said. "I'm making breakfast."

"Okay. I'll come back by later."

He seemed uneasy. *What was wrong?*

Suddenly, Eli smiled. "I have this memory of kissing you while I was distracted. Do you remember that?"

Only forever. "Yes."

"Mind if I try it again?"

"I don't mind."

Pulling her close, Eli placed his lips on hers, feather light at first, then with increasing firmness. He smelled like shaving soap and the cold air from outdoors, and tasted like peppermint. A delicious combination.

Maggie wrapped her arms around his neck. Gathering her closer to his chest, Eli deepened the kiss. Several times during their pretend courtship she'd been swoony, but now Maggie was breathless in a way she'd never experienced.

When Eli finally drew back, he leaned his forehead against hers and stared into her eyes. Then he turned away and opened the door, stopped, turned back, and pulled her close again. Hands framing her face, he kissed her. "That was even better than I thought it would be," he whispered.

Maggie was glad he seemed as off balance as she was. He opened his mouth to say something else when they heard footsteps on the porch. They stepped away from each other before Ruthie appeared at the back door.

"From my Mama," the girl said, holding up a jar. "Plum jelly."

Face burning, Maggie took the jar. "Tell your mother I said thank you."

Eli winked at Maggie, said bye to Ruthie, and was gone. The little girl left a moment later.

Maggie resumed the breakfast preparations, peeling potatoes to pan fry, glad to have some time alone to gather her composure. She smiled at Eli's last words. The kiss, or kisses, had been even better than she'd imagined, too.

She looked down to see that she'd peeled the potato nearly to nothing. Better keep her mind on her work.

When breakfast was ready, and there was still no sign of Cordelia Calhoun, Maggie began to worry. In the hall, she listened at the door. Nothing.

A gentle tap on the door prompted a soft reply. Had she said come in? Maggie eased the door open to find Mrs. Calhoun dressed in the clothes that Peg had loaned her. She was sitting on the edge of the bed, hands folded in her lap. She raised anxious eyes to meet Maggie's gaze.

"Good morning," Maggie said.

"Morning."

It took a moment for Maggie to realize what was happening. Cordelia wasn't used to doing anything without specific instructions. Heart hurting, Maggie pulled a chair away from the wall and sat down closer to the bed. Last night's attempts at normal conversation couldn't be repeated.

"I made some breakfast," Maggie said, "and I have hot coffee, or tea, if you prefer. You can eat here, or in the kitchen. Whatever you feel comfortable doing."

"I appreciate it," the woman said, but still seemed unable to make a decision.

"Is it okay if I bring some tea in for both of us?"

Cordelia smiled at her. "Yes."

Maggie brought a tray and placed it on the bedside table.

Once they were both holding a cup, Maggie said, "You have a lot to adjust to, and I'll be glad to help you in any way I can. I also wanted to share with you that I, too, have recently been confined to an asylum."

Mrs. Calhoun gaped at her in astonishment.

"It was for several weeks," Maggie continued, then told her about Hollis Anderson, and the fire at Fair Haven, and how she'd escaped, and how her sons had helped her since then.

Cordelia listened to Maggie's story, never once offering a comment, but her facial expressions revealed a genuine interest and concern, and an empathetic nature. She smiled when Maggie talked about what wonderful men Eli and Nathaniel were.

"Do you mind if I ask how it happened for you?" Maggie finally asked.

The woman opened her mouth several times before any words emerged. "It was so many years ago, but I remember some."

Maggie listened in growing horror as the woman told her about the Indian raid, and then the man who'd harmed her instead of helping. And then when she'd thought the worst was over, how he'd given her to the Indians.

"They tied a rope around me and made me walk behind them as we left," Cordelia said. "If I fell, they dragged me."

A knot formed in Maggie's stomach. She didn't want to hear more, but this woman needed to tell someone.

"I knew there was worse in store," Cordelia said. "When we got to their village one of the squaws demanded they get rid of me. Normally, the women didn't have any say in that sort of thing, but she was furious. I couldn't understand what she was saying, and I don't think she was trying to spare me. But she wanted me gone, that was clear. And I wanted to oblige her. While they were arguing about it, one of the littlest kids clustered around began crying. Nobody was paying him any mind. Without thinking about it, I picked the boy up and placed his head on my shoulder, rocking him back and forth. He hushed up immediately. That Indian woman looked at me with the strangest expression."

"Like what?" Maggie said.

"Like maybe I was magical or something. The child had been sick, and no one could get him to quit crying. She decided then and there that I could stay. I was with them for years. Wherever they went, I went. I practically raised that little boy. Life wasn't easy. I tried to get away a few times, but was always caught. And disciplined. Then I got sick. I found out they planned to kill me."

"Kill you?" Maggie whispered.

"Yes. In their eyes it was the merciful thing to do. They were moving on, and I wouldn't be able to travel."

Maggie had no words.

"Then, the boy I'd helped raise—he was still young, but he'd grown up strong and healthy—waited until everyone else was asleep and then threw me over his shoulder and took me away. He tied me to a tree, and left me there with some food and water, and said that someone would find me. He told me there were soldiers nearby, for me to wait until he was gone, and then to yell for them. Then he disappeared into the woods. I did yell for help. No one came. I don't know how long it was. It felt like forever, but was probably only a few days or I wouldn't have survived. By the time they found me, I had a bad fever. The best I can figure, that made me talk crazy. They took me to the asylum."

"I'm so sorry," Maggie said.

Mrs. Calhoun took a sip of tea. "After I got well, I tried to convince them that I had a family. I asked everyone who came through there to help me. The ones in charge had heard outlandish tales before. They didn't believe me. And I admit, my memory and even my speech were a little garbled at first. It was hard to communicate. I got better with time, but I still couldn't get anyone to believe me. Eventually I gave up."

"Until you saw Caleb Calhoun."

Cordelia nodded, tearful now. "At first I thought I was dreaming. Then I just knew it was one of my boys. My heart soared. Then I saw that his eyes were the wrong color. I was heart broke."

She looked at Maggie. "I don't want my sons to know what I told you about the Indians. I already said more than I should have on the train, but there are some things that I don't ever want them to hear."

Maggie understood. Sometimes you kept secrets to protect yourself. Sometimes it was to protect others.

CHAPTER THIRTY-EIGHT

OVER THE NEXT few days Maggie marveled at how well Cordelia Calhoun adjusted to her new life in Moccasin Rock. She refused to sit idly by and insisted on helping with the laundry, cooking, and even holding and feeding the baby. She still seemed unsure of herself at times, and waited for others to make the first move in any situation, but clearly she was improving.

Peg and Cordelia hit it off immediately, despite the fact that most of what they had in common was tragedy.

Both women had known sorrow and suffering. Both had lost spouses and children in differing circumstances, yet each had a strength and dignity that was evident in everything they said and did.

Maggie had worried about Cordelia meeting Dovie, but after a few awkward moments in Peg's kitchen, the two seemed to reach some sort of understanding. *Was there something in a person who'd suffered that made them recognize it in others?*

Mrs. Calhoun's meeting with Caleb had also been a source of concern. It couldn't be easy to find that your husband had remarried and fathered another child. Caleb had sat down with her and patiently answered all her questions, and they seemed to be forging a unique friendship and bond. They were not related to each other at all, but they'd both loved Amos Calhoun.

And Cordelia simply doted on Brody. "I missed so much of my own children growing up," she told Maggie. "It's enjoyable to be around a growing boy."

"I know there's no way to make up for the years you lost," Maggie said, "but they have wonderful memories of what time you did have."

At Cordelia's quizzical look, Maggie told her about overhearing Eli's conversation with the baby. Tears filled the woman's eyes, but she continued on with her work with a smile on her face.

That evening when Eli and Nathaniel stopped by, Cordelia hugged them so fiercely that Eli glanced at Maggie over his mother's head with a questioning look. She smiled and moved to another room to give them some privacy.

Although Maggie was thrilled for the Calhoun family, she was still worried about her father. She'd sent letters to him, but he hadn't responded. *Was he even getting them?*

Avalee reported to her that she'd gone to the Radford house, pretending to believe that Maggie would be home. Hollis had once again answered the door and refused to let her come in.

Even though she hadn't seen Hollis since the day he'd appeared in Peg's kitchen with the Fair Haven sheriff, Maggie still couldn't shake the feeling that he was out there watching her. *When would Hollis give up?*

At dinner that evening, Maggie noticed the look of interest on Cordelia's face when Peg made a casual comment about Maggie and Eli's courtship. *They'd forgotten to explain what was happening.*

As Maggie was feeding Lucinda before bed, Cordelia told her how happy she was that her oldest son had found someone.

Maggie hastened to clear up the misunderstanding. "This was a way that Eli came up with to keep me safe. We're only pretending to be in love."

Cordelia smiled. "Are you?"

After Mrs. Calhoun left, Maggie admitted the truth to herself.

She wasn't pretending at all. *How did Eli feel?* The two of them had not had another moment alone since the kiss. He liked her and was definitely attracted to her, but was he interested in anything more? All she knew to do was to wait and pray to know the Lord's will.

⚘

Maggie was outside at the clothes line, battling a freshly dried sheet in a gusty wind, when the leaves crunched behind her.

Thinking it might be Adger Wilson's pig again, she sidestepped, holding the sheet above her head to keep it from being soiled.

Suddenly she found herself gripped by strong arms, a gloved hand clamped down over her mouth.

Dropping the sheet, she wrenched her head aside, struggling and twisting as she kicked at her captor, but he held tight. The sheet was wrapped around her legs, hindering her further. She bit the hand that was pressed to her mouth, screaming the instant it was removed. Curses filled her ears as the hand once again clamped down, and she was dragged toward the woods.

Maggie wasn't sure what his ultimate destination was, but she couldn't let him take her. She had to keep fighting the man.

"Get a hold on her," a deeper voice barked.

"I got her."

There were two of them. She didn't stand a chance fighting both. Maybe she could outrun them. But she had to get him to loosen his grip.

Maggie let herself go limp for a moment, catching her captor off guard. His steps faltered, then halted as he tried to regain his grip.

With her hands momentarily free, Maggie turned and dug her nails into the first thing she could reach. He screamed, hands flying to his injured face. She ran straight into the woods. He lumbered along behind her.

Where was the second man?

As branches slapped at her face and snagged on her dress,

memories of fleeing the asylum assailed her. But Maggie had several things in her favor this time—she had on the moccasins to protect her feet, she wasn't in pain, and she wasn't carrying the baby.

Catching her toe on a tree root, she went sprawling, landing hard. Struggling to breathe, she scrambled up and took off again— just seconds ahead of her pursuer.

Whoever Hollis had hired wasn't giving up. Maggie dodged, and went further into the thicket. Barely able to make her way. Running blindly, she finally pushed through, and then stopped. She'd reached a clearing.

Panting, gaze swinging left and right, she searched for a hiding place. Maggie wasn't sure what lay on either side of her, but in front of her stretched the Brazos River. Then she remembered that Eli had said something about people living in tents out here—but she was turned around. Which direction should she go?

Running out of time, she dashed to her left, and tripped on her skirt. Sprawled flat on her stomach again, lungs straining for air, Maggie looked up, straight into the furious eyes of a man with a scar on his chin and a gap between his teeth.

"I had planned on going easy on you," the man said. Then he pointed to his face and to the bloody scratch that Maggie's nails had inflicted. "But not now."

The last thing Maggie saw was a fist flying toward her face.

CHAPTER THIRTY-NINE

ELI ENTERED THE front room of Peg's house and smiled at the sight of his mother holding Lucinda. It took him a moment to realize that his mother wasn't smiling.

"What's wrong?"

"I don't know," she said. "Maggie was out back bringing the laundry in. When I heard a scream, I thought maybe she fell or something, so I went outside to check."

She raised worried eyes to his and a chill rolled down Eli's spine.

"There's no sign of her out there, Son. There's a note, but it doesn't make any sense to me. I was wrapping the baby up to come and find you."

Didn't make sense?

Eli rushed down the hall, through the kitchen and onto the back porch. The laundry basket was tipped over and sheets were scattered around.

Fear hit him like a punch to the gut. *Hollis had Maggie.* A piece of paper was stuck to one of the porch posts, whipping in the wind, held in place by a pen knife.

He read the words, ice cold panic twisting his insides. *"Let's play a little game. I have someone you want. All you have to do is find her. It will end where her troubles all began."*

His mother had followed him out.

"Where's Peg?" he asked.

"Running some errands. She should be home soon."

"Mama, are you okay to watch the baby alone for now?"

"Of course, I am. What are you going to do?"

"I'm going to get Maggie."

Eli didn't have time for anything besides that hurried statement and a prayer as he ran to the jail. Grabbing a rifle, he explained to Bliss what was going on.

"I'm going, too," Bliss said.

Eli started to say no, then thought better of it. Bliss was a good fighter, and even better with a gun.

"Good. Where's Caleb?"

Bliss frowned. "He stopped by earlier, looking for you, said he'd gotten a message about some land he was interested in buying. Wanted to know if you'd go with him. Not sure when he'll be back."

Eli had been counting on the help. "I can't wait. We'll go on without him."

His second moment of pure panic came when they got to the livery stable.

"Your horse is limping," Eagan said. "Not sure what happened. I'll tend to him. Don't think it's anything serious. But he can't be ridden."

"Then saddle me another one," Eli said. "And one for Bliss."

"Strangest thing," Eagan said. "Remember that man I told you about, the one that asked about all my animals? Well he came back and hired out every horse I had, and even most of the wagons and buggies. Had a group of men with him. The only thing I have left is a little pony cart. And I don't have a pony."

Eli spun around, but then didn't know where to go. There were plenty of people in the area that he could borrow horses from, but it would take too long. Nathaniel came running up while he was still trying to decide what to do.

"Mama told me what was happening. I'm going with you."

Eli nodded. "We have to take the train." With the others following, he retraced his steps and headed for the depot.

Walter Miller stepped out of the hotel lobby, carpenter's apron on, hammer in hand and asked what was going on. Eli couldn't slow down. "Maggie's been abducted. Going to get her." He wasn't surprised when Walter tossed the hammer inside and tore his apron off. "I want to help."

Eli *was* surprised to see Peg waiting at the depot, along with Brody and Avalee Quinn, Maggie's breathless friend from Fair Haven. "What are y'all doing here?"

"I came to see Maggie," Avalee answered in a quivery voice. "Mrs. Harmon and your mother were in a tizzy about what was happening. Poor Maggie."

Peg Harmon gave Avalee a disgruntled look, but directed her remarks to Eli. "I've never been in a tizzy in my life. I'm going with you. It's that simple. Maggie's come to mean a great deal to me."

"I'm going, too," Brody said.

Eli didn't have time to argue with the boy. "You sure you're up to it? Don't want you to lose ground."

"The doctor said I'm fine."

Nathaniel nodded in agreement and Brody added, "I'm tired of resting. Please let me go."

"Okay."

Avalee still stood there, ticket in hand.

"Well, you're not going," Eli said.

Her eyes widened. "I can't go home?"

Eli rubbed his temples. "Sorry, I thought you were offering to help find Maggie."

"I would love to help," she said. "What do you need me to do?"

Before Eli could refuse her offer, Bliss blurted, "Peg Harmon, you're not going off to Fair Haven to get yourself shot at."

Peg's eyes flashed. "Who's going to stop me?"

For the next several minutes everyone talked and no one moved.

Eli debated pulling his gun and shooting up into the air to get their attention. Instead he growled, and started shoving them all toward the train.

Once the train was underway, Eli took another look at the little makeshift posse he'd assembled: Nathaniel, who wanted to heal, not harm; Walter Miller, who looked grimly determined and scared to death; Peg, Brody and Avalee—a midwife, a boy and a flirt; and Bliss. Eli supposed he should be grateful that his mother was taking care of Lucinda, or no doubt she'd be here, too.

He wanted to send them back, but they were all staring at him, solemn-eyed and determined. And truthfully, he might need help. Again, not who he would have chosen, but the fact that they all came running when Maggie was in trouble, meant a lot.

They'd each come to care about her, while his own feelings, as much as he tried to deny them, went far beyond that.

Peg and Bliss were still bickering, and it was turning in to a real humdinger. They were speaking in hushed tones, but Eli had over-heard enough to know that Peg had discovered that her husband's pension had really been payments sent from Bliss. Let them fight it out. It kept them from trying to talk to him.

God, please don't let any of them get hurt. And please help me find Maggie.

"I don't want any of you to put yourself in danger," Eli said as the train pulled into Fair Haven later. "I don't believe that Hollis Anderson was armed the times I saw him, but he could be now."

"We'll be careful," Peg assured him. The others nodded their agreement.

"Just tell us what needs to be done," Nathaniel said.

But, as was often the case of late, Eli didn't know what needed to be done.

CHAPTER FORTY

UNLIKE THE OCCASION of his previous visit, the Radford home had a neglected and empty feel that sent Eli's heart racing. He'd stationed the others at various intervals around the yard, and resisted the urge to check and make sure they were in place.

What was he up against? He was certain it was a trap, but to what end? Was Hollis watching him approach the house? Had he harmed Maggie? If Hollis was desperate enough to kidnap her, he was desperate enough to kill her, and anyone else who got in his way.

With no idea what he was facing, Eli was unsure whether to tap on the door like this was a normal visit or kick it in. He was surprised to see the door already ajar.

Easing the Colt from his holster, Eli pushed the door further open with his boot, and then braced for gunfire. When nothing happened, he eased forward. The hall looked the same as the last time, but somehow felt different. The whole place did. There was no hustle and bustle of servants, no sounds coming from the adjoining rooms. The first room he checked was empty. The second one had one old man sitting in front of a cold fireplace.

Eli had only gotten a glimpse of Nelson Radford before, when he'd stopped Maggie from running up to the porch, now he studied the man—brown hair, graying at the temples, a slim build, and a face that might have looked better without the sorrowful expression. He was staring into the empty fireplace as if he were watching flames dance around.

He turned to face Eli. "Who are you?"

"I'm Elijah Calhoun, the sheriff of Moccasin Rock. I'm searching for Hollis Anderson. He's kidnapped Maggie."

The man jerked back. "What?"

"Hollis is not the man you believe him to be. He's taken her from Moccasin Rock. She's in danger."

"I don't know what you're talking about," Radford said, "but I do know Hollis doesn't have her."

"How can you be so certain?"

"I just know."

Eli looked around. "Where is everyone?"

"They walked out."

"Why?"

Nelson faced the fireplace again, refusing to answer.

"I'm going to search this house from top to bottom," Eli said, "and if I find Maggie you're going to regret lying to me."

The man gave him a frustrated look. "Don't you understand? I want you to find her. She's not here."

"Then where is she?"

"The last I heard, she was with you. I guess she ran off again."

Jaw set, Eli left the room before he said something he'd regret. He made quick work of searching the bottom floor, and the basement. *Nothing.* Before heading upstairs, he stepped out the back door, whistled, and waited until his brother reached him.

"Any sign of her?" Nathaniel asked.

"No. I've still got to search the second floor and the attic. Will you check on everyone else?"

Nathaniel nodded, and then stepped back and blended in to the lengthening shadows.

With a sense of dread that was growing by the minute, Eli

bounded up the wide oak staircase and searched every room—each larger and more lavishly decorated than the last.

He stepped in to the biggest room so far and knew immediately it was Maggie's. Perfume bottles, jewelry and a leather photo album on the vanity top, a huge oval mirror on a stand, little fans and hat boxes. Plush rugs, overstuffed pillows on the huge four-poster bed, a chaise lounge, and several elaborately carved wardrobes—filled to capacity with fancy dresses and shoes. Up on one of the wardrobes there was a china doll with a fancy dress that probably cost more than his clothes. No doubt Maggie would be handing that down to Lucinda someday—along with most of these other things. *She must have missed all this.*

Eli shook that thought off, and searched the room, even checking for hidden panels that might lead elsewhere. The adjoining water closet was even more elaborate than the bedroom, featuring all the most modern amenities, including an enormous copper tub with hot and cold running water. Eli shook his head in amazement.

By the time he'd finished searching the whole house, he had a more complete picture of Maggie's life, but still no idea where she was.

Downstairs, he tried again to convince Mr. Radford to tell him where Hollis Anderson might be. "If I'm wrong," Eli said, "all I'll face is a little embarrassment and the possible wrath of Hol—."

Nelson interrupted. "I will admit I made a mistake about him loving her, but I cannot believe that he would harm my daughter."

"For the sake of argument, let's just say you're right. If I wanted to talk to Hollis, to clear the air, where else might he be? An office? A friend's house?"

Grudgingly, the man answered. "Hollis has a business on Oak Street, not far from the depot. Anderson Investments. But I'm telling you, I saw the man a little while ago. There's no way he has Maggie, and I can't understand why you think he does."

Out of sheer frustration and aggravation, Eli told Nelson

Radford about the note, and then about the asylum and the guard. Nelson's face went ashen as he sagged forward.

Rushing to the back door, Eli signaled again for Nathaniel. "I think I know where Hollis has taken Maggie, but her father's in a bad way. Can you check on him?"

"Sure."

"And after you see to him, will you make sure that everyone else gets home?"

Nathaniel's brows rose. "Don't you want us to go with you?"

"No, I'm getting more and more uneasy as this drags on. Just get everybody home safe. I'll handle it."

The front door of Anderson Investments was locked, but through the window he could see light spilling from a room somewhere towards the back. Instead of knocking, or calling out to Hollis, Eli glanced around, making sure he was alone on the street. He then kicked in the door, stepped inside and hurried down the hall toward the light.

He halted when he caught sight of Hollis Anderson.

In contrast to his usual perfect posture and pristine attire, the man was slumped over his desk, clothing disheveled, and a nearly-empty whiskey bottle in his hands.

Hollis glanced up at Eli, then leaned back and let his head drop against the padded leather desk chair. That move was followed by a groan. The bottle had probably been full when Hollis started drinking. The man's usual smugness was gone, and in its place was a resigned look.

"If it isn't the conquering hero," Hollis murmured. "You've already won the damsel in distress, Sheriff. Did you come to finish off the villain?"

Eli glanced around the room. No sign of Maggie. Not that he'd expected this reprobate to have her sitting here beside him.

"Where is she?" Eli growled.

Hollis ignored that question, and continued whining. "If you've come to finish me off, I'll save you the trouble, Sheriff Calhoun. I'm done. And if you had any sense, you'll give up on her, too. She's not the wealthy woman you think she is."

Holstering his gun, Eli studied him. "You figured out a way to get all her money, even without marrying her? Somehow, I'm not surprised."

"No, I didn't get a cent."

"Then what are you talking about?"

"How can I put this so that someone of your ilk would understand?" Hollis snapped his fingers. "I know. You might say I've counted my chickens before they hatched."

Eli frowned at him. "Maggie told you all along that she wouldn't marry you."

"That's not the counting I'm talking about." Hollis Anderson's laugh had a hollow sound to it. "I won't bore you with the details, let's just say that Nelson Radford wasn't as naïve as I thought. But he was careless, for years, which resulted in his financial ruin."

Understanding dawned. "Are you saying that Maggie is…"

"That's right, Sheriff Calhoun. She's broke. Busted. Destitute. And so is her father. Don't you see? There wasn't any money. Nelson Radford lost everything. By trying to arrange my marriage to Maggie, he and I were both after the same thing."

So she had been a pawn of two desperate men. "Does Maggie know?"

Another bitter laugh escaped his lips. "No. Her father hasn't told her. I found out today, by accident. I confronted Nelson, and he admitted that he wanted money he thought I had so he could regain his financial footing and see to Maggie's future, while I was counting on getting my hands on his finances to begin building an empire and my social status. Fortunately, I know a couple of other rich women. Not as easy on the eye, but far easier to tame than the fiery-tempered Miss Radford."

Eli's head was reeling, but he couldn't worry about the implications now. "I don't care about all that. Where's Maggie?"

Hollis shrugged. "I have no idea. And I no longer care."

Drawing his Colt, Eli stepped around the desk, cocked it, and aimed it at Hollis Anderson's head. Anderson's eyes widened and his face paled.

"I'm going to ask you one more time," Eli said, "where's Maggie?"

Hollis dropped the bottle and straightened in the chair. He seemed far more sober than he had a moment ago. "I…I'm serious. I really don't know. Why do you think I would?"

Fishing in his pocket with his free hand, Eli withdrew the note and tossed it on the desk. "Didn't you leave this for me?"

With shaking fingers Hollis Anderson unfolded the paper, read it and then glanced up at Eli. "I've never seen this before. I'm not sure what's happening, but I had nothing to do with it."

Eli leaned in closer. "I promise you, if you're lying to me, or if you hurt Maggie in any way, I will hunt you down again. Even if it takes the rest of my life."

Confusion flickered across Hollis's face. "I wouldn't hurt Maggie."

"Right," Eli sneered. "You'd pay someone else to do it."

Hollis stared at him, brow furrowed. "What are you talking about?"

"The bruises. The cracked ribs. Abuse that the asylum guard administered on your behalf."

Hollis's mouth dropped open. "Are you saying that guard beat Maggie?"

"Like you didn't know."

The man shook his head and then groaned again. Running a hand across his forehead, he looked up. "I had no idea. I admit that I tried to force Maggie to go along with my plan, and may have lost my temper a time or two, but I would never condone physical violence."

Eli studied Hollis and the horror on his face. *He was telling the truth.* Now what? Where could Maggie be? And who had her? It wasn't Hollis Anderson, and Tiny was in jail.

Eli grabbed the note and read it again. This time, something clicked. "The asylum."

"The asylum? Who would do that?"

Eli headed for the door. "I don't have time to explain, but it's someone even more despicable than you."

CHAPTER FORTY-ONE

MAGGIE STRAINED AGAINST the ropes binding her wrists, heart pounding as pin pricks of fear jabbed at her.

A dapper silver-haired man leaned against the doorway, smiling as if they were facing each other across a dining table.

Who was he? How had she gotten back to the asylum? Maggie remembered being struck in the face, but recalled nothing after that, including how she came to be tied up in a chair in this room littered with debris. She'd only been here once. This was Dr. Mitchell's office. What was left of it anyway.

Her head throbbed as she tried to think. Had she been drugged? How long had she been gone? Did anyone know she was missing?

The man straightened. "Still trying to work it all out?"

"Who are you?" she asked. "How much did Hollis Anderson pay you for this?"

The man's smile widened. "I'm not acquainted with Mr. Anderson, although I know who he is. I've gone to a great deal of effort to learn everything I can about Elijah Calhoun, and those around him."

Maggie tried to grasp what the man was telling her. "You know Eli?"

"Yes, you might say that he and I are old friends. Met him when he was still a kid. He was a pain then, and he hasn't changed at all."

This was J.L. Slidell! "Jasper," she whispered.

"I see Eli told you about me. How flattering."

"Eli won't fall for this," Maggie ground out as she resumed her struggle to free her hands. "He's too smart for you to trap him."

The man stepped further into the room. "I believe you misunderstood me, my dear. There's nothing to fall for. I'm not trying to lure him into a trap. I'll be gone by the time he arrives to try and rescue you. And I don't doubt that he will survive the fire, that kid has nine lives."

Maggie stilled, but her heart thudded faster than ever. "Fire?"

"Yes, this place will be fully ablaze when he gets here."

Terror swept over her. "Why are you doing this?"

"It's simple. He can't possibly rescue both of you in time."

Maggie's heart lurched. "Both of us?"

Jasper nodded. "His mother's a guest here, too. I've got her safely tucked away in a room on the other side of the building. Sign on the door said solarium." He looked around. "This was a fancy set-up at one time. Too bad it will be reduced to rubble in a matter of hours."

Maggie closed her eyes, blocking out the sight of Jasper's smug grin, but she couldn't block the feeling of helplessness and horror that swept over her. After everything that Cordelia Calhoun had been through. To be rescued and reunited with her sons, and then snatched away again. Then another terrifying thought hit her. Cordelia had been alone with Lucinda.

"Where's the baby?"

He looked confused. "What baby?"

Nausea hit Maggie in waves as she pulled against the ropes. She could move her fingers enough to determine that the bindings were thicker than twine, but not as large as regular rope. "If you've harmed her, I promise you—"

"Oh, calm yourself," he said. "I let Mama Calhoun drop the brat off with the squaw next door. I had planned on taking you and Mrs. Calhoun at the same time. But then you ran, and by the time I doubled back for Eli's mother, he was there. Stomping and storming around the back yard. I have to admit, that was fun to watch."

She stared at him in disbelief. Reasoning with him wasn't going to work. Could she keep him talking long enough to delay what he had in mind? Give someone time to rescue them. Someone had to know they were missing by now.

Jasper straightened and sauntered into the room, stepping past the overturned furniture, through the broken bottles, abandoned medical devices and papers strewn about. He kicked at the debris, sending a bottle spinning into Maggie's foot.

He squatted down beside her chair.

"Losing his fiancé will be a blow Eli won't soon recover from, at least that's what I'm hoping for. I even shot at you once."

Maggie shuddered when he smiled and shrugged. "Unfortunately, I've never been as good with a gun as that meddlesome kid grew up to be. So I tried to think of other ways to hurt him. While I was nosing around, I discovered that those boys found their mother again after all these years. Now, that tickled me to death."

Jasper's voice dropped. "You see, Eli will have to choose. And no matter what choice he makes it will haunt him for the rest of his life. Because one of the women he loves will be dead. And maybe, if I'm lucky, he'll die trying to rescue you both."

No! "He doesn't really love me," Maggie blurted. "It was all a show to keep me safe."

"Not buying it."

Maggie stifled a sob. "You won't get away with this."

He chuckled. "But I will. There's nothing to connect me to any of it. I've had helpers doing most of the leg work. And I have several witnesses who will swear I never left town today."

"Please, if you have any decency, let us go. You're holding a grudge about something that happened years ago. He was only a kid. Stop before it's too late."

"Sorry, I can't oblige you on that." He touched her hair. "I have to admit, it is a shame to destroy such beauty, but sometimes that's the way it works."

Maggie jerked her head back. How could someone who looked so angelic be so evil?

"When Elijah Calhoun comes rushing to the rescue I want him to struggle over what to do," he said. "I want it to tear him apart."

Jasper pushed to his feet again. "I'll be setting fire to the sides of the building, but not the front. The door will be unlocked, and open. Waiting for him to rush in like the hero he envisions himself to be. By that time, flames should literally be licking at your feet. And when he hears you screaming, and then hears his mother screaming, he won't know which way to go."

Please, God. Help us. "What makes you think he'll even show up?"

"Oh, he'll show. That's one thing you can count on; Eli always does the right thing. I left him a message with enough information to get him out here. To make things even more interesting, and to make sure he can't come thundering in with a whole posse, I arranged for there not to be a single horse around and for that lawman brother of his to be gone."

"You've been planning this for awhile."

He seemed proud of himself. "Yes. When I found out that he planned on taking in that kid, I pushed the boy into the creek. I should've stuck around long enough to finish him off."

Maggie gasped. "Did you have anything to do with Ruthie wandering away?"

"No, that was a happy coincidence. Again, it was fun to watch. Easy to blend in with the crowd of folks out by the river and watch all the hysteria. And Eli Calhoun trying to help."

He pulled out his pocket watch and frowned. "I thought he'd be here by now. Oh, well. If he doesn't get here in time, I'll go to the funerals. His grief should provide plenty of entertainment."

Cold chills raced across Maggie's skin. This is what a true lunatic looked like.

J.L. Slidell, well-known businessman and politician, was crazier than any of the women in the asylum.

Laughing, he waved at her and left the room. Maggie listened to the sounds of his footsteps receding. Fighting for calm, she also struggled to breathe, drawing in deep gulps of air, remembering the last fire here. The smoke could render her unconscious before the fire ever reached her. She had to do something. She renewed her efforts to break free of the ropes.

Maggie wasn't sure how much time had passed before she smelled the smoke. Her wrists were raw, and the ropes were damp now. Blood.

Footsteps sounded, someone racing up the stairs. Was he coming back?"

"Maggie! Where are you? Holler if you can hear me so I'll know which way to go."

Eli had found her!

She opened her mouth, but before she could reply, she heard him say, "Mama?" in a disbelieving tone. Maggie couldn't hear Mrs. Calhoun, but apparently Eli could. She'd been hoping that it was all a bluff on Jasper's part.

Maggie remembered the agony in Eli's voice when he'd told of finding their cabin in flames as a boy, of trying in vain to reach his mother. She couldn't let that happen again. Couldn't let him make a decision he'd regret. No matter what.

He was shouting to both of them. Rescue was just a breath away. For one of them.

"Maggie! Can you hear me?"

"Eli, Jasper tied your mother up in the solarium," she shouted. "It's on the east side of the building. Go get her. I've worked myself free. I'll be out of here in a matter of moments."

Please Lord, let him hear me…let him believe me.

Her prayers were answered. "Get out now, Maggie," he shouted. "Run. I'll get Mama and meet you outside."

She sent up another prayer, asking for peace with whatever happened. When she opened her eyes, smoke was billowing in under the door. A moan escaped her. Hanging her head, a broken bottle near her foot caught her eye. One last hope, and no time for second thoughts.

Tipping her chair over, she landed with a thud in the debris. Scooting around until her fingers grasped the glass, she maneuvered it into position.

She sawed at the ropes, desperately, her fingers nearly numb and slippery with blood. Her hope soared when the rope gave way. Shaking the bindings loose, she fumbled with the rope at her ankles. Clearly, Jasper had not expected her to free her hands. The ones at her feet were loosely tied.

Maggie stumbled when she stood, and fell when she took the first step. Crawling toward the door, she was aware of the glass and debris cutting into her hands and knees, but she didn't truly feel it.

She opened the door. Flames had engulfed the hall. The sound was deafening. She slammed the door shut, coughing and straining to breathe.

The window. Sobs tore from her throat as flames appeared on the wall near the door. Maggie grabbed the chair she'd been tied to, and broke the glass. There were still tiny jagged shards protruding from the glazing. She snatched up several newspapers and old rags from the debris and pressed them over the frame. Then she climbed up, and perched there.

In the glow of the flames from the rest of the building she could see people milling about below, but her gaze focused on one. Eli. Standing directly beneath the window, beckoning to her.

Maggie squeezed her eyes shut. Smoke swirled around her. Coughing, choking, she couldn't make herself let go.

Eli shouted, "Come on, darlin'. I got you."

A part of the ceiling collapsed behind her, sending flames, ash and debris in a cloud toward her. Maggie closed her eyes, breathed *Please, God,* and jumped.

The jarring impact left her disoriented for a moment. But she wasn't dead. She eased up, only to realize she was lying on top of Eli. He was flat out on the ground, eyes closed. He'd broken her fall. And she'd broken him.

Was he dead? "Oh, Eli. I'm so sorry."

Joy filled her when he mumbled, "I knew you could break my heart, but I didn't realize you could break my bones."

Then he lost consciousness again.

CHAPTER FORTY-TWO

ELI OPENED HIS eyes to see the asylum fully ablaze, and Caleb hovering over him. Trying to sit up, Eli looked past his brother for other faces. A searing pain in his left arm took him down again.

"Easy now," Caleb said. "Your mother and Maggie are fine."

Inhaling deeply, Eli waited as a coughing spell racked his body. "You sure they're okay?" he wheezed.

"Yes, Nathaniel's looking them over to be sure, but they're well enough to be throwing conniption fits in their effort to get to you."

Eli closed his eyes, thanking God with all his heart. When he opened them again, Caleb had moved back and Nathaniel was kneeling beside him.

"You hurt?" he asked.

"Feels like someone tried to rip my arm off."

"Let me look at it."

"In a minute. How are Mama and Maggie?"

Nathaniel proceeded with the examination, but he did answer the question. "They inhaled some smoke, and Maggie has lacerations to her hands and knees."

"Lacerations? How?"

"She crawled through some debris. There are also rope burns on her wrists, and a bruise on her cheek. She got socked pretty hard."

Eli ground his teeth together so tight he wondered if he'd

cracked any. And it had nothing to do with the way Nathaniel was moving his arm. He was going to hunt Jasper Slidell down and end this once and for all. Now.

But not if he passed out. "Hey, careful there," Eli growled, "that hurts like h—

Nathaniel cut him off. "Yep, and it'll get worse before it gets better. You've got a dislocated shoulder."

"Didn't need a doctor to tell me that. How's Mama doing?"

"Like I just told you, she took in some smoke. But she shouldn't have any long term problems."

Eli searched Nathaniel's face. "How is she doing, though? As far as...oh, you know what I mean."

Nathaniel nodded. "I know. Has it set her back? I don't think so. But I think it's aged me about fifty years." Voice husky, he said, "When I realized that y'all were inside that burning building it took three people to hold me back. Caleb was literally sitting on me at one point. When I saw you coming out of there with her, I've never been so glad to see anybody in my life."

He squeezed Eli's good arm. "Now let me do what I need to do to fix you up, or I'll have to sedate you."

Despite his pain, Eli tried to grin. "It's going to take more than three people to help you do that. By the way, why didn't you go home when I told you to?"

Nathaniel shrugged. "You're not my boss.'"

"Mine either," Caleb said from over Nathaniel's shoulder.

"How did you know to come here?" Eli asked.

"That little ragtag posse didn't return home; they followed you to Hollis Anderson's office and he told them about the asylum. When I got home, Abby told me what was happening. I took out after y'all. I still had a horse."

"Any sign of Jasper?"

"No."

"When I find him," Eli said through clenched teeth, "and I will find him, I don't want you interfering."

Caleb raised his hands in surrender. "Nathaniel filled me in on what all this was about. Why didn't y'all tell me what was going on?" Caleb's glance slid back and forth between his brothers.

"We should have," Eli admitted. "But it seemed personal, like something we needed to tend to."

Bliss walked up, gun in hand, and a sober look on his face.

"What's wrong Bliss?"

"Jasper Slidell's out back there."

Eli struggled to sit up again. "Don't let him get away."

"He's not going anywhere. He's dead."

"What happened?"

"I saw him standing there watching the fire," Bliss said. "Laughing. Didn't figure that was happenstance. Knew he had to be involved. I drew my gun and called out to him. The idiot went for a derringer that he had in that fancy waistcoat. I filled him full of lead."

Regret hit Eli. Not for Jasper, but for Bliss. "He's a powerful man," Eli said. "Killing him could bring all kinds of trouble and attention your way."

"I'm not a bit worried about it," Bliss said. "Nathaniel told me what this was about, and I wish you'd confided in me earlier. I coulda told you that Jasper Slidell had more enemies than he did friends. Some of them might make a show of grieving, but believe me there won't be many a tear shed for the man."

"You knew him?"

"We've had a few run-ins through the years."

Nathaniel moved Eli's arm just then, and Eli sucked in a breath between his teeth. "Hey, watch it."

"Sorry, Eli, but this has to be done," his brother said.

Maggie was now hovering behind Nathaniel. Eli stared at her as several emotions warred with each other in his mind: Regret that

she'd been hurt again, happiness that she was going to be okay…
and a deep sorrow that he'd have to let her go.

He'd never wanted a penny of her money, but he'd been glad
she had it for her own sake—to live the life to which she was accustomed, which she deserved. He could not provide that for her.

Eli was thinking all that, but what came from his mouth was,
"Maggie, love."

He reached out to touch her face at the same time he heard
Nathaniel say, "This is going to hurt."

That's the last thing Eli remembered.

∽

Maggie gathered her hair in one hand, smoothed it and let it fall
back to her shoulders. She'd washed it several times before the smell
of smoke was gone, but it was finally clean. She'd pulled it back with
a ribbon, a blue one that matched the dress she wore.

Eli would be here any moment. They'd not been alone since
the night at the asylum, and had rarely seen each other even in the
presence of others. She missed him.

When he tapped on the door, Maggie reveled at the sight of
him. Even with one arm in a sling, and a worried, tense look on his
face, he was the most handsome man she'd ever seen.

Wait, why was he worried?

For a few minutes they discussed all that had happened, and
again Eli apologized for what Jasper Slidell had done. And again,
Maggie assured him that it wasn't his fault. Jasper, and only Jasper,
was responsible for what had happened.

She wasn't sure Eli agreed with her, but he finally moved on.

"What will happen to your father?" he asked. "Hollis made it
sound like he was destitute. Sure am sorry about that."

"It's true that he's nearly broke, but Papa had a few assets left.
He should be able to stay in the house for several months as it's
readied for sale. Fortunately, it turns out he had some friends, real

friends, not like Hollis Anderson. He's a good man, helped many a businessman get his feet under him. Not everyone forgot that. His life will be different, that's for sure, but he'll get by."

"Good," Eli said. "Did he tell you about Hollis Anderson?"

"Yes, he mentioned that Hollis had a sudden yearning to return to the east. Good riddance."

Eli nodded, perched on the edge of the sofa—like he planned to bolt and run at any moment. *What was wrong?*

He drew in a deep breath. "Maggie, I think it's time for our pretend engagement to end."

Relief flowed through her. He was nervous about asking her to marry him.

"The sooner any talk about us dies down," Eli said, "the easier it will be for you to get a real fiancé."

Maggie blinked. "What? You don't love me?"

He shrugged. "That doesn't matter one way or the other. I'm not good enough for you, plain and simple. You're an educated woman. You're beautiful. You'll have your pick of men. All better choices than me."

Didn't he realize how absurd that was?

"Don't worry, Maggie, you won't be alone for long. All you have to do is watch your attitude and temper. Remember, a little sweet talk can go a long way with potential suitors."

She stared at him in disbelief. He couldn't have made her angrier if he tried. Then it hit her. *That's exactly what he was trying to do. Why?*

"What's really going on here, Eli?"

"I'm trying to be a friend to you, and Lucinda. I've come to care about you both. Once you get back to Fair Haven you'll not be lacking for masculine attention."

There was something about the way he looked when he said Fair Haven that had her puzzled. "So you really want me to go?"

His shoulders relaxed. "Yes. I want you to go."

Maggie pushed to her feet. "I think I'm starting to see the light here. You want me gone because it'll be better for me."

Eli nodded.

"And easier for you."

He tensed up again, but didn't say anything.

"You're a chicken," she said softly.

He stood. "I am not."

"Yes, yes you are. You're scared."

"I don't know what you're talking about."

Hands on her hips she glared at him. "This has nothing to do with my attitude or my temper, or your imagined shortcomings. Or even your ability to provide for a family. You are scared. Plain and simple."

"Now wait just a minute. The reason I want you to go is because that's what's best for you and Lucinda."

Tears welled up in her eyes.

Looking as if she'd hit him, Eli reached out to her, then lowered his hand and stepped back. "Please don't cry, Maggie. It'll work out better for everybody this way."

Maggie swiped at her eyes. "I'm not going to cry. I'm frustrated and angry. I can't believe that you're going to let your past ruin any chance of a future."

His eyes widened. "My past? What's that got to do with anything?"

"That's why you're scared. You said that you learned never to get attached to anybody, and never to get your hopes up. People leave. People die. Isn't that what this is really about?"

Lips a thin line, he said nothing.

She poked a finger at his chest. "Admit it."

He stood there, clutching the brim of his hat, knuckles white now.

"You're not the only one who worries about the past," she said. "I was a pawn of my father and Hollis, but I'm willing to take to a chance on marriage."

She couldn't stop the little sob that escaped her. *Why was he being so stubborn?*

Well, if she couldn't make him change his mind, she sure wasn't going to make it easier for him.

"I've got news for you, Elijah Calhoun. I'm staying right here in Moccasin Rock and I'm going to marry the first man that asks me. And we're going to have a dozen more babies."

He jammed his hat on his head and glared at her. "You'd better be on that train tomorrow morning, Maggie." His tone turned pleading. "If you don't, you'll regret it someday. When you find the man you want to spend the rest of your life with."

I found him.

"And no matter what you're thinking, it's not me."

Despite Maggie's best effort, the tears she'd fought brimmed over and ran unchecked down her face.

Eli turned and ran.

CHAPTER FORTY-THREE

HE'D MADE MAGGIE cry. Eli knew she'd probably shed many a tear in private, but she'd never let him see. She hadn't cried when he met her—despite what she'd been through—and she'd not shed a tear over losing her fortune. And yet she'd cried because of him.

He turned over and stared at the ceiling, calling himself every name he could think of, and then starting over. He was spending the night in the cabin so he wouldn't be tempted to show up at the train station in the morning. She and Lucinda had to go. But he couldn't watch them leave.

Every time he closed his eyes he was assaulted by mental pictures of Maggie growing older, and more beautiful, and the baby growing up. Who would be there for them? He'd been trying to do the right thing by making her leave. Hadn't he?

But it had definitely not turned out right. What if Maggie really did marry the first man who asked her? What if the fellow was a scoundrel? A criminal? Worse than Hollis Anderson? What would become of her and Lucinda?

By the time morning rolled around Eli's head ached nearly as much as his heart. He waited until he was sure the morning train had come and gone, and then headed into town. At Bony Joe's he drank two cups of coffee, and poked his fork around in the food placed in front of him, but he had no appetite.

After leaving there, Eli stopped by the mercantile to make sure Brody was okay. He'd spent the night with Jamie Wilson's family and was spending the day helping Silas Martin. The boy would start school after the new year, but for now he was excited to earn some money for Christmas presents.

As he was leaving the store, Eli saw Adger Wilson's pig and mule pass by, headed in the direction of the church. That was all he needed today. Stalking after them, Eli was determined to get them off the street, even if he had to lock the silly critters up to do it. He slowed when he realized that a couple of boys were running along behind the animals—two of Adger's sons.

"Sorry, Sheriff," Jamie panted, "they followed me when I headed to town."

It took only a few minutes to help the boys herd the animals in the direction of the Wilson's house.

After they'd gone and the dust had settled, Eli stood near the picket fence at the grave yard, looking at the markers. There were men, women and children buried here. At least one old preacher and two outlaws. Except for the youngest among them, they'd probably all had plans, hopes and dreams. Some lived to see them, others didn't.

But they all had one thing in common. Whatever they did or didn't do, it couldn't be changed now.

Whatever had been left unsaid, or undone, was that way forever.

That's when it hit him. *Maggie was right.* He'd wanted an absolute guarantee that everything would work out. That there'd be no loss and no heartache.

Eli had wanted it all, and he'd wanted it his way. But he'd been losing control for weeks—of his life, his emotions, his thoughts and actions. Control he'd fought hard for since he was old enough to fight.

And the tighter he'd held on, the harder it had gotten. He had to let go. Truly surrender everything to God.

Pastor Wilkie's message from Matthew flashed through his mind. *Don't worry about tomorrow.*

Eli turned on his heel and headed straight for the train station. If Bliss hadn't been walking by, Eli might not have told him his plans.

"Where you going?"

"I'm going to Fair Haven. To get Maggie and the baby."

The old man grinned. "Sounds like a right fine idea to me."

Despite his confident air, Eli wasn't sure of Maggie's reaction. He'd hurt her. She might need time to get over that.

He also wasn't sure exactly what he'd say, but it would start with an apology and end with a proposal. Eli practiced both all the way to Fair Haven.

Unfortunately, Maggie wasn't easy to find. It hadn't occurred to him that he didn't know where she would live. Once again, Nelson Radford was alone in the big house, surrounded by boxes, crates and barrels. Obviously he was preparing to vacate the premises.

"Where can I find Maggie?" Eli asked.

"She told me she was staying with the woman who's taken her in. A Mrs. Harmon, I believe. That's the last I heard."

Eli didn't want to worry him unduly, so he nodded and turned to leave. Then he stopped. He wasn't sure he liked Nelson Radford, but the man was Maggie's father. Best get things settled now.

"I plan on marrying your daughter when I find her," Eli said. "Do you have any problem with that?"

Nelson eyed him with a look of amusement. "No objection. But it seems to me you'll need to do a better job of keeping up with her. You've already lost her again."

Grumbling, Eli left, stopping next at the sheriff's office. Shiloh Clark hadn't seen Maggie either. After several other stops, Eli went by Maggie's friend Avalee's house. It was of similar size and style to the Radford place.

Even from the front porch Eli could hear the buzz of activity inside—she must be hosting some sort of gathering. The door was opened by a frazzled looking man who pointed to a door on his right when Eli asked to see Miss Quinn.

Eli stepped through the doorway and nodded to Avalee. She was surrounded by other giggling girls of every shape and size. But none of them was Maggie.

When every eye turned his way, Eli tugged on his collar and thought about backing out into the hall. There was a table full of food laid out, and Eli had a feeling that a single man would be snatched up faster than one of the little pink cakes piled up in the center.

"I haven't seen her," Avalee said when Eli asked. "She sent word that she was okay and had survived her ordeal. That's the only thing I've heard."

Avalee clutched her throat and closed her eyes. When she opened them there were tears. "You don't think she was abducted again, do you?"

Realizing that Maggie's friend was truly concerned, Eli felt bad about the thoughts he'd been having. "No. I don't think so. Believe me, if I thought Maggie was in trouble, I'd be tearing this town apart, not going through it at this pace."

Avalee smiled at him in a knowing way. After he was outside on the front porch, he heard a burst of excited babbling erupt from within. Well, that should give them plenty to talk about for awhile.

After searching every other place he could think of, Eli headed home. He should've checked with Peg Harmon first. Maybe Maggie told her where she was going. Even if she hadn't, Eli would find her.

Because no matter how he looked at it, he couldn't imagine a future without Maggie.

✍

Eli pushed open the door to Nathaniel's office, and heard his brother's deep laugh coming from the living quarters at back, and then an answering feminine giggle.

Despite his weariness, Eli smiled. His brother was certainly having a better day than he was.

"Nathaniel?" Eli shouldered open the door to the kitchen and froze.

The laughing girl was Maggie. She sobered when she saw him, and then gave him a defiant glare as she placed a plate of food in front of his brother.

"What's going on here?" Eli asked.

"We've been fishing," Nathaniel said, looking at Maggie with a big smile on his face. Aggravation shot through Eli. Not only was that his girl, he'd taught her to fish!

Both of them stared at him as he pushed further into the kitchen. Maggie had the grace to look embarrassed, but Nathaniel kept on smiling.

"Come on in," he said, "and make yourself at home. Maggie fried up the fish, and boy, let me tell you, it is good."

Eli tried to get words out, any words. All he came up with was, "Why?"

"What's that now?" Nathaniel never stopped grinning.

"What is she doing here?" Eli finally managed. "I thought she left on the train."

"She was about to, was all packed up and everything. I stopped by to tell her and Lucinda goodbye when it dawned on me that I didn't want them to leave."

"*You* didn't want them to leave?"

Nathaniel shook his head. "Nope, I was real disappointed that Maggie wasn't going to be my sister-in-law. I got to thinking that since you didn't want her, maybe I could talk her into staying here as my wife."

"Your wife?" Eli couldn't believe his ears.

"Yep."

Maggie was standing there, twisting a dish towel in her hands. Nathaniel reached out, looped his arm around her waist and pulled her close. "You gotta problem with that, brother?"

Eli didn't stop to think about the fact that Maggie immediately pushed away from Nathaniel, or that his brother's tone and expression were goading. In fact, he didn't stop to think at all. In one swift move he was across the kitchen, had Nathaniel by the collar and was jerking him from the chair.

Nathaniel didn't seem a bit surprised. "If I didn't know better I'd think you were jealous, Eli. That maybe you wanted Maggie for your own wife. Could it be?"

"Yes, blast it! I spent the day searching all over Fair Haven for her and then raced back here to get ready to go out again, wherever I had to go, until I found her."

All the mirth was gone from Nathaniel's expression. He pushed away from Eli, straightening his shirt as he stepped back. "Perhaps you should tell Maggie that."

Nathaniel picked up his jacket, nodded to Maggie and headed for the door. "I was only teasing about asking her to be my wife. All I did was offer her a shoulder to cry on until you came to your senses."

Eli hung his head, embarrassed to look at Nathaniel as he left, scared to look at Maggie. The silence was deafening. He held his breath when he heard her move across the room, and then let it go when she stopped beside him and slipped her hand into his.

"Is it true?" she asked him.

"What?"

"What you said to Nathaniel, that you want to marry me. Or were you lashing out in jealousy?"

Eli snorted. "Oh, I was jealous all right, but I meant what I said. Before I can ask you anything, though, I need to clear up things with Nathaniel."

Maggie nodded. "I'll be here. By the way, I had no idea he was going to say all those things. There's nothing between us."

"I know that. I'll be back as soon as I find him."

Eli didn't have to look far. Nathaniel was sitting outside on the bench. He gave Eli a rueful smile. "I planned on leaving you two alone for awhile. Then I realized I'd stormed out of my own house. I have a patient coming by later so I'd better stick around."

They sat there in silence for a moment. "You don't really have any feelings for Maggie, do you?" Eli asked.

Nathaniel eyed him warily. "Why?"

"Well..."

Nathaniel bolted to his feet, jaw tight. "If you're about to tell me that if I want Maggie then you'll walk away, so help me, I'm going to haul off and punch you right smack in the nose."

Eli jerked back. "What?"

"You're trying to do what you always do," Nathaniel said.

It was clear that his brother was angry, angrier than Eli had ever seen him, but he didn't understand why. "What are you talking about?"

"Let me ask you something," Nathaniel said. "When we were kids, and we only found enough food for one of us, if there was only one crust of bread, who got it?"

Eli looked away.

"Me, that's who. I was too little and too messed up to know what was going on back then. Once I figured it out, I wanted no part in it."

Nathaniel's voice dropped to a whisper. "Do you honestly think that I could just pick a woman and child to replace the ones I lost? I would give anything if it worked that way. If it were that easy. It's not."

Eli started to voice his agreement and then stopped. *A child? What was he saying?* He stared at Nathaniel.

"Yes, our baby died, too."

Eli felt as if he'd been kicked in the gut. "I'm so sorry. I never knew."

Nathaniel stared off into the distance. "Someday I'll tell you about it. I can't yet."

Throat tight, Eli looked at him, not knowing what to say.

Nathaniel sighed. "You can't fix everything for me, Eli. But thank you for the times that you could, and did. I think Maggie is a wonderful woman, and that baby is something special. But they're not for me. And more importantly, Maggie's crazy in love with you. Now get on back in there and do whatever you have to do to grab onto the miracle that God has dropped into your life."

Eli did something he hadn't done in years. He hugged Nathaniel and then started back inside.

Hand on the doorknob, he looked back at the man he knew better than anyone else on earth, and yet in some ways, didn't know at all.

"Just for the record," Eli said. "I do want the best for you, but I wasn't about to step aside. I would have fought you for Maggie."

Nathaniel grinned at him. "I'm glad to hear that. Now go."

Back inside, Maggie was sitting at the table, staring up at him over the forgotten supper. "I had planned on proposing in a much more romantic way," he said. "Now, I guess I'm desperate to get the words out there. All the pretty phrases have flown right out of my head."

She stood and walked around the table. "Tell me what's in your heart, Eli. It doesn't have to be pretty words."

Eli took a deep breath. "I want you buried beside me in the cemetery," he blurted.

Maggie stepped back. "What?"

He groaned. "That sounds crazy. Let me try again. What made me realize I didn't want to live without you was a stop by the church this morning to chase away Adger Wilson's pig and mule."

Her patient look had turned to one of confusion. "I don't understand."

Eli ran a hand along his jaw. He was trying to sweet talk her and so far all he'd done was mention graveyards and stray animals. "While I was there, I looked at the gravestones. I could see the span of people's lives. Couldn't help but wonder what they'd done with it. That's when it hit me. However much time God gives me, I don't want to waste any of it by trying to control everything. And I want you by my side. And however long that is, one day, one year, or fifty years, I want you to know I loved you every minute of it."

Her eyes filled with tears.

Eli took a deep breath and hurried on. "And I want to know that when your time finally comes, which I pray is many, many years from now, that you'll be laid to rest beside me in the Moccasin Rock Cemetery."

"What if I go first?" she asked, her tone teasing, despite the tears.

"Then I'll be counting the days until I can join you."

He kissed her then, a tender kiss full of love and promise.

"I'm moving forward in faith," Eli said, "but I'll admit I'm still worried about you not having the kind of money you're used to."

"I'm not."

"Maggie, please understand, even if I worked at everything I could think of, or find to do, from sun-up to sundown, I'll never make that kind of money."

"I'm not worried," she said. "But, I'll tell you what, if I decide I need more money, I'll make it myself."

His eyes widened. "How?"

"I don't know," Maggie admitted. "But I can assure you that it won't be illegal, or immoral. Do you doubt that I can do it?"

Eli smiled. "Maggie, darlin', I have no doubts about you at all."

EPILOGUE

ELI STEPPED INTO the Fair Haven church and stopped in his tracks. He and Maggie had been here yesterday, making arrangements for today, and the place had looked nothing like this.

They had agreed in the interest of time, a simple wedding would be best.

Now there were bows, wreaths and candles...everywhere. It was beautiful, but who was responsible?

He caught sight of Caleb's wife, Abby, and Jenna and Avalee scurrying back and forth through a side door. The three of them had been busy. They had all celebrated Christmas together just a few days ago. The women must've saved all the decorations for today.

Looking around, he noticed that some of their family and friends had also arrived in Fair Haven. Eli had agreed to the ceremony taking place in Maggie's church. That was the only thing she'd asked for. Since it was about all he could give her, he had readily agreed.

He'd been touched when Wilkie Brown had agreed to travel from Moccasin Rock and help in any capacity needed. It would be the two preachers conducting the ceremony.

Eli was surprised to see Bliss and Peg sitting in the same pew. He thought Bliss was watching over things in Moccasin Rock.

"Don't get your drawers twisted," Bliss said when Eli approached them. "Silas and Big John are keeping an eye on things. I'm heading back right after the wedding."

Silas? Big John? Eli was glad the men were willing to assist, but how would Moccasin Rock fare? Silas might have half the town locked up by tonight. Thankfully, after the wedding was over, Caleb would be helping Bliss enforce the law until he and Maggie returned from their honeymoon.

His gaze was drawn to his mother as she entered the church. Maggie had helped her get ready for the wedding, making sure she had a beautiful dress, and fluffing up her hair somehow so that it seemed fuller, softer. She looked so happy and content.

Eli kissed her cheek, grateful beyond words that he had an opportunity to do that.

He headed to the front of the church, and turned toward the back where Nelson Radford was standing. Eli realized he would need room for his mother, and a father-in-law, in his new house. He'd barely finished, and already he was adding on to it.

There were times in his life when the thought of such responsibility and commitment would have scared him to death. But the feeling uppermost in Eli's mind was gratitude.

God had blessed him more than he'd ever dreamed, and more than he deserved.

An organist began playing a wedding tune at about the same time that Nathaniel, Caleb and Brody joined him. He was grinning at the sight of them all polished up, when Maggie stepped into the back. Eli forgot everything else.

Taking her father's arm, Maggie pressed a kiss to his cheek, then all eyes watched as she made her way up the aisle—head high, smile wide. Breathtakingly beautiful.

Then she was standing beside him. Eli wasn't sure he'd been this nervous before a gunfight.

He listened as Wilkie Brown spoke about making God a priority in your marriage, and then Maggie's pastor, Alfred Campbell, began his part with "Dearly Beloved." For the next several minutes, Eli replied when prompted, pledging to love, honor and cherish Maggie for the rest of his life, and hoping he had many years to do that.

Then the preacher turned to Maggie. "Do you, Magnolia Eileen, take this man to love, honor and obey, for as long as you both shall live?"

Eli was watching Maggie, waiting for her reaction to the "obey" part, when it dawned on him what the preacher had said. *Magnolia?*

She grinned at him, one eyebrow quirked. He wasn't sure if it was from his obvious surprise at her name, or at the thought of obeying him. He wasn't worried. Life with Maggie would keep him on his toes.

After a kiss that Eli wished they could've shared without the curious onlookers, he and his bride left the church arm-in-arm.

Outside, Maggie exchanged tearful, though happy, goodbyes with her father, Peg and his mother.

Then she fussed over Lucinda, clinging to her like they'd be gone a year. He marveled at how different they both looked from the day he'd laid eyes on them. Especially Lucinda. She was healthy now, and growing like a weed. He leaned down and gave the baby a kiss. She smiled, gurgled and batted at his chin.

Eli reached out and drew Brody into the loop. The boy had also gained weight. "Be sure and leave that new rifle in the box until I get home and teach you how to use it," Eli said. "Can't have you getting hurt."

Brody grinned. "I'll wait."

Eli slapped him on the back. Peg and his mother were going to look after Lucinda and Brody until Eli and Maggie returned home.

Maggie kissed the baby again, then hugged Brody again, and several other people again. *They were going to miss the train.*

Eli glanced over to see Caleb and Nathaniel grinning. He shook his head as they joined him.

"Why are you in such a hurry to leave?" Caleb asked.

"Yeah, it almost seems personal," Nathaniel said.

"It is. Very."

His brothers laughed. Then Caleb grew serious. "I have a business proposition for you." Then he looked at Nathaniel. "You, too."

"Business? What kind of business?"

"I want to start a cattle ranch, and I want you two to go in on it with me."

They both stared at Caleb in amazement.

"I've worked on ranches a time or two," Eli said, "but that doesn't mean I know anything about running one."

Caleb seemed unconcerned. "So we'll hire people who do."

"You're throwing some words around that sound real good," Eli said. "But to hire people, you have to have money, and I don't. And to invest in a business, you need to have money, which—as I mentioned—I don't."

"But I do," Caleb said.

Eli didn't even have time to get aggravated at him before Caleb hurried on.

"What I'm trying to say, is that we'll treat this as a partnership. We'll each invest what we have, be that money, time or experience. I want to build something, together. In fact, there'll be plenty for every member of the family to be involved in, if they want. Even our kids can get in on it." Caleb glanced at Abby, her waist a little thicker now. Of course he'd be thinking of the next generation.

"You should know I'm adopting Brody and Lucinda," Eli said. "They're Calhouns. They'll be part of anything I'm a part of." He'd hired Murphy Patterson to search for any family that Brody might have, but it seemed the boy truly was alone in the world. Or at least he had been.

Caleb smiled. "I'm good with that. I knew they'd end up Calhouns before you did."

"Yeah, me too," Nathaniel said.

Eli stared at them. "I'm that easy to figure?"

They laughed. "About this, yeah," Caleb said. "So what do you think about my idea?"

The other two considered it, then exchanged a look and a nod. "Why not?" Eli said.

"I think we should call it the Calhoun Cattle Company," Caleb said.

"Exactly where do you plan to do this?"

"Out by your place. I've bought up a lot of land out there."

Their discussion was interrupted by Maggie. "You ready?"

Without a word, Eli grabbed her hand and set off for the train station, surprised to see that everyone was following.

As they reached the depot, they passed a man with a handlebar mustache who was standing beside a tripod and several large cases.

"We have a surprise for you," Caleb said.

At first Eli assumed that by "we" Caleb meant himself and Abby. Then he noticed *everyone* staring at him and Maggie, looking excited. *Surely none of them were going with them*!

He and Maggie weren't getting to go far, or be gone for long. Time and funds were limited. Eli had planned on enjoying every single second of their time away…alone.

Then he realized that the man with the mustache was also staring at them.

"We hired a photographer," Caleb said with a grin. "He was supposed to get here for the wedding, but there was trouble somewhere down the track. The train will be leaving a little behind schedule, so he's going to take some pictures here before y'all leave."

The next while was a flurry of activity as a photograph was taken of Eli and Maggie, and one of everyone who'd attended the wedding. Then someone lined up the brothers: Eli, with Maggie in front of him, Nathaniel in the middle, then Caleb, with Abby in front of him. Nathaniel protested at first and tried to step away, but Eli pulled him back. *Hang in there, brother. You'll find someone again.*

Next was a picture of Eli, Maggie, Brody and Lucinda, then one of Eli with Nathaniel and their mother.

For the last photograph, at Maggie's suggestion, Eli and Caleb took off their suit coats and strapped on their guns, and once again, the two of them tugged Nathaniel into the picture. Even as Eli stared solemnly at the camera, he felt a little silly. What would their kids and grandkids think someday?

Bliss seemed to be traveling the same line of thought. "Just think, you'll be able to look at these things in the future and remember what y'all looked like when you were in your prime."

Several people chuckled, including Eli, until he tracked the old man's gaze to Peg. The expression on his face was so sweet and hopeful that it was almost painful to see.

Bliss didn't need a picture to remember what Peg looked like in her prime. It wouldn't surprise Eli if Bliss still saw her exactly the same. Two of the finest people he'd ever known. Hopefully they'd come to some understanding about the past and find happiness together.

Eli then turned to Maggie, knowing that even when she was old and gray she'd have that spark of sass and stubbornness that had fascinated him from the beginning.

Maggie caught him staring at her. "Everything okay?" she whispered.

"Just thinking about our future. No matter what it brings, I will always love you."

She smiled. "Is that a promise?"

"It's a Texas promise."

AUTHOR BIO

A seventh-generation Texan, Laura Conner Kestner spent 25 years in community journalism before pursuing a career in fiction. Her first novel, Remember Texas, was published in 2018, and the sequel, A Texas Promise, in 2019.

Laura's won several writing awards, including a Genesis Award from the American Christian Fiction Writers, a Daphne du Maurier award for excellence in mystery/suspense from the RWA KOD chapter, and a RWA SARA Emma Merritt award. She's a three time GOLDEN HEART® finalist, a 2019 HOLT Medallion finalist, and a 2019 WILL ROGERS MEDALLION AWARD finalist. For more information, or to contact Laura, please visit http://lauraconnerkestner.com